happy
families

Janey Fraser has been a journalist for over twenty-five years and contributes regularly to national newspapers and magazines including the *Daily Telegraph* and *Woman*. This is her third book following *The Playgroup* and *The Au Pair*. She has also published books under the pen name Sophie King.

happy
families
janey fraser

arrow books

Published by Arrow Books 2013

2 4 6 8 10 9 7 5 3

Copyright © Janey Fraser, 2013

First published in Great Britain in 2013 by
Arrow Books
Random House, 20 Vauxhall Bridge Road,
London SW1V 2SA

www.randomhouse.co.uk

Addresses for companies within The Random House Group Limited can be
found at: www.randomhouse.co.uk/offices.htm

The Random House Group Limited Reg. No. 954009

A CIP catalogue record for this book
is available from the British Library

ISBN 9780099580850

The Random House Group Limited supports the
Forest Stewardship Council® (FSC®), the leading international
forest-certification organisation. Our books carrying the FSC label
are printed on FSC®-certified paper. FSC is the only forest-certification
scheme supported by the leading environmental organisations,
including Greenpeace. Our paper procurement policy can be found at:
www.randomhouse.co.uk/environment

Typeset by SX Composing DTP, Rayleigh Essex, SS6 7XF
Printed and bound by CPI Group (UK) Ltd, Croydon, CR0 4YY

This book is dedicated to my wonderful children, William, Lucy and Giles, who between them have:

- accidentally broken the car window with a cricket ball, minutes before going on holiday;

- handed me jeans to be washed and dried in ten minutes flat, so they can wear them to a party;

- visited the tattoo shop without written parental consent;

- had to be rescued from an angry nightclub owner, after being found in possession of four fake IDs (*one* is excusable but *four* was pushing it);

- made me overdrawn;

- given me big warm hugs to make it all worthwhile.

Happy Families is also dedicated to my husband, who makes me laugh every day.

ACNOWLEDGEMENTS

Grateful thanks to:

My agent Teresa Chris, who declares that my books should be used as contraceptives because the children are so naughty.

Gillian Holmes, Richenda Todd and everyone at Random House involved in the complex labour preparations required to give birth to a novel – and feed it.

Betty Schwartz, who helped me conceive, in a literary manner of speaking, many years ago.

In memory of Jane, my much-missed friend and children's godmother.

PERFECT PARENTS' SCHOOL! SIGN UP NOW!

<u>EIGHT WEEKS TO CHANGE YOUR KIDS – OR YOUR MONEY BACK!*</u>

IS YOUR FAMILY LIFE IN A MESS?

DO YOUR CHILDREN REFUSE TO BEHAVE?

THEN YOU'RE NOT ALONE!

BUT THE GOOD NEWS IS THAT CORRYWOOD'S PERFECT PARENTS' SCHOOL IS HERE TO HELP!

CLASSES FOR ALL AGES RUN BY ~~IN~~EXPERIENCED PARENTS

*Certain conditions apply.

Chapter 1

BOBBIE

'I'm not telling you again, Jack! Put it back. NOW! Before I count to three. One. Two. Two point five . . .'

Bobbie felt like screaming. Correction. She *was* screaming. Why wouldn't Jack do what he was told?

She'd tried everything. Hypnotherapy. Reflexology. Cranial osteopathy. Dairy diets. No-dairy diets. But Jack was the kind of child who simply couldn't leave things alone. Including the Action Man Easter egg in his hands right now.

'Two point seven five . . .'

An older woman in the queue ahead, wearing gold hoop earrings and bright pink leggings, was turning round to stare. Don't blame me, Bobbie wanted to say. Supermarkets shouldn't be allowed to display sweets (let alone Easter eggs when it was barely February!) right by the checkout. How was a parent meant to cope?

Jack, with his blond mop of hair (just like his father) might only be seven but he had a will of iron. Just look at the way he was hopping from one foot to another, challenging her with a gappy-toothed mischievous try-and-stop-me grin that would melt anyone's heart. Anyone that is, who wasn't related by blood. 'Put that back,' she repeated.

Jack leaped up and down, shaking his head. 'What's the magic word, Mum?'

She gritted her teeth. 'Please.'

Jack tossed the egg in the air and then caught it. Why were small boys like rebellious fleas? Always zooming around as though their batteries were on speed. Constantly pushing your buttons. 'Say it again, Mum!'

Anything! Just to stop him. '*Please.*'

There was a rumble of disapproval from behind her, followed by a 'Kids are allowed to get away with anything nowadays!' How true! Just look at Jack who now – despite two 'pleases' – was peeling off the shiny silver and purple wrapping, cracking off Action Man's head and stuffing it in his mouth while still jumping around from one foot to the other as though in a boxing ring.

'WE HAVEN'T PAID FOR IT YET!'

Oh dear. Everyone in the queue was turning round. Quite a few more were mumbling loudly about 'respect' and 'in my day' apart from a weasel-faced, tattooed youth who was yelling, 'Go for it, kid,' accompanied by a loud wolf whistle.

'JACK! I'LL TELL YOU ONE MORE TIME!'

Was that really her, shouting like that? She must, Bobbie told herself, have been mad to have come here in the first place. A busy supermarket on a Saturday morning with a borderline hyperactive seven-year-old in tow? It was asking for trouble. But she'd been desperate for a birthday card and some wrapping paper for this wretched party. Not to mention a pair of tights and an instant colour wash to brighten up her hair, which had looked horribly mousy when she'd looked in the mirror this morning.

'I'm sorry,' she blustered to the crowd at large. 'I've got him on a no-sugar diet and . . . NO, JACK, NOT ANOTHER ONE! COME HERE!'

Bobbie hurled herself forwards but Jack had already rushed past, diving into the empty Reduced Bread shelf. Now the crowd was gasping with horror mixed with excitement. '*Get out of there or you'll hurt yourself,*' she hissed, bending down on all fours to try and extract him. But he was out of reach. Only someone so small – and unmanageable – could do this.

Then suddenly his right arm and leg came out from the shelf at exactly the same time and back again – rather like synchronised swimming. She tried to grab him – nearly! – but the arm and leg shot back, accompanied by loud giggles from the perpetrator. Then out again. And in. Missed once more!

Oh no. He was flicking bogeys now. This was Jack's favourite party trick when in trouble.

'Anyone got a camera?' giggled a voice behind her. 'This would look great on YouTube.'

Bobbie wanted to curl up and die. If she'd done this at Jack's age, her mother would have given her a jolly good smack. But it wasn't allowed nowadays. The only way was to give in as quickly and gracefully as possible, before this got any worse. Bugger that. She'd got him this time. By the elbow.

'Stop, Mum,' wailed Jack as she finally dragged him out of the shelf. 'You're hurting!'

'Then behave yourself or else there'll be real trouble!' Even as she uttered her empty threat, Bobbie was aware of a general sucking in of breath from the audience. Please don't let there be anyone she knew here! Someone from school or a neighbour perhaps, who had witnessed yet another example of her poor parenting skills. Bobbie was all too aware that within a few weeks of starting their new school, both her children had built up an impressive reputation at Corrywood Primary – and not for the right reasons.

Desperately, she tried to restore her credibility. 'You'll have to pay for the egg out of your pocket money.'

'But you stopped it,' protested Jack, trying to wriggle out of her grip. 'Cos I bit Daisy.'

That was true. Wow, it was hard to hang on to him! Her son was twisting and turning so that her arm was in danger of being yanked out of its socket. They'd moved to the front of the queue now as if, by unspoken agreement, everyone else had let them go first, keen to despatch them. Meanwhile, all that was left of Jack's crime was a silver and purple wrapper on the floor and a brown gooey smear round his unrepentant, grinning mouth.

'I'm afraid,' said Bobbie, flushing furiously, 'that my son has eaten some of our shopping before we could pay for it.'

The checkout kid gave them a disapproving glare. 'You've got to give it back. That's the rule.'

Short of giving him an enema, that might be a bit difficult. 'But he's eaten it! Can't we just pay for it?'

Dubiously, the checkout kid eyed the wrapper on the floor. 'Only if I have the bar code.'

Bending down, she picked up the packaging. But the chocolate had smeared the numbers – and now her hands! 'I'll get another,' offered Bobbie quickly. 'Stay there and don't move. Not *you*. My son.'

Quickly she dived out of her place, horribly aware that the some-parents-let-their-kids-get-away-with-murder rumbles were getting louder, belted down the aisle and raced back up with a substitute Action Man egg. Bar code intact. 'I do wish', she said hotly, 'that shops wouldn't put sweets so near the checkout. Can you have a word with your manager about that?'

The kid gave her a sharp look. 'I *am* the manager.'

What? For a minute, Bobbie was tempted to demand proof of age. Not that she, Bobbie, had ever been asked for verification of her own thirty-nine years. Sometimes she felt even older. Recently (horror of horrors), she'd actually begun to notice the beginnings of eye bags! Mind you, it was no wonder, after eight years of sleepless nights and impossible behaviour. Rummaging through her untidy purse to find her card, she was dismayed to find hot tears trickling down her cheeks. How could she be such a rubbish parent? How was it possible that she, Bobbie Wright, former PR manager, who had once been known for her cool, calm, efficient manner, have become this screaming fishwife of a mother?

'Why can't you behave?' Bobbie pleaded as she marched Jack towards the multi-storey car park. Even as she spoke, she realised she shouldn't be pleading. She should be *telling*. Who was in charge here? Don't answer that.

Jack flicked a bogey at her. 'Piss off.'

Stunned, she stared at him. Where had he got that from? It definitely wasn't a phrase they used in their house. Nor was it in the national curriculum – but then again, you never knew nowadays. 'WHAT DID YOU SAY?'

'NUFFING!'

Sensing he'd gone too far this time, Jack did a little twist, ducked out of her grip and shot off away from the walkway and into the road, narrowly avoiding a neat little blue sports car with, if she wasn't mistaken, the disapproving woman with gold hoop earrings at the wheel.

'JACK! COME BACK! For God's sake, you nearly got killed!' The shock, as she caught up with him – plus the effort of an emergency sprint – made her go hot and cold at the same time. The thought of life without Jack or Daisy was impossible. But if only she could be the nice rational mother she yearned to be, instead of this miserable, inconsistent failure who said 'no' one minute and 'yes' the next, just to keep the peace.

It wasn't that she was weak, as she'd tried again and again to explain to Rob. It was simply that two children in close succession was hard work. It might have been all right if they'd been the kind who did what they were told, like her sister-in-law's girls. But their own children had such strong personalities . . .

Jack with his indignant 'nuffings' was always arguing with his sister. He was incapable of sitting still. Constantly making demands, especially when she was on the phone for work. Only able to sleep if she lay down with him or stood outside his bedroom door, uttering empty threats such as 'if you don't stay in your bed, there'll be trouble'.

As for Daisy, her daughter – currently queening it at Saturday gym – she was just plain bossy! Eight going on eighteen. Convinced she knew better than anyone else. Not afraid of answering back, whether it was to her mother or teacher. *Shows lack of respect to authority*, her last report had said, as though this was her parents' fault. Was it because some of her generation treated their children as friends or equals instead of putting that parent/child distance between them as her own had done? Or was it because she, Bobbie was so inexperienced at mothering? After all, she'd never even picked up a baby before having her own – unsurprising, given

7

that she was the first out of her career-minded friends to get pregnant.

Of course, there were good moments. Well, seconds, if you were talking daytime. At night, when they'd finally dropped off, they both looked like little angels curled up in bed – Jack with his thumb in his mouth. Then she'd reproach herself for having yelled at them earlier on. But the next day, they would wake up, fully charged, and the arguments would start all over again.

Maybe, Bobbie told herself as she headed for her slightly dented, rather dirty Volvo estate with a protesting Jack firmly gripped by the scruff of his collar, they should have stayed put in Ealing. But moving out to Corrywood three months ago had seemed a good idea. More house for the money. Fresh air. A semi-rural environment that was just under an hour from London where Rob still worked. Not far from Pamela, her husband's sister, who would, he had assured her, be a 'real help'.

Bobbie still wasn't sure about that. Nor was she sure about Corrywood Primary where Jack had already got a black mark for pinching someone else's packed lunch and Daisy had upset the support teacher by correctly pointing out that the capital of Australia was Canberra and not Sydney.

How she missed their old school, not to mention her friend Sarah whom she'd known since antenatal days! If Sarah had been here, she'd have made her see the funny side. But right now, that was the last thing she felt like doing.

'Get in the car. NOW.' She almost pushed him into the back seat. 'I don't want to hear a word out of you until we've picked up Daisy from gym. Got it? Then we've got exactly one hour to change before we go to Aunty Pamela's. And if you two don't behave, you've had it. I really mean that.'

'Sorry, Mum.' A little pair of repentant arms reached up towards her. 'I didn't mean to be naughty.'

Was this the same child? Sometimes it felt as though there were two Jacks. The one who could be absolutely impossible, and the one who was merely mischievous and who gave her big warm cuddles. Bobbie's heart melted. 'I didn't mean to shout. But you must . . .'

Just then her jeans pocket vibrated. Bobbie's heart leaped at the name on the screen. At times, she would give anything to have her mother nearby. But in the meantime, they had to make do with phone calls. 'Mum! How are you?'

'Quite good, actually!'

That was a relief. Since her father had died more than ten years ago, Mum had been on her own and even though it hadn't been a great marriage, Bobbie knew she got lonely. Every school holiday, she and the children drove up north to see her (Rob was usually tied up at work) but it wasn't really enough. She could just see Mum now, she thought guiltily. Sitting at her little kitchen table, teapot by her side, pictures of the grandchildren on the fridge and a meal for one in the oven since there was 'no point' in cooking a big meal now there was only her.

'Actually, I've got some news. I've started to see someone.' Mum gave a nervous little giggle. 'He's called Herbert.'

'Really?' A slither of apprehension slotted itself into Bobbie's chest. No. That was selfish. Why shouldn't Mum have a life of her own?

'Yes! I won him at the WI raffle!'

'What?'

'I won a date with him, darling.' Mum was babbling like an excited teenager who'd just secured her first date. 'And we got on so well that we're still seeing each other. Herbert's actually rather famous. In fact, you might have seen him on television.'

'NO, JACK, NO! Sorry, Mum. Jack's trying to get out of the car. No, I'm not driving at the moment. Not this time. Please. Go on.'

'He's that famous psychoanalyst who goes into people's homes every week to get their children to behave.'

Bobbie felt herself break out into cold, shivery goose bumps. 'Not Dr Know? JACK, I SAID "STOP IT".'

'Yes! You'll like him. I know you will. In fact, I want you

both to meet. Herbert's very busy with his filming for a couple of months but we wondered if we could come down after that. I thought it might be nice to see you on Mothering Sunday.'

She'd love to see Mum too, but on her own. Not with Dr Know: that awful so-called expert, whom some critics reviled while others adored. The one who made parents weep when he accused them of inconsistency. The man whose name was constantly in the headlines with varying degrees of puns along the lines of 'Know-it-all' or 'Dr No' because of his firm views on discipline. The doctor who had written all those bestsellers on childcare. This was horrendous!

'There's just one tiny thing, dear.'

Bobbie could feel that slither of apprehension growing and growing, as she tried to hold her son back. 'Yes? NO, JACK!'

'It's a bit awkward, really.' Bobbie could just imagine her mother at the other end, twisting her hands nervously. She gave a good impression of being rather mouse-like to strangers. But every now and then, Mum proved she was made of stronger stuff. That's what Dad used to say, anyway.

'To be frank, dear, I was wondering if you could keep Jack and Daisy under control. Don't take it the wrong way but I'd like us all to make a good impression on Herbert. You do see what I mean, don't you? Bobbie? Are you still there? *Bobbie?*'

There was a young mum who lived in a shoe –
Though it felt, at times, just like a zoo.
There were kids always fighting
Or kicking and biting.
Oh what, oh what should she do?

Chapter 2

'What on *earth* are you wearing?' demanded Bobbie, staring in horror at her daughter, who was tottering down the stairs in silver sparkly tights, pale blue ballet leotard and a pair of black high heels pinched from her own wardrobe. 'We're going to Aunty Pamela's! Not an Ann Summers' party!'

Daisy flicked back her long straight blonde hair, adjusted the plastic fairy tiara on her head, leaped off the bottom step and gave a coquettish twirl. 'Who's Ann Summers?'

Hastily, Bobbie tried to backtrack. 'She's a sort of friend who wears very grown-up clothes. Clothes that aren't suitable for children.'

Her daughter pouted, just like her heroine on that loud American television comedy she was addicted to. Daisy, with her new adult front teeth that dwarfed the old babies on either side, couldn't wait to grow up. How well Bobbie remembered that stage even though she hadn't been allowed to do half the things her daughter got away with. 'I'm not a child. I'm eight! And I don't want to go to Aunty Pamela's anyway. She smells funny.'

Why did kids always tell the truth when they *shouldn't*? And *not* tell it, when they should?

Her sister-in-law did indeed reek: with a heavy expensive perfume that gave Bobbie a dull headache. Nor did it help that Pamela (never Pam!) treated her with a slightly bemused air of condescension, constantly referring, even after all these years, to Rob's previous girlfriend: a minor actress who still appeared in bit parts on television. Pamela's teenage daughters had inherited their mother's aloof, superior manner. Rob, of course, thought they were perfect. Not like his own kids.

Still, she could at least try to fail gracefully. Just for today.

'Can't you wear the Topshop tunic we bought specially for the party?' begged Bobbie. 'You loved it in the shop.'

'I've changed my mind.' Daisy's cool blue eyes met hers with the determination of a professional who had been walking over her mother for years. Daisy, like her brother, had a mind of her own. 'I want to wear *this*.'

Why sweat the small stuff, as her friend Sarah always said? There was no point in arguing – not when they had twenty minutes to get there. A smart lunch with Rob's goody-two-shoes sister, to celebrate her birthday, was the last thing she needed on a lovely crisp day like this! How much nicer it would be to go out for a walk along the canal, and allow the kids to run off some of this energy. Maybe go to the woods where the daffodils were bursting out. Or bung them in front of their Nintendo 3DS for some peace and quiet.

Instead, she'd have to try and make sure they behaved in company. Maybe it could be a practice run for Dr Know's visit. Bobbie still found it hard to believe Mum was really serious about this man. Then again, she'd always been a bit star struck. A real sucker for anything with the word 'celebrity' in it. Perhaps it was an escape from her fairly humdrum life. 'If only you all lived a bit nearer,' Mum often said wistfully.

One more thing to add to her guilt trolley! Along with Not Good Enough Mother, Nagging Wife and Frantic Freelance Market Researcher, Trying to Stay Sane. Meanwhile, Daisy, flushed with success at having won the clothes battle, did another look-at-me! pirouette in the sitting-room mirror, followed by her trademark dramatic pout. 'Where's Dad?'

She might well ask. Now they'd moved out of London, it took Rob much longer to get home. Last night it had been well past midnight when she'd heard his key in the door. And right now he was heading a Saturday morning 'team strategy brainstorming session'. When you were an advertising account manager, it was expected. Or so he said.

'But it's your sister's party!' she'd complained when he'd told her about today's meeting this morning.

'I'll get there as soon as I can,' he'd said, dropping a kiss on top of her head before dashing out of the door for the train. She'd sat at the table for a minute, wondering what had happened to the *proper* kisses he used to give her. The ones before the children had been born. They loved each other – of course they did. And at least they still 'did it' every now and then, unlike some of her old friends back in London. But there was no getting away from the fact that the kids had completely changed their relationship. Still, didn't that happen to everyone?

'Dad's going to meet us there.' Bobbie took another look at her daughter's outfit and shuddered. 'Let's get going, shall we?'

Another twirl! 'Only if I can give Aunty Pamela her present!'

Blast. She'd forgotten to wrap it. Bobbie picked up the huge cut-glass vase she'd bought at great expense for Pamela. It was always a challenge to find something for the woman who had everything. The last thing she'd got her (a rather pretty red floral cardigan) had ended up in that second-hand designer shop in town. Bobbie had come across it soon after moving here. The place had some nice stuff; including, or so it would seem, unwanted gifts.

Grabbing some leftover wrapping paper from her emergency supply under the stairs, she rifled through her bag for the car keys. 'Ready? Where's Jack gone now? JACK? JACK?'

Why did you always have to say everything *twice* when you were a parent?

'He's in his room. Dying on the Wii.' Daisy was eyeing her suspiciously. 'What's happened to your hair, Mum?'

'I put a rinse on it,' began Bobbie, glancing in the mirror. No! It had gone pink. Not chestnut as it had said on the packet in the supermarket. But bright fuchsia pink. Almost as bright as her daughter's sunglasses. But not nearly as removable.

Her sister-in-law Pamela and husband Andy lived at the other end of Corrywood: the 'posh' part with electric gates and parking space for three cars. Rob and his older sister had always been close, even though they were so different. Her husband was more easy-going; at least he had been when they'd first met.

Then again, so had she, Bobbie reminded herself as she stood at the door, trying to hang on to Jack's hand. Kids changed you. It was inevitable, just like sagging boobs and dwindling sex lives. And anyone who claimed otherwise was lying.

'You're late!'

So her husband had actually got here before her! Quite some time before, in fact, judging by the empty wine glass in his hand and open shirt without a tie. Sometimes, when Bobbie saw her husband outside the home, she realised with a jolt that he really was extremely good-looking, with those blond golden looks that ran in the family.

'And *you're* early,' she retorted, aware they were squabbling again. They seemed to be doing rather a lot of that recently. Maybe it was the job. Or the move. Or the kids. Or all three.

'Well, I said I'd try, didn't I? What on earth have you done to your hair?'

'Don't ask! It didn't do what it said on the packet.'

'My God, Daisy!' He was turning to his daughter now. 'What have you done to your face?'

'Red felt tip,' said Bobbie quickly, deciding to gloss over the furious who's-going-to-wrap-aunty-Pamela's-present? argument in the back seat. 'They wrote the card with it. Don't ask.'

Daisy circled her arms around Rob's waist, hugging him. Bobbie could remember doing the same with her father. There was something very special about the relationship between a little girl and her daddy. Even if the latter hadn't really deserved it, like her own. 'It's all over the car, Dad! It wasn't my fault! Jack wouldn't believe me when I said red was a primary colour.'

'IT ISN'T.'

'YES IT IS, STUPID.'

15

'Don't argue! Not as soon as we've got here!' Rob threw a disappointed look at Bobbie. 'Couldn't you have made the kids wear something more suitable? Jack's got chocolate all over his T-shirt. He looks an absolute mess!'

Clearly, he thought the same about her. Bobbie glanced at her reflection in her sister-in-law's French gilt hall mirror. Even if you ignored the pink streaks, it wasn't a pretty sight. Her mascara was smudged from where she'd burst into tears after Jack had dug the scissors into the car seat. And, oh no, there was red felt tip, which matched Daisy's, on her new blue shift dress, an outfit which had seemed perfectly presentable in the shop but which seemed downright dull compared with the pale green chiffon affair that was now floating up.

'Ah, you're here!' Pamela gave her an air kiss, avoiding (as usual) actual skin contact. You only had to look at her, marvelled Bobbie, to guess she had been a model. How did anyone get those amazing chiselled-out cheekbones? Her own looked like a clown's. Maybe that last-minute dab with the blusher had been too much.

'Interesting hair, darling. Now, Natasha, do go and get your aunt something to drink.' She glanced at her silver bracelet wristwatch. 'There's just about time before we eat.'

Pamela was one of those hostesses who wrote down exactly what she had served at which dinner party, so you never had the same meal twice. Bobbie on the other hand, had a repertoire of six dishes; two of which were pizza. Burned and just about edible.

'And, Melanie,' continued Pamela brightly, 'why don't you take Daisy to your bedroom so she can change out of her fancy-dress outfit?'

Bobbie took a deep breath. 'Actually, I'm afraid that we don't have anything else. Daisy insisted on wearing this.' She gave a small, scared smile. Her sister-in-law might once have been a world-famous name, but she had dedicated the last eighteen years to bringing up her perfect family. Frankly, it made Bobbie feel hugely inadequate. So too did her home,

16

which she had secretly nicknamed Princess Pamela's Palace. It was a vision of white carpet, artfully distressed walls, chrome fittings and priceless modern paintings. When Bobbie had first come here, she'd assumed the David Hockney in the downstairs loo was a print.

'Daisy *insisted*?' Pamela's immaculately painted mouth tightened. 'Oh dear, Bobbie. I've told you before. You really have to stand your ground as a parent.'

'Mum says I look like a friend of hers,' chipped in Daisy.

'Really? And who might that be?'

Daisy beamed. 'Ann Summers!'

Oh God.

Pamela's deep blue eyes – bearing no sign of lines or, heaven forbid, puffy bags – widened while Natasha and Melanie, both impossibly long-legged and blonde like their mother, began to snigger. Their mother silenced them with a look. Instantly, they stopped.

Neat! How did she do that? Bobbie felt like asking for the recipe.

'Look smart, Natasha, will you?' Pamela seemed different today. Tenser than usual. Almost as though she was waiting for something to happen. Knowing Jack and Daisy, that wouldn't be long. 'Let's take our guests into the drawing room for drinks, shall we?'

Guests? Bobbie stiffened with alarm. This was meant to be a family party. A 'small' affair to mark Pamela's birthday even though she didn't look a day older than when Bobbie had first met her. Judging from that line-free face, she wasn't averse to a spot of Botox. Bobby trailed behind her hostess as they walked along the spotless white carpet (whoops – Jack was leaving muddy sock prints!) and past the enormous kitchen where a flurry of caterers were at work, into the massive drawing room with its antique chandelier and original eighteenth-century fireplace, which Pamela had personally sourced from an architectural-salvage specialist.

Nervously, Bobbie took in the small group of navy-jacketed

men and women in cocktail dress perched on the edge of Pamela's beautiful pale yellow sofas from Harrods. A big party would have been all right! You could, she'd learned from experience, camouflage your kids in a crowd. But not today. Not when her lot were the only children there.

'Little ones!' squealed one woman in a high-pitched girly voice. She reached her hand out – were those nails *real*? – to touch Jack as though he was a zoo exhibit. 'How utterly adorable! How do you do, little man!'

Her son just stood there, scowling. After scoffing two chocolate Easter eggs, he was now in his sullen post-additive stage. 'Go on, Jack,' said Rob encouragingly with a slightly desperate edge to his voice. 'Shake hands.'

'Shan't.' Jack's hands remained silently stuffed in his jeans pocket. Belatedly, Bobbie wished she'd dried his smart trousers in time.

'Please,' she whispered urgently, horribly conscious that her mothering reputation was on the line here.

'Why?'

'Because it's polite,' hissed Rob and Bobbie at the same time. At last! They finally agreed on something.

Jack eyed the woman's red talons suspiciously. 'She might not have washed hers. You're always saying we've got to do that before we touch stuff.'

'I'm sorry,' said Bobbie, going puce red. 'Our son's rather shy. Sensitive too.'

There was a loud sound. An unmistakable rip. Followed by the most horrendous smell.

'Jack's farted again!' sang out Daisy.

'NO I DIDN'T.'

'YES, YOU DID!'

Bobbie couldn't even bring herself to look at anyone's face or to try and stop the arguing. When her lot yelled in capital letters, it was impossible to be heard.

'IT'S PONGO,' thundered Jack.

'Who's Pongo?' asked Red Talons faintly.

'He's our pretend dog.'

'When Jack makes a smell, Mum always pretends he's done it. It's cos it's less embarrassing. We'd love a real dog but we're not allowed one.'

Red Talons was frowning. 'But if you don't have a dog, how can you pretend he's making a smell?' She was addressing her question to Bobbie. 'It doesn't make sense.'

'Parenting *doesn't*!' Bobbie heard herself giving a slightly hysterical laugh. 'Believe me, you have to be mad to work there. Come on, you two. Let's give Aunty Pamela's present to her, shall we?'

She held out the large box, which looked as though it had undergone an emergency caesarean with criss-cross bandages of Sellotape and 'Happy Christmas' written on the wrapping paper. Whoops.

'I want to give it,' announced Daisy bossily.

'No. Me!' Jack charged in, his body colliding with his sister's.

'Do it together,' pleaded Bobbie. 'Please.'

'I'M THE YOUNGEST!'

'I'M THE ELDEST!'

Crash.

There was a silence as the vase flew out of the box (it looked as if the wrapping hadn't been very secure) and smashed straight into a rather lovely rosewood desk, shattering into several pieces.

For a moment, there was a hushed silence of horror.

'My Davenport!' gasped Pamela. 'It's dented!'

Then Daisy began to yell. 'MY HEAD HURTS!'

Jack's yell was even louder. 'SO DOES MINE!'

To Bobbie's horror, he flew at his sister. There was nothing for it but to dive in herself.

'Let go!' Bobbie begged, prising Jack's fingers off Daisy's nose.

'HE'S HURT ME!'

'NO I DIDN'T, TWIT FACE!'

'For a shy, sensitive kid, he's not slow at defending himself,' said one of the navy-jacketed men jauntily, as though trying to defuse the situation. Bobbie couldn't bring herself to look at her husband, who was standing on the edge of the circle, pretending that his children had nothing to do with him. If there was one thing Rob hated, it was being made to feel stupid. Especially in public. Just as well he hadn't come shopping with them that morning.

'SHE DID IT FIRST!' Jack was wailing now, to get sympathy.

'NO, I DIDN'T!' shrieked back Daisy, her small face puce with fury.

'Any serious injuries?' asked a pleasant, calm voice. 'No blood or signs of concussion? That's all right then.'

For a minute, Bobbie hardly recognised this kindly, not-very-tall, boyish-faced man. Andy – Pamela's husband – was rarely at family occasions. He had the kind of job that involved being away for weeks at end, in order to earn the fantastic amount of money that must be needed to run a house like this; not to mention that weekend pile in Devon where they'd been asked to stay a few times. He was also more normal than his wife; warmer and without that smart, clipped accent that smacked of expensive schools and pony clubs. One of those men who, despite not having particularly prepossessing looks, was actually rather attractive.

'Would you mind moving over here, everyone?' Andy was saying now. 'Thanks. Natasha and Mel will sweep it up. Then we'll have lunch. Meanwhile, how about another drink?'

After that, Bobbie knew that lunch would be a disaster. What kind of woman asked a seven- and eight-year-old to an otherwise all-adult birthday celebration? A woman who wanted to show up her sister-in-law, that's who. Yet Rob adored his older sister. In his eyes, she couldn't do any wrong. It was utterly maddening!

'Sit still, Jack,' she muttered fiercely for the umpteenth time as her son jumped up and down from his seat.

'But I want to watch that DVD you brought to shut me up.'

'And don't eat with your mouth full. I mean, *talk* with your mouth full.'

One of her nieces giggled again but was instantly silenced by one of Pamela's Looks. Wow! She ought to patent that.

'I'm sure your mother didn't mean that, dear.'

'Yes she did!' Daisy had now united with her brother to strengthen the opposition. Her manoeuvres could teach the UN a thing or two. 'She always lets us eat in front of the television so she can get some p and q.' Daisy put on her bossy look. 'That's "p" spelt with one letter. Not like the other one that's spelt "p" and then "e" and then another "e" . . .'

There was a gasp from the woman with the irritating little-girl voice.

'That's quite enough!' butted in Rob with the false jovial voice he adopted when pretending that this kind of behaviour was a mere blip in the otherwise serene radar of family life. 'Why don't you eat up this delicious lunch that Aunty Pamela has prepared?'

Pamela? Prepared this? Bobbie almost snorted. Hadn't Rob seen the team working their socks off in the kitchen? If she had as much help as Pamela had had over the years, she could have brought up a perfect family too! Instead, she had to work. Not her old lucrative PR work, which didn't fit in with school hours or holidays, but as a telephone market researcher, earning peanuts by making cold calls about anything from nappy rash cream to holidays. That reminded her. She still had to finish her quota by tomorrow night.

'It's disgusting!' Bobbie's attention was brought back to her daughter, who was poking the salmon suspiciously. 'I don't want it.'

Rob was going red. 'Daisy, that's very rude.'

'I can't help it. It tastes funny. And it's the same colour as Mummy's hair.'

Too late, she heard the fatal words coming out of her mouth. 'If you don't eat it up, you can't have any pudding.'

'Quite right,' muttered one of the other guests, shooting daggers in their direction.

Pamela nodded tightly. Her hands were clenched under the table, Bobbie noticed. 'The key to good parenting is to be consistent.' She glanced across approvingly at her two perfect daughters who were sitting, straight-backed, on the other side of the table.

Andy put an arm around his wife. Interesting! Pamela was visibly stiffening at his touch. 'Did I tell you', he said with a proud edge to his voice, 'that my wife has volunteered to run a Perfect Parents' class at the girls' school?'

'A parenting class?' squeaked the woman with the little-girl voice. 'I've heard about those! You can get free vouchers, can't you? My niece did it. Before her breakdown.'

Pamela nodded like a modest prefect accepting an honour. 'The PTA asked if I would be a volunteer. I've done a day's training, of course.'

'Not that she needed it!' Andy cut in. 'Pamela is a natural.'

Everyone nodded their heads although Bobbie couldn't help seething silently. Anyone could be a natural if they had kids who did what they were told. Just look at Mel, who was clearing the plates without being asked.

'In our day, parents didn't need help like this,' boomed a man in a pink shirt. His eyes fell on Jack's empty place. 'But today's generation gets away with anything.'

As he spoke, there was the sound of loud voices from the room next door. Loud American cartoon voices. 'The DVD player,' said Pamela, appalled. 'Someone's switched it on.'

Suddenly, Bobbie realised that Daisy's place was empty. And Jack's! She'd been too busy admiring her nieces' exemplary behaviour to notice her own two slipping off. 'COME BACK YOU TWO! THIS INSTANT!' A table of appalled-looking faces turned their gaze at her as though in one. Had she been yelling again? It was so easy to do it out of habit.

'Excuse me,' she said, pushing her chair back and running into the den next door. It was a room designed for the girls and their friends, Pamela had explained airily when she'd had it decorated – no doubt at huge expense – by an interior-design company from Knightsbridge. A room where they could relax on black leather sofas and listen to that incredibly complex silver high-tech system on the wall. The one with the wires that Jack was fiddling with right now.

'Stop! You might electrocute yourself. Come back to the table!'

Her son made a face. 'But I want to see what happens next!'

'Jack! I said leave those wires alone.'

'I can't. They won't go back properly.'

Desperately, Bobbie picked up a handful of spaghetti cables and shoved them behind the screen. 'Stay there,' she willed. The picture flickered and then went out altogether. Great. Now they'd bust the entertainment system.

'LOOK WHAT YOU'VE DONE, MUM!'

'Shhh.' Bobbie put a finger to her mouth. 'Don't say anything. Just come back to your seats. Everyone's waiting for you. It's SO embarrassing.'

Daisy folded her arms. At this rate, her daughter would have to be Prime Minister when she grew up. Or a teacher. 'Only if we can have pudding.'

'OK.' Instantly, Bobbie knew she shouldn't have given in. 'I mean no.'

'Then we'll tell them you broke the television. It's new. Mel said it cost thousands.'

'ALL RIGHT. YOU CAN HAVE PUDDING THEN!'

There was a gleam of triumph in Daisy's eyes. 'Come on, Jack.'

Everyone, apart from Andy, glared at them as they trooped back into the dining room. 'We've been talking,' her husband began, with an edge to his voice.

I bet you have, she almost said. She could just imagine how the tongues had been wagging during their absence.

'Why don't you join Pamela's class?' Rob glanced across at his sister as if for affirmation. 'You might pick up some useful tips.'

Bobbie could hardly believe it! 'Are you saying I'm not a good-enough parent?'

Pamela smiled smugly. 'We all need help, darling, from time to time.' She threw a disdainful look at Jack, who was picking his nose. 'Don't you think?'

Talk about patronising! 'Why', said Bobbie through gritted teeth, 'doesn't *Rob* sign up?'

Her husband shook his head as though she'd just suggested something really, really stupid. 'I work! How would I have the time?'

'I work *too*,' she retorted indignantly.

'Yes, but only from home.' Pamela's voice was silky smooth: serene again, without that tension Bobbie had noticed earlier. If it weren't for the fact that her sister-in-law was teetotal, she might have suspected she'd just knocked back a gin or two. 'Why not give it a go, Bobbie? Mel will babysit, won't you, darling?'

The two of them were treating her like a kid! If the children weren't here, she'd say something. But Daisy was looking at her with a please-don't-argue-with-Dad-again look.

'OK,' she said, gulping down half a glass of wine. It was like being dumped on the naughty step. On the other hand, it would be an evening off from the kids. *And* it might give her some tips before Mum arrived with Dr Know.

But she wouldn't tell anyone. Not even her best friend Sarah. After all, parenting classes were for parents who couldn't cope, weren't they? And no one, least of all her, wanted to admit to that.

Even if it *was* all too true.

There was a gran from Inverness,
Who told her daughter she knew best.
She came to stay –
But lasted one day,
Before being expelled as a pest.

Chapter 3

VANESSA

Vanessa was so upset by the scene in the supermarket that she had to force herself to concentrate on the road. That poor mother in the supermarket! She really had her hands full with that little monkey, thought Vanessa as she drove slowly back along the busy high street and into the part of town that wasn't quite as chic as the rest of Corrywood. There was a parking space right outside. For a second, she just sat there, gazing up with a quiet sense of pleasure and pride at the yellow awning with VANESSA written across it in clear black loopy letters.

Then she swung her legs out of her little car – a present to herself for her forty-fifth – and made her way into the shop. It was teeming with keen-looking customers, brows furrowed, all skimming through her rails with one eye over their shoulder, in case someone else should discover a bargain before them. Just the way she liked it!

At the back, near the racks of shoes and hats and handbags and costume jewellery – including that rather striking feathered peacock brooch that someone had brought in – there was a small group of children playing 'dressing up' with the box of clothes and shoes that she put out specially for them. If the kids were amused, she reasoned, their mothers were more likely to relax and buy something.

'Everything all right, Kim?'

Her assistant nodded. 'We sold the Norman Hartnell this morning,' she whispered excitedly. 'For the full price!'

Really? When Vanessa had discovered the incredibly glamorous cream sequinned satin evening dress in a pile that had been handed in by an extremely elegant regular (pushing eighty if she was a day), she had been astounded. But then again, nothing in this business ought to surprise her any more.

The shop had been a brainwave some years ago when she'd been addicted to Trinny and Susannah. Vanessa hadn't always agreed with their tastes, but they had proved that one woman's style could be another woman's disaster, and vice versa. At the time, she'd been a cleaner: a job she'd loved. Nothing like the satisfaction of shiny sinks, shiny floors and the smell of polish – not to mention the perks.

Vanessa had been amazed by the number of cast-offs that her generous, well-heeled clients pressed on her. 'Have this,' they would say when she'd finished cleaning their houses for them. 'Please! I don't wear it any more.'

And then she'd gawp at the Zandra Rhodes silk top or Armani evening dress which had been casually dumped into her arms almost as a tip (for she was good at her job and everyone knew it) and wonder how it was that anyone could have the money to buy such a gorgeous outfit and then only wear it once or twice or not at all. 'Where there's muck, there's brass,' her own mother used to say. But what could she do with these beauties? After all, it wasn't as though she had the kind of life where she could wear these clothes herself.

So she'd hoarded them up and taken out one of those business start-up loans which, together with her savings, had been just enough to start a small second-hand designer clothes agency in the old hardware shop that was going cheap because of its short lease.

Initially, some of the women of Corrywood had been a bit sniffy about wearing other people's cast-offs or, indeed, being seen at the wrong end of the high street. But word got around that these weren't just any old hand-me-downs. They were all designer names in fantastic condition. Vanessa was very fussy about that. And before long, her little business really took off.

Vanessa glanced down at the pink leggings she was wearing right now. A bit bright maybe but she still had the legs to wear them, so why not? She'd accepted them from a rather beautiful but aloof regular, who used to be a famous model some years ago. Vanessa always worked on a 50:50 commission rate. Her customers would wait, awkwardly, while she sorted through the bags they brought in, and then tell them if she was willing to give them hanging space. Only when they sold did she pay out. That way, she didn't have to buy stock. It was brilliant.

Part of her felt rather empowered as these women waited to see if she wanted their stuff or not. Another part of her felt sorry for them. It was amazing how many women really seemed to need the money nowadays although they tried not to show it. Even aloof customers like Pamela Gooding, who had pocketed that twenty-pound note the other day with surprising alacrity.

She was one of the locals who didn't want to be seen in a second-hand shop. So Vanessa would pick up her clothes from her house and then drop off her 'earnings'. Pamela had never actually invited her in, but Vanessa had snatched a quick glimpse from the imposing glossy black front door. The hall alone was bigger than her own two-bedroom maisonette.

'Mummy! Mummy! Look at my shoes!'

Vanessa couldn't help laughing at the sweet little girl shuffling along proudly towards her very pretty plump blonde mother who was jostling bosoms with a line of intent size fourteeners. They must have sold quite a few of the larger sizes that morning: the rail was looking distinctly sparse.

She frowned. 'Do we have any more new stock?'

Kim nodded half-heartedly. 'In the back room. Want me to go through them?'

'No thanks. I'll do it.' Vanessa ran her eye over the new window display which Kim had cobbled together that morning. Her assistant simply didn't get it when it came to colours. The bright red handbag looked positively garish next to the yellow dress! And as for the black boots, she'd already told Kim that they needed to go back to their original owner. If stuff didn't sell in eight weeks max, it had to be returned. Black boots were winter stock. They'd had their chance.

You had to be pretty ruthless in this trade, Vanessa reminded herself as she sorted through the various carrier bags in the back room, holding each item up to judge it for 'Corrywood appeal'. This Karen Millen dress was rather nice, although it had a stain on the sleeve. And this white Reiss jacket was brand new. Vanessa shook her head with disbelief. Still, didn't everyone have clothes like this? Outfits which had seemed like a good idea at the time but which ended up at the back of the wardrobe for one reason or other?

She spent the next hour deliciously distracting herself from that unsettling experience in the supermarket this morning while Kim handled the front end of the shop. By the time she finished, Vanessa had a small but prestigious pile of Yes's and a rather large pile of No's. If only, she thought as she finally locked up the shop and drove home with the bottle of Bombay Sapphire from the supermarket clinking in the boot, she could be so successful in her own personal life.

Had someone told Vanessa, years ago, that she'd lose touch with her only child, she would have laughed in their face and told them that nothing – nothing – would come between Brigid and her. Nor would she have believed them if they'd told her that 'her' Harry, whom she'd wed on her twenty-first birthday, was already married to someone else. But life was a strange thing.

Now, as Vanessa began to lay the table, putting pretty tea candles out to make up for the fact that she hadn't actually cooked dinner herself (one of the joys of living alone was that you no longer felt guilty about that sort of thing), her mind went back over the past in a way that she normally didn't allow herself to do.

She hadn't found out about the first wife until the woman had turned up at the house seven years later, furiously waving a wedding certificate. On closer inspection, it was horribly obvious that Harry – whom she'd fallen for, hook, line and

29

sinker, at the local ballroom dancing class – was indeed legally tied to this angry Irish redhead, spitting and swearing on her doorstep.

Brigid had just turned three, then. 'I don't want to lose you,' Harry had spluttered just before she'd thrown him out, declaring that she never, ever wanted to see him again. Only later did Vanessa wonder if she'd been too hasty. She had loved Harry, with his mop of black hair, bright blue eyes and clever way with words, not to mention numbers. Really loved him. And he had loved her. She was certain of that. But he'd lied and Vanessa had seen her own father do that once too often. Never would she allow another man to ruin her life. Not now. Nor in the future.

Privately, Vanessa blamed herself for being such a poor judge of character. She might have been young when she'd married Harry but she should have been savvy enough to have seen through him. Hadn't she had enough practice when growing up in her east London estate?

Still, if there was one thing her mother had taught her, it was how to survive. So Vanessa had picked herself up, moved out of London to a town where rents were cheaper and taken on cleaning jobs to fit in with nursery hours. At first, Brigid (named after Harry's mother at his insistence) had been a doll of a little girl with big round blue eyes and her father's mop of black hair. But it soon became apparent that she had also inherited his temper. Was it because she didn't have a father figure in her life?

But when Vanessa tried to get in touch with Harry so he could resume, rather late in the day, his parental responsibilities, she drew a blank. Letters came back to her marked *Return to Sender*. And his boss at the accountancy firm where she'd assumed he still worked, said he thought Harry had taken a job abroad but wasn't sure.

By the time Brigid was fourteen, with her heavy eyeliner and dreadlocks, she not only refused to go to school, she also refused to tell Vanessa where she was going in the evenings. 'It's none of your business,' she would yell.

30

'It is if you're living under my roof,' Vanessa would shout back.

'Not for much longer!'

Then Brigid had stormed out, leaving Vanessa to worry herself sick all evening until she finally returned in the small hours. This pattern went on for two years until one evening, Brigid had come in, white-faced, with a pregnancy kit in her hand.

She didn't want to think about the next bit. It was too painful. In fact, she shouldn't have allowed herself to have gone as far as this. Besides, there wasn't time. Vanessa felt a delicious shiver go through her. If she wasn't mistaken, tonight might just be the night! Then she began to tremble. Was she really, finally ready for this? It wasn't just the sex. Any fool could do that. It was the other thing.

Maybe, Vanessa told herself, putting the final touches to the table before getting herself dressed, this wasn't such a good idea after all. Perhaps she ought to ring and cancel.

'Coward,' whispered a voice in her head.

That did it. 'I might have made some wrong decisions but I'm not afraid of anything,' she said out loud, almost as if to convince herself. Besides, she had other things to think about tonight.

There was a young girl called Jo,
Whose favourite word was 'no'.
      She yelled and she cried
      And she went all boss-eyed,
Till her brother stamped hard on her toe.

(Then she belted him back and they're still arguing.)

Chapter 4

Vanessa had always loved the long-drawn-out preparations for a date. Even though she felt particularly nervous tonight, the clothes helped to calm her down. The oyster-coloured silk undies which she could now afford to buy brand new. The red jersey dress which she'd kept for herself from stock, rather than re-sell it. (Red was her favourite colour at the moment because it made her hair look even blonder.) And then the matching heels which had come from another regular client but which could have been made for the dress.

She spent a long time putting each one on, savouring the ritual. It was part of the deal she had made with herself a long time ago. The more you occupied yourself, whether it was working or dressing yourself up for a blind date, the more you could block out the past in your head. She'd made a mistake that morning in the supermarket, allowing that freckled-faced boy and his frantic mother to take her back in time.

But now, as she sat in front of her dressing table, carefully applying a tasteful line of fake eyelashes, she felt more like her old self. More like the Vanessa who had told herself, five years ago, that if she was going to survive, she had to re-invent herself.

Part of this re-invention process had been to start internet dating. Of course everyone did it nowadays but when Vanessa had started, wasn't quite so common. Rather daring in fact. She'd taken some risks, she could see now. Gone out with men without leaving her phone number with anyone although, to be honest, she wasn't the type who had lots of friends anyway. People could let you down. It was simpler to have lots of 'good acquaintances' but never allow them to grow too close.

She'd had the same attitude towards the men she'd met. 'Are you looking for a husband?' one of them had asked hopefully in the early days. Vanessa had run her eyes over the small, sandy-haired man with glasses and tried to compose a tactful reply in order to save his feelings.

'Afraid not. I just want a bit of companionship, that's all.'

And it was true. She might have added that she also wanted to be admired. To be assured that she was still attractive in bed. But then again, she'd never let them get that far. Sex, in Vanessa's view, was something that had to be saved. Saved for the right person if he ever came along. Not that she was looking, mind you. When you'd been bitten once, it took a long time to trust again and Vanessa hadn't been sure until last autumn that that would ever happen.

But then she'd met Brian Hughes.

It had been through one of those sites which promised to match you up with local applicants. Until then, Vanessa had preferred dates that were outside her area. London or Milton Keynes. Places that she could get to easily enough but where there wasn't a likelihood of bumping into someone after a date that hadn't worked out. But her eye had been drawn to this one, perhaps because it didn't promise miracles like so many.

Meet a friend, it had said simply. That was it. No expectations of roses or champagne or wedding bells. Just meet a friend.

Later, Brian said that the wording had grabbed him too. 'It wasn't threatening,' he had said in the succinct way that had attracted her right at the beginning. His matter-of-fact manner of speaking, which had seemed slightly abrupt on the phone, was, she decided when they met in person, a mask for a rather nice, shy man, who was (according to his profile) in his mid-fifties. Not too old but not too young either, unlike some of his predecessors.

He was stocky rather than tall, and she didn't care much for his dress sense – ghastly maroon jumper! – but she still got good vibes about this man as he shook her hand firmly and said it was very nice to meet her. Vanessa also had this strange feeling that she'd seen him before.

To her relief, he hadn't bought cinema tickets at all (she hadn't cared for the somewhat violent film on offer) but suggested dinner instead at a rather nice little Italian round the corner. Italian was her favourite and, as it turned out, Brian's too.

'So,' he said after they'd ordered whitebait for starters followed by lasagne and then smiled, rather hopefully, because their tastes were so similar, 'what's your story?'

Vanessa wasn't used to this. Usually, internet dates initially hopped around banalities, like 'What do you do?' and 'Have you ever done this before?' But Brian got straight to the point. Instinctively, she felt there was no side to this man who spoke so courteously to the waiter (she'd dropped a previous date for being rude in a restaurant) and who now settled back in his chair, waiting for her to talk.

So she'd given him the sanitised version of her story, minus the bigamy. Married young. Marriage didn't work out. Husband left when daughter was three. Daughter now 'doing her own thing'.

Brian had listened, nodding at the right bits without saying anything and then, when she'd finished (how she hated men who interrupted!), leaned back in his chair and said, 'My wife died five years ago.'

Vanessa's heart had sunk. She'd had widowers before. Usually all they wanted to do was talk about their departed loved one and weep into their wine glasses before confessing that they could never forget their dead wives but that they missed having someone to talk to. When this had first happened, she'd been sympathetic. But after a few widowers, she'd realised that the 'someone to talk to' had been a euphemism for something else. And when she'd said she didn't want the bed part yet, they hadn't bothered getting in touch again.

'We didn't have a great marriage.' Brian's next words, steady and clear, shook her. 'Should never have got together in the first place, to be honest.' He made a rueful expression. 'But we stuck together for the sake of the kids. The kids we tried to have.'

Then his voice changed. 'By the time we gave up, it seemed too late to split. Couldn't bear the idea of hurting each other.'

This was a good man, she realised. Honest too.

'Still missed her when she went,' he added, shaking his head. 'Funny thing, that. Despite our differences, I always thought we'd grow old together. But I get round it by keeping myself busy.'

He suddenly jerked up his head to look her straight in the eyes. 'Not many people know this. From the outside, Mavis and I looked like the perfect couple. But there's something about you, Vanessa, that makes me feel I can tell you anything.'

She was flattered. Careful, she told herself. Not so fast.

'What do you do?' she asked, wondering if she was being too nosy. 'If you don't mind me asking, that is.'

'Not at all.' He sat up straight as though taking pride in what he was about to say. 'I used to teach, for my sins. Headmaster, actually, but I had to take early retirement due to health.' Then he leaned forward; clearly wanting to make a point. 'I'm much better now they've got my medication sorted. Fit as a flea, in fact.'

'A headmaster?' she repeated. 'Round here?'

He nodded enthusiastically. 'Corrywood. Do you know it?'

She took a deep breath. 'My daughter went there. Brigid. Brigid Thomas.'

Something flickered in his eyes. 'Thought I'd seen you before!'

She bit her lip. 'Me too.'

'I remember her quite well. Clever girl.'

'Yes.' Vanessa looked away. This was getting too close to home. Uncomfortably close. How much did he know exactly?

There was a brief silence. 'So what do you do, Vanessa?'

She seized the opportunity to change the subject. 'I run a shop. Vanessa's in town. It sells second-hand designer clothes.'

'What a great idea! I'm all for recycling. Got quite green since my retirement, I have!'

'Really?' She was glad to steer the conversation back to him. That coincidence about Bridget had thrown her. 'So what do you do, now you're retired?'

Now he had a schoolboy twinkle in his eyes. 'Actually, I own half a racehorse.'

Was he kidding? Vanessa had never, ever met anyone who owned a horse, let alone a racehorse. Racehorse-owners were the kind of people who wore smart jackets at Ascot on the telly: always a good time for business because regulars like Pamela Gooding usually needed a new outfit for Ladies' Day. She glanced at Brian suspiciously in that maroon jumper with worn-away elbows. 'Half a racehorse', he had said. Sounded like a fantasist to her . . .

'Please,' he said, putting out a hand as she stood up. 'Don't leave. I'm not winding you up. It's like this.' His eyes – a rather nice blue with green flecks – grew slightly dreamy. 'When I was a little boy, growing up in Kent, my dad used to take me to the bookies. I loved it!' His face shone with such delight that Vanessa knew he was telling the truth. 'Loved the air of excitement as we all hung round the desk, listening to the radio. Loved the big board with all those names and numbers next to it. Loved it when my dad won and we got fish and chips for tea. Felt desperately sorry for him when he came back empty-handed and my mum would have a go at him for spending the rent money.'

He stopped. Vanessa was hooked. 'It was after one of their bust-ups that I decided.' His eyes met hers again, serious this time. 'I was going to save up for a magic horse that would win every race. I'd give the winnings to Mum and then she'd never have to worry about paying the rent again.'

'That's lovely,' exclaimed Vanessa, her lasagne lying forgotten and cold in front of her. 'So what happened?'

'I got into teaching because it was a safe job and because I like kids. At weekends, I'd hang round the local stables, offering to muck out free of charge. Drove Mavis crazy, it did. But I loved the smell. Loved the way that horses listen

37

without judging you. Loved the warmth when you put your head against them.'

'But how on earth did you afford one for yourself?' It was, Vanessa couldn't help thinking, a bit like her buying Harrods. Nice thought but completely out of reach.

He put his elbows on the table. For a minute, she could see an excited little boy. 'There was another bloke at the stable who wanted to buy this sixteen-hand gelding with potential. He couldn't afford to do it on his own so he was looking for someone else to go halves.' Brian shrugged. 'Mavis had died by then. I'd got my health back and frankly I was bored with retirement. So I blew my life savings! Best thing I ever did! There's nothing like the thrill of watching a race and knowing that yours is in it! Got myself a little van too, so I can travel round the country watching Upper Cut.' He grinned. 'That's his name.'

Wow! She'd never have thought it of him. Not from the outside, anyway. 'That's amazing!' she breathed.

'You think so?' Brian looked pleased as he topped up her glass with house red. 'I could never have done it when my wife was alive. We led a very safe life, Mavis and I. But after she went, I thought: Well, why not take a few risks in life? It's not as though I have anyone to let down any more, is it?'

Just what she'd thought when she'd opened the shop. She couldn't have risked that business loan if she'd had Brigid to support. And even then she might not have done it if she hadn't decided it was time to live life dangerously.

Brian leaned back in his chair and gave her the kind of look that you usually only gave someone you'd known for a while. Not a first date. 'Being on your own has its perks but it's nice to share successes with someone, don't you think?'

This was moving too fast! Much faster than she usually did. To mask her embarrassment, Vanessa took a sip of wine which turned out to be a gulp. The gulp became a cough and suddenly she was spluttering all over her dress. All over her plate. And all over Brian's jumper.

'Hey, it's OK.' He passed her another napkin, not seeming to worry about the mess on his clothes. 'Honest. We've all done it.' He grinned. 'At least I'm wearing the right colour! Now, how about pudding? Great! I've got a bit of a sweet tooth, I'm afraid. Another one of my sins.'

His large hand closed over hers on the stained white linen cloth. It felt warm. Friendly. Secure, yet exciting at the same time. 'I'd really like to see you again, Vanessa. What do you reckon?'

Of course she wanted to see him again! Over the next few weeks, Vanessa – rather to her surprise – found herself bursting out into song every now and then in the shower or on her way to the shop; snatches of tunes that she thought she'd forgotten. 'You seem happy,' Kim had said suspiciously when she'd caught Vanessa at it in the stock room.

Yes she was – but she wasn't telling why! Both she and Brian, by mutual agreement, withdrew their profiles from the dating site. Once a week, they'd meet up for dinner or a film. It wasn't always a Saturday because that was often a race day and Brian could be anywhere in the country, watching Upper Cut from the owners' box.

'Come with me,' he would say but Vanessa needed to be in the shop. Besides, it would be too big a commitment, she told herself, to be seen out and about by all Brian's friends.

Just as it would be too big a commitment to go to bed with him.

They'd talked about it, of course. Not in words but in gestures. Brian kissed in a way she had never been kissed before. The first time, she'd been completely blown away. It was like being taken into another room in her body that she had never entered before. Who'd have thought it? He didn't seem that kind of man from the outside.

They'd gone further but not much. When she thought about it, Vanessa got a funny tingle running down her spine as though she was a teenager again. But every time he tried to unbutton her top on her sofa (she wasn't very keen on *his* house, which smelt musty and had Parker Knoll chairs) she gently steered his hand away. 'I'm sorry,' was all she would say. And to her amazement, he accepted it.

This couldn't go on for ever, though. Several months of dating without sex would have been the right thing to have done if she'd still been a teenager. But they were both grown-ups. Tonight, Vanessa thought nervously, while spraying on her usual Chanel No. 5, she needed to tell Brian the truth.

As if on cue, the bell rang with its jolly waterfall chimes. Vanessa took a deep breath, checked her Silky Sienna lipstick in the mirror, pressed her lips briefly against the photograph of a teenage Brigid by her bed – something she often did, as a comforting ritual – and went to open the door.

'Did it hurt?' asked Brian, looking across at her.

They were lying, naked on her bed, the gourmet meal for two lying uneaten in the cooker. Earlier that evening, when he'd arrived, it was as though he knew exactly what she was thinking. Wordlessly, he had taken her by the hand and led her to her own bedroom, which she had had the foresight to tidy up first.

For the last two hours, they had done nothing but touch. She hadn't realised it could be so erotic.

Now she nodded, watching him draw his finger along the neat scar where her right breast used to be. 'Yes. I was scared too. But – and I know this sounds awful – the worst bit was losing my hair. It came back a different colour and the texture was different.'

He nodded, glancing at the line of wigs on her dressing table. The wigs that she alternated every six months. Then he ran his fingers through her real hair: short, spiky and mouse-coloured. 'I like this as well. It's natural. Did you find the lump in the shower?'

She nodded.

'My wife did the same.' He spoke quietly. She hadn't realised it was breast cancer. It had been one of those subjects they'd steered clear of.

40

'When?' he said, moving his hand to the other breast. For the first time as long as she could remember, Vanessa felt a quickening below her waist.

'Five years ago. I've got the all-clear now. One of the nurses at the hospital told me that I could do two things. Worry myself to death in case it came back, or put it behind me and live each day to the full.' She smiled to herself at the thought of that kind woman; one of so many. Say what you wanted about the NHS, there were some amazing people in it. 'I chose to do the latter,' she added.

He nodded, gently turning her to one side so that his naked body spooned hers. She could lie like this for ever, she thought to herself. The great thing about going to bed with someone your age was that they didn't have a perfect body either. But at the same time, she could feel herself sweating with anticipation.

'Is that why you haven't slept with anyone since Harry?'

She whipped round to face him. 'How did you know?'

He smiled down at her, tracing the outline of her face with his thick index finger. 'Instinct.'

She nodded. 'I wasn't ready before and then when I was, I got this.' Forcing herself, she looked down at the scar. It might be neat but it was a constant reminder that she had nearly copped it. Not that anyone would have cared if she had. She had felt weird, being unable to put a name in the next-of-kin box. No point in putting Brigid's.

'I think it's beautiful.'

Beautiful? 'You can't really mean that.'

'I do.' His tongue gently licked her scar. Slowly. Carefully. Exploring her. 'It's a sign of bravery. And a medal to show that you have won.'

Then his mouth came down on hers and his hands began to do things that she had never known possible. 'Headmaster,' she murmured. 'Are you feeling my legs, like you size up a racehorse's?'

'Absolutely,' he murmured back. 'And I think we've got a real winner here . . .'

They were still in that lovely post-sex companionable silence when the doorbell went. 'I'll ignore it,' she mumbled hazily and Brian had sleepily nodded his agreement. But the waterfall chimes continued. Again and again. Someone wasn't going to give up.

Then a thought hit her and she sat up. What if the shop had been broken into? It had happened to the curry place next door last month, courtesy of some lager-happy louts. Consequently, she'd had a new alarm fitted that went straight through to the call centre. It might be the police!

More alert now, she slid out of bed, slipping on her pink silk pyjamas and pulling a cream rose-print wrap around her shoulders. Brian had gone back to sleep, sprawled over most of the bed. Part of her felt tempted to wake him up and tell him to do his man stuff. But then again, she'd managed so far on her own, hadn't she? They might have slept together, and yes, it had been pretty amazing, but it didn't change things. Independence was the only way forward if you weren't going to get hurt.

The doorbell was even more persistent now. 'All right, all right, I'm coming.' She made her way through the kitchen, taking a knife from the box set just in case. She could see a figure through the glass door. A tall figure which looked as though it was holding something.

Slipping the safety chain in place, Vanessa opened the door a chink. 'Who is it?'

Bloody hell! She'd been right to bring the knife. The man on the other side looked like the kind of youth you would definitely cross the road to avoid. Tall with a dark complexion and knotted dreadlocks partly covered by a dirty yellow beanie.

'Are you Vanessa? Vanessa Thomas?'

'I might be. Why?'

'Brigid told me to give you this.'

Her daughter! For a minute, Vanessa's heart soared with disbelief and wonder and hope, all mixed in one. 'You know her? Where is she?'

'Gone away.' The youth's voice was impatient. 'That's why she's left you this. Now, are you going to take her or not?'

Her?

It was only then that Vanessa saw that the large bundle in the man's arms wasn't just a dirty old blanket. My God! It was a child. Fast asleep. Her throat tightened so much that she could hardly speak.

'What's going on?' Brian's deep voice was behind her. 'Get back, Vanessa. I'll handle this.'

'No!' Vanessa heard her voice rising. Brian's intervention, well meaning as it was, annoyed her. This was a family matter. Nothing to do with the man whom she'd allowed to share her bed. Quickly, she undid the safety chain and snatched the bundle before the youth could take it away. The child opened her eyes (emerald green!) as though she'd been pretending to be asleep.

Vanessa gasped. This child was the perfect miniature of Brigid at that age. Quite a lot smaller – as though she was four instead of six – but with the same little nose and dark hair just like Harry's side of the family. There was no mistaking the resemblance.

'What's your name?' she whispered.

'Sunshine.'

The word came out quite clearly and then the eyes closed again.

'Is she ill?' demanded Vanessa, suddenly scared.

The youth sniffed. 'Just tired. We've been travelling.'

'And where is Brigid?' Her voice came out like a squeak.

'I told you. Gone away.' He handed her a letter. 'She wants you to look after her now. It's all in here.'

Then he was off. Swallowed up into the darkness like some kind of ghostly hoody apparition with a backpack.

'Who was that?' asked Brian, looking down the path.

'I don't know. But this', she said, looking tenderly down at the shock of matted black hair, 'is my granddaughter.' She stroked the little soft cheek gently. Yearning, desperately yearning, to kiss the child but at the same time not wanting to wake her. 'At least I think she is.'

43

There was a young mum from Whitehall,
Whose kids drove her clean up the wall.
    She begged, 'Do as you're told
    Before I grow old!' –
But the order was far too tall.

(So she's still on the ceiling.)

Chapter 5

ANDY

Andy Gooding knew perfectly well that if anyone asked his wife what her husband did for a living, she would wave her beautiful tanned arms in the air dismissively and say something airy about 'finance'. It wasn't that Pamela wasn't interested, as she'd once explained, it was just that she'd had enough of 'that kind of thing' in the past.

'That kind of thing' meant work. When Andy had met Pamela, she'd been famous as *the* girl in the lingerie adverts. You couldn't go anywhere without seeing her on giant posters or inside glossy magazines or reading about her lifestyle in broadsheet newspapers as well as the tabloids. The whole nation (and most of Europe) was in love with this beautiful eighteen-year-old who had been discovered in the student canteen at LSE.

Brains as well as beauty, one caption had said, drooling over this long-limbed, honey-skinned blonde whom every woman in the country wanted to be – and whom every man dreamed of bedding.

Of course their paths would never have crossed if Pamela's agents hadn't used his firm for financial advice. Even then, a meeting wouldn't have been on the cards if he hadn't used his senior position to wangle an invitation to the agency Christmas party at Stringfellows (Stringfellows!) in the hope that he might catch a glimpse of the famous Pamela. Never Pam, as she told journalists firmly. Always Pamela.

But then she'd spilt a drink down him at the bar. At first he hadn't even realised it was *her* because there were so many beautiful people around. 'I'm sorry,' she had said in an impeccable Home Counties accent which Andy himself had been trying to cultivate for years. He'd assured her that it didn't matter one bit and, in doing so, managed not to have just one word with her but at least ten.

Then she'd glided off to talk to someone else but, as she did so, she had looked back and given him another lovely smile as though he was some strapping ex-public-school boy instead of a man with a boyish grin, a too-short hair cut and traces of an Essex accent who was only (just) an inch or so taller than she was. And that's when Andy knew he had no chance. No chance whatsoever. Because, despite his experience with women gleaned from evenings in sleazy Soho bars – or maybe because of it – this gorgeous creature really was out of his league.

But miraculously – all these years later, he still couldn't believe this! – she was outside the club when he left, standing by the pavement and looking for a taxi. A couple of men had come up to her, pestering for autographs. Then one of them made a suggestive comment. Andy might seem like a medium-sized, mild-mannered man on the outside but he'd learned how to fight his corner. 'That's enough,' he'd said firmly. 'She's with me. Now clear off, both of you.'

Andy was embarrassed by the 'She's with me' words that came out of his mouth but as he flagged down a taxi, Pamela stepped into it and then reached across to beckon him in as though she expected him to follow. 'Thank you,' she said.

Andy fought back the urge to apologise for having been so forward just now in declaring that they were together and, instead, reached across for her hand in the silence of the back of the black cab. Incredibly, she didn't take it away.

Not many people knew exactly why Pamela, at the height of her career, dropped everything to marry a rather quiet, not particularly good-looking but extremely wealthy financial whizz-kid. After all, if it was gold she was after, she could have had her pick of playboys. 'I know I'm young but I'm ready to settle down and start a family,' was all she would say to the magazines who hounded her for interviews.

Andy himself was astounded by his luck, despite the little warning voices in his head. 'She's using you,' they said. 'You'll regret it. You'll see.' But he'd shoved the voices to the back of his mind and as the years had gone by he'd realised how right he'd been to do so. Pamela was the perfect wife. She was a wonderful home-maker. The house always looked immaculate. Even though they sometimes used caterers, she would cook herself for important business dinner parties.

Every now and then, one of his clients would have the nerve to ask if his wife really was *the* Pamela. The model who used to be so famous. And then he'd make one of those faces that indicated it was indeed true but that he couldn't possibly discuss it. Inside, the recognition made him feel special: something that Andy hadn't had a great deal of in his life until now.

Sometimes, when Pamela's credit-card statement was way over the limit, Andy would feel a little start in his chest. Then he told himself not to be so boring. So what if she enjoyed spending money? They could afford it and, besides, it gave Andy pleasure to know that he was able to provide his beautiful wife with the standard of living that she was entitled to. Even if it did mean working so hard that, ironically, there wasn't much time to enjoy the family life he had always yearned for.

It went without saying that Pamela was a brilliant mother. Incredible really, given that she and her brother had been brought up by a string of au pairs and nannies. 'That's why I want to look after our girls myself,' she was always saying. Sometimes Andy was worried because Pamela didn't seem to have any close friends: she had little time for socialising with the other mothers at Corrywood High apart from her PTA and fund-raising activities. 'I want to concentrate on my family,' she'd say sweetly. 'I need to be the lynchpin while you're away, earning the money.'

It was all so very different from his own background: a childhood which no one knew about, not even Pamela. A childhood where all he'd ever wanted was a pair of warm, loving arms around him. How he had yearned – still did, to be honest – for a mother's tender kiss on his face. A home to come back to after school where someone would listen to his day and cook him tea. A brother or a sister maybe, whom he could talk to. Really talk to. Somewhere safe. Somewhere where no one could hurt him.

It had been his wife's nephew at the lunch party who had brought back all the memories. Jack! His mouth twitched. Little scamp! Not that Pamela had seen it that way. 'Such badly behaved children,' she had shuddered. 'I blame Bobbie. She lets them get away with murder.'

Privately, Andy felt sorry for the pretty but exhausted-looking woman; a fresh-faced, natural girl-next-door type, who had clearly been so embarrassed after the broken vase incident. 'Some children are harder to deal with than others,' he'd said casually while helping Pamela to load the dishwasher.

'Rubbish,' his wife had retorted. 'It's all a question of being firm at the beginning. And please don't do it that way, Andy, or the cutlery won't get washed properly. Just go and sit down, will you! I'd rather do it on my own.'

So he had. Not exactly sat down, because Andy wasn't the sitting-down type, but he did have some paperwork to do in his office: a rather nice room at the back of the house, overlooking the lawn, with an expensive mahogany desk and a large studio portrait of Pamela and the girls staring down at him approvingly. Every time he looked at that picture, it gave him inspiration. This was what he was working for. This was what he had achieved, despite everything.

The first time he'd seen his step-dad hit his mum really badly was on his tenth birthday. (In those days, his name had been Barry.) The argument had been his fault. Barry knew that because his mum said so and she was never wrong. 'If it wasn't for you, I wouldn't have to stick around in this hole,' she had yelled at him, nursing her black eye with an already bloody dishcloth.

In the event, she didn't stick around. When Barry woke up

48

the next morning, shivering under the thin, scratchy blanket on the sofa where he slept because there was only one bedroom in the flat, she had gone. 'See you tonight,' his step-father had mumbled, pressing a tenner into his hand. With hindsight, Barry should have realised something was up. Neither his mother nor step-father had ever given him money before and he fingered the dirty note with reverence because it was the very first birthday present he had ever been given.

When Barry came back from school and found his step-father wasn't having his usual pre-shift kip, he used some of the money to buy fish and chips. A real treat! Rather oddly, his step-dad didn't come back the next morning and there was still no sign of his mother. Not sure what else to do, Barry just took himself off to school. This went on for a week until he finally asked his teacher if she could lend him some money for tea as the tenner had run out and he didn't know where his parents were.

'Weren't you worried, dear?' asked the headmistress as he stood waiting in her office for social services to arrive. Barry hadn't liked to say that no, he hadn't been. That it was actually a relief not to be belted by his mum if he said something she didn't like.

The foster home was all right, really. For the first time in his life, he had a proper bed. Barry was so excited that he couldn't contain himself. 'You've ruined the mattress!' yelled his foster mother the next morning. 'Look, it's soaking wet. What are you? A baby?'

After that, it seemed Barry could do no right. When he made the mistake of exploring a top shelf in his room, all hell broke out. 'I just wanted to know what was inside,' he'd tried to explain when they found him with bits of a model train scattered all over the floor. How was he to know it had belonged to his foster parents' son, who had died years ago?

That was the beginning. It was very easy, Barry soon learned, to earn a label. He might as well have worn it round his neck. *Bad boy*. The one who gave lip. 'Don't answer back,' snapped his foster mother when he'd pointed out that it wasn't he who had picked at the cold meat in the fridge which was meant for the next day, but the other foster kid they'd also taken in.

'Why do they have us if they don't like us?' Barry asked him during an uneasy truce that night.

'Cos they get paid, stupid,' the boy had replied.

It wasn't long before the foster parents decided he wasn't worth the money and he was sent to a children's home. It was colder there with a continual, over-riding stench of urine but he didn't mind too much. He made some good friends: boys that taught him it was his right to take stuff even if it didn't belong to him. 'Why should it all go to people who speak posh?' demanded one of his new mates. There seemed a certain logic in that.

After Barry was put up as the kid who smashed the window of the local off-licence while his mates ran in and grabbed as many bottles as they could carry, he was sent to another home that stank of urine and cabbage. He met new friends there. Got into more trouble; some of which was too painful to recall. But then the place got a new manager. At least that's what they called him, although he seemed more like a friendly headmaster to Barry.

'What do you want to do in your life?' asked the man when he called Barry into his office after yet another fight in the dorm. By then, Barry was fourteen. He couldn't read very well but he did like figures. For some reason, they reached out to him during maths lessons; they were clean cut; they said what they meant instead of pretending to be his friend and then turning on him.

'I want to do something with numbers,' Barry heard himself saying.

He'd expected the manager to laugh. To tell him that he was far too stupid for a job with numbers. But instead, the man looked at him hard before nodding. 'Good idea. Let's see what we can do, shall we?'

Before the year was out, Barry was one of the few kids in the home to sit a proper maths exam. By the time he was sixteen, and old enough to move into a hostel, the head had helped him find a place at college. Barry never looked back. He changed his name from Barry to Andy, after one of his football heroes. And he worked harder than any of the other students, driven by the excitement that, at last, he was good at something! He refused to drink because that's what had helped him get into trouble in the first place. But he did start to go out with girls. And he discovered quite a flair in that department.

At thirty, the new Andy wouldn't have given the old Barry a second glance, although he always stopped when he saw a homeless person sitting in a London doorway to toss him a few coins. He had his own two-bedroom mews house, thanks to some shrewd investments based on tips that he'd gleaned from the sleazy Soho bars. Then had come the biggy. The tip he'd heard while sitting on the office toilet. A whispered conversation between his boss and another man by the urinals when they thought no one else was listening. A name. One name. That was all. But it was said in such a way that Andy found himself risking all his savings. For a few heart-stopping hours, he was so nervous that he had to go home sick. But the following day, the financial papers proved him right. Right to go against the advice that he could have taken in the Gents. Overnight, Andy became a wealthy man. Far wealthier than his boss, who was on a five-figure salary.

And that was exactly the stage he'd been at when he'd met Pamela. Beautiful Pamela who had grown up with a brother, two parents, a pony and an au pair in a gracious Georgian house in the country. Her lovely face had frowned with concern when he told her that both his parents had been killed in a car crash when he was a baby and that he had been brought up by a maiden aunt, who was also long dead.

But deep down, he couldn't quite get rid of that naughty little boy inside. The one who whispered into his ear every now and then. The one who kept asking him how he could live this lie and wasn't it time, before too long, to rebel? Because somehow, life with its daily grind of meetings and

51

emails, wasn't much fun any more. And although he still needed to provide for his beautiful wife and daughters, Andy Gooding couldn't help wondering if this was it. If this was all there was to life.

A mum* there was, whose kids drove her to drink.
Each night, a bottle or two she would sink.
   She drank from a beaker
   While smoking a reefer –
Then threw it all up in the sink.

*Now working as a relationship counsellor.

Chapter 6

After Andy became a wealthy man overnight, he bought out the senior partner, who had been wanting to retire for some time. At first, it was a novelty to tell others what to do, including some of the sharp know-it-alls who had taken such delight in ordering him around previously.

Before long, he had widened the client base; brought in business from abroad, which meant quite a lot of foreign travel. Although he didn't like being away from home it was a novelty. To think that the furthest he'd been away as a kid was Southend!

He made some other changes too. Fresh fruit was made available at all times in the office. (His craving for oranges came from the care home where anything that wasn't a tin was 'too expensive'.) And the recruitment selection process was revised. No longer were successful applicants taken only from the Oxbridge pile. At Andy's insistence, interviews were also granted to school-leavers who showed potential. Boys like him. The old him.

It wasn't long before Andy got used to being rich and having other people around him who did what he wanted. But every now and then, something would remind him that life hadn't always been like this. It might be an article about kids and delinquency rates. Or it might be a discussion on Radio Four about teenage illiteracy.

On the Monday after his wife's birthday lunch, it was the front page of his newspaper which had grabbed his attention. Below a huge article reporting the lavish funeral of a very famous elderly photographer was another piece. Smaller. Far more important. GANG OF TEENAGERS SENT TO YOUNG OFFENDERS FOR TERRORISING SHOPKEEPER, screamed the headline. Then it added: YOUNGEST ONLY 12!

Andy, who was reading the paper in the back of his car, had felt like tapping the window between him and his driver and asking his driver to pull in because he felt sick. That kid could have been him! *What kind of kids do this kind of thing?* demanded the woman journalist who had written the article.

'Kids whose parents don't know how to be parents,' Andy wanted to yell.

By the time he got into the office, he was still upset. His secretary, a sensible woman in her fifties who was good at both her job and remembering birthdays, gave him a strange look. 'Are you all right, Andy? You look upset.'

Hastily, he gathered himself. 'Just preoccupied, that's all.'

She still looked apprehensive. 'There's a Harry Screws here to see you. He's in reception.'

Screws' was their main competitor in the area. Recently, to Andy's disconcertion, some of their clients had defected. Now the head honcho had turned up in person, without an appointment. Bloody cheek. The kind of strategy Andy might have adopted in his position.

'Do you want to see him?' added his secretary.

Did he want to see him? Bloody hell. Wasn't this just what he'd been angling for?

'Sure. We'll take the Green Room.'

'Don't you need a bit of time to prepare?'

Andy didn't need to prepare. Instinctively, he knew what Harry Screws was going to offer. Funny really. If it hadn't been for that article in the paper – not to mention Pamela's little nephew, whose face still haunted him – he might have told this arrogant bastard where to get off. But now, he was more than ready to discuss the options.

'Won't you get bored?' asked his secretary when he told her to organise the necessary paperwork without even consulting his financial adviser, who he knew would be dead against the deal. 'No sum of money', he could just hear George, his financial adviser, say, 'is worth losing a job for. However large.'

He shook his head. 'I've worked hard, really hard over the years. And I've missed out on family life as a result.' He stopped for a minute, thinking about his beautifully behaved girls. How lucky he was! Seeing Bobbie and her uncontrollable kids at the weekend, plus that ineffectual brother-in-law of his, had really brought that home. 'This will buy me some time to be with them before they grow up and go away.'

'That's so sweet!' His secretary made an 'Ahhh' sound. 'You're right! Families do need fathers. Did you see that piece in the paper? About the thugs who smashed the shop window? They were only twelve. Twelve! And did you read about their family backgrounds?' She shook her head.

Andy wasn't able to say anything to that one. Instead, he just gave her a curt nod and went off to the next meeting that his secretary had already organised. The one where he was going to tell the rest of his colleagues that he had agreed to the sell-out. Everyone's jobs would remain the same, apart from his own.

Already, Andy could feel a buzz of excitement that he hadn't felt for a very long time. Pamela would be thrilled! Not that she moaned about him never being there. She was far too supportive a wife to do that. But now, at last, he could go with her to those race meetings at Ascot. He could take her out for lunch. Be there for the girls. Go to all those school concerts he'd always missed before. Be at home in the afternoon. Starting from today!

'It's all right, thanks,' Andy told his driver. 'I'll walk back.' It normally took just under an hour by car to reach the green leafy suburbs that were now home. But he needed the fresh air! Had to breathe it in greedily; gulping down a freedom that he hadn't realised he had needed so much until today.

Peeling off his suit jacket, Andy threw it on the ground and jumped over it like a child. A dog walker gave him a strange look but Andy didn't care. It was like leaving the home, all over again!

'You've sold the business?' Pamela frowned at him. Pamela never frowned. It was, as she was constantly reminding the girls, a waste of all those facial exercises which she had taught them to do, along with going to sleep on their backs so they didn't get pillow marks.

But now, standing in the hall with her tennis racquet after returning from the club (where the membership fees would have paid a small mortgage), a cluster of horizontal lines had gathered across that smooth skin just above her immaculately shaped eyebrows. A clear sign of disapproval even though Andy had convinced himself she would be thrilled.

'You're just going to stay at home?'

His wife's deep blue eyes, which had wowed millions into buying silk underwear and inspired many a man both in bed and out of it, locked with his. Her lack of enthusiasm was all too clear.

Nervously, Andy's hand went to loosen his tie before remembering that he had whipped it off and thrown it in the hedgerow in those moments of utter abandonment as he had walked jauntily home. It had been a pink silk tie which Pamela's mother had given him last Christmas. He cared little for either the present or the donor. 'Only for a few months. Until I've decided what I really want to do.'

'But I thought you were *doing* what you wanted to do!'

Did his wife really know him? Or was it because he'd never given her the chance, guessing it had been too risky? She wouldn't care for the real Andy. Might not even want to be married to him. 'I just feel . . .' he began hesitantly, 'that there has to be more to life than working hard all day, every day. I want to be able to relax a bit.'

Like you, he almost added.

Pamela was sitting down on the bottom step of their staircase now, displaying her long legs under her short tennis skirt; the type which were really shorts. Her trainers would be sitting neatly in the downstairs closet. Pamela never, ever allowed anyone to go through the front door without taking

57

their shoes off. It had taken her ages to get rid of Jack's sock prints on the white carpet after the lunch party!

'But what will you do all day?' This time, her voice had more of an accepting air to it, albeit an irritated one.

He seized on that with relief. 'Be with *you*! Spend more time with the girls. Do something with that golf membership. Help the gardener.'

'The gardener? John's a professional. He doesn't want any help. Besides, you don't know anything about plants.' She muttered something. It sounded like 'Or teenagers'.

Fair enough. He *didn't* know much about teenagers because he'd been away so much. But that was going to change now. He was ready to learn!

'I thought you'd be pleased,' he said slowly, sitting down next to her on the soft wool carpet which Pamela had had hand-made by an Italian firm; the type that didn't list their prices in their brochures. He reached out his hand for hers. There was a moment of hesitation and then she gave his a quick squeeze before retracting it.

'I am.' Her voice was small. Almost, if he didn't know her better, a little scared. 'It's just that I'm used to my own company.'

Then before he knew what was hitting him, she gave him a big hug. A hug that smelt of the expensive perfume he always bought her (at her request). A hug that was a welcome change from the cool Pamela. Recently, her moods had swung from tense to exuberant and, occasionally, something in between. It was an early menopause, she'd explained during her better moments. Women were so unpredictable! And nature really did seem to have it in for his wife of late.

'The girls and I have had to get used to managing on our own,' she continued, showering the top of his head with little kisses. Wow! What he done to deserve such attention? 'We've never complained about it because we knew you were doing the important bit. But I suppose the idea of you being here with us is going to take a bit of getting used to. That's all.'

She looked at him now with those beautiful china-blue

eyes, expecting him to understand. And he did. Up to a point. Pamela had always been honest. That had been one of the conditions of their marriage. He'd made that clear at the start.

'You're wrong, you know,' he started to say. 'I don't do the important bit. You do that. It's called bringing up the children. And you do a great job.'

Her eyes melted. 'Oh Andy, you're so sweet.' Then she kissed him. Full on the mouth, which was something she hadn't done for a while: usually he took the lead. And as she kissed him, Andy felt his body flooding with happiness. He had done the right thing in accepting that offer!

'In fact,' added Pamela, jumping to her feet, 'this might have come at exactly the right time. Mummy rang this morning.'

Andy's happiness deflated as though someone had pierced it with a pin. Pamela's mother was a very strong-willed widow who had loathed Andy at first sight. She was one of those people who always managed to turn the conversation round to herself, whatever the subject.

Camilla was also a frightful snob. When they'd first met, she had quizzed him relentlessly about where he'd gone to school. Her mouth had narrowed when he'd told her about his parents dying in a crash and the aunt who was now dead. 'She doesn't believe me,' Andy realised with terror. Even now, Andy expected Camilla to triumphantly present him with proof of his real past.

'Is she coming to stay?' he asked, trying to sound enthusiastic. Pamela adored her mother, from whom she inherited her honey-gold skin and beautiful blonde hair. The difference between them was that Camilla was a bitch who had pushed her daughter forward as a model (having always wanted to be one herself) and now seized every opportunity to bemoan the fact that her daughter had 'given everything up' to be a 'housewife'. She didn't need to add that in her view, all this was down to one person. Andy. Or, as she insisted on calling him, Andrew.

Thank God she lived in Sussex and not round the corner.

'No, darling.' Pamela patted his shoulder comfortingly, much as one might pat a small dog: something that Andy had always yearned for but would never be able to have as his wife was allergic to pet hair. 'Her arthritis is playing up again and her au pair has just walked out.'

Hah! Camilla was one of a new breed of grannies who had au pairs to look after them. But as soon as they realised what a spoilt, demanding woman she was, they were off. Andy didn't blame them. 'She wants to know if I could go down. I told her it was impossible because I needed to be here for the girls.' Then she gave his arm a little squeeze. 'But if you're going to be around, then maybe you could spare me for a few days.'

'Well, yes but . . .'

'Great!' Pamela was already running up the stairs. 'I'll pack a bag and you can pick up the girls from school. Natasha will need to go straight to athletics club so you'll need to wait there before collecting Melanie from extra French. She'll want to drive you back – her instructor says it's crucial for her to practise – so make sure you take the L plates.'

Andy tried to take all this in. He'd suggested, years ago, that the girls went to a private school. Weren't all state schools crap? Just look at his own early experiences. He might have come through all right but he was one of the lucky ones.

But Pamela had been adamant that they went to Corrywood High, an 'excellent' state school that was just round the corner, where she had also volunteered to be on the PTA. She'd had enough of public school education herself, she told him. She wanted the girls to have a 'normal' life. The fact that a famous actress was also on the PTA had nothing to do with it.

'Don't worry,' trilled Pamela as she flew back down the stairs, cheeks flushed and an unusually excited glint in her eye. 'I'll be back in time to run my parenting class next week.' She gave him a kiss. Not one on the mouth this time but a quick brush on the cheek. 'If you're interested, take a peep at the leader manual. It's in the den. And don't forget to pay Mrs C. She's changed her hours, by the way, so she'll be in at nine tomorrow instead of eight to do a general clean-up. Bye, darling. I'll keep my mobile on! But the battery's a bit low so don't worry if you can't get hold of me.'

Home alone! Andy heard his wife rev up her car, feeling a mixture of freedom and apprehension. He'd never, as far as he could remember, been in the house without anyone else at three o'clock in the afternoon. He ought to make use of it! Go and play squash, or just chill out on the sofa. Then again, from what Pamela had said, there wasn't much time before the school run. Andy felt excitement racing through his chest. His daughters would be so pleased to see him!

'What are you doing here, Dad?' Natasha eyed his T-shirt with undisguised horror. What was wrong with the Grateful Dead? He'd forgotten he'd even possessed it but after Bobbie had gone, he had rifled through his drawers in holiday mode and put it on to remind himself that he really didn't need to wear a suit any more. At least until he decided to get another job.

'Mum's gone to stay with Gran and I've got some time off work.'

Natasha gave him a little push. 'Don't stand here. Not so close to the gates. Everyone will see you. God, Dad. You're so embarrassing! Did you bring my athletics stuff?'

Pamela hadn't mentioned that. Or had she? There'd been quite a few 'don't forgets' on her way out.

'Fuck, Dad! I'm going to get thrown out of the team if I don't have my kit. I've already got two strikes.'

Fuck? He'd never heard the girls swear before.

Natasha frowned at him. 'I mean it, Dad. You'll have to go back and get it.'

What happened to the 'please'? If his daughter didn't look the same as usual with her blonde hair tied back in the regulation ponytail, he might have thought she was a changeling. His Natasha never spoke to him like this.

'I can't! We've got to pick up Melanie.'

Natasha snorted. 'She's got detention again, which means she won't be out for another hour.'

Had he heard right? 'Detention? Again?'

His youngest daughter rolled her eyes. 'I know. I did tell her. If you're going to have a fag, do it when they're all tied up in a staff meeting. Not at the back of class.' Natasha put her hand to her mouth. 'Whoops. I didn't mean to say that.'

Andy began to feel he was in a bad dream.

'Mr Gooding?'

Swivelling round, he found a tall, gawky young girl with a slightly harassed look on her face, a bouncy ponytail, metallic braces and a folder in her hands. 'I'm Judith Davies.'

Should he know her? 'Are you in Melanie's class?'

Natasha let out a groan. '*Dad!*'

The young girl smiled. 'Actually, I'm one of the English teachers well as being in charge of pastoral care. I don't believe we met at the last parents' evening. Would you mind giving this to your wife? It's for the parenting course tonight.'

'Tonight?' Andy was confused. 'My wife said it started next week.'

'It was going to but we had to change the date at the last minute.' The young girl looked worried. 'We sent everyone an email.'

When would people realise this wasn't always a reliable method of communication? Still, he couldn't help feeling for the girl. She was looking pretty distressed, twisting her hands this way and that. 'I don't think Pamela could have got it. She's away at the moment.'

'No! We were banking on your wife. We've got two parenting classes running, you see. One for the primary school which I'm in charge of and one for the main school which your wife is doing. She was the only parent who volunteered.'

Andy could see why. Who would want to put themselves up there as an authority on how to be a perfect parent? When Pamela found out about Mel's detention, she'd be very upset.

'Of course, whoever leads the course won't exactly be giving help,' added the girl. 'They'll just be the facilitator.'

That put a different complexion on it! 'So you just need someone who can go through the text book and set exercises?'

'Exactly!' The young girl's eyes gleamed. 'Look, Mr Gooding, I hate to ask you this, but I'd be really grateful if you could step in, just for this evening!'

Him? Andy Gooding leading a 'How To Be a Perfect Parent' session? It was a joke. Surely. Except that this young teacher wasn't laughing. Nor was his daughter, who was mouthing, 'Don't do it, Dad. It's soooo embarrassing!'

'We're pretty desperate, Mr Gooding. And it won't take too long to read the leader notes.'

Andy hesitated. For a moment there, he had a distinct whiff of urine and cabbage, mixed with his foster mother's voice: 'You'll never come to anything, you little sod.'

He'd show them! Prove them wrong, the lot of them. 'It will be a pleasure,' he said, hardly believing his own words. 'Happy to help.'

PERFECT PARENTS: SESSION ONE

SETTING GOALS!

MAKE A LIST OF BEHAVIOURAL ISSUES THAT
YOU WANT TO CHANGE IN THE NEXT EIGHT
WEEKS! E.G.:

EATING WITH MOUTH FULL.
NOT GOING TO BED.
NOT GETTING UP.
FIBBING.
ANSWERING BACK.
REFUSING TO WEAR SELECTED CLOTHES.
BEING UNABLE TO SPEAK, UNLESS IN
    ONE-SYLLABLE WORDS WHILE TEXTING AT
    THE SAME TIME.

Chapter 7

BOBBIE

Rob wouldn't stop nagging her about that hideously embarrassing lunch party at his sister's. It was really getting on Bobbie's nerves. On and on he went for the rest of the weekend, while nursing his BlackBerry, even in bed.

Why couldn't the kids behave? It's not as though they were babies any more. How could they have let him down in front of his sister and her husband? And – the worst bit – why couldn't she, Bobbie, control them? She was with them all the time at home, wasn't she?

Sometimes Bobbie felt that her husband was just an onlooker when it came to family life; exonerated by his demanding job that kept him safely away from the real action at home. It made Bobbie turn away at night, furious with both him and for herself for having agreed to move away from their friends into the boring, semi-rural countryside and a new school which the kids hated.

The only upside was the house. How she adored their beautiful semi-detached Victorian honey-bricked home in a lovely shrub-lined road, with those wonderfully airy square rooms and sash windows overlooking a good-sized lawn. They could never have afforded it in London. It was – along with the school's fantastic reputation – the only reason she had allowed herself to be dragged, kicking and screaming, from Ealing. Now she wished she'd stuck to her guns.

Then, as if that wasn't enough to spoil her weekend, there was a huge piece on Dr Know in one of the Sunday supplements which she took with her into the loo to read, one of the few places where she could have a minute to herself.

WOULD YOU LET THIS MAN REPROGRAMME YOUR KIDS? ran the headline. Afterwards, there was a whole page of interviews with parents who had been on his television show. Some swore that his no-nonsense advice worked a treat. Others declared he'd ripped their families to shreds through his Jerry Springer-type interview methods and they were still recovering.

Bobbie shivered. She had to do something. Fast. For Mum's sake, although heaven knew what she was doing with a man like this. A celebrity crush was one thing, but dating a child expert who thought couples should have to pass a parent-suitability test before they were even allowed to conceive was something else.

Mum, however, was either unaware of her new boyfriend's reputation or didn't care. In fact, she'd sounded deliriously excited when she'd rung during pre-school panic hour on Monday morning. Bobbie had been haring around getting ready whilst at the same time looking under general household debris for clean knickers and trying to get the kids up. ('Now, Jack. PLEASE')

'I'm having such a wonderful time, darling! Herbert took me to this *brilliant* party in London last night and we met all kinds of famous people including . . .'

'JACK! GIVE DAISY BACK HER MOSHI MONSTERS. NOW! Mum, that's great but I've got to rush. We're late for school and Jack will lose his golden time again. Damn!'

Bobbie began to choke as clouds of chemicals engulfed her. Bugger. She'd just put on fly spray instead of hair spray. That's what came of trying to do five things at once. And of not unpacking all this stuff that was still in a box in the corner of the bathroom after the move.

'What's golden time, dear?'

'They get an extra five minutes on the computer and – NO, DAISY. DON'T CLEAN JACK'S SHOES FOR HIM OR YOU'LL GET POLISH ALL OVER YOUR SCHOOL UNIFORM.'

Too late. 'Mum, I've got to go. Bye, you two!'

Sometimes the only way to get the children to school was to pretend you were going without them. 'I'M IN THE CAR!' she yelled out, still in the hall.

'AND JACK'S IN HIS BOXERS!' yelled back Daisy from upstairs. 'HE CAN ONLY FIND ONE SOCK!'

So what was new? Socks divided themselves in this house before you could say 'Not on the floor – in the bin.'

Bobbie rustled around in the tumble dryer. Yes! A matching pair. Pink was cool for boys nowadays, wasn't it? Eventually, she managed to bundle both kids into the car (school was just too far to walk), lob a couple of cereal bars into the back and put on the *Mandarin for Juniors* CD to drown out the arguments.

'I WANT THE ONE WITH NUTS IN IT!'

'NO, I DO.'

'I'M THE ELDEST. TELL HIM, MUM. TELL HIM!'

Would they ever reach a stage where they actually sat still in the car and made polite conversation, wondered Bobbie as she double-parked out of desperation next to a people carrier in the school car park. Maybe when they were thirty. If they all got that far.

'Quick! Run!' she instructed, shooing them out with a kiss that somehow missed. Jack hared off, straight into a squat freckle-faced boy who began squawking. 'He's hurt me! He's hurt me!'

'Jack!' began Bobbie, getting out of the car to apologise. The boy's mother, who was quite obviously pregnant, glared, her piggy eyes narrowing.

'Isn't your kid the new one who nicked my Wayne's gluten-free packed lunch?'

'I'm so sorry!' She looked down at the boy whose screams had begun to subside although there was a massive bruise developing on his right knee. Jack meanwhile had shot out of sight, as had Daisy.

'So you should be! If you can't bloody well look after your kids properly, don't bloody well have them.'

The bell! Saved by the bell, which was ringing out from

the cosy-looking, red-roofed building with 'Corrywood Primary' on the board outside. 'Sorry,' Bobbie repeated again, dashing back to the car where the owner of the enormous people carrier was honking her horn furiously. Oh God. There was a notice on her windscreen. Probably another complaint.

<u>IMPORTANT!</u>

THE CORRYWOOD PERFECT PARENTS' COURSE
WILL START ONE WEEK EARLIER THAN
ADVERTISED!
PLENTY OF PLACES STILL AVAILABLE!
THERE WILL BE ONE SESSION FOR PARENTS OF
THREE- TO ELEVEN-YEAR-OLDS AND A
SEPERATE ONE FOR AGE TWELVE PLUS.
BOTH WILL BE HELD AT THE MAIN SCHOOL
AT 7 P.M.
SEE YOU THERE!

It was a sign! (One that had been written by the teaching assistant, judging by the spelling.) So her sister-in-law was running the older group, not the one for Jack and Daisy's age. Maybe she *would* go then. Even if the course didn't improve her parenting skills, it might at least help her make some friends . . .

'Hi, everyone!' The young teacher with the bouncy ponytail beamed brightly. They were a smallish group with one or two familiar faces from the school gates, including – help! – the pregnant woman from the playground this morning. The one with the squat, freckled son whom Jack was always upsetting.

What bad luck! Desperately looking around for an escape, Bobbie took in the classroom with its map of the world on one wall and a chart displaying the current members of the cabinet by the window. The chairs had been seated in a horseshoe shape away from the desks. Was it too late to make a bolt for it? Pretend she'd just received an emergency message from Mel, who was babysitting? No. That wouldn't work. Mel would only tell Pamela and it would all get back. Bobbie might still be new here but she could already see how the mother mafia worked!

'Some of you will know me as Miss Davies.' The young teacher flicked back her ponytail as she spoke and Bobbie noticed that her hands were shaking slightly. Poor thing was nervous! 'But for the purpose of these sessions, please feel free to call me Judith. Sorry about the change of date, by the way. I'm afraid someone made a mistake in the office.'

There was a sniff of disapproval from Pregnant Mum along the lines of bloody well having to find a babysitter at the last minute.

'I'd also like to add', continued Judith with the earnestness of a sixth-form prefect, 'that this is a new parenting programme which we've drawn up ourselves, here at Corrywood. So we're open to any suggestions and comments. Remember – we're here to help *you*.'

'I don't really need any help,' murmured a very tall, scarily skinny woman with a small mauve butterfly tattoo on her arm and blue streaks in her hair. (Thank goodness her own pink highlights had washed out now, Bobbie thought.) 'I just, er, want to take it in.'

Another mum who felt awkward; Bobbie felt a surge of relief.

'Some of you', began Judith slowly, 'might feel a bit embarrassed being here. You might think that parenting is something we ought to be able to do without help. Try seeing it like building a house. You wouldn't do that without being taught how to lay bricks, would you? It's even more important to learn how to lay the foundations for a family.'

Wow! Put like that, it made sense.

'Actually,' flustered the mum with the butterfly tattoo, 'I *could* do with some advice. But only if it doesn't involve star charts or the naughty step. That kind of twaddle only works if your kids will sit on it in the first place – and mine won't, whatever that Dr Know on telly says! Not unless I glue them by the seat of their pants.'

There was a loud mutter of agreement. If only they knew. Bobbie still couldn't believe Mum was actually dating the man – let alone coming to lunch with him. Maybe, with any luck, their relationship might fizzle out before then. No. That wasn't fair. After all, Mum seemed so happy . . .

Judith, meanwhile, was taking notes. Her handwriting, Bobbie could see, was very small and neat. 'I'll do my best. Now, let's introduce ourselves, shall we? Just a bit about yourselves and why you are all here.'

Help! She was looking straight at her. It was like being back at school. Did she really have to go first? 'Er, I'm Bobbie. Short for Roberta. Mum had this thing about *The Railway Children.*'

Only Judith seemed to get it. 'I have two children,' she continued, feeling a bit stupid now. 'Well, three and a half actually, if you count my husband and his BlackBerry.'

This time, there *was* a burst of laughter. Actually she wasn't being funny. It was the truth. 'I'm here because I'd like to change my family. Preferably for someone else's. Anyone want to do a swap?'

Silence again. Didn't they realise she was joking? Bobbie had never regarded herself as a naturally funny person but since having children, she found herself coming out with some crazy things. Maybe it was an internal mechanism trying to keep her sane.

'Seriously,' she added, 'I'd just like them to do what I say. You know. Go to bed when I ask. Eat what I put in front of them. Live together without trying to murder each other. Go shopping with me without eating stuff before we've paid for it. Stay at the table when we're eating. Do their homework on time, too.'

There was a wave of enthusiastic nodding.

'I'd like my kids to go to bed when I say, too,' sighed a woman with what looked like baby sick on her shoulder.

'Especially my Alfie. He's the worst. But it's difficult when you've got eight of them.'

'Talk about too many kids!' whistled Pregnant Mum. 'Are you Catholic or just plain careless?'

'Both actually.' She glowered. '*And* proud of it.'

Heavens, you could almost smell the gunpowder.

'When are *you* due?' asked Bobbie quickly, instinctively trying to keep the peace.

Pregnant Mum glared. 'I'm *not*.'

Shit. Bobbie sank into her seat. Now she really *had* made an enemy for life. But the woman really did look as though she was four, if not five, months gone.

'I'm sorry,' she whispered. 'I'm still trying to shift post-baby weight too.'

'It's not that.' The woman glowered. 'It's me fibroids.'

Horrifically embarrassed, Bobbie kept only half an ear on the rest of the introductions. The woman with the butterfly tattoo had a son and daughter. 'My son's addicted to his laptop. On it all night, he is! Then he won't get up for school in the morning. The last time I took it away, he hit me.' She pointed to her tattoo. Flipping heck! It was a bruise.

'How old is he?' asked Judith gently.

'Nearly nine.'

They all tried to hide their shock at that but it was pretty obvious, looking round the group, that they were thinking the same. Not 'How could she let him get away with that', because, as any parent knew, there was no stopping a kid at times, but 'What was wrong with children nowadays that they tried to hurt their own parents?'

Was this the first step to Borstal? Bobbie thought of Jack in the Reduced Bread shelf, clutching his stolen Easter egg, and shivered.

'My daughter's fifteen,' added Butterfly Mum. 'She's from my first marriage. She keeps getting tattoos and I think it's a cry for attention. In fact, I wasn't sure which group to come to; this one or the one up the corridor for the older group. I might slip in and out if you don't mind.'

'Me too,' added Too Many Kids Mum. 'Why don't I just take notes for you?'

Judith nodded doubtfully. 'We could give it a go.'

The only man in the group was a dad who was bringing up his ten-year-old daughter alone. His name was Matthew and he wanted some advice on how to stop worrying. 'I get really panicky about whether Lottie's eating the right stuff; if she's been run over when she's home late; or if a headache is really the sign of meningitis or a brain tumour.' His face crumpled and for a minute he looked like a little boy. 'Her mother died of cancer and, to be honest, it's made me a bit paranoid.'

Poor man! Then Not Really Pregnant Mum said she was bloody well fed up with her children swearing at her and that she wished her kids would shut up sometimes and give her some peace. To think *she'd* criticised Bobbie! And a mum with an American accent said, in a broad Southern accent, that she'd like some advice on how to stop breastfeeding.

'This course is for toddlers upwards, I'm afraid,' said Judith, colouring furiously.

'Sure. I get that. But Byron's just turned six! In fact, he's exactly six years, two months and four days.'

There was a collective gasp and several muffled sniggers. 'Maybe our later session on "Letting Go" might help,' said Judith nervously.

Wow! Surely no parenting programme on earth could provide magic answers to this lot. But Judith was nodding her head up and down excitedly as though they had all just gained grade As. 'Excellent! Now I want you to keep that list and at the end of the course, we're going to go back to it and see how far we've come.'

'Do you have kids of your own, Judith?'

This was from the woman whom she'd mistakenly thought was pregnant. The girl shuffled her papers as if embarrassed. 'No, but I've been a teacher for some years now and I've done the Perfect Parents' training course.'

There was a snort. 'Then you don't know what it's like, do you?'

'Give her a break.' Bobbie heard herself say. 'Let's just see how it goes, shall we?'

Not Really Pregnant Mum's eyes narrowed. 'Well of course, you're the expert, aren't you?'

Judith Davies gave a little cough. 'I think we'll have a film now.' The lights began to dim and Bobbie felt her eyelids grow heavy. Don't go to sleep, she told herself urgently. But it had been *such* a long day . . .

'So, Bobbie!' Judith's chirpy voice woke her with a start. 'What did you think?'

Think? Think about what? Too late, she could see the end credits on the whiteboard in front of them. 'The film about positive praise,' repeated Judith slightly stiffly.

Positive praise? Had she missed out on something here?

'Would anyone like to help Bobbie out?' Judith smiled tightly around the rest of the class.

'Sure.' The good-looking widower in the suit was speaking up. 'Positive praise is finding something in your children's behaviour that you can flag up.'

'So what can you praise in your own children, Bobbie?'

She racked her brain, horribly conscious that all eyes were on her. Bobbie's mind flew back over the previous week. Daisy and Jack must have done *something* right! 'Er, I could praise them for being alive.'

Judith frowned. 'Would you like to expand on that?'

'Well, Jack nearly ran out in front of a car the other day and I only just saved him.' She shivered. 'It was awful.'

'Actually,' said the man in the suit quietly, 'that's exactly the sort of thing I'm terrified about.'

'Right,' squeaked Judith, 'time for some role play, I think. Is everyone comfortable with that?

No. Please don't pick me. *Please* . . .

'Bobbie! I'd like you to pretend you're Jack. I'll be the mother. OK? I've just asked you to go to bed. Now, how would Jack react? Put yourself in his shoes.'

Suddenly, Bobbie found herself lying face down, nose to

the ground. Her arms and legs were flaying furiously: all the frustrations of the last eight years were coming out. 'I'M NOT GOING TO BED BEFORE DAISY! IT'S NOT FAIR.'

There was a nervous titter. 'Now, Jack! Daisy's older than you so it's only fair.'

'PISS OFF!'

There was a gasp. 'That's not very nice.'

'YOU'RE NOT VERY NICE EITHER!'

Judith sounded as though she was struggling. 'If you don't go to sleep, you'll be too tired for school.'

'DON'T WANT TO GO TO SCHOOL! I HATE IT! AND I HATE MISS DAVIES!'

There was another gasp. Had she gone too far? Bobbie staggered to her feet. Suddenly she was a mother again. A very embarrassed mother. 'He doesn't really mean that. It's just that he misses his old school and his old teacher.'

Miss Davies was nodding uncertainly. 'Right. Of course. Now, Matthew, how about you doing the same exercise? The point is to try and listen calmly to your children – just as I did there – without getting down to their level.'

Bobbie slunk back to her seat.

'Is it really like that at your house?' whispered the American woman.

'Course not.' Bobbie gave a hysterical little laugh. 'It's much worse.'

The class was ending now, thank goodness. 'Remember to practise positive praise for homework!' Judith glanced at her notes. 'It says here that we should all give each other a good-luck hug. Is that all right with everyone?'

Bobbie drove home, kicking herself. What a fool she'd been! Why hadn't she toned Jack down in that role play? Now his reputation would be worse than it was already – not to mention hers. Still, that positive-praise stuff sounded as though it might have possibilities. Maybe, she told herself, creeping into the house so as not to wake up the kids, she'd give it a go in the morning.

'You're still up!' Bobbie stared at Jack sitting too close to the television on a bean bag that belonged to his bedroom. Daisy was at the far end of the room, cuddled up on the sofa with Melanie.

'I had to put her next to me to stop them fighting,' said her husband's niece, shrugging. 'Don't like each other much, do they? They didn't want to go to bed either.'

Well, of course they didn't; that's why parents were invented. To make kids do stuff they didn't want to. 'We watched this cool film,' piped up Jack. 'They cut off this monster's legs and all this green gunk spewed out.'

How could Melanie have let them watch a programme like that? And how could the kids have played up? They'd promised to go to bed on time.

'I'm very . . .' she started. And then stopped. Positive praise! If she was going to give this course a chance, she had to find *something* to praise them for.

But what?

'I'm very pleased that you've brushed your hair,' she ventured. It was one of their bugbears. Jack hated the feel of anything on his skin.

Her son stared at her. 'But I haven't.'

'Well, the thought might have been there.' Bobbie turned to Daisy. 'And well done for, er, sitting nicely.'

Daisy's eyes narrowed. 'Are you feeling OK, Mum?'

Her husband's niece was giving her a strange look too. Standing up, she put something away in her handbag. 'Think I'll go now. Don't worry, I'll walk.' As she spoke, there was the sound of the key in the lock. Rob! At last! Back from yet another late meeting. He looked tired: too tired obviously to even kiss her cheek.

'You lot still awake?' His gaze fell on his niece. 'Thanks for babysitting, Melanie.'

'Mel,' said his niece sulkily. 'I've changed my name.'

'Right. Mel it is.' He shrugged before finally giving Bobbie a peck on the cheek. There was a faint whiff of something alcoholic. Advertising meetings always seemed to involve drink. 'How did the parenting course go?'

77

Praise him! Praise him! Don't have a go at him for being late when he'd promised, absolutely promised, that he'd be back ages ago. 'I like the fact that you've been thoughtful enough to ask,' she said brightly.

Rob was frowning. 'There's no need to be sarcastic,' he said in a low voice.

'I'm not!' Bobbie could feel her cheeks burning. 'It's called positive praise. And if you'd made the effort to come on the course with me, you'd know how to do it yourself.'

Appalled, she stopped. Mel was looking distinctly uncomfortable although luckily, Jack and Daisy were scrapping with each other over the remote control and hadn't heard. Rob's face was stony. 'I'll run you home, Mel. Thanks for babysitting.'

'See you next Monday then!'

'Actually,' Bobbie heard herself saying, 'I won't be needing you, I'm afraid.' Then she eyed her husband challengingly. 'I don't think the course is for me, after all.'

STILL STUCK ON POSITIVE PRAISE?

HERE ARE SOME EXAMPLES!

I ADMIRE YOUR TEXTING SKILLS EVEN THOUGH WE'RE MEANT TO BE EATING.

SO YOU'VE WRITTEN ON YOUR BEDROOM WALL? WOW! HOW ARTISTIC!

YOU ARE A BRILLIANT COMMUNICATOR! I CAN SEE THAT FROM YOUR MOBILE-PHONE BILL!

YOU'VE PEED ON THE FLOOR AGAIN? GREAT AIM!

Chapter 8

VANESSA

Vanessa carried the filthy old grey blanket carefully into the lounge, looking down with awe at the little face that had gone back to sleep after the exchange with the rough chap on the doorstep. Very gently, she laid her granddaughter on to the sofa, kneeling down next to her and taking in the snub nose, rosebud mouth and those two little dimples, just like her own. She really was very small for her age.

'What do you mean, you *think* she's your granddaughter?' Brian asked, confused.

'I've never actually seen her before,' she admitted.

But despite the sun-tan and the heavily matted hair wound into tightly plaited braids with red and blue beads, there was no mistaking Brigid's child. You only had to look at the dark, almost gypsy-like Irish look which had come from her husband's side of the family. This child could have been her own daughter, twenty years ago. A Brigid who hadn't yet learned to rebel. Who had wrapped her arms around her and said, 'I love you, Mummy,' over and over again.

A large lump formed in Vanessa's throat. If only she had known then how things would turn out, she wouldn't have been so hasty. Wouldn't have said all those terrible things.

'I don't understand,' said Brian quietly beside her. 'Why haven't you seen her?'

'Because I wasn't allowed,' she replied shortly. Why couldn't he just go? All the earlier tenderness between them had disappeared now. Instead, Brian felt like an intruder. She needed to be alone with her granddaughter, to find out what on earth had happened. But she couldn't wake her, even though she was desperate to find out where Brigid was. It wouldn't be fair. From the look of that filthy – and smelly – shift dress she was wearing, the child might well have been travelling for some time.

'Funny name, isn't it?' added Brian. 'Sunshine, I mean. Quite nice though. I like it.'

What right had he to pass judgement on her granddaughter's name as though he knew her? Besides, Sunshine was quite ridiculous! So typical of Brigid!

'I hate my name,' she used to complain as a teenager. 'I don't care if it belonged to Dad's mum. It's not as though that lot have ever had anything to do with us, is it? When I'm a mother, I'm going to call my kids something pretty. *And* I'm going to bring them up differently!'

The memory made Vanessa smile. Why was it that every generation of children was determined to 'do it differently' from their parents? When it came to it, they often ended up repeating the very behaviour that they had once criticised.

Suddenly the child woke up. So quickly that Vanessa was taken by surprise. Those catlike green eyes – such a contrast to her dark looks – focused steadily first on her and then on Brian. But she didn't look troubled – not at all! Vanessa wondered suddenly if this little girl was used to waking up next to people she didn't know.

'It's all right,' she said softly. 'I'm your grandmother.' Even as she said the words, a wonderful warmth flooded her body. For six long years, she had yearned to say those words! Nearly seven if you went back to the day that Brigid had come home, white-faced, with the pregnancy-testing kit. Of course she had said some things she hadn't meant. They both had. But she hadn't expected her daughter to turn on her heel and never come back.

The child stared at her as though she was taking her in rather than the other way round. 'I know.' She spoke very clearly, pronouncing each word as though it had a space around it. 'Mummy told me.'

Mummy! Vanessa felt her heart soar with excitement and nervousness. 'Where *is* Mummy?' she asked urgently.

'Gone away.' The little one spoke without emotion, as though this was perfectly normal. 'She said you would look after me until she came back.'

'Came back from where?' asked Brian.

Vanessa wished he wouldn't ask questions too. It might scare the child. Stop her from talking. But she didn't seem to mind. 'I don't know.' She shrugged prettily and Vanessa was struck by how narrow and thin her shoulders were under the shift dress. 'She'll be back soon. She always is.'

So this had happened before! Vanessa felt anger mixed with resignation. For years, she had fretted and worried about her irresponsible teenage daughter. After Brigid had walked out, she'd done everything to find her. Gone to the police, and even the Missing Persons section of the Salvation Army. But to no avail. How on earth would her daughter manage to bring up a child on her own when she was no more than a child herself?

And now she, Vanessa, had been proved right. This little one hadn't been looked after – just look at her clothes and dirty fingernails. She'd been abandoned, probably for some holiday or a boyfriend who didn't want a child in tow. It was appalling! Brigid didn't deserve to be a mum.

Besides, the letter – or rather the note – spoke for itself. *Please look after her.*

As though she was Paddington Bear!

There was a passport too, giving Sunshine's surname as her own (Thomas) and her place of birth as London. Vanessa felt a pang. So her daughter had given birth in this country then, without even bothering to tell her. That really hurt.

In the emergency-numbers section, there was Brigid's name but no address or contact number. The second contact was her own. Maybe her daughter did care for her after all? Or perhaps there simply hadn't been anyone else to put.

And, hang on, there was another note at the back of the passport, also in Brigid's handwriting. *To whom it may concern. I give authority to my mother Vanessa Thomas to look after my daughter Sunshine Thomas until further notice.*

There was no date or witness's signature.

Further notice? What on earth did that mean?

'Who was that man, Sunshine? The one who brought you?'

The child's eyes widened as though the answer was obvious. 'One of Mummy's friends.'

Vanessa shuddered. Brigid's friends, over the years, had been a motley crew. She could just imagine her daughter giving her child, as though she were a parcel, to this grubby backpacker, whoever he was. How irresponsible.

Sunshine began to shiver. Quickly, Vanessa put the note back in the passport. She needed to sort out the child first. She was cold. And no wonder, in those rags. Her mind began to race. She didn't have any clothes that would fit. Besides, she needed to clean her up first. And feed her too. There was nothing to her! All skin and bones.

'Are you hungry?' she said as the child sat up, fully awake even though it was the small hours of the morning.

She nodded.

Vanessa felt a stab of panic as she tried to recall what was in the fridge. What did children eat nowadays? Then she remembered – that was it! Brigid had loved her soldiers.

'Would you like a boiled egg?'

That snub nose wrinkled with disgust. 'Mummy and I don't kill things. We're vegans.'

Vegans?

Vanessa stared at Brian in horror. No wonder her granddaughter looked so thin.

'What do you eat then?' she asked hesitantly.

'Beans.' There was the sort of look that indicated Vanessa should have known that.

'Shall I go to the garage?' suggested Brian. 'The twenty-four-hour one?'

'I don't think she means Heinz.' She glanced down at Sunshine – such a wacky name – who had fallen asleep again. 'But thanks, anyway.'

Brian nodded; his large face soft with compassion. 'Want me to stay?'

'If you don't mind, I need to be alone for a bit.' Vanessa looked up at him now, hoping that he'd understand. She liked him – more than that – but now this had happened, and it was big. She had her granddaughter back. How long for, she didn't know. But she couldn't mess it up as she had with Brigid. And if that meant giving up the personal life she had only just made for herself, so be it.

'I'll ring you,' said Brian uncertainly.

Vanessa hardly heard him letting himself out. Instead, she curled up on the sofa next to Sunshine – Sunshine! – and snuggled into her. She might smell, but she was still her granddaughter. Only then did she notice that the child's right hand was clasped tight around something. Gently, Vanessa unfurled it. It was a whistle! A simple clay whistle with three holes and a bit of grubby string attached. Sunshine muttered something in her sleep and, closing her fist, turned away. It reminded her of a mouth organ that her daughter had had as a teenager. She used to blow it tunelessly all day long: it had driven the neighbours mad.

'Mummy,' murmured Sunshine, still asleep.

Mummy. Vanessa's heart twisted with pain. 'Oh Brigid,' she said out loud. 'What have you done *this* time?'

When Vanessa woke the next morning, Sunshine wasn't there. Her first thought was that it must have been a dream and a huge cloud of disappointment billowed up in her chest. Then she saw the old blanket lying on the ground. It was true then: her granddaughter really was here! But where had she gone?

Her mind raced wildly round the possibilities. Sunshine had unlocked the front door and run off in search of her mother. What could be more natural than that? Anything could have happened! She might have been run over. Snatched by some evil person. Got lost! She'd be scared – crying her eyes out. For God's sake, what was she doing just standing there in her dressing gown? She needed to ring the police!

Dashing into the kitchen to grab the phone, she glanced

out of the window. It was open, even though she was sure she'd shut it last night. Sunshine was sitting in the middle of the lawn, cross-legged, playing that little clay flute. For all the world, she looked like a small faun in that filthy thin brown shift dress and braids. Vanessa's initial relief was swiftly followed by embarrassment. It was five o'clock in the morning – what would the neighbours say?

Hastily, Vanessa unlocked the back door and ran out, barefoot, over the patio, which she'd built herself last summer. 'What are you doing?'

A pair of green eyes lifted up to hers. There was no emotion there, Vanessa realised with a start. Just . . . well, nothing. 'Mummy and I always play our flutes when the sun has woken up.' The words were said steadily, as though she was explaining something obvious. 'Then we sit and listen to ourselves for a while.' She patted the grass beside her. 'You can sit with me, if you like.'

The grass was damp and the curtains next door were already twitching, but something inside Vanessa made her sit down next to Sunshine – funny, the more she said it, the less odd it sounded – and wait. The child was chanting something quietly to herself. It sounded like 'peace' repeated over and over again. Was she meditating? Had Brigid joined some kind of cult? Vanessa felt a pang of panic. Despite her strong personality, her daughter had all too often been led astray by unsuitable friends.

'Do you know who I am?' Vanessa asked gently, wondering if the child recalled the conversation they'd had last night when she was barely awake.

The little girl nodded. 'Van Van.'

Vanessa laughed. 'Nearly. It's Gran, actually.' She made the sound. '*Gr*. Like that!'

There was a solemn nod. 'I know. But Mummy said your name is Vanessa. So I've always called you Van Van.'

Always? So this little mite had been thinking of her for all these years when she'd been doing the same? Vanessa felt a mixture of agony and happiness.

Then the child stopped and looked up at her expectantly. 'Are we going to wash in the river now?'

Wash in the river? What kind of life had her granddaughter been leading? 'Actually,' she said gently, leading her towards the back door, 'I thought you might like a shower.'

'What's that?'

If the question hadn't been asked in such a sweet way, Vanessa would have thought she was having her on. Such a poppet! 'I'll show you. Look. Here's the bathroom.' Then she felt awkward. 'You'll need to take off your clothes first.'

Without hesitation, Sunshine neatly stepped out of the brown shift dress. She was wearing knickers made out of some kind of hessian. Even though this child was her flesh and blood, it still seemed odd to see her naked. Trying not to look, Vanessa turned on the power shower. 'You see—' she began but Sunshine started to scream.

'It's the rains!' She clung to Vanessa, burying her face in her chest. 'Help! We're going to be flooded again!'

'No. It's all right.'

But however much Vanessa tried to reassure her, it was no good. Eventually, she turned it off and ran a bath instead. That seemed to appease her granddaughter. 'It's like the pond,' she said, splashing herself.

Just the cue that Vanessa had been waiting for. 'What pond, Sunshine?'

Another look of surprise. 'At home, of course.'

'And where *is* home?'

There was a shrug. 'Near the pond.'

She mustn't push her too fast. Not yet.

'Let's wash your hair, shall we?' she said brightly, putting a dollop of shampoo in her hands.

That little nose wrinkled. 'If you don't wash it, it stays clean. Mummy says so.'

That old wives' tale! Vanessa had been itching to do something with Sunshine's hair ever since she'd arrived. 'Let's just try it, shall we?'

'Ow! My eyes hurt!'

86

'Sorry. Here. Take this flannel.'

Even as she spoke, Vanessa realised that her granddaughter probably didn't know what a flannel was. Besides, she was yelling so much that she couldn't hear. It was almost impossible to wash those tightly knitted braids. Maybe she could get her to the hairdresser tomorrow, during her lunch hour. That was a point – how on earth was she going to open the shop with her granddaughter in tow? She'd have to ask Kim to step in.

Somehow she managed to wash Sunshine. But what could she put her in? The thin shift dress she'd arrived in was hardly suitable for this weather. In desperation, Vanessa tried a pair of size six jeans from a bag of shop rejects by the front door, but they were far too big. How about this sky-blue jumper? It went down well below Sunshine's knees and the colour suited her. Brought out those green Irish eyes. Teamed with a pair of long socks, it would do until she could get to the shops.

She also managed to find some organic muesli at the back of the cupboard (a free sample which she'd never opened) which seemed to go down all right. But now what? Vanessa looked at her granddaughter sitting cross-legged on the floor with her cereal bowl – she'd seemed reluctant to sit at the table and Vanessa hadn't wanted to force the issue – and felt a wave of apprehension.

She hadn't looked after a child for more than twenty years and she'd made a real hash of it then. Sunshine would need to go to school; she'd need to be registered at the doctor's. Where on earth should she begin?

By the end of the following day, Vanessa had signed up Sunshine as a temporary patient (thank heavens for her passport which had helped with the paperwork); bought a book called *How to Raise the Perfect Child* by an author called Dr Know; and made an appointment with Joe Balls, the headmaster of Corrywood Primary, the local junior school. Funny to think that Brian had once been in his seat.

Mr Balls was a nice man, whose wife Gemma sometimes popped into the shop, along with her three small children.

'Officially, we shouldn't accept Sunshine without properly validated written consent from the parent or, in the case of a carer, something called a Parental Responsibility Order,' he told her in his small office, which was lined with books in alphabetical order. 'But if this is just going to be a temporary arrangement, I'll take her in as an emergency measure.' He gave a little sigh. 'It's not the first time this has happened in my experience, I'm afraid.'

Vanessa felt mortified. What must he think? Brigid's irresponsible behaviour reflected on her, too. 'To be honest, I'm not sure what my daughter is up to,' she said worriedly. Then she dropped her voice, conscious that Sunshine was outside in reception. 'Brigid's always been rather unpredictable.'

Mr Balls nodded as though he understood, rather than being shocked. 'If Sunshine's mother hasn't returned by Easter, we'll have to reconsider the situation. Meanwhile, I can give your granddaughter a place in Year One, starting tomorrow.'

'That's wonderful!' Vanessa felt a huge weight lifting from her shoulders. 'She needs stability at the moment. All she wants to do is sit and play her flute. She doesn't even want the television on!'

Mr Balls gave her a sympathetic look. 'All this must be rather different for you too.'

'It is.' She nodded, thinking how her life had changed in the space of forty-eight hours. 'I still can't believe it! I mean, I'm thrilled to have her, but it's all so sudden and I'm out of practice. What time do six-year-olds go to bed nowadays? What do they do for entertainment? What do they wear?'

Mr Balls laughed. 'If they're anything like ours, they want to do exactly what *you* don't want them to do! That reminds me.' He pushed across a small flyer with a picture of a smiling mother with her arm around an equally happy-looking child. 'You might be interested in this. It's a new parenting course that we're running on Monday evenings here at the school. You've missed the first one but there's no reason why you shouldn't join in next week. It might help you get into the swing, don't you think?'

There once was a sister and brother,
Who wouldn't stop fighting each other.
'Stop that,' snapped their aunt.
'What do you mean, "Can't"?
By the way, I'm really your mother.'

Chapter 9

ANDY

WELCOME TO THE FIRST SESSION OF OUR PERFECT PARENTS' COURSE! PLEASE GO TO ROOM 1A FOR THE THREE TO ELEVEN GROUP AND ROOM 10A FOR TWELVE YEARS UPWARDS.

Andy looked at the crudely written sign on the blackboard in the reception hall of Corrywood High. That was *him*! He was the one who was running the teenage lot. How utterly terrifying! It wasn't the prospect of an audience that scared him witless. He had been used to that at work: standing up at meetings and, every now and then, in front of huge conferences as the keynote speaker. No. It was the place that scared him. He and schools had never gone together. Even on the rare occasion when Andy's work had permitted him to accompany Pamela to parents' evenings, he'd felt distinctly uncomfortable, waiting for a teacher to leap out and cane him.

Andy wiped his clammy palms on the side of his beige trousers, which he'd put on along with a smart navy jacket. The nature of the audience was unnerving too. He could fob off predatory women in an office environment (amazing how many didn't seem to care that he was married!) but school mums posed a different problem. They'd know far more about bringing up children than he did.

Still, he'd promised to do it, so do it he would. Mentally visualising a positive outcome (a tip he'd picked up from one of many business courses), Andy paused outside room 10A – it was buzzing with high-pitched chatter – and then strode in.

Just look at that wall chart. Andy began to sweat as he took in the various organs of the human body, and another with a list of foreign words that could have been Russian for all he knew. Languages were something he'd never had the opportunity to learn. For a moment, Andy was a small boy, poised to do a runner: anything to get out of the classroom . . .

Then he became aware of a smallish group of women, seated in a horseshoe of chairs, swivelling round to focus on him expectantly, as though he was going to solve all their problems in two hours flat. Problems that he wasn't qualified to solve.

'Make them laugh,' said the voice in his head. 'Make them laugh like you did in the home.' It was something he still did in tricky work situations; it defused the atmosphere. Threw the opposition by making them see you in a different light.

'You might be wondering if Pamela has had a sex change!'

There was a silence.

Help.

'Pamela,' he began again. 'Pamela Gooding – my wife – was meant to be running this class. But she had a domestic emergency so I'm afraid you've got me instead.'

To his relief, a horsey-looking but attractive redhead, wearing an extremely low-cut clingy jersey that showed the top of a black lacy bra, made an 'ahh' sound. 'That's so sweet!' Her voice was much posher than her racy outfit suggested. 'You wouldn't get many husbands doing that.' She rolled her eyes. 'Mine certainly wouldn't. It's why I'm here. It's not easy when you're an MSP.'

'MSP?'

She gave him a provocative smile. 'Married single parent, darling. It's when you have a husband in name but he does sod all to help. By the way, I'm Audrey.'

'I know what you mean,' piped up another, who seemed to have come straight from the gym in black Lycra shorts and sweat band round her head. 'Sometimes I think it would be better if I was on my own. Then I wouldn't have someone

91

telling me I'd got it all wrong.' She sniffed. 'And I'm not just talking about how to bring up the kids.'

'Come on, Paula!' whispered the pretty blonde woman next to her, wearing a red sweatshirt with JILLY'S AU PAIR AGENCY emblazoned across the chest. 'Nigel said he was sorry, didn't he? Besides, this isn't Relate. That's tomorrow night. We're here for the kids. Remember?'

These women were utterly terrifying! Exactly the kind he could never have married. Thank heavens for Pamela with her calm, efficient, steady manner, even if it could be misinterpreted as cool. 'Anyway, my wife will be back next week.'

'Shame,' he heard Audrey whisper loudly to her neighbour. 'Rather cute, don't you think? Wouldn't mind him for a bit longer!'

Andy had never quite understood why his boyish good looks (as one admirer had once put it in pre-Pamela days) went down well with 'the ladies'. It wasn't as though he was tall either. But they did seem to appreciate the way he listened to them, as well as his self-deprecating humour.

Usually Andy ignored women who gave him come-on smiles. But it was difficult to blank out this posh Audrey who simply wouldn't stop talking and looking at him in that provocative manner, thrusting out her chest meaningfully. Power bosoms! That's what he called them secretly. He only hoped hers were properly cooped up.

'What I really want from this course,' she was now saying, 'is to get my kids to do exactly *what* I tell them, *when* I tell them.' She waved a hand, encrusted with diamonds, around in the air. 'Simple as that. When I was a child, I'd have got a jolly good hiding if I hadn't obeyed my mother.'

There was a murmur of 'me too's. 'Actually,' said Andy, desperately trying to recall the first chapter of the handbook which he'd been mugging up since 4 p.m. that afternoon, 'I was going to start with goals and objectives.' He turned to the whiteboard. That was better! He felt safer now; as though he was doing a presentation at work. 'What do the rest of you want help with?'

'Bedtime! I can't get the little buggers to stay in their beds!'

Audrey again. If he wasn't careful, she was going to dominate the rest of the sessions. Still, he was used to that at meetings. You had to target the non-talkers to remove the spotlight from the hoggers.

He turned to a very skinny woman, wearing a too-short skirt over black leggings (the sort of thing that a teenager might wear), a leopard-skin spotted scarf artfully wound round her neck and long, dangly green earrings. Very bohemian for Corrywood, wasn't she? Living with a houseful of women had taught Andy to notice clothes and make-up and other girly stuff like that. 'What would you like help with?'

She ran her long, thin fingers through her hair, which was scrunched up in a loose knot. 'I've always tried to be a friend and not just a mum to my kids . . .'

'Grow up,' muttered someone.

'I could never tell my mother anything. She was always criticising me. So I've gone the other way with mine.' She fiddled awkwardly with one of her earrings. 'The other night, I let my fifteen-year-old's boyfriend stay over.'

There was a gasp from the others.

'It's OK!' Bohemian Mum smiled reassuringly at them all. 'She *is* on the Pill. But when I ask them to do something, like their homework, they ignore me. It's like they don't have any respect for me any more.'

Was that surprising? 'That can't be easy,' he began. 'But you know what we can do?'

They all looked at him with hope in their faces. Fuck, thought Andy. What *can* we do? He glanced at the manual, which he'd left surreptitiously at his side to use as a prompt. Big black letters jumped out at him.

WHAT KIND OF CHILDHOOD DID YOU HAVE? HAS IT AFFECTED THE WAY YOU PARENT NOW?

Andy felt a cold dread descending on him but immediately batted it away. His own experiences were irrelevant. This wasn't about him. It was about *them*. 'I'd like you to write down some childhood memories,' he said, more positively

93

now. 'Then we'll discuss how your own parents' methods of bringing you up have formed you as parents.'

'Come again?'

It was Sweat Band Mum. That was another thing Andy had learned from his business-skills conferences. If you found it difficult to remember names, you gave them a mental badge that summed up their appearance or attitude.

'This isn't going to be some kind of psycho session, is it?' She made as though she was going to get up. 'Because if it is, I'm out of here. I had to pay my au pair extra to babysit for this!' She waved away her blonde neighbour, who looked as though she was about to intervene. 'No, Jilly. I'm telling him straight. What I want is some practical advice.'

She was right. 'OK.' Andy was really getting in the swing now. 'Forget the handbook. Let's take one problem at a time. Bedtime, for instance. How old are your kids? And what time do you make them go upstairs?'

'Not everyone has an upstairs!' pointed out Bohemian Mum.

'There's no need to interrupt!' butted in the woman next to her. 'Mine are five and fourteen. It's the older one who's the problem. He goes to bed when he wants to because he won't listen to me.'

Whoa there! This lot were getting really vociferous. 'Then you need to *make* him listen,' he suggested calmly.

'And how exactly do we do that?'

Everyone was facing him now, each one with the same questioning look. Andy thought of his own two girls who were always in bed when he rang from foreign trips to speak to them. 'You just *tell* them.'

They spoke in one breath: 'But it doesn't work!'

Quickly, he tried to think on his feet. Solve it like a business problem. That was it: 'Give them a bonus,' he declared enthusiastically. 'Offer them something they really want if they'll go to bed.'

'It doesn't work!' Sweat Band Mum repeated, loud in her indignation. 'I bribed mine with a new games console each but they still stay up later than me and then they won't go to school in the morning. We want proper answers.' She looked round the room and everyone nodded. 'That's why we're here. It's because nothing else has worked. And as for those ineffectual parenting books – has anyone read Dr Know's latest? – don't even get me started!'

This was really getting out of control! Andy briefly wondered how the young teacher was getting on down the corridor with the three-to-eleven group. Maybe they could do a swap. Her class couldn't be worse than his.

Then Audrey spoke up. 'Come on, you lot. Let's give Andy a chance, shall we?' She sat forward confidentially so Andy could see the dip between her ample breasts. They were tanned and smooth. Quickly he looked away. 'I like your idea of talking about childhood, Andy. It *does* make a difference in the way you bring up kids. My mum was a control freak. She wanted to know exactly what I was doing with my friends, and where, right up to when I left home. To be honest, it's made me the same with my own. Sometimes they come back reeking of fags and other stuff. When I ask if they're doing drugs, they tell me to sod off and then that leads to another argument.'

Phew! She'd finished. Andy's head was reeling. But she had a point. Quite a lot of them. Very deliberately, he took his mobile phone out of his pocket and dropped it on the floor. There was a gasp from his audience as it came apart, scattering the battery and other bits under the chairs.

'What did you do that for?' gasped the woman wearing the JILLY'S AU PAIR AGENCY sweatshirt.

'To show that patterns can be broken.' Andy knelt down on the floor and gathered his phone together. It was a technique he had witnessed once before at a work conference; they'd all been quite impressed by it. 'You can get very attached to something, like many of us are to our mobiles or to a way of doing something. But you can also break that pattern if you want.'

He looked at the redhead. 'Your mum might have been controlling but recognising that is the first step to recovery.

Next time you find yourself wanting to tell your daughters what to do, remember how you felt at their age. Angry, maybe. Trapped, even.'

There was a wave of uncertain nods and Andy felt a quiet hum of satisfaction followed by panic as they all waited expectantly for his next trick. Now what? Yes! He could play the DVD which accompanied the handbook. 'Mind dimming the lights, please?'

What a relief! This would buy him thirty minutes of peace and quiet. After that, they would have a discussion. Then they could all go home and he'd never have to do this again. Still, it made him realise what a brilliant job Pamela had done. He'd always been appreciative but now he was more grateful than ever. He'd buy her something to say so. Another diamond eternity ring perhaps. Or maybe a pair of earrings from her favourite jewellers in Old Bond Street.

Andy slipped off into a daydream about how he would treat Pamela. After that, they might spend the night at a nice hotel somewhere. Pamela was always more receptive in hotels. 'The girls might hear,' she would say when he suggested something different to just going to sleep at home. Not that there was much chance of that in their huge house where the girls had their en-suite bedrooms at the far side. But the principle was right: the girls had to come first. There was nothing more important than family and even though he didn't like his mother-in-law, he admired his wife for rushing off to help her.

The film was coming to an end now and the redhead was jumping up to turn on the light like teacher's pet. 'That was extra*ord*inary,' she started to say just as the door opened and a large, burly man lumbered in.

'Sorry I'm late, mate. The name's Kieran, by the way.'

Andy glanced at the man in an orange, oily boiler suit. Corrywood might have a great reputation but you got a real mixture of people here, like this one with his rough accent and bald head with no neck. 'Take a seat, will you?' There were certainly enough empty ones!

The man stared, his eyes narrowing. 'Don't I know you from somewhere, mate?'

'I don't think so,' began Andy. But then he stopped, taking in the long silver scar on the newcomer's right cheek. The tattoo of a red flame on one side of his neck, and a matching blue one on the other side. For a minute, he was overwhelmed by the smell of urine and cabbage and Brussels sprouts. No, he said fiercely to himself. No. It couldn't be!

'Barry, isn't it?' the man persisted.

'Andy actually,' he replied pleasantly. Politely. So as not to reveal his shock. 'I'm afraid you've missed most of the session but perhaps the rest of you would like to tell Kieran here about the film and any tips on compromise that you've hopefully picked up.'

The newcomer took a seat but his beady black eyes remained firmly fixed in his direction. He's recognised me, gulped Andy, feeling sweat gushing down his back. He's recognised me.

What if Kieran questioned Pamela at the next meeting? What if Kieran insisted that he was sure he knew Andy from the past? The questions began to throb in Andy's brain before he'd even got into his Porsche, parked carefully under a streetlight to deter thugs.

Pamela, who had always been intrigued by his lack of family, might make her own enquiries. Then all his carefully built-up secrets would come tumbling down! It wasn't just the fact he'd been in care. It was the Thing that had happened there. The Thing which even now he couldn't bring himself to think about or else he would go mad. Think of something, he told himself urgently, pressing the security button at his gate. Think of something.

The house was horribly empty. Usually when Andy got back late, exhausted from work or a trip, Pamela was waiting for him in her silk dressing gown, drink in hand. There'd be a meal in the oven if he hadn't already eaten and Classic FM playing quietly in the background. But now it was silent apart from a drone of television from Natasha's bedroom, which stopped before he reached the top of the stairs.

Natasha barely looked up from her desk when he put his head round the open door. She was doing her coursework, from the look of the computer screen. Such a conscientious child! A real relief after some of the tales he'd heard tonight.

'Thought I heard the television,' Andy said.

Natasha's eyes widened. 'I've been doing some online French tutorials. Want to look?'

She was kidding! There was no way he wanted to display his ignorance. 'No thanks. Where's Mel?'

'Still babysitting for Aunty Bobbie. But Mum rang. I took a message.'

She handed him a heart-shaped piece of paper from her jottings pad. *Need to stay on for an extra week or two. Please don't ring tonight. Am going to bed early.*

Andy felt an odd feeling in his chest. 'An extra week or two? Why?'

Nattie shrugged. 'I don't know. But she did say there were plenty of home-made meals in the freezer. Shut the door, can you, Dad? I've got to get on with my work.'

There once was a father from Deal,
Whose children would tell fibs and steal.
'Will you please tell the truth
Or I promise – by struth –
You'll forgo your very next meal.'

(Of course he didn't mean it, so they're still at it.)

PERFECT PARENTS: SESSION TWO

<u>LEARN THE SECRET OF REFLECTIVE LISTENING!</u>

REPEAT YOUR CHILD'S WORDS AND SHOW THAT YOU REALLY DO UNDERSTAND.
BELOW IS AN EXAMPLE.

CHILD: 'F— OFF AND LEAVE ME ALONE.'
PARENT: 'I UNDERSTAND THAT YOU WANT ME TO F— OFF AND LEAVE YOU ALONE. I'D LIKE SOME PEACE AND QUIET TOO. BUT I'M THE ADULT SO YOU BLOODY WELL HAVE TO DO AS YOU'RE TOLD.'

(NB Last sentence to be used only under extreme duress.)

Chapter 10

BOBBIE

'Just look at the time! We're going to be late for school! What do you mean you can't find your shoes, Daisy? Where did you last throw them? Jack! Get out of bed now.'

'But I'm comfy, Mum.'

'I said, NOW!'

Nag, nag, nag! That's all she ever seemed to do nowadays. Sometimes Bobbie thought she was two people. The crazy one when the kids were around and the normal one when they were at school.

'Sit up and eat your cereal, Jack! Not like that! You'll get your foot stuck in the back of the chair. See! Wiggle your toes to the right. To the *right*! That's it. No, there isn't time for more breakfast. You'll have to eat a banana on the way. All right. Dip it in peanut butter first if you *have* to. No, we're *out* of the crunchy sort.'

Thank heavens no one else could see them now, thought Bobbie as she hustled the kids out of the house. Shit! She'd shut the door before picking up her keys from the kitchen table! If they'd still been in London, her friend Sarah would have had a key. Now she'd have to break in or find a locksmith when she got back. Meanwhile, they'd have to *walk* to school.

'But it's raining,' pouted Daisy. 'Did you know that if it rains like this for another week, Britain will have enough water to fill a thousand swimming pools? It said so on my Clever Clogs app.'

'That's not going to get us to school on time, is it?' Bobbie heard herself snapping back in a way that she didn't like. Then again, she hadn't liked herself for a long time. Being a parent had turned her into someone whom she wouldn't want to be friends with. To think she'd hoped that the course would help! She'd been right to jack it in. That first session had only made her feel even more of a failure.

And no wonder! It wasn't designed for kids like hers who yelled in capital letters or parents who screamed back with exclamation marks. She'd just have to muddle on until they were eighteen. Longer than some life sentences.

'Don't push your sister like that!' Bobbie felt like smacking Jack but managed to hold back. It was so easy to lose it. Frighteningly easy. 'Just walk nicely, can't you? And hurry up!'

They were taking the quick route to school along the canal, past the brightly coloured barges with the flowers on top and pretty names along the side. This was one of the good things about moving out of London. Corrywood had the Grand Union running through it: perfect for walks, she and Rob had told themselves excitedly when they'd first arrived. The truth was that family walks always degenerated into family arguments. Like now.

'HE'S STILL PUSHING ME, MUM!'

'THEN MOVE OVER!'

There was a scream followed by a terrific splash. 'Daisy!' shouted Bobbie. Kneeling down on the muddy side, she grabbed hold of her daughter and hauled her up, coughing and spluttering. 'Are you all right? SAY something!'

The ear-splitting yell suggested that her lungs were still working. But it took a few seconds for the relief to catch up with Bobbie's heart, which felt as though it was throbbing in her throat. 'You naughty boy, Jack. Your sister could have drowned.'

'I'M WET, MUM! I'M WET!'

'IT WASN'T MY FAULT! SHE SHOULD HAVE MOVED OVER.'

A jogger gave her a critical look as she ran by. Don't blame me, Bobbie wanted to say. I didn't ask for kids like this. I'm trying my best.

Hanging on to Jack with one hand and a sodden Daisy with the other, she made her way to school. She'd have to dry her off there, now she'd locked them all out of the house. That would be one more black mark against the Wright family. How on earth was she going to sort them out before Mum arrived with Dr Know?

'I wish you'd never been . . .' began Bobbie. Then she stopped, appalled with herself. She'd come close, so close, to saying that she wished Jack had never been born. Of course she didn't mean that. But sometimes kids did things that made you say stuff you never thought you were capable of. 'I wish you hadn't pushed your sister over the side,' she said lamely.

Jack nodded. For once, he looked penitent. 'I'm sorry, Mummy.'

'It's your sister you need to apologise to!'

'But she pushed *me*!'

Daisy, soaking wet, was still sobbing. 'He did it first.'

'STOP!' Bobbie heard herself screaming just as they reached the school gates. 'BOTH OF YOU.'

A woman with a baby in her arms and a toddler in each hand gave a little wave from the other side of the road. It was Too Many Kids Mum, that mother with eight children. Now she'd tell all the others in the group what an appalling parent she was.

One more reason for not going again.

It took nearly two hours to find a locksmith, which meant that Bobbie didn't sit down at her desk until nearly lunchtime. She'd fallen into the market-research job through her friend Sarah from London. Both had been looking for something to do that fitted in with school hours and holidays. Then one of the other girls from their old antenatal group had told them about an agency who needed articulate women to make cold calls and ask questions, usually about medical or psychological subjects.

Some of them could be really embarrassing. A few weeks ago, Bobbie had had to find people who were happy to talk about piles. The week after that, it had been contraception. Last week it was fungal nails. This week it was tranquillisers. Not surprisingly, it was difficult to find interviewees with both the time and inclination. Bobbie was quite used to having the phone slammed down on her or being verbally abused. This job wasn't for the faint-hearted.

'Hello, is that Mrs Grant? How are you today? My name's Bobbie and I'm ringing on behalf of Research Trivia . . .'

No? One more refusal with fifty-four more names on her list to go. All too often, Bobbie didn't even get as far as giving her company's name. Consumers were becoming increasingly smart at recognising cold callers and she didn't blame them. The last thing she would want herself was a market researcher ringing up out of the blue.

But every now and then, you hit gold. Someone who was lonely. Someone who actually wanted to talk because they didn't have anyone else to chat to.

'Hello, is that Mr White? Who's calling? Actually, my name's Bobbie and I . . . Yes, actually, I am from a market-research company and I'm doing a survey on . . .'

No? Fair enough. Fifty-three to go.

On an average day, Bobbie would get at least five lots of surveys done. Usually, her pleasant voice (the one she saved for those who weren't related to her) charmed even those who weren't very keen on divulging their social or medical habits. But today, at this rate, she was going to need some tranquillisers herself. Desperately she worked her way down the list, without any takers. Was that really the time? She hadn't even had lunch and now she was going to be late for school pick-up.

Dashing to the school, Bobbie found Daisy and Jack waiting in the playground with a none-too-pleased duty teacher who didn't seem impressed by Bobbie's excuse that she'd been 'delayed at work'.

'But you *don't* work,' trilled Daisy right in front of her.

'Yes I do! From home.' Bobbie had given up expecting others to accept she had a proper job even though she didn't go out to an office. But it would be nice if her own husband

and children saw it as that. 'Come on,' she said, chivvying them into the car. 'We've got to get back. How was school today?'

'I wrote about Jack trying to drown me in the canal,' announced Daisy, who was wearing a too-big navy tracksuit to replace the saturated school uniform. 'My teacher gave me eight out of ten. She also wants to see you.'

Great.

'I didn't try to drown you,' retorted Jack. 'You fell in yourself.'

'No I didn't. And stop flicking bogeys at me.'

'I'm not.'

'Yes you are.'

'STOP ARGUING!' Sometimes Bobbie didn't even know she was shouting until she felt her throat getting sore. 'I had enough of that this morning. Now when you get in, I've got some work to finish before tea. I won't be long. Promise.'

'Hello, is that Mr Bigger? My name's Bobbie and I . . . Yes, actually, I am from a market-research company and I'm doing a survey on tranquillisers. I was just wondering if you'd mind answering a few questions about . . . You will! That's wonderful! Thank you so much. Can you tell me when you first started taking—'

'MUM! I'M STARVING.'

Not yet! Not yet! Desperately, Bobbie turned round from her desk in the spare room and tried to bat away Jack. 'Just one minute,' she mouthed. 'Please.

'I see. You started when your wife died. I'm so sorry. And can you tell me the name? Florence? Actually, I meant the name of the tranquillisers.'

'MUM, I'M HUNGRY!'

'In a minute, I said. No, not you, Mr Bigger. Sorry. Do you spell that with one "t" or two? Not your name; the tranquillisers. Right. Got it. And did they help? JACK, I'LL BE THERE IN A SECOND. No, Mr Bitter. I mean Bigger. This isn't a hoax call. It's part of a market survey and . . .'

Too late! He'd rung off. She'd lost him. The only person who had been happy to talk to her that day! Bobbie felt like weeping with frustration. That meant she wouldn't reach her target so she'd only get her telephone expenses. How were they going to manage?

'I'm hungry, Mummy,' bleated Jack plaintively. Of course he was! Shocked by herself, Bobbie put her arm around her son. What kind of mother was she to put her work before her children? A lousy mother, that's what. Still, if in doubt, switch on Sky. How did mothers manage before?

'WHAT DID YOU SAY?' thundered a voice from the screen.

Oh my God. There he was! Dr Know! Right in front of her! A male cross between Supernanny and the devil with those forbidding eyebrows, knitted together with derision as a mother from the studio audience cowered before him. 'You let your son go to bed at WHAT time?' he was roaring.

Jack began to whimper. 'I don't like this programme. It scares me.'

Her son was actually hiding behind a cushion! Nothing *ever* frightened Jack.

'That's Gran's new boyfriend,' began Bobbie.

Daisy fixed her with a scornful look. 'Don't tell lies, Mum, or your nose will get bigger.'

'I'm not.'

'Mum!' Her daughter grabbed the remote to switch channels. 'I'm not going to tell you again!'

A screen of flying pink pigs appeared before them. That was better. Both kids settled down into their bean bags, cans of fizzy drink at their side (she'd given up on that one) with a distinct air of relief. Dr Know had been banished. But they wouldn't be able to get rid of him so easily when he came to the house!

What am I going to do? she texted her friend Sarah after she'd finally got them to bed and was still waiting for Rob to come home. Sarah would understand. Her son Tom was

108

just like Jack. Both live wires. They had supported each other ever since their boys were born; told each other that it was the wild ones who would make something out of their lives. All they had to do as parents was to make sure they survived until they were grown up. Poor Sarah! It was much worse for her now that she was on her own.

It's not just Mum's boyfriend, she added. *It's me. The kids have turned me into a monster.*

Know what you mean, Sarah texted back. *That's why I've just joined this new parenting class. Really great! Have made some new friends too. You ought to see if there's one in your area.*

New friends? Bobbie felt a surge of jealousy as well as surprise. She'd never labelled Sarah, who had such strong opinions, as the kind of person who would take advice from a parenting class. Maybe, just maybe, she ought to give it one more go.

She was late. They'd already started.

'Listen and encourage,' Judith was saying with the shining face of a convert. Bobbie found herself glancing at the teacher's bare left hand. No wedding ring. No children. A non-parent with no commitments and all the answers. Hah!

'Children often feel that their parents aren't listening,' continued Judith excitedly. 'This week, we're going to help you to do that through the art of reflective listening.'

Bobbie shuffled in her seat. Phrases like this were all very well but she'd love to see this woman handle Jack. When she'd left her son half an hour ago with Mel, he was still rooted to his DS game after a furious put-that-down-and-go-to-bed argument which she'd lost, hands down.

If only you could switch kids off and then on again, like the computer. Maybe they'd work then.

'You don't look very convinced, Bobbie,' said Judith, suddenly addressing her.

'I'm not, actually.' She flushed as everyone turned to look, including Not Really Pregnant Mum and someone new: a

109

small, blonde, older-looking woman with hooped gold earrings, wearing a very chic pair of black trousers and silky mauve top. Now where had she seen her before?

'I tried out the positive praise on my children after last week's session,' continued Bobbie. 'I did it on my husband too. They all thought I was being sarcastic.'

Judith nodded. 'You missed the beginning of the session, unfortunately, when we had feedback on how our "homework" went. The general consensus was that it takes time to break the patterns of a lifetime. But it's vital that we persevere. You might have better luck with reflective listening.'

'Not if your kids yell as much as mine,' muttered Butterfly Mum, whom Bobbie had renamed Battered Mum. 'My ears have been ringing since the day they were born. I just can't get used to the shouting.' She nudged Bobbie. 'By the way, I thought you were very brave to do that role play last time. My kids are much worse than yours but I didn't have the gall to act it out.'

Really? That made her feel better!

'Shall I repeat that?' Judith was fixing her with a you-weren't-paying-attention-were-you? look. 'Reflective listening means listening to your children while making eye contact at the same time – that's essential – and then saying a phrase which shows that you understand how they are feeling.'

Not Really Pregnant Mum sniffed. 'Pity some mums can't do that.' She threw Bobbie a filthy look. 'Did you know that my son is diabetic? He can only eat certain food.'

So Jack hadn't just stolen a lunch box. He'd nicked someone's lifeline.

'My son's a picky eater,' piped up one of the others. There was a chorus of 'My kids are like that too.'

Judith was nodding again. Did she ever stop? Those nods must be a nervous habit. 'We're diverting slightly here but how about encouraging him to make his own supper – under your guidance, of course. You never know' – she gave a silly giggle – 'he might be the next Jamie Oliver!'

Make their own supper! Had this woman any idea of what

it was like at teatime? It was chaotic enough with the 'sit down's and the 'don't fight's and the 'have you learned your Mandarin vocab', without showing them how the microwave worked.

'I haven't time to let my son cook!' said the woman indignantly. 'He'd burn himself or make a real mess. Besides, he'd get under my feet!'

Bobbie almost felt sorry for Judith, who was becoming really flustered. 'Maybe it's time for the film,' she said, fiddling around the laptop. As the lights dimmed, Bobbie was aware of the new woman looking at her curiously. That was it! She was the woman from the supermarket. The one with pink leggings who had been staring when Jack had been playing up. Great! That was all she needed. Someone who had witnessed her lack of parenting skills in action. She looked, at a guess, as though she was in her mid-forties. A slightly older mother who thought she knew best.

Bobbie slipped out of the session as soon as the post-film discussion was over. Homework was to practise 'reflective listening' and 'encouraging' children by picking up the skills they were good at and praising them. Fat lot of good that would do.

'Hi!'

Bobbie turned round at the friendly voice. Andy! That was a surprise. It seemed strange to see her sister-in-law's husband at school and not in that white-carpeted mansion with chrome fittings and a chill in the atmosphere. Perhaps he was here to support his wife by being part of the group or maybe help her with the PowerPoint. What a nice man!

He glanced across at the *Perfect Parents' Guide for Juniors* in her hand. 'How's it going?'

She groaned. 'Put it this way: I was hoping for some magic answers but so far I haven't got any.' Then she stopped, not wanting to cast any aspersions on poor Judith, who was doing her best. 'How's Pamela's course going?'

He nodded briskly as though she'd touched a nerve.

'Actually, I'm having to do it for her, on a temporary basis. It was meant to be for one session but somehow I seem to have ended up running the second one too. Pamela had to go to her mother's and is staying a little longer than she'd intended. Camilla's new au pair isn't settling in very well. Oh, and her arthritis is playing her up too.'

He gave her a loaded look. Interesting, mused Bobbie. Sounded as though Andy cared as little for their mutual mother-in-law as she did. Camilla was an overbearing woman always talking about herself, who'd made it clear that Bobbie wasn't what she had expected as a daughter-in-law. Only a carbon copy of her own daughter Pamela would have done for her son!

'Didn't Rob tell you?' added Andy.

'I don't think so.' Bobbie didn't like to confess that her conversations with her husband were very much of the 'Guess what Jack's done *now*' variety rather than normal stuff. 'To be honest, I haven't seen much of him. He's been working really late again. So how did your session go?'

Andy made a wry face. 'So so. We've been so lucky with our girls that I'm not really sure if I'm able to give the right advice to parents like . . .'

He stopped, awkwardly. Bobbie knew exactly what he was going to say. 'To parents like me, you mean, with kids that smash vases and leave filthy marks on white carpets?'

'Actually, I was thinking of someone in my class.' Then his face cleared. 'Hey!' He touched her arm briefly in a show of family affection. 'They're just kids! I was a little rascal at your son's age.' Then he stopped again as an odd, unreadable expression flitted over his face. 'Fancy a coffee before you go home?'

Bobbie was about to decline and then stopped. Why not? Rob wasn't going to be back for ages and Mel was a responsible babysitter. Besides, it would be nice to get to know Andy a bit better, away from Princess Pamela's Palace. She could certainly do with some solidarity at family gatherings in the future.

'I'd love a coffee, provided your daughter doesn't mind babysitting for a bit longer.'

'I'm sure she won't.' Andy glanced at his watch, looking pleased. Bobbie felt an odd tingle of excitement. One that grew bigger, for some reason, as he placed a hand briefly in the small of her back. 'There's a nice little place round the corner. At least it *looks* nice; I haven't actually been inside. Shall we give it a go?'

DON'T EVEN BOTHER . . .

Phrases that won't work on the kids

How many times have I told you not to do that?
Wait until your mother comes home.
Euros don't grow on trees.
Give me back my iPad.
Let me finish my sentence.
I'll buy you a bike if you get a good report.
When I was your age, we listened to our parents.

Extracted from www.toptipsforineffectualparents.com.

Chapter 11

Sunshine was such a quiet child at times, but at others, she was a real little chatterbox. So reflective listening was a bit hit and miss.

'Would you like tea now?'

'No thank you.'

'No thank you?'

'I'm not hungry.'

'You're not hungry?'

'No.'

So polite! It was almost unnerving, rather like Sunshine's habit of observing everything: staring around her; taking it all in; picking up a cushion from the sofa and examining its stitching or reaching up for a blue vase on the mantelpiece and holding it up to the light. She clearly had a good eye for colour. Brigid had been arty too.

But at this age, her daughter had been an open book. Sunshine could chat away – and how! – but she seemed to clam up when asked questions. The important ones. 'Why did Mummy not come with you, Sunshine?' Vanessa prodded every now and then. Or 'Where is she now?'

But all she could ever get out of her granddaughter was a shake of the head in answer to the first question and a shrug for the second.

'What about her passport?' Brian asked when he rang to see how things were going.

Of course! It would have a stamp, wouldn't it? To say where she'd been. Heavens! This child had travelled! South America, Morocco, Istanbul and, last of all, Goa.

What a breakthrough! Vanessa had, by chance, seen a documentary on India the other month, including a short spot on Goa, which, the enthusiastic presenter had declared, was not just a favourite holiday destination but also a popular spot for ex-pats who 'wanted to drop out'.

That sounded like her daughter all right. But did that mean Brigid had simply handed over Sunshine to that dirty friend of hers in India and got him to bring her over to the UK? Why? And, more importantly, how could she get hold of Brigid and find out exactly what was going on?

Maybe someone at the local council offices might help. It took her a while to reach the right person who said, no, it was the Foreign Office she needed to speak to. So she'd hung on for a while before eventually emailing them, full of hope; only to receive a standard reply informing her that her 'query' had been received and would be dealt with 'within twenty working days of receipt'.

'How could you do this, Brigid?' Vanessa had asked out loud in a cross voice that wasn't like hers at all. 'How could you be so selfish as to leave your child like this? And why with *me*, when you haven't bothered keeping in touch?'

Meanwhile, she was torn between wonder at meeting her granddaughter and annoyance at all the hasty adjustments that now needed to be made to the life she'd so carefully built for herself since Brigid had stormed out all those years earlier.

For a start, Sunshine woke so early! Vanessa could hear her moving around from 4 or 5 a.m. in the spare room next to hers, which she'd transformed into a child's bedroom by buying a pretty rosebud duvet and a few other bits and pieces that a little girl might like. (She'd also brought some of Brigid's toys out of the understairs cupboard, which had given her a bit of a funny feeling in her chest.)

It wasn't that she came into her room when she woke. But just hearing her sit there and chant made it impossible for Vanessa to turn over and go back to sleep.

Sunshine seemed to chant at least twice a day: a low

sing-song chant that sounded a bit like a nursery rhyme except that it was difficult to make out the words. Maybe she was a Buddhist? Vanessa had once watched a programme on different religions and been rather taken by the chanting side. Did she do it at school? Not according to Miss Davies. 'Sunshine seems to be settling in nicely. She's beginning to talk much more than she used to. And she's a very good reader for her age, isn't she?'

Was she? Vanessa had been out of the parenting loop for so long that it was difficult to know. But she *had* noticed that when Sunshine wasn't chanting or playing that dirty old flute (which never left her sight), she had her face in a book: one of a pile which Vanessa had brought down from the attic along with the old toys.

Nor did she read with a finger underneath each word as a new reader might but sat there, cross-legged on the floor, glued to the pages, which she turned quite quickly. Her daughter seemed to have done quite a good job as a mum, considering the reading and polite manners. Rather surprising really.

That was the other thing about being a mum all over again. You forgot how warm and excited you felt when someone praised your child. Or how easy it was to take it as a personal insult when your own flesh and blood did something wrong.

Another thing she'd forgotten was how long it took to get a child ready, even though Sunshine was very good and stood there waiting patiently by the door in her crisp new school uniform and shiny brown lace-ups while Vanessa locked up her little maisonette and ensured she had everything she needed for work that day.

Then as soon as she dropped off her granddaughter in the classroom, feeling distinctly old compared with all these young things rushing in and out with prams and baby slings, Vanessa would tear off to the shop. Only there would she feel normal again. Like her old self. Except that something was different; at the back of her mind was always the looming responsibility of a 3 p.m. pick up at school.

When she did arrive at the school gates, puffing slightly, Sunshine always seemed quite happy; chatting away to the other children with that wonderful beaming smile of hers. Maybe Miss Davies was right: she *was* coming out of herself. 'Friendly little soul, isn't she?' said one mum. Too friendly! Sunshine was now beginning to say hello to everyone they passed in the street. Perhaps it was what they did in Goa.

Meanwhile, closing the shop early for the school pick-up wasn't great for business, even though her assistant Kim had reluctantly agreed to do a couple of afternoons a week. Maybe, when this wasn't all so new, Sunshine could join her in the shop. Perhaps by then Brigid might even have turned up to collect her child. Or maybe the Foreign Office would track her down to remind her of her maternal duties. Meanwhile, she'd just have to wait.

Since her diagnosis, five years ago, when that lump had appeared so unexpectedly in her right breast, Vanessa had learned to take one step at a time and to live life for the day. Thanks to a mixture of luck and her amazing medical team, Vanessa had been one of the fortunate ones. As a result, she'd sworn that she would enjoy every extra minute of life that she'd been given – including this bonus time with the granddaughter that she'd given up hope of meeting.

They were already falling into a routine. After school, Sunshine would walk back home with her, hand in hand, for tea. Her favourite was haricot beans and plain pasta. She also loved raw broccoli and fruit, although she seemed to think the bananas were very funny. 'Big,' she laughed, stretching her hands out. 'Very big!'

Vanessa thought back to the tiny, tasty bananas she had had the other year in Sri Lanka when she had gone on a singles package holiday. Maybe Sunshine had a point!

Another surprise was the television. When Vanessa turned it on for her favourite teatime quiz, Sunshine let out a little shriek, holding her hand against her eyes and pointing. 'Look, Van Van. Look! There are people inside!'

Vanessa laughed until she realised the child was genuinely

scared and thought that the figures on the screen really were trapped inside her pink telly. Only when she switched it off did Sunshine calm down. Better leave that for a bit, Vanessa told herself, feeling rather cheated at having missed her programme.

After dinner, she would sit down on the floor again to do her homework (her granddaughter seemed to find chairs uncomfortable) and then start to yawn just as the sun went down. What kind of a life had she been leading? Vanessa would wonder. She had a vision of a mud hut in the middle of nowhere. Yet from the travel brochures she'd got from the agency round the corner, Goa looked quite civilised with some beautiful hotels. Maybe that was just on the surface.

Often at night, when Sunshine was asleep, Vanessa would creep into her room and kneel down by her side, watching her breathe evenly. She always had her thumb in her mouth – just as Brigid used to do – and her eyelashes were thick and dark, betraying her Irish roots. Just like all the photographs of her daughter, which were still in the sitting room. Sometimes Vanessa imagined to herself that this was Brigid and she was being given a chance to start all over again.

'Doesn't she miss her mother?' Brian asked during one of his regular how's-it-going? calls. They had decided, both of them, that they wouldn't see each other for a bit until things had settled down.

'She doesn't talk about her,' marvelled Vanessa. 'Strange, isn't it? She just seems to accept everything just as it is.'

'Maybe she's used to being left alone,' suggested Brian. Vanessa didn't like the sound of that although she privately agreed. She had a vision of Brigid leaving her granddaughter for hours at a time while she went out to work (what kind of work?) or (another horrible thought) entertained boyfriends in a room next door.

Dr Know's book had a short section on latchkey kids. It consisted of one word. *Don't*.

Then something happened that gave her another perspective on Sunshine's former life. They were walking down the street, back from school towards the shop. Kim couldn't come in today so Vanessa had had to shut it for an hour to collect Sunshine. 'You're going to help Granny at work today,' she had said, phrasing it like a big treat. It was a tip she'd picked up from that parenting class, which had been quite useful actually.

Sunshine had nodded as though she had been told this before. Vanessa could just see her daughter and granddaughter sitting by a dusty road, selling berries. Or maybe dealing behind closed doors with Sunshine acting as a lookout. She shivered. And then suddenly a car backfired right next to them and Sunshine fell to the ground, covering her head with her arms and crying. Not just a child's cry but a terrified scream that chilled Vanessa's blood. 'It's all right,' she soothed, wrapping her arms around her. 'It's only a car.'

'Gun, gun,' insisted Sunshine, shaking all over. 'They're coming to kill us.'

Vanessa's mouth went dry. What kind of environment had the child been living in?

'No, poppet,' she said firmly. 'No one's coming to kill us. You're safe with me. I promise.'

But the child refused to be consoled and by the time they got to the shop, she was still crying. There was someone waiting outside too. A customer, from the look of it, with a bulging carrier bag in one hand and a small boy in the other who was tugging and trying to get away. It was the fresh-faced woman from the parenting class, Vanessa realised. The same mum she'd seen at the supermarket when the little boy had hidden on the bread shelf.

From the awkward expression on her face, it was clear the woman recognised her too. Vanessa could see why she looked uncomfortable. They'd all said stuff in class. Stuff that didn't belong outside the classroom. She suspected, too, that this young mum was still embarrassed about the supermarket scene. She'd have felt the same.

'I didn't realise you worked here. JACK, DON'T DO THAT.'

'Actually, I own the shop.' Vanessa felt that glow she always experienced when customers took her for an ordinary assistant.

'Really? JACK! COME AWAY FROM THE ROAD! AND YOU TOO, DAISY.'

Vanessa hadn't noticed the little girl skipping ahead.

'Sorry, have I come at a bad time? Only when I popped in the other week, another woman who served me said you bought clothes.' The young mum glanced down at her bag. 'I've got some stuff I don't wear any more. Perhaps you could tell me what it's worth.'

'Come on in,' said Vanessa encouragingly, turning round for Sunshine. She'd been there a few minutes ago! Where was she? Her heart missed a beat. But then she saw her, sitting on the pavement. 'What on earth are you doing there!'

Her granddaughter, Vanessa saw with surprise, was hanging on to the older girl's hand and gazing up with an adoring younger-sister look. 'Daisy's my friend,' beamed Sunshine.

'We sit next to each other in the orchestra,' added the other child.

'What does your daughter play?'

'The flute, but she's not my daughter,' said Vanessa lightly. She'd thought everyone had realised that at the parenting class. 'She's my granddaughter. I'm . . . looking after her while her mother is away.'

As she spoke, the two girls had already run ahead into the shop. 'Hang on,' called out Vanessa. 'Don't touch anything, please!'

But they were already sitting cross-legged on the floor, as good as gold. The older girl had taken her recorder out of her bag and was showing Sunshine how to play it.

'JACK, COME OUT OF THERE! I SAID NOW!'

Heavens. The little boy was ducking and diving in the window display! Undressing one of the models and trying on clothes! 'Put that hat down, Jack,' called out his sister bossily. 'You know what Mum said! You can't put anything near your head until you've finished your lice treatment.'

Lice?

121

'I'm so sorry.' The young mum was beetroot with embarrassment as she dragged her son out of the window, knocking over a mannequin in a cranberry-coloured jumper and black leather skirt. 'And ignore Daisy. Jack's clear. The nurse checked him yesterday.'

Vanessa's heart went out to her. 'It's all right. Honestly. My daughter', she added in a low voice, 'was very hard work when she was little. I know what it's like when people stare at you. That's why I felt sorry for you in the supermarket the other day – that *was* you, wasn't it?'

The woman nodded. 'I'm Bobbie, by the way. I think we missed the introductions at parenting class the other night.'

She put out her hand. 'Vanessa.' She turned to the small boy with the closely shaved head who was now trying to yank his sister's recorder out of her mouth. 'And your name, if I'm not mistaken, is Jack. Would you like a biscuit? Then your mum can show me what's in that bag.'

She was lucky, Vanessa told herself on the way home. Compared with that little scamp, Sunshine was really very easy to deal with, apart from the odd panic over backfiring cars and television programmes. She didn't run off. She didn't shout and scream when she didn't get her own way. She didn't . . .

'Hey! Aren't you Brigid's mum?'

Vanessa stopped as a very thin, weasel-faced youth with huge plug earrings and a clutch of silver nose rings stood in front of her, blocking her path.

Her pulse began to beat in her throat. Wasn't he one of the 'bad' crowd that her daughter had hung out with as a teenager? She hadn't seen any of them for a long time and had presumed that they had moved away, probably to London where things were livelier. Pity he hadn't stayed there, she thought, looking up at this man, determined to stand her ground. He didn't seem nice. Not nice at all.

'Heard she'd gone abroad,' he now said, looking at her challengingly.

Vanessa had been about to storm off but now she stopped. What did this man with his rough accent and nose ring know about her daughter? 'I believe so,' she answered evenly, trying to sound cool even though her heart was pounding.

'Don't know where she went, do you?' he persisted. 'I've been looking for her, like.'

'I don't.' Vanessa felt a wave of disappointment. So he knew as little as she did!

Sunshine, sensing her unease, was now tugging at her hand. 'Come on, Van Van.'

He scowled. 'And who is this?'

'Sunshine!' Her granddaughter's face beamed up at him – so trusting, so open. 'But Van Van sometimes calls me poppet!'

The man knelt down so that his weasel face was level with her granddaughter. His skin was like a pimply crater and he stank of stale BO. She tried to pull Sunshine away but the child was standing firm.

'Poppet, eh? And how old are *you*?'

Sunshine treated him to one of her big wide smiles. 'I'm six.'

'Six?' He looked up at Vanessa, his eyes narrowing again. 'That's interesting. Your daughter and I were stepping out together around that time. Did you know that? *Granny?*' He said the last bit in a nasty sarcastic way. Then his eyes narrowed. 'At least, I guess that's what you are.'

'Go away.' Vanessa heard her voice come out in a growl. 'Leave us alone.'

He scratched his chin thoughtfully. It had, she noticed with disgust, a few straggly hairs on it; the kind that men got when they couldn't grow a beard. What on earth had her daughter seen in this rude, uncouth lout?

'I wonder,' he was saying, looking at Sunshine. 'I wonder . . .'

'I said: Leave us alone!'

'Everything all right?'

Vanessa swung round to see Brian. Her heart filled with relief. Never had she been so pleased to see him! 'No. It's not.'

Brian's eyes narrowed. 'I recognise you, don't I? Jason, isn't it?'

'Keep your hair on, Granddad!' The youth spat on the ground. 'You're not my headmaster now.' He focused his narrow eyes on Vanessa again. 'Got to go away now on a job. But I'll be back. Still live in the same place, do you?' He glanced down at Sunshine. 'Cos something tells me that this little lady and I need to be better acquainted.'

There was a grin. A stained yellow-toothed grin. 'Dads have legal rights too, you know. And I've always fancied being one. Reckon I'd make a good father. Don't you?'

SUGGESTED TOPICS FOR FAMILY CONFERENCES

The recent 'You have exceeded your allowance' email
from broadband.
Missing tenner from your purse.
Unmade beds.
Foul language.
School detentions.
Lost PE kit.
Unsavoury friends.

Extracted from www.perfectparentsnevergiveup.com.

Chapter 12

ANDY

Andy didn't think he'd miss the office. Hadn't he been desperate for a break? On the whole, he *was* enjoying the rest. He really was, even though it felt odd not to check his emails every five minutes or hold back-to-back meetings. Even so, he invariably found himself downloading *The Times* on to his iPad after breakfast so he could check the business pages.

There had been a small piece the other day about him selling the business to Harry Screws and it had given Andy an odd pang to see their names in print. It didn't seem real to be reminded of his old world. Not when he was sitting in the kitchen, surrounded by the girls' half-empty coffee mugs and dirty cereal bowls. It felt like playing truant: an experience he hadn't been unfamiliar with as a kid.

It also seemed weird to put the bowls in the dishwasher: Pamela hated anyone else helping her. But she wasn't here. Andy couldn't remember the last time his wife had been out of the house for so long. It was always him. Not her. As for the girls, they didn't have as much time for him as he had hoped. Always rushing in and out. Always on their phones or laptops.

Maybe that's why he had enjoyed his coffee with Bobbie so much. It had been nice to talk to someone. Good to get to know his sister-in-law on a one to one. Whenever they'd met before, it was at family gatherings; usually in their house rather than anywhere else because they had more room, as Pamela would point out. Privately, he knew it was because his wife loved playing the gracious hostess. And why not? She was a good one.

Even so, he'd often felt sorry for Bobbie at these do's. (The ones that he was around for, that was.) He'd noticed her trying to keep her children quiet while Rob would be mingling, glass of wine in his hand, as though he was a single guest, but every now and then shooting a disapproving look at his lively offspring.

Still, that was the family that both he and Bobbie had married into, as they had agreed the other night in that little bistro round the corner from school. 'They're different, don't you think?' he'd asked, knowing from snippets he'd picked up over the years that Bobbie came from quite a modest background herself. 'Imagine having nannies from birth and then being packed off to boarding school before your ninth birthday. It's given them a sort of edge, if you know what I mean. Very independent.'

Almost unfeeling, he'd nearly added.

Bobbie had nodded earnestly over her cappuccino. 'Rob loves the kids, I know he does, but he assumes that they come out of their packaging ready to behave.'

He'd laughed. 'I like that.'

'Then when they don't, I'm the one to blame. He thinks I'm too weak.'

Her eyes had grown misty. She was really upset! Andy found himself patting her hand reassuringly. 'Better than belting them.'

She looked up and he suddenly noticed how clear her green eyes were. He was wrong to have put her down as the girl-next-door type. She was the kind of woman who seemed quite ordinary at first but, when you looked closer, was stunning in a natural way. 'Is that what happened to you as a child?'

'No,' he wanted to say but the lie stuck in his throat. It had been one reason why he'd suggested coffee with Bobbie, to be honest. He needed time to compose himself before going home; he'd spent the whole class on tenterhooks that Kieran, with his bald head and tattoos, was going to turn up again; his nose had been full of that mental smell of urine and cabbage and Brussels sprouts which Kieran had brought back.

'I got caned every now and then,' he tried to say in a casual manner. Her eyes grew concerned so he forced himself to make a dismissive gesture, suggesting it was no big deal. 'But that happened to boys in my day. You know. Heads down the toilet – I mean loo. It was standard school stuff.'

Bobbie looked more reassured. 'Rob's told me a bit about that. He said it was just a bit of fun that helped him to grow up.'

Yeah, right, thought Andy. Bet his brother-in-law's posh boarding school didn't have quite the same approach as the home.

'But you were brought up by an aunt, weren't you?' Her eyes were locked on his sympathetically. 'Was she nice to you?'

Ah yes! The mythical aunt. Andy tried to remember the tales he had woven over the years. It was difficult, sometimes, to recall all the elaborations. 'Yes. More or less. But I didn't see much of her.'

'So you went away to school too?'

'For a bit.' He needed to change the subject. 'Tell me about you. How did you meet Rob?'

Her eyes grew dreamy. 'We were both at Durham.'

Of course. One of the good universities. Andy couldn't help feeling a surge of jealousy. He'd have loved to have done a degree himself.

'We met at freshers' week and it was love at first sight.'

Andy nodded. 'I felt that way about Pamela when I saw her.'

'Really!' She smiled. You should do that more often, he wanted to say. It really lit her up, made her look even more attractive. Then Bobbie's face changed. 'Camilla didn't approve of me. I wasn't an Hon. like Rob's previous girlfriend and although my parents were educated, they didn't have much money. Camilla made it very difficult but Rob said that if he couldn't marry me, he wasn't marrying anyone. But then we had kids and it all changed.'

He leaned forward to catch her quieter voice. 'In what way?'

She stirred the froth on top of her second cappuccino and then sucked the teaspoon. Totally natural. Pamela would never do that.

'Motherhood wasn't what I expected. Daisy had a mind of her own, from the minute she was born. When she was a baby, she wouldn't stop yelling unless we took her into bed with us. Then Rob said he couldn't sleep so he moved to the spare room.' She stirred the froth more vigorously now. 'Still does every now and then when he gets in late.' Then she looked nervous. 'Please don't tell anyone I said that. I don't know why I'm telling you, if I'm honest.'

He touched her hand briefly. 'It's because I'm family.'

She nodded, biting her lip. 'And Jack, well, Jack! What can I say!' She began to laugh, but in a troubled way. 'He's uncontrollable! Utterly fearless! Jack does what he wants in life and there's no rhyme or reason to his logic. Rob says that things have got to change. That's why we've moved out here. To a new area with better schools. Jack was almost expelled from the last one and now it looks as though he's in trouble again.'

Sighing, she ran her hand through her hair; something she did rather a lot, he noticed. It was nice. 'As for Daisy, I'm always getting complaints about how bossy she is. That's why I signed up for the parenting class. To try and make our family work. Otherwise I don't know what will happen. And, to make it worse, I've simply got to make them behave by April!'

'Why's that?'

'You've heard of Dr Know?'

Of course he had! The man was a genius. There'd been a profile on him in the *FT* the other day, under the heading CHILD EXPERT MAKES A KILLING AS NEW BOOK TOPS BESTSELLER LIST. Apparently he was raking it in.

Bobbie was shaking her head ruefully. 'My mother's dating him. Or stepping out, as she puts it.'

'You're kidding!'

'Wish I was. She's bringing him to lunch on Mothering Sunday and I don't want to let her down.'

'I can see that!'

She had tears in her eyes now. 'I feel as though I've told you too much.'

'Of course not.' He handed her the napkin on the table to dab her eyes, wondering if it would be appropriate to give her an it-will-be-all-right hug. Maybe not. 'It will be our secret. I promise.'

Poor Bobbie, Andy had told himself as he drove home. Part of him wanted to shake his brother-in-law and tell him to take more of a hands-on role in his little family. Then again, hadn't he been an absent father himself until recently? Never back until late. Expecting Pamela to do it all. At the time, he had seen it as a badge of honour to be able to provide for them all. But now he wasn't so sure.

Did he miss work? Bobbie had asked. Yes and no, he'd answered truthfully. But he had another job now! The most important one in the world: bringing up children. Well, teenagers.

Pamela had been right to leave him in charge. What had she said the other night on the phone when he'd rung to see why she was extending her stay? 'It will do you good to see more of the girls,' she'd declared in that clipped posh voice that still did it for him after all these years. 'Besides, Mummy needs me at the moment and as you're at home I can afford to give her some of my time. You do understand that, don't you?'

What he *did* understand was that what Pamela wanted, Pamela got. It was the way she worked; the kind of woman she was. And he went along with it because – well, because he idolised her, didn't he? Not just for being so beautiful and choosing him over everyone else, but because she had given him something he had always wanted. A family.

Andy clenched his fists. He'd be buggered if Kieran destroyed everything he'd built up. He'd have to stop him – whatever it took.

The following morning, Andy had woken with a start. He'd been having a horrible dream in which Kieran had pushed

130

his head out of the old crumbling window and then pulled down the sash so that his neck snapped in half.

'No. NO,' he'd shouted before realising that it was a dream. He wasn't back in the home. He was here, in his lovely house in their huge king-size bed with the heavy yellow brocade curtains at the far side of the room and Pamela's dressing table, laden with pots and bottles, on the left. On the right was the door leading to their enormous en suite. On the bedside table sat the extremely expensive watch which Pamela had given him on his fortieth: 8.20 a.m!

Trying to put that horrible nightmare behind him, Andy had stretched out before putting on his Harrods silk dressing gown (another Pamela present) to go downstairs and make a cup of tea. It had been years since he had got up at this time. It felt odd yet really liberating. Then he remembered. School! The girls were going to be late. And wasn't that Nattie's alarm going? How could she sleep through that?

Pausing by his younger daughter's bedroom door, he debated whether to knock or just go in. There was something rather awkward about invading the girls' privacy now they were older. Besides, they were usually so good at getting themselves up. Or so it had seemed in the last week that they'd all been together.

The alarm showed no sign of stopping, so he opened the door and peeked in. Bloody hell! She was still in bed. Eyes closed. A terrible colour, too. Horribly white. 'Nattie!' He shook her urgently. 'Nattie! Are you all right?'

There was a groan as she turned over. Thank God for that! Then relief turned to fear. Was she ill? He reached out to feel her forehead.

'Piss off and leave me alone.'

Andy stepped back just in time to avoid her angry arm. She'd never, ever spoken to him like that before. 'What's wrong, Nattie?'

Then he saw it. Lying on the stained duvet. An empty bottle of wine.

'Chill out, Dad. She's just sleeping it off.'

Andy whipped round to see Mel standing in the doorway, still in her pyjamas. 'What do you mean, she's sleeping it off?'

His daughter shrugged. 'She had a few friends round last night, that's all.'

Friends? But he'd checked his daughter when he'd come back from his coffee with Bobbie and she'd been fast asleep. A nasty feeling crawled through him. Had she been out cold even then?

'She only had half a bottle.'

'Half a bottle!'

'Well, three-quarters then.' Mel shrugged again. 'Mum lets us.'

'She does?' Andy's temples began to throb. The girls were always allowed a glass of wine at Sunday lunch when they all sat down as a family but no more than that. At least not to his knowledge.

'Mum says we need to learn our limits.'

Well, yes. But not this way. Kneeling down, he tried to gently shake his daughter, who had gone back to sleep. 'Nattie! Wake up! You've got to go to school.'

'I wouldn't bother, Dad. When she's like this, she's out for ages. You'll have to write a note. Mum often does that.'

This couldn't be right.

'It's true, Dad.'

He had a flash of the young Pamela: the girl he'd met all those years ago at the club. Cool. Calm. Aloof. Never without a glass in her hand. He turned to his eldest daughter. 'And what about you? Were you drunk too? Is that why you're not at school?'

Mel shrugged again. 'I've been suspended. It's only for two days.'

'ONLY FOR TWO DAYS!'

'Don't shout, Dad or you'll wake her up. Nattie needs to sleep it off.'

'What did you *do*?'

Yet another shrug, accompanied by a roll of the eyes. 'I didn't hand in my coursework.'

But his girls always did their work on time. Didn't they? 'Couldn't you ask for an extension?'

'I'd already had one. Two actually. That's why I've been suspended.'

Andy was still trying to make sense of this. 'But shouldn't there be a letter from school?'

Mel shrugged. 'Forgot to give it to you. Sorry.'

This wasn't acceptable. It really wasn't. 'We're going to have to talk about this,' he began but as he spoke, his mobile bleeped with a text.

In hospital with mum. She's broken her arm. Will ring wn been seen. Wnt be back until next week earliest. Lv P.

'Did you know Granny had broken her arm?'

'Oh yeah.' Mel spoke as though her grandmother was someone she didn't know very well. 'Mum texted just now. It woke me up. And don't bother trying to get hold of her. She's switched off her phone.'

She had too! Andy wasn't often at a loss for words, but this was too much. Things had to change around here and he was going to do it. The first thing he'd do, was to . . . Do what exactly? Let Natasha sleep it off? Then read her the riot act on drinking? Make Mel do her coursework and write a letter of apology to the relevant teacher? That would do for starters. There was no way he'd allow them to mess up school as he had done.

And then he needed to talk to Pamela. How could she have been so crafty? How could she have built up this perfect family charade during his long absences without telling him what was really going on?

As for the parenting class: forget it! There was no way he could tell others what to do. Not if his own kids had been behaving so badly. That would be hypocritical. He'd just have to bow out.

Besides, it was the perfect excuse to avoid Kieran before working out what to do.

'But we've had such fantastic feedback!' Judith Davies had looked genuinely upset when he'd gone into school with a

133

sick note for Natasha, claiming that she had a 'headache' and a note of apology which he'd made Mel write. The girls had insisted that he didn't have to take the letter in by hand ('It's so embarrassing, Dad!'), but Andy's experience at work had taught him it was often better to have a face-to-face. Now he was beginning to wish he'd rung instead. Judith Davies might be young but she was very persistent.

'I've had emails from two of the parents in your group, saying how wonderful you are!'

Andy squirmed.

'They say that you're honest and not afraid of bringing in your own experiences!' Judith's eyes shone. 'It's just what we need.' She lowered her voice – they were standing in the corridor next to the pupils' lockers. 'The truth is that we had a very low take-up rate when we asked for volunteers to help out. Parenting classes can be a bit tricky. No one likes to admit they can't cope or claim that they're good enough to tell others how to do it.'

You could say that again!

'Your wife was the only person who agreed to do the teen class, and we were thrilled. Don't take this the wrong way, Mr Gooding, but we wanted someone whose children weren't perfect, otherwise everyone else in the class feels inferior. That's why we were so worried when she couldn't do it at the last minute – I'm sorry about her mother, by the way. If you hadn't offered to step in, we'd have had to cancel the whole thing!' Her young face was pleading. 'Please, Mr Gooding! We'd all be so grateful if you continued.'

Andy hesitated. It was only for a second but it was enough. Judith Davies was sharper than she looked. 'Thank you,' she cried, seizing the opportunity. 'Thank you.'

God, that poor girl, so young to be a teacher, had looked desperate and Andy had always been a bit of a sucker for women in distress. He'd just have to brazen it out with Kieran. Insist he didn't know him. And he'd cancel that golf session at the club. It would give him more time to mug up the parenting handbook. Maybe buy Dr Know's book too.

After all, how difficult could it be to bring up kids? Surely it was just a matter of setting the rules and making them stick to it. You'd get the odd blip, like he'd had with the girls, but the key was consistency and organisation. The same skills that had got him where he was today in business!

There was, thought Andy walking out to the car park, something comforting about applying business tactics to this new strange world of school-run mums that he'd had found himself in.

'Oy! You!'

A large burly bald man in an orange boiler suit was getting out of a heavily dented Mondeo and whistling at him. Andy froze. It was Kieran! Quickly he started up the engine.

Too late. Kieran was striding towards him now, grinning and waving. Reluctantly, Andy put down the window. 'Nice to see you, mate. Sorry I had to miss the last class – had to do some overtime. You're a natural, know that? Emailed school, I did. Told them how good you were and how it was great to have a bloke in charge to represent a dad's point of view. Reckoned that might get them to keep you on, instead of your wife.' He grinned, revealing a big gap in his teeth at the side. 'It would be a shame if we didn't see you again, wouldn't it? By the way, I wasn't kidding before. You really do look like a geezer I used to know. Odd how some people have a double, isn't it?'

Andy had still been shaking from the encounter when he got back home. His earlier good resolves had vanished. Instead, he felt stressed. Worried. Apprehensive. Like the old Barry. The kid he'd shut away all those years ago.

'Don't start having a go at me yet, Dad,' said a white-faced Natasha, sitting at the breakfast bar, cupping a mug of coffee. 'I'm sorry. It was a one-off. Honestly.'

'That's not what your sister told me,' he began. Then his eye fell on the post. It wasn't the postcard he noticed, from his old secretary who was having a week in the Scilly Isles. It was the envelope with the word *Urgent* typed in red through the address window.

'Sorry. I opened it by mistake.' Nattie had a funny edge to her voice. 'It's for Mum.'

He picked it up, intending to put it in his wife's dressing room, off the main bedroom. But when he got there, something in him, prompted perhaps by all the odd things that had been happening recently, made him take out the piece of paper that was poking out of the envelope anyway. It was a final demand. From a loan company he wouldn't trust with a barge pole.

A demand for £10,000.

Plus £1,000 for interest.

PERFECT PARENTS: SESSION THREE

THE THREE-CARD RULE!

LEARN HOW TO PLAY GAMES – AND GET THE KIDS TO DO JUST WHAT YOU WANT!

IT'S MAGIC! HONESTLY!

ARE THE CHILDREN WRECKING YOUR MARRIAGE?*

When did you last have a meaningful conversation
  with your husband?
1. In between kids' arguments.
2. In your sleep.
3. On skype.
4. At the divorce court.

When did you last make love?
1. Six weeks after the last baby.
2. Six months after the last baby.
3. Six years after the last baby.
4. Still counting.

When you go on a family holiday, do you:
1. End up sleeping with the kids to make sure they're
   safe in a strange place.
2. Refuse to let them join the kids' club in case they
   pick up germs.
3. Get cross with your husband because he leaves it
   up to you to watch them in the pool.

*There are no right answers. But it might make you
think . . .

Extracted from *Charisma* magazine.

Chapter 13

BOBBIE

'GIVE ME BACK MY DS.'

'IT'S MY DS!'

'NO IT'S NOT!'

'That's enough!' Bobbie felt like banging the children's heads together. 'It's bedtime, anyway. So neither of you can have it.'

Daisy shot her a don't-be-stupid look. 'It's only seven o'clock.'

Why had she bothered to teach them to tell the time? Or to read? Or to talk? If she'd encouraged them to stay mute, they wouldn't be able to answer back or challenge orders. God, she needed a drink. Bobbie went into the utility room, ostensibly to put on the washing machine. 'Because Daddy and I are having a special meal together,' she called out.

'Is that why you're opening a bottle *before* we've gone to bed?' Daisy appeared at the door, both hands on her waist in full teacher mode. 'I *saw* you, Mum! It's there! Hiding in the soap-powder cupboard.'

A glass of wine was one of the few pleasures she had left nowadays! Something that Dr Know, no doubt, would deeply disapprove of. But she needed *something* to unwind after a day of 'don't do that's.

'Actually, it's beetroot juice.'

'In the laundry room? Let me taste it then.'

'Sorry. All gone.' Hastily Bobbie swigged the rest of the evidence and bustled her daughter back into the kitchen. 'Tell you what! Why don't you help me tidy up?'

The kitchen table was groaning with a week's worth of post that she hadn't had time to open. She'd tried to make a start this morning but had got diverted by a disturbing marriage survey in her favourite magazine. Oh heck. There was a school note too. About not double-parking. It all needed clearing unless they were going to eat off the floor.

'I'm not tidying up!' Daisy sounded like a mini-terrorist. 'I want to cook!' She eyed the packet of ready-made fish pie on the side. Before she'd had kids, Bobbie had attempted to make everything from scratch. But who had time any more?

'OK. But make sure you put the packaging at the bottom of the bin.'

'Why?'

'Because . . . just because, that's all.'

Daisy eyed her suspiciously. '*Why* are you and Daddy having a special meal together?'

It was as though she was being interrogated about a date! Bobbie thought back to the message she'd left earlier, with Rob's secretary, reminding him that she needed him home early for 'a rather important family matter'. Hopefully the secretary would get the point. That magazine article had really unsettled her.

'Because we need some time to talk.'

'But you talk when you argue!' Daisy's eyes narrowed as though she was eighteen and not eight.

Was this the example they'd been setting? 'No we don't.'

'Yes you do, Mum!' Her daughter flicked back her hair – oh for the days when she'd tied it up in bunches! – and eyed her suspiciously. 'Why aren't you wearing jeans?'

Bobbie smoothed down her black evening trousers which she only wore on special occasions. The elasticated waistline made up for the extra stone that she'd never quite been able to shift after Jack. 'Because it's nice to dress up sometimes.' She wouldn't put it past her daughter to have X-ray vision and demand to know why she was wearing the new silk undies she'd splashed out on earlier, just in case she and Rob got that far. 'Now why don't you go up to your bedroom and download a film?'

Bobbie hadn't ever meant to be one of those parents who

got a laptop each for her kids but she'd given in last year because 'everyone else has one'. Rob had said it was 'ridiculous' and that had led to yet another argument. Nowadays, nearly all their disagreements seemed to be about the children. Or him getting home late. Or her work which wasn't bringing in enough money.

Shit. That reminded her. She still had some calls to make if she was going to get her quota. She hadn't reached it last month and her pay statement, which was based on performance, had been even smaller than usual.

Thankfully, Daisy had actually done what she'd asked! Strains of *My Real Mother Is an Alien* (a favourite in this house) filtered down the stairs. Jack was quiet. Good quiet or bad quiet? Bobbie hesitated. If she didn't disturb him, she might just squeeze in a couple more calls.

This week's survey was about personal hygiene wipes. It was proving a bit of a challenge.

'Hello. Is that Adrienne Tilling? It is? Hi. How are you? My name is Bobbie and I'm doing a survey on . . .'

One down. Twenty-two more to go.

'Hi. My name's Bobbie and I wondered if you had a few minutes to . . .'

No. Right. On to the next one.

Damn. Now her mobile was going. *Mum.* At last! She'd been trying to get hold of her for ages. She desperately needed to hear her soothing voice. A reminder that Bobbie wasn't really a grown-up after all. Was she the only middle-aged mum who didn't feel old enough for all this responsibility?

'Darling! Are you there? So sorry I haven't been in touch before but Herbert and I have been on a tour, promoting his new book!' Mum sounded so excited, like a young girl describing a date. 'It was wonderful! Everyone made a great fuss of us.'

Bobbie felt an unreasonable rush of jealousy. 'That's great.' Then she remembered. 'Look, I'm on the other phone for work. Sorry, are you still there? No, not you, Mum. Hello? Hello?'

Bugger. She'd lost both of them.

'Who are you talking to?' Rob was standing at the doorway, tie dishevelled and face strained.

'Mum and work at the same time.' Suddenly aware of a burning smell, Bobbie dashed to the oven. A billow of grey smoke came out. 'Dinner's ruined!'

He flung his tie on the chair. 'You shouldn't have left it in for so long.'

That wasn't fair. 'I was trying to get some calls in.'

'Tell me about it! My secretary said I had to get back early. What's up?' He glanced at the candles and the table with proper cloth napkins by the side of their best place mats. 'I haven't forgotten our anniversary, have I?'

'No.' Bobbie felt her voice coming out flat. 'I just tried to make an effort, that's all. Have some, you know, couple time.'

'Right. Sure.' His voice softened. 'That would be nice. But I have to say that I'm not that hungry, I'm afraid. I had to take a client out. It would be nice to sit down and chat, though. In fact, I've got something to tell you, I may have to go to—'

'DADDY!' There was the sound of mini-elephants stampeding down the stairs. Daisy flung herself into Rob's arms, closely followed by Jack, determined not to be outdone.

'Can you watch the film with us?'

'Can we eat dinner with you?'

'I helped Mummy make it!' Daisy was beaming triumphantly. 'The packet's at the bottom of the bin.'

Two hours later, when she'd finally got the children down, Bobbie peeled off her lace undies and crawled into bed. Rob was already flat out, breathing noisily. The house was silent: the first bit of peace she'd had since getting up that morning at six thirty. But she couldn't sleep. For some reason, Bobbie kept wondering what Andy was doing right now. She couldn't imagine her own husband being in charge of the kids while she went away.

'What are you doing?' mumbled Rob sleepily as she reached out for him.

'Just trying to cuddle up.' Bobbie turned over, hurt, listening as the loud snores resumed.

So much for couple time. Perhaps she'd left it too late? Maybe Rob had gone off her completely. It wouldn't be surprising. Even she could see that the always-rushing-around, often snappy, ineffectual mother of Daisy and Jack was completely different to the happy-go-lucky Bobbie that Rob had met at university.

Had she tried so hard to be a good mother that she'd forgotten about her husband?

'It shouldn't be like that,' agreed her friend Sarah. 'But it is.' They were walking through the park by her friend's home in Ealing, west London. It was a teacher training day at Corrywood so Bobbie had seized the opportunity to catch the train with the kids and visit her old friend. 'At least that's how some men see it,' she continued. 'They can't cope when all your attention is on the children and then they find someone else who'll give them more time. Pathetic really.'

When Sarah had been married to Ross, her investment-banker husband, they'd had a lovely three-storey home in Islington overlooking the park. But after he'd gone off with the MD, she'd ended up with a two-bedroom maisonette. Ross had been able to afford a good lawyer.

'And I have to say,' she added, deftly avoiding a used condom in their path, 'Rob shows all the signs. The wrong ones.'

Bobbie felt her heart thumping in her throat as she watched Jack and Daisy hare off through the damp leaves left over from the winter. Tom, Sarah's son, who was Jack's best friend, was streaming ahead, shouting excitedly. They couldn't hear. The coast was clear.

'Go on.' Bobbie braced herself. 'Remind me.' She'd been around when Ross had gone off only a few months after Tom had been born. But although she'd tried to help, Bobbie had been up to her eyes with a new baby and demanding toddler.

'Well . . .' Sarah stopped as an ambulance screamed by. Bobbie had forgotten how noisy it was in London. 'There was the getting back late all the time. Not having sex. Not appreciating special couple dates at home – yes, I tried that one too. Arguing over Tom's bedtime. I tell you, Bobbie, it might be difficult on my own, but I've realised from the other mums in my parenting class that it can be easier to be single. At least you don't have someone telling you that you're doing it all wrong.'

Bobbie could see that. A picture swam into her head of herself bringing up a subdued Daisy and Jack who only saw their father at weekends. It had its attractions! Then again, had they really gone that far down the hill without her realising? 'He *has* got a new secretary,' she ventured.

'Oh dear!' Sarah bit her lip worriedly. 'How old?'

'I'm not sure.'

'Married?'

'He doesn't say much about her.'

'Not good. Could mean he feels guilty.' Sarah gave her a hug. 'Or it might be that he isn't interested. Hard to tell. Mind you, there is one thing you could do if you're really worried.'

Bobbie listened carefully. It was an audacious idea, not one that Bobbie could really bring herself to contemplate. Besides, she'd get sacked or reported if she got found out. 'Up to you.' Sarah shrugged. 'After my experience, I wouldn't trust anyone again. Ever.'

As she spoke, there was an ear-splitting cry ahead. At a distance, Bobbie could see two small boys wrestling each other on the ground. 'They're arguing!' Bobbie threw Sarah a horrified look. 'But our two never argue.'

Sarah's face was taut as they began running towards them. The closer they got, the clearer it was that Jack was the aggressor. 'He's taken my phone, he's taken my phone,' Tom was saying.

'GIVE IT BACK TO HIM,' Bobbie began to shout.

Sarah laid a hand on her arm. 'Shouting doesn't work. I've learned that on the course. You have to try empathy management.'

She knelt down next to the boys. 'Jack, I can understand that you envy Tom for having the latest smart phone. And Tom, I understand that you don't like Jack any more because he has a daddy at home and your irresponsible father abandoned us when you were a baby. Now you're older, you're beginning to realise the full implications of that. Is that right?'

Bobbie gasped. Talk about bad-mouthing the absent parent! But Tom, whose little face was caked with mud, was nodding. So was Jack's.'

'The thing is, Jack, that Tom's daddy gave him the phone out of guilt during his last access weekend. So why don't you hand it back and we'll go to that ice-cream parlour on the corner.'

'OK.'

To Bobbie's amazement, both boys stood up.

'How did you do that?' whispered Bobbie.

Sarah shrugged. 'We've got a great teacher. It's a real pity you live so far away.' Then she tucked her arm into Bobbie's again. 'Cheer up! You might not have anything to worry about. Well, you do with Jack, obviously. And with Dr Know. There's no way I'd have that man at *my* table! But when it comes to Rob, you know what to do now, don't you?'

Her husband was very quiet for the rest of the week. Not that she saw much of him. He had to be in the office all weekend too. That new campaign again – or so he said. Daisy and Jack seemed to pick up on her vibes and by the time Monday evening came, Bobbie was more than ready to go to parenting school, if only for a break from the house.

Vanessa had saved a seat next to her. Bobbie had changed her views about this bright little blonde woman after she'd been so nice about Jack demolishing her window display. 'Your Daisy was brilliant today,' she whispered. 'She helped Sunshine find her flute when it went missing in orchestra.'

'Nice to hear my daughter's done something right,' whispered Bobbie back.

'Tonight,' chirped Judith, 'we're going to talk about how to get your children to do what you want without any arguments.'

'If there's a recipe for that, we ought to gold-plate it,' said the pretty frail woman with the bruise. (The butterfly bruise on her arm had faded, but she had another one now on her cheek.) 'I got this yesterday. All because I told my son there wasn't time for piano practice. And then I got this one on my thigh from my daughter because she wanted to eat curry *and* spag bol at the same time.'

Judith bit her lip. 'Oh dear. Maybe the three-card rule might help.'

'Isn't that something to do with football?' demanded Not Really Pregnant Mum huffily. She really ought to call her by her real name, thought Bobbie guiltily. But somehow 'Angie' didn't seem quite as suitable. It suggested someone who was more delicate, both in looks and mannerisms. 'By the way, Bobbie. Your Jack got sent off for tackling my Wayne this morning.'

Oh God.

'Got a whopping bruise on his shin, he has.' Her eyes narrowed. 'My Wayne's got very sensitive skin.'

'Perhaps you can both discuss that later. Is that all right, everyone? Good! Now, the three-card rule can really work a treat! Let's say your child doesn't want to go to bed. You give him a yellow card and ask him again nicely. If that doesn't work, you give him a blue card and explain that if he still says no, you'll give him another. Then if that doesn't work, you give him a red card. That means a punishment.'

There was a stunned silence. 'And you think they'll listen?' asked Too Many Kids Mum, incredulously. 'I don't want to be rude, Judith, but if you had children, you'd know it doesn't work like that. Not on my lot anyway.'

'Really?' The girl looked hurt. 'If you don't find that useful, there is another idea in the book. It suggests that if your child won't go to bed at a certain time, you tell them that that's fine, but that they have to go to bed a quarter of an hour earlier the next night.' She smiled excitedly. 'If they refuse, then they go to bed a quarter of an hour earlier than that on the following night. Clever, don't you think?'

'Bollocks!' Not Really Pregnant Mum snorted with derision. 'At this rate, my lot will be going to bed when they should be getting up. They'll meet up with themselves.'

'Actually,' said Vanessa, putting up her hand tentatively, 'my problem is that my granddaughter, who used to live abroad, gets up when the sun rises and goes to bed when it goes down. It's not always very convenient.'

Too Many Kids Mum leaped to her feet. For someone who'd had so many children, she was amazingly slim. Maybe running around after her kids kept her fit. 'Don't take this the wrong way, anyone, but I'm just off to the teenage class. See you next week.'

'Already?' Judith looked hurt again. 'But we were just about to play the film and have a discussion.'

But she was off. If only the rest of them could join her . . . 'By the way,' whispered Vanessa as the film started. 'I'm about to advertise for some help in the shop; Kim, my assistant, is going on a mid-life-crisis gap year. I don't suppose you know of anyone who might be interested in applying, do you?'

Me! Me! she wanted to say. But then again, she didn't have any relevant experience. Only a degree and three years in PR. 'I'll ask around,' she promised.

Bobbie had been hoping to have another chat with Andy after class but his session was still going on, from the sound of the animated discussion drifting down the corridor. So she drove home, trying to remember everything she'd learned that night.

Listen.
Think before you make empty threats.
Remember what it was like at their age.
Put yourself in their shoes.
Negotiate so that somehow they do what you want,
    without realising they've given in.

147

Talk about Mission Impossible!

'Hi, Mel—' she began as the door opened.

But it wasn't her niece. It was Rob. His face was serious. Grave. 'Thank God you're back. I've got something to tell you.'

WHAT KIND OF PARENT ARE YOU?

If you and your husband disagree over a parenting issue, do you:

1. Discuss your differences over a glass of wine, followed by hot, make-up sex.
2. Save up for a divorce.*
3. Tell your other half that he/she is a useless parent.
4. Ring Dr Know's helpline.

Answer: (If this looks upside down, you've drunk too much already.) You are a rubbish parent, regardless of whichever one you picked.

*Average waiting time, approx. twelve years with current interest rates.

Extracted from I Can't Cope With My Kids *magazine.*

Chapter 14

VANESSA

She should have come clean tonight. Why hadn't she had the guts to stand up in class and say, 'Look, everyone, I've got a real problem. My granddaughter has turned up to live with me and I've completely forgotten how to bring up kids. I made a hash of it with her mother anyway so it's not as though I've got much experience to go by. Sunshine – funny name, I know – seems to have settled, but recently she's started to have nightmares in her sleep. Now her father, or at least that's what he says he is, has turned up out of the blue. I'm scared he's going to try and take her away from me. My friend Brian used to teach him and says he's bad news. Oh, and I still don't know where my daughter (Sunshine's mother) is.'

Then again, thought Vanessa, would they have understood? Everyone else in the class had normal problems like trying to get their children to go to bed on time or making them eat their vegetables. How she wanted to tell them that none of this was important! The only really crucial bit about parenting was to keep talking. To communicate. To make sure that they didn't run away when they were sixteen.

When Brigid had walked out all those years ago, Vanessa had been convinced she would come back just as she had done before. Every time the phone rang, Vanessa would dive for it, desperately hoping it was her daughter. Each day the postman came up the path, she fell on the post in case there was a letter in familiar handwriting. But there never was. And although the Salvation Army, as well as the police, had put up Missing posters, showing a sullen Brigid in her Goth stage, there had been no response.

'You might have to prepare yourself for the worst,' said one of the police counsellors who had tried to help.

'She's not dead,' Vanessa retorted. She tapped her chest. 'If she was, I would feel it here.'

Then nearly a year after Brigid had left, an envelope bearing that distinctive swirly writing fluttered through the door with an indecipherable postmark, Vanessa had seized it, fingers trembling as she tore it open. A photograph fell out. Just a small one. A baby. A tiny baby, lying on a blanket from what she could see.

Feverishly, Vanessa had turned the photograph over. *This is the granddaughter you wanted me to get rid of. Don't try and contact us.*

That wasn't true! She *hadn't* wanted Brigid to have an abortion. She'd merely pointed out that it was one option. But her daughter had misread her reaction. Vanessa comforted herself with the thought that at least Brigid still cared enough to send a photograph. Maybe she would ring next time or send another picture.

But as the weeks and then the months and then the years went by, Vanessa reluctantly accepted the fact that her daughter was never coming back. She would never be allowed to see her granddaughter whose photograph she kept by the side of her bed; whose little face she kissed every night.

Now, however, even worse was the uncertainty. Why had Brigid sent her daughter here with some scruffy stranger who had just vanished into thin air? Was her daughter ever going to turn up to get Sunshine? And if she did, would she just whisk her off again?

Vanessa couldn't bear the idea of that. Sunshine might not have been with her for very long but, already, she couldn't imagine life without her. Yet it was that horrible ex-boyfriend of her daughter's who really worried her. That was the most important thing to deal with right now. She needed to find out – fast – whether he had any legal rights to her granddaughter.

'There's a solicitor on the high street who's quite good,'

Brian told her during one of their late-night telephone conversations. 'He'll tell you the score. Might cost you, mind, but I could help out if you'd like.'

'I can afford it, thanks,' Vanessa had said hurriedly. Brian was a good man – she was pretty certain of that – but she didn't want to be indebted to anyone.

'Anyone claiming paternity rights has to be able to prove it,' the solicitor told her. 'Has this young man suggested a DNA test?'

Vanessa shook her head, her mouth dry. Sunshine was sitting on the floor beside her, quietly reading one of her books, oblivious to the fact that her future was being discussed. Bobbie's son would be jumping up and down and touching those legal files. Sometimes, Sunshine was unnerving. 'He hasn't been in touch since.'

The solicitor raised a quizzical eyebrow. 'That doesn't mean he won't. The best advice I can give you is to try and get hold of your daughter. You say you've contacted the Foreign Office?'

She nodded.

'Then I don't know what else to suggest, to be honest.' There was a sympathetic look. 'I feel for you. I'm a grandfather myself.'

It wasn't sympathy she wanted, it was practical help!

That had been a few days ago. Since then, Vanessa had been trying to distract herself by concentrating on her granddaughter. 'How about a game of Snakes and Ladders? Mummy used to like that at your age.'

But Sunshine seemed quite happy to sit and play her flute with a haunting foreign melody. Then one morning on the way to school, she began jumping up and down and pointing at a teenager whizzing past wearing a silver and red safety helmet. 'Look at that bike,' called out Sunshine excitedly. Her face was shining in a way she hadn't seen before. 'It's like Mummy's! We used to ride together!'

'Really?' A picture of her daughter and this little mite,

cycling through some mud village in Goa, formed in Vanessa's mind.

'We can ride too!' Sunshine was still jumping up and down. 'You and me!'

Vanessa roared with laughter. 'I don't think so, poppet. It's been years since I was on one.'

'Yes, Van Van. Yes.' Sunshine was tugging her hand. 'We can get them now instead of going to school.'

She was serious too! 'Tell you what. I'll try and find you a second-hand bike and we'll go for a ride in the park another day. How about that?'

In fact, it only took her a few hours to find one; it turned out that the woman over the road still had her daughter's blue and silver Raleigh in the garage. Vanessa got it checked over by the local bike shop where she also bought a helmet, and before she could say, 'On you get then,' her granddaughter was off, screeching with laughter, down the cycle lane in the park with Vanessa running after her, flapping her arms and calling at her to come back. The message was plain. If Vanessa wanted to keep up, she needed to get a bike of her own.

It was the perfect weather for it. This year's spring, as everyone was remarking, was more like summer with warm balmy days that were just right for cycling to and from school through the park. Vanessa hadn't laughed so much in her life: she felt like a teenager again. And, even better, Sunshine was giggling like a normal kid. 'Faster, Van Van!' she kept saying. 'Faster!'

There was only one problem. Great as it was to play with her granddaughter, she also needed to be in the shop. Kim wasn't going to be there much longer and Vanessa needed help fast. She'd have to ask around. The business needed more than one pair of hands if it was going to carry on being successful and goodness knows, she needed the income. New shoes and school uniform and all the other expenses soon added up. Still, what was that compared with having her granddaughter?

*

One evening, as Vanessa sorted through yet another bag of designer cast-offs in the shop while Sunshine curled up quietly at the back, reading an eight-year-plus book, her mobile went.

'Brian!' she said, feeling her spirits soar. He hadn't called for a few days and she couldn't help thinking she'd put him off with her constant excuses about being 'busy'. But Sunshine had to be her first priority. Besides, part of her was scared. Much as Vanessa liked Brian, she didn't want him to creep through the armour she'd built up; she couldn't afford to let anyone hurt her again.

'It's good to hear your voice, Vanessa.' That might have sounded smarmy coming from someone else but the way he said it made her feel like a million dollars.

'What have you been up to?' she heard herself saying like a nervous adolescent.

'Hanging around the stables. That's why I'm ringing actually. Upper Cut is running at Ascot next Thursday. Want to come?'

She'd have loved to. But who'd look after Sunshine? Vanessa felt a twinge of frustration. She'd been so used to doing what she wanted, *when* she wanted. But she had responsibilities now.

'I understand, Ness. How about tonight then? I could come round with a bottle.'

'That would be lovely!'

It would too. Some men might have been put off by Sunshine's arrival. It wasn't every man who could cope with another woman's child, let alone a grandchild. The 'Ness' bit made her feel rather warm inside. He'd called her that when they'd been . . . well . . . together and, to her surprise, she'd quite liked it.

'What time does little one go to bed?' he asked.

'Any time after the sun has set! I'm not joking. From what I gather, that was the kind of life my granddaughter has been leading.'

He chuckled, the nice warm chuckle that made Vanessa feel things weren't so difficult after all. 'Not a bad way of

154

doing it, if you ask me. Early to bed and all that. Shall we say 8 p.m. then?'

Vanessa felt something tingle inside. That evening in bed with Brian, on the night that Sunshine had come into her life, still gave her the shivers in the nicest way. He'd been what some of her romantic novels described as 'masterful' but 'considerate' at the same time. Nor had he seemed repulsed by the neat scar where her right breast used to be.

Eight o'clock! Vanessa smiled to herself as she went about Sunshine's bedtime routine; a routine which was now becoming strangely familiar. She couldn't wait!

They'd been lying next to each other for about half an hour in that lovely post-lovemaking glow when Brian heard it. 'What's that noise?' he said, sitting bolt upright so that her head, which had been nicely positioned on his broad shoulders, fell on the pillow.

'I can't hear anything,' she murmured sleepily, still aware of his imprint inside her. For the first time in years, Vanessa felt beautiful. At least, that was one of the words that Brian had murmured while they were exploring each other's bodies. It wasn't true, of course, but it had been a lovely thing to say.

'A chanting noise. There it is again. Hear it? It's getting closer.'

'Quick!' Instantly, she pushed him off the side of his bed and threw his trousers at him. 'Get into the wardrobe. Now!'

He'd only just closed the doors behind him – the type with slats in them so he could breathe – when Sunshine wandered in. Her eyes had a strange glazed look to them and Vanessa knew she was sleepwalking, while chanting that low 'ummm' sound at the same time. She was heading straight for Brian's side of the bed as though she knew exactly where to go. 'It's all right, Sunshine,' she whispered, holding out her arms. 'I'm here.'

'Mummy!' The word came out as clear as day. Sunshine was looking straight at her with that weird expression as though her eyes belonged to an old china doll Vanessa had once owned. 'Mummy!'

She thinks I'm Brigid! realised Vanessa with a start.

Then the child's eyes snapped shut and she curled up in a ball, her back facing the wardrobe. Vanessa waited a few minutes until she was certain that Sunshine really was asleep. 'You can come out now,' she hissed.

Slowly the wardrobe doors opened and a somewhat dishevelled Brian emerged, bare-chested and still in his underpants (maroon like that flipping jumper!), clutching his trousers. Vanessa, trying hard not to giggle, held a 'sshh' finger to her lips.

'I'll give you a ring, shall I, Ness?' he whispered.

She nodded, hoping that he would. Lying there, stiff with nerves, she waited for the click of the front door. Then she glanced down at Sunshine, noticing that her hand was, as usual, firmly clasped round her flute. How she loved her: this mini version of her daughter who was so much more biddable. Yet clearly, she wasn't adapting as well as Vanessa had thought. Sleepwalking was usually a sign of inner turmoil. She'd have to book an appointment at the doctor.

In the morning, she woke to find Sunshine wide awake, looking at her in a strange way. Suddenly, Vanessa realised that her nightdress, which she'd slipped on just before her granddaughter had come in, was open at the chest.

'You have a scar!' Sunshine was tracing it with her finger, her eyes soft with sympathy. 'Poor Van Van. Did you get a nasty cut?'

'Not exactly,' Vanessa started to say but Sunshine was nodding her head.

'Yes, nasty cut. Like Mummy.'

She was talking baby language; something that she did when upset about something, Vanessa had noticed.

'Like Mummy?' Vanessa repeated faintly.

But the child was still tracing the scar with her finger. 'Make better,' she said, smiling up at her. 'I'll make it better now.'

'Sunshine!' Vanessa was sitting upright, every nerve in her

body on fire. 'What did you mean about Mummy? Has someone hurt her?'

But the child's face had clamped down now. She started to play the flute: a jolly, familiar tune about ten little ducks which Vanessa hadn't heard her play before. A tune she had taught Brigid to sing when she'd been very small and one which her daughter must have taught her own child.

'Please tell me,' whispered Vanessa. But Sunshine carried on playing. What on earth should she do now?

WHAT KIND OF PARENT ARE YOU?

If your kids won't do their homework, do you:

1. Do it for them because it's 'quicker' – even if you do get a D.
2. Write a sick note for the computer.
3. Explain that if they don't pass their exams, they won't get a job. Do they want to end up like you? Stressed, overworked and unable to control their children . . .

Answer: (If this is the right way up, you haven't had enough to drink.) You are a devious parent, regardless of whichever one you picked. Well done.

Extracted from I Can't Cope With My Kids *magazine.*

Chapter 15

ANDY

Andy leaned back in his soft black leather chair by the window with one eye on the gardener pruning the rose bed and the other on the *Team Leader's Guide to Perfect Parenting for Teens*. It was so hard to concentrate! How could he sit on his arse like this when that man was working so hard? It didn't seem right.

Twice he'd offered to help, but the youth had looked offended and quietly said that it was all right, thank you. He'd had his brief from Mrs Gooding, just as he'd had for the past two years, and he was sure that Mr Gooding must have enough on his plate anyway.

That was the problem: Andy didn't. Apart from looking after the girls and, of course, gemming up on the theory. Tonight was Session Three. Two weeks since Pamela had gone. Amazing that the girls weren't missing her more.

'Mum often goes out,' Nattie had said airily. 'We're used to it.'

Were they? What did she *do* when she went? And where did she go? Did it have anything to do with that ten thousand pounds? he wanted to ask Pamela. But every time he rang, her phone was off. Nor was she replying to any of his *PLSE RING ME* texts in capital letters to stress how urgent it was.

'She's out with friends,' Camilla had told him coolly the last time he had called. 'If you want my advice, Andy, you'll give her some breathing space.'

Breathing space? Why? Andy took a deep breath. 'Is she . . . is she having an affair?'

There was a nanosecond pause. Not much. But just long enough. 'Of course not,' scoffed Camilla.

Was she telling the truth? Andy didn't trust his mother-in-law and, until very recently, he had trusted his wife implicitly. The £10K loan plus the girls' behaviour had dented that trust but, call him naive, he'd be happy to stake his last fiver on Pamela being faithful to him. Hadn't that been one of the ground rules that he and Pamela had set? Amongst others, that was. And he was pretty sure that, just like him, she didn't want to lose everything they had worked for.

At least he didn't think she did.

Andy looked around the sitting room with its claw-legged sofas, deep white carpet, the original Andy Warhol over the marble fireplace (although he preferred the David Hockney in the loo) and the elegant rosewood table with the latest copy of *Vogue* on top: all of which bore his wife's hand. 'I don't want to model any more,' she had told him with a rare tear in her eye all those years ago. 'I want to be a home-maker and a mother.'

He so wanted to believe her! And in fact, nothing in the next eighteen years had given him cause to think otherwise. They had a great physical relationship on the nights when Pamela wasn't too tired. In addition, he provided the financial stability while his wife ran an immaculate home; entertained crucial business guests; and brought up two beautiful daughters whose behaviour was, until recently, exemplary. Andy shifted uncomfortably in his chair at the recollection of Nattie's drunken stupor and Mel's suspension. Those were just blips, surely? A reaction to their mother being away for longer than she had ever been before. As for the £10K, well, Andy had never known his wife to get into debt before. Perhaps she was helping out her mother. There had to be a good reason for it. Surely?

Mind you, if there was one criticism he could make of his wife, it was that, even after all these years of marriage, she still had that detached air of superiority, even towards him. She wasn't warm and easy to talk to, like Bobbie. On the few occasions when Andy had disagreed with Pamela (he still didn't see the point of the sauna hut in the garden!), she had given him a look that reminded him how lucky he had been to marry her: Pamela, the face of lingerie, whom everyone still remembered all these years later.

Was this, Andy asked himself now as he turned over a page of the perfect-parenting handbook, the reason why he hadn't stormed down to Sussex to have it out with Pamela? The fear that she might leave him because he didn't really deserve her?

And was that why he thought it was probably better to wait until she got home and talk to her face to face about that ten thousand? Camilla was right. Pamela needed space. And he'd give it to her. Meanwhile, he had other problems on his mind. Tonight – if Kieran turned up – he was going to have to face the man who could ruin his life.

Try as he had, Andy simply hadn't been able to come up with a plan to stop him. Even though something inside warned him that time was running out.

'I might be a bit late back from the class this evening,' he told the girls.

Neither bothered to reply. They were sitting with trays on their laps in front of the giant wall-mounted flat-screen TV. (They had one in almost every room.) Eating while watching would never be allowed if Pamela were at home. But tonight Natasha had insisted that she 'had' to see something on Sky for homework. It turned out that the 'something' was one of those American soaps where the kids knew much more than their ineffectual parents.

'Homework?' he had questioned.

'Yes, Dad!' Nattie had fixed him with a Pamela look. 'My English coursework is about American humour in twenty-first-century scripts. I've told you that before.'

Had she? 'Perhaps your coursework should be something about the perils of under-age drinking,' he retorted.

His youngest daughter scowled. 'Just because some of my

friends came round . . .' She stopped as though realising she'd said too much.

'*Some* of your friends?' he questioned. Was that why he'd found more bottles in the bin outside? If so, they'd cleared up pretty well, he had to say. If they could cover their tracks like that, what else were they hiding?

'Come off it, Dad.' Mel was talking as though she was the parent and he was the unreasonable child. 'Didn't *you* have fun as a kid?'

Her words stopped him in his tracks. Brought back that whiff of urine and cabbage and Brussels sprouts mixed with an image of a bald man with a tattoo on his neck. 'Of course I did,' he retorted lightly. Then he noticed that Mel was texting furiously while talking. How did kids do that so fast? It took him ages to send a message.

'Aren't you going to be late?'

His daughter barely raised her eyes. 'Late for what?'

'Babysitting Daisy and Jack.'

'I'm just going, Dad. Stop nagging!'

'Nag, nag, nag! That's all you ever do!'

Audrey was wagging her finger at Bohemian Mum, the one whose kids had rats in their bedrooms because of the takeaway leftovers under the bed. ('I'm trying to show them that they need to clear up themselves.')

'But, darling! If you'd only let me tidy up a little bit—'

'I need my privacy!' Audrey was stamping her feet and waving her mane of red hair around. Blimey! She was really getting into this role play. Any minute now and she'd turn into a real kid.

'I do understand but don't you think things have gone a bit too far?' Bohemian Mum's voice tailed off and she turned to Andy, her hands clasped as if in meditation. 'I'm sorry. But I just can't do this. I'm not very good at being strict. That's half the trouble really.'

You could say that again! 'It takes practice. Besides, everyone has, er, different parenting styles. How about swapping over.'

Andy looked around. Thank God Kieran wasn't here again this evening! With any luck, he might have dropped out.

Then he nodded at Audrey, who was looking even horsier tonight with a bright orange lipstick that accentuated her wide mouth. 'Can you play the adult who is trying to tidy up her teenager's bedroom?'

'Sure!' She grinned in what she presumably thought was a winsome manner. 'Ready and waiting!' Within a flash, she rounded on Bohemian Mum. 'If you don't let me into your room, I'll break the door down.'

'Fuck off.'

There was a shocked silence. 'I say,' breathed one of the other mothers, taking off her thick glasses to wipe them on her suit jacket before putting them back on again. 'That's a bit uncalled for, isn't it?'

Bohemian Mum shrugged. 'I encourage my children to express their feelings.'

They all looked to Andy as though seeking permission to continue. 'Good! This is, er, good stuff because it's realistic. So, everyone, what do you do when your kids swear at you?'

'Make them spell it out,' suggested Audrey.

'For God's sake,' groaned the woman with glasses, who looked like one of the lawyers from his old company: the intellectual sharp sort. 'Get real. Withdraw their privileges. Mind you, when I told Julius he couldn't have his laptop for a week, he borrowed mine.'

'Change the password,' said someone else.

'I did. Twice. In Latin *and* Greek. But Julius got it both times.'

'How about the good old-fashioned swearing tin?' said Audrey brightly.

'Tried that. But then he "borrowed" the money.'

'Talking of nicking, have you read the latest about Dr Know?' said someone else. 'He got that mother to shop her kid to the police and now the child's gone into care.'

'I think that man is great! It's about time we started getting stricter.'

'You're kidding! He's a monster!'

Bobbie's mum's boyfriend always got a reaction. It was certainly raising his profile. Suddenly the door burst open to reveal a man with a very thick neck and tattoos. 'Sorry, mate,' he said loudly. 'Had to work late at the garage.'

Kieran! Andy silently groaned. 'We're in the middle of doing some role plays about how to handle confrontation in the family, actually.'

'Sounds good. I could do with some advice on that.' He grinned. 'Tell you what. We're the only blokes here, aren't we? So why don't you and I have a go? We could pretend we're brothers.'

Audrey bounced up and down in her seat, letting out a delighted cry. 'What a wonderful idea!'

Andy felt his throat go dry. 'I'm not sure.'

'Go on.' Intellectual Mum frowned. 'If we can do it, it's only fair that you do too.'

Kieran was already on his feet, fists up at the ready as though they were in a boxing ring. 'I hate you,' he scowled. 'You really get on my wick!'

Had his old enemy started the role play already? Or did he really mean it? For a minute, Andy began to quake as though he was twelve years old again. Then his adult side took over. 'You're a bully, Kieran. A pathetic miserable bully.'

A purple vein sprang up on his opponent's face. 'You're going to regret that!' Kieran's fists balled up before him. 'Really regret it!'

This was for real, Andy realised. Kieran meant every word.

'Go for it, boys!' Audrey was banging on the chair with excitement.

'Come on then,' roared Andy. 'Bring it on!'

'Everything all right here?' Both men stopped as the door opened and a tall, well-built man with a deep voice strode in. It was Mr Balls, the primary head. Rumour had it that he used to be big in banking but had chucked it in for teaching. If so, Andy respected him for that. At the same time, he knew instinctively that he wouldn't want to get on the wrong side of him.

'We're just doing some role play,' said Andy quickly.

Mr Balls raised his eyebrows. 'Sounded very convincing but keep the sound down, can you? We've got a governors' meeting in the next room.' He made an amused, wry face. 'By the way, we're still auditioning for the parents' Christmas panto if either of you are interested. You both look like pretty good actors to me!'

Kieran let out a nasty laugh. At least, Andy knew it was nasty although it might not have seemed that way to someone else; someone who didn't know him. 'You could be right there, mate! You could be right.'

It took a while for the class to disperse that evening. All the women wanted to stop and tell him that they had 'really enjoyed' the session.

'Fantastic performance, Andy!' Audrey was virtually shoving her chest up against Andy in her enthusiasm. 'I love a man who is masterful. See you next week!'

She slung an expensive-looking suede bag over her shoulder and turned back with a wink. God, she was terrifying!

'So, Barry, that was good stuff.'

'Thanks,' replied Andy without thinking.

'Aha!' Kieran cackled. 'Caught you there, didn't I? It *is* Barry, isn't it?'

Bloody hell. How could he have been so stupid? How could he have dropped his guard after all those years? But the role play had unsettled him; taken him back to the child he used to be. 'The name's Andy now,' he hissed. 'How did you find me?'

There was another nasty laugh. 'I didn't find you. It's one of those coincidences. You and me, we just decided to bring up our kids in a nice area near a good state school.' He slapped Andy on the shoulder. 'Come a long way, both of us, haven't we?'

Andy stepped back. 'Don't touch me. You're vile.' He shuddered. 'Truly vile.'

'Is that right?' Kieran raised his head: for a minute he looked as though he was going to snarl like the animal he was. 'Think you've forgotten something, Barry. You were there. You saw what happened. We might only have been kids but that kind of stuff stays with you for the rest of your life.'

How horribly true! Every bone in his body wanted to get back to the safety of his home and his family. But something had to be done. 'Let's go and chat about this somewhere, shall we?'

Kieran grinned. 'Planning on getting rid of me, are you?'

'Don't be daft. I just think we need to talk.'

'Maybe you're right. Next week then, after the session. I've got to get back to my kid now. Have to hand it to you, Barry. You're looking pretty neat. And I hear you've done well for yourself too. Very well.'

Then those eyes hardened. Grew cold. 'Still, you've got a bloody gall, running a parenting course when you were such a difficult brat yourself. But maybe that's the point.' He grinned again. 'We know how to push the buttons, don't we? And we know how to hurt people too. Really hurt them. Don't you agree?'

Andy's hands shook on the steering wheel all the way home. His mobile rang just as he turned on to the drive and in his flustered state, he stalled the car.

'Andy! Have you got home yet?' Bobbie sounded breathy. Upset.

'Almost. Why?'

'I'm so glad I've caught you. Look – I don't know how to say this. Rob got home early tonight.' Bobbie's lovely voice hesitated. 'Before me. He smelt something funny.' Then she stopped. 'Oh dear. This is so difficult.'

'Please.' He could hardly get the words out. 'You must!'

'All right.' There was the sound of a deep breath. 'Mel was

smoking in the garden. But it wasn't just an ordinary cigarette. It was something else.'

'Cannabis?' He heard a voice coming from his mouth that didn't seem his.

'Yes.'

Her voice was so quiet that he wasn't sure if he'd heard correctly. 'Are you sure?'

'Rob seemed to be. And apparently Mel admitted it. I just wanted you to know before you saw her tonight. I'm so sorry, Andy. So very sorry.'

WHAT KIND OF PARENT ARE YOU?

If you can't get your kid up in the morning, do you:

1. Apply cold flannel to face while asleep.
2. Tickle toes.
3. Install three alarm clocks out of arm's reach.
4. Remove duvet.
5. Unplug laptop, which will be under the duvet.

Answer: Haven't you got it yet? Nothing works.

Extracted from I Can't Cope With My Kids *magazine.*

Chapter 16

BOBBIE

'When I'm older, I'm going to smoke like Mel!'

Bobbie nearly stalled the car as Daisy's assured voice piped up from the back seat on the way to school.

'That's very silly.'

'I'm going to do it too,' announced Jack, who had recently taken to copying his sister. This was not a good thing. The two were far more dangerous on the same side than when they were trying to kill each other.

This was all Mel's fault. How could she have smoked in front of the children – well, as good as? The garden was just as bad. The children could have got high through passive contact or whatever it was called. (Bobbie had to confess she didn't know much about drugs and didn't want to either.) It was utterly outrageous!

Yet a small part of her had been silently pleased that Princess Pamela's eldest wasn't quite so perfect after all. Was that why she had told Andy about the cannabis? Rob had been furious. 'You had no right to interfere! It was up to me to tell my sister when the time was right. This is family business.'

It had led to a huge argument: one that had woken the children so that they'd had to stop and reassure a stricken Daisy and Jack (who seemed so vulnerable and biddable when they were half asleep) that it was nothing really. Mummy and Daddy weren't rowing! Of course they weren't. Just talking.

Now, a few days later, she and Rob weren't even doing that. Just speaking to each other in terse sentences. They were sleeping at opposite sides of the bed. It wasn't good, Bobbie told herself now as she joined the queue of late drop-and-run mums. But she was damned if she was going to make up without her husband apologising too!

'Why is it very silly to smoke?' piped up Jack again just as she missed a parking space thanks to a dinky little car with a 'Granny On Board!' sticker that had nipped in first.

'Because it can give you cancer.'

'What's that?'

'I know! I know!' Daisy was bursting with enthusiasm. 'It's something that we can avoid if we eat five a day and do lots of healthy stuff. We're doing it in Pee Ess Eee.'

'It's not quite that simple,' began Bobbie but her words were obliterated by hooting behind. 'Quick, out, both of you! Don't forget your lunch box, Jack, and don't pinch anyone else's again, will you? Or commit any more football fouls. Daisy, here's your recorder. Kiss?'

Briefly, their little warm faces collided with her nose, one at a time. 'Love you, Mum,' said Jack and her heart lifted. It was moments like this that made it all worthwhile.

'Love you!' replied Bobbie just as a tall, well-built man came striding up to the car. 'Not you. Sorry. I mean I love my son!'

As a newish parent, Bobbie was still getting used to everyone's names, including the teachers. But everyone knew Mr Balls, head of primary. A decent, fair man, according to the school-gate gossip. Not afraid of giving praise or of telling someone (whether it was a child or parent) when they were stepping out of line.

'Mrs Wright, I wonder if you'd mind coming in to school for a minute?' He glanced at her car, which had, by now, caused quite a backlog of irritated parents at the wheel. 'It might be an idea to park somewhere sensible first.'

Bobbie followed her children's headmaster meekly into the reception area, feeling as though she was back in school uniform herself. She had rarely got into trouble when she'd been at her local grammar, apart from one detention when she and a friend had bunked off for a music festival.

Consequently she'd assumed her own children would behave too. Some hope!

'Shall we go into my office?'

It wasn't so much a request as a command. Bobbie took a seat opposite Mr Balls's desk, feeling like a condemned woman.

'Cup of tea? The kettle's just boiled.'

She nodded. 'Thanks.'

He stood up and went to the side of his room where there was a little kitchen. Somehow, she had expected a secretary to do the honours. 'Bourbon biscuit?'

Her favourite! Maybe this man wasn't so forbidding after all.

'Now,' he began, putting a KIDS R GREAT mug in front of her, 'I know it's not easy when children start a new school. But we still have some teething problems here, don't we?'

Oh God. 'Has Jack been biting again? I'm sorry. I thought he'd got through that stage although I'm afraid he still does it every now and then to his sister.'

'Actually it's not Jack I want to talk about. Although, now you mention it, I did hear that he's still trying to turn the sandpit into concrete.'

Bobbie went bright red. 'By, er, weeing in it again?'

It had been Jack's party trick as a toddler: one that he hadn't really grown out of.

'Afraid so. Bit too old for such behaviour, don't you think? Mind you, change often makes us act in a childlike manner.'

That was true enough. 'I'll have another word with him.'

'Thanks. Otherwise I'm afraid he'll be banned.'

'From school?'

'Just the pit!'

Thank heavens for that. Home schooling would completely tip her over the edge. Imagine having the kids at home all day, every day!

Mr Balls put down his mug. 'It's Daisy I really want to talk about.'

Bobbie groaned. 'What's *she* done?'

'It's not her.' He looked apologetic. 'It's us, the school, that needs to pull its socks up.'

Bobbie stared at him. 'I don't understand.'

'Your daughter is very bright, Mrs Wright. We did some IQ tests the other day and she came out streets ahead of the others! That's why, in my opinion, she's sometimes seen as being "outspoken".'

Mr Balls's voice grew excited and he began to tap his fingers on the desk as though playing a musical tune. 'She's bored. Needs stimulating. I'd like her to join our new Gifted and Talented stream, if that's all right with you. Best to start after Easter when there'll be a couple of other new faces too.'

'Bored? Needs stimulating?' she repeated. 'So it's my fault?'

'Not at all!' For a moment, Mr Balls looked as though he was going to pat her hand. 'It's natural for parents to blame themselves. My wife and I do it all the time. But no, you've done a great job. Bright children aren't always easy to handle.'

Bobbie thought back over the litany of disasters she'd gone through with her two. That behaviour at Pamela's lunch party had been just the tip of the iceberg. 'Is Jack bright too?' she asked hopefully.

Mr Balls made a sympathetic face. 'Actually his IQ was average.'

Blast. So she couldn't blame his bad behaviour on that.

'But he's a real character, isn't he?'

Phew! He said it in a way that was a compliment rather than a criticism. 'My wife and I have got one of those too – always into everything!' He glanced at the family photograph on his desk, showing a clutch of glowing faces in matching blue anoraks. 'In our experience, it helps if you can find something to channel a child's energy into. Is there anything that might make him feel him feel good about himself? Like a sport, for example? Our eldest is really into skateboarding.'

Jack might be great at throwing vases but he was only average at football, unless it came to illegal moves. Still, maybe she'd try his suggestion: it might help him let off steam.

'If you'll excuse me,' said Mr Balls as the school bell clanged, 'I've got to take assembly now. Getting back to Daisy, we'd like to move her up next term. Obviously you'll need to discuss this with your husband so perhaps you could email me?'

Then he paused. 'By the way, I gather you're on the Perfect Parents' course. How's it going?'

Bobbie was torn. If she admitted it really wasn't doing very much for her at the moment, he might think it was *her* fault – especially after what he'd just told her about Daisy. 'Fine, thanks. Fine.'

'Good.' He nodded. 'Judith Davies was very keen on running the younger group. I was a bit worried, between you and me, as she isn't a parent herself. Nice to know it's working out.'

So Daisy was gifted! Well, very bright! Bobbie almost skipped out of school. If that was the case, she could put up with any amount of bad behaviour. Well, up to a point. She couldn't wait to tell Rob – it might help to mend bridges. Nor could she wait to tell Princess Pamela! That would wipe the smile off her face along with the news about the cannabis-smoking daughter.

Oh dear. That wasn't very nice. Parenthood made you so horribly competitive at times. She should resist the urge to join in, Bobbie told herself as she headed for the dry cleaner's to drop off Rob's suits. Shouldn't be smug about her daughter's status, tempting as it was to plaster it over Facebook. But she was dying, absolutely dying, to tell someone! No good trying to get hold of Rob: he was always in a meeting. And Sarah's phone was going through to a new, unusually chirpy, message: 'Hi! You know what to do! Leave your details and I'll ring you back.'

Not for the first time, as she dumped the suits on the counter and put the ticket away in her bag, Bobbie wished she had a friend in Corrywood. Someone to confide in. Someone who would understand her problems.

173

Turning round in the queue, she almost bumped into a small pretty blonde clutching a bag of clothes in each hand. 'Vanessa!'

'Oh. Hi, Bobbie.'

She didn't seem that thrilled to see her, which made Bobbie feel stupidly hurt. She'd grown to like this woman whose granddaughter idolised Daisy. Bobbie had thought Vanessa liked her too. Maybe she was one of those women who blew hot and cold.

'Sorry.' Vanessa's face was flustered. 'I was miles away.' She had her mobile in her hand and kept checking it as she spoke. 'Look, I don't suppose you could do me a huge favour, could you?' She touched Bobbie's arm. 'I've got to shut the shop early to sort out some, er, personal business. Would you be able to step in, just for today?'

It was very short notice and she was meant to be finishing off that list of phone calls for Research Trivia, but Vanessa really did look distressed. 'I'll pay you,' her new friend added, naming a figure that was far more than she got paid for her interviews. Still, that wasn't the point. Bobbie wanted to help out. And maybe she could make her calls between pick up time and Rob getting home.

'All you have to do is to make a note of all the clothes that customers bring in to sell. There's a book on the desk to write down details. Explain I'll come back to them with a price when I've been through everything. As for the selling, just let them browse, although you could add an encouraging word.' Vanessa gave her a pleading look. 'Is that OK?'

Bobbie nodded nervously. The last time she'd worked in a shop was when she was seventeen and then someone had walked out wearing an outfit without paying for it, declaring she was going to 'show my husband'. Perhaps that was something she wouldn't mention to Vanessa.

'Thanks so much! If you come with me now, I'll let you in and show you the ropes.' Her voice was close to tears. 'I can't tell you how grateful I am.'

Bobbie took her hand. 'Vanessa, are you all right?'

'Not really, to be honest. But I don't want to talk about it. Not yet.'

Bobbie had a brilliant time at Vanessa's. No wonder kids loved 'playing shop'! Quite a few women came in with carrier bags stuffed with some gorgeous stuff. 'I don't need them any more,' they'd say with a slight tinge of regret in their voice. Then they would add, 'How much do you think you can sell this for?'

It was amazing how many well-dressed, would-be sellers seemed to need money. Others clearly had an eye for a bargain, like the woman who clicked through the rails with a decisiveness that suggested she was a pro before pouncing on a pale pink cocktail dress. 'Is this a genuine Ghost label?' she demanded.

Bobbie was a bit taken aback. 'I think so.'

'Think or know?'

Talk about being sharp! 'I couldn't tell you, I'm afraid.'

'Hmmmm.' The woman, in high heels and soft elegant tapered beige trousers, slammed down a crisp twenty-pound note. 'Then I'll give you that for it.'

What! 'The label says forty pounds.'

'That four looks like a two to me.'

Rubbish!

'If you don't want it, I'll have it!' declared a small woman, homing in.

'I didn't say I didn't want it!' Tapered trousers snatched the hanger away from her rival. 'I was just checking it was an original. All right, I'll take it. Here's the other twenty.'

Nothing like a bit of rivalry to push a sale along! Two other customers were having a similar tussle by the size-16 rail. With any luck, it would result in another ringing up of the till. At least she hoped so. Maybe Vanessa was worried because of money. If so, this morning's takings, which were really quite good, should help.

Bobbie spent the rest of the day chatting to customers,

some of whom seemed startlingly candid about their private lives. 'That colour really suits you,' she said to a middle-aged woman who was trying on a clingy red jersey dress. It did too; made her skin look less sallow.

'Do you think so?' The woman eyed herself doubtfully in the mirror. 'That's the first compliment I've had since my husband left me for his secretary. I used to buy her presents, you know, at Christmas! I never dreamed anything was going on. And to think that's what he was doing when he was having late meetings! I tell you, my dear, if I had my life again, I wouldn't be so trusting.'

Late meetings? Bobbie felt a cold chill go through her. No. Surely Rob wouldn't do that. Would he? Pushing aside the thoughts, Bobbie distracted herself by sorting out the rails after the woman had gone. That was better! Now what else could she do? Vanessa hadn't asked her to rearrange the window display but it seemed to Bobbie that the black dress was a bit severe to pull customers in. With the warmer weather, that yellow skirt would look rather jaunty, and perhaps she'd put the hyacinth-blue silk top next to it.

'That looks wonderful!' said Vanessa when she got back after lunch. She still seemed a bit flustered but not quite as bad as this morning. Maybe she'd sorted out whatever it was that had upset her.

'So you didn't mind me changing the window display?'

'Not at all. It shows initiative.'

'I dropped a couple of the prices too. Not much but it helped one or two customers to make up their minds. Hope that was all right.' She showed Vanessa the figures.

To her relief, her 'boss' nodded approvingly. 'Listen, I know this is putting you on the spot again but I've got to go up to London tomorrow to see someone. Are you able to help me out? And maybe over future weeks too?'

Bobbie had been partly hoping for this. 'I'd love to. But I need to be free for the school run.'

'Supposing we share? I'll pick up your children – although I like to walk rather than drive if that's all right with your

176

two – and you collect Sunshine. I wouldn't ask anyone else but she adores Daisy.'

She and Rob could certainly do with the extra money. She'd just have to squeeze in the market research too.

'Great.' Vanessa's phone began to vibrate and instantly that worried look returned. 'See you tomorrow then.'

Bobbie almost felt like dancing when she drove home with the children. She had a job – a proper job, outside the home! OK, so she might be over-qualified, but it fitted in with the kids. And that's all that mattered. At least it was when you were a working mum.

'How was your day?' she sang.

'I was the spelling-bee queen today,' said Daisy casually, 'although I was told off for talking. It wasn't fair. I was just helping the others.'

It didn't matter. Daisy was bright. She could forgive her for anything. Well, almost. 'How about you, Jack?'

'I saw him fighting in the playground,' cut in Daisy importantly. 'He had to go and see Mrs Davies.'

'*Miss* Davies,' corrected Bobbie. Great. The leader of their parenting class. That would really help her reputation. 'Why were you fighting, Jack?'

'Dunno.'

'There must be a reason.' She glanced in the driver's mirror to see her son shrugging. Right, she told herself. Let's use a bit of perfect parenting here. Empathy. 'I can understand why you might want to hit someone. . .' she began.

No. That wasn't right.

How about the three-card method? 'If I hear you've been in a fight again, I'll . . .'

She stopped, wondering which punishment to use this time.

Maybe this was a case for positive praise instead. 'It sounds like you're rather good at fighting, Jack.'

Both children were staring at her in amazement as she parked outside the corner shop. 'Are you feeling all right, Mum?' asked Daisy sharply as though she was the adult and Bobbie the child.

'Yes. No. Just stay there. I've got to pop in to get a tin of something for dinner.'

A good mother, Bobbie told herself, as she stood in the queue with her basket of baked beans and cheddar, would have had a proper meal ready. But working outside the home meant it was difficult to do that. As for . . .

Oh my God! Where was the car!

'Are those your kids?' shouted a man tearing past. To her horror, Bobbie saw the Volvo slipping steadily down the hill with Jack at the wheel. She'd left it in reverse, she clearly remembered, with the handbrake full on. The little devil must have crept into the front seat.

'It's all right, he's got them,' yelled someone else as Bobbie raced past. Thank God! Somehow the stranger had caught up with the car, opened the door before it had gathered any more speed and yanked on the brake.

'Thank you, thank you,' she said, tears in her eyes, before turning to her son. 'You naughty, naughty boy!'

'It's not the lad's fault, it's yours!' The man, with the bald head and thick neck with tattoos, glared at her accusingly. 'I wouldn't leave my kid in the car. For two pins, I'd call social services.'

'I'm sorry,' she stammered. 'I won't do it again. Honestly.'

'Don't tell Dad,' she instructed both Daisy and Jack firmly when they'd got home.

'Why?' they chorused.

'Because. That's why. No, don't ask any more questions. Just go and take your tea and eat it in front of the television. Have you washed your hands?'

'I'm trying to build up my immunity,' flashed back Daisy. 'We're doing that in Pee Ess Eee.'

Was it any wonder that the kids played up, Bobbie asked herself as she fitted in a couple of work calls. Something had to give when you had two parents who were working their socks off to pay the bills, and discipline was top of the list. Ah! At last! There was Rob's key in the lock. Finally.

Jack flew through the door and into his arms. 'Daddy, Daddy, I drove the car today!'

'Really?' Rob frowned. 'How did that happen?'

'He's making it up, Daddy!' Daisy beamed at her. 'Isn't he, Mummy?'

Oh God. So much for her so-called honest approach to life. Now she'd turned her daughter into a liar!

'We'll tell you about it over dinner.' As she spoke, Bobbie realised she'd been so busy with work calls that she'd forgotten to make anything, just as she'd forgotten to get the kids to bed. 'Baked beans all right?'

'Actually, I've eaten.' Rob sounded apologetic. 'Sorry. We got some food brought in during the pre-conference conference.'

'Pre-conference conference?'

'Didn't I tell you about it?' He ruffled Jack's hair. 'Probably got interrupted by the children as usual. The actual conference is next weekend. In Geneva.'

'No you didn't.' Bobbie's heart began to beat. She'd been looking forward to telling Rob about her day in the shop but now it didn't seem so important.

'The whole office is going,' he said, as though this made it any better.

'Including your secretary?'

'Yes. Why do you ask?'

'No reason,' said Bobbie quickly. 'No reason at all.'

'By the way.' He tossed a magazine at her. One of those free London give-aways. 'Thought you might like to see this.'

Bobbie stared in horror at the picture of her mother, gazing in adoration at a small man with a goatee beard, knitted eyebrows and a glare that would terrify any child into instant submission.

DR KNOW FALLS FOR GLAMOROUS GRANDMA ran the headline.

Glamorous? Actually, Mum *did* look rather good. She'd had her hair streaked and layered and was wearing a sparkly low-cut dress. In fact, she didn't look like Mum at all.

PERFECT PARENTS: SESSION FOUR

KIDS LOVE RULES!

PARENTS NEED BOUNDARIES TOO! E.G.:

NO SLEEPING WITH SOMEONE ELSE'S PARTNER
NO NICKING OTHER PEOPLE'S CAR-PARKING
   SPACES AT SCHOOL
NO LYING TO THE CHILDREN
NO STAYING LATE AT WORK TO AVOID FAMILY
   BATTLES
NO TAKING SOMETHING BACK TO A SHOP
   WHEN IT'S BEEN USED
NO SWIGGING WINE IN THE UTILITY ROOM

(With special thanks to *I Can't Cope With My Parents*
magazine: a new sister publication to *I Can't Cope With
My Kids*.)

Chapter 17

VANESSA

Vanessa hadn't been able to function properly since Sunshine had dropped her bombshell. 'Scar,' she had said, tracing the part of her body where Vanessa's right breast used to be. 'Nasty cut.'

What did Sunshine mean exactly? Was Brigid a self-harmer? Had someone attacked her? Or was it just something simple; an accident where she'd cut herself by mistake, like the time her daughter had knelt on a pair of scissors at the age of nine?

'What if it means something sinister?' she asked her GP, whom she had come to see as a friend over the years. 'Perhaps that's why Brigid sent her here! Not just because she was an inconvenience as I'd originally thought, but to protect her from danger. I know it sounds a bit far-fetched but . . .'

Her voice tailed away in distress. 'Not at all.' Her doctor nodded understandingly. 'I think the best thing is for Sunshine to see someone.'

'A psychologist?'

'Possibly.' She was making some notes.

Vanessa didn't like the sound of that. 'Bit extreme, isn't it?'

'Nowadays art therapy is very popular. Some children find it easier to draw a picture of what they're thinking, instead of talking about it. Let's see what we can do, shall we?'

Meanwhile, Sunshine seemed perfectly happy with her new life. She loved school where she was always Reader of the Week. She enjoyed playing her little flute in the orchestra and chatted away excitedly about the summer concert (would she still be here by then?). But most of all, she adored going out on her bike in the park.

'Come on, Van Van,' she'd call out, her plaits flapping in the wind. (Vanessa had taken her to the hairdresser who had managed to get rid of those awful beads that had made the other children stare at school.) 'I'm going to beat you!'

She'd also discovered the joys of television, which she no longer suspected of containing locked-up cartoon figures. Vanessa would sit beside her to watch sometimes, her arm around this little mite who had shaken up her world. If she closed her eyes, she could pretend that it was Brigid all over again. At other times, she kept them open and roared with laughter.

Children's television was so different now from her daughter's day – some of those presenters couldn't string two words together! – but other things, like the cartoons, had stayed exactly the same. 'Look, Van Van,' Sunshine would say. 'Jerry's escaped but Tom's after him now!' Then she'd squeal with excitement and jump up and down.

The only sign that something wasn't right was the low murmuring that came from her bedroom at night. 'Mummy, Mummy,' Sunshine would whimper restlessly as she tossed from one side to the other.

'It breaks my heart,' Vanessa told Brian during their phone calls. Since that scare when her granddaughter had so nearly found them in bed together she'd reluctantly told him that maybe they ought to take a break for the time being.

'Poor little mite,' Brian had said understandingly. 'Goodness knows what she's been through. Pity there's such a long waiting list for this art therapy.'

In the event, as luck would have it, there was a cancellation and within a few days, Vanessa found herself taking Sunshine to a small Portakabin, close to the hospital, where a bright, bustling young girl (why was it always young things in charge nowadays?) suggested that 'Granny' might like to sit next door while they made some 'pretty pictures'.

Sunshine had pouted, Daisy-style. 'She's called Van Van. And I want her there with me.'

Vanessa couldn't help feeling a rush of pride. 'Perhaps I

could sit at the side,' she suggested, not wanting to get in the way. Sunshine seemed happy with this arrangement. In fact, from where she was sitting, Vanessa could see her granddaughter was really getting into her drawing: leaning over the piece of paper, pushing back one plait with impatience, bottom lip sucked in with concentration. Goodness! She was actually rather good! Mind you, Brigid had been arty too.

'What's that?' asked the bright enthusiastic girl, pointing to something on the drawing that Vanessa couldn't see.

'The sun, silly!'

Vanessa resisted the temptation to tell her granddaughter that it was rude to call someone 'silly'. She'd noticed that Sunshine had picked up some expressions that she hadn't used before, like 'cool' and 'awesome', courtesy of Bobbie's kids.

'And what about this?'

'Be quiet. I'm still doing it.'

'Sunshine!' Vanessa started to say in disapproval but stopped as the girl gave her a please-don't-talk glance.

There were a few minutes of silence and then Sunshine leaned back in her chair with a sigh of satisfaction. 'There!'

'That looks like a person to me!' said the girl jauntily.

'It is, silly. It's my mummy.'

Vanessa held her breath.

'What's she doing in your picture, Sunshine?'

'She's smiling! My mummy is always smiling. She sings too and she plays tunes, just like me.'

Instinctively, Vanessa thought of the little clay flute which was tucked into Sunshine's pocket, as usual.

'What else does your mummy do, Sunshine, when she's not singing or playing tunes?'

'She looks after me, of course! And she looks after other people's children too.'

Really? Vanessa tried to imagine the angry-faced teenager she'd last seen in charge of a group of children.

'Does she do that in your home?'

Sunshine was shaking her head so that her plaits flew in the air with indignation. 'No. She does it at school.'

Really! How long had Brigid been a teacher? Had she gone to college after all, despite those I'm-not-doing-my-A-levels arguments. How incredible! Her daughter had really made a life for herself. Vanessa's heart was bursting with pride.

'What's that mark on your mummy's arm, Sunshine? The big red one.'

Silence.

'Can you tell me, Sunshine?'

'No.'

Her granddaughter's head was now bent over the sheet of paper, drawing something else.

'What's that?' asked Vanessa, unable to stop herself.

'It's my school!' Sunshine beamed. 'I've drawn a picture of it. Then, if Mummy sees this, she'll know where to pick me up like all the other mummies!'

Vanessa felt as though her heart was going to break.

The jaunty girl had a brisk edge to her voice. 'Would you like to come back again to do some more pictures?'

'No.'

Goodness. For a moment, that could have been Brigid speaking. '*No, I won't be back by midnight.*' '*No, I won't tell you where I'm going.*'

'Are you sure?'

The little head nodded firmly. Then she tucked her hand into hers. 'Come on, Van Van. I don't want to do any more drawing. It's stupid. Let's go bowling instead.'

'So,' said Bobbie quietly as they settled into their chairs in the classroom, waiting for Judith Davies to arrive. 'Sunshine isn't going back to the art therapist then?'

Vanessa shook her head. 'She refuses to. Stubborn – just like her mother. And grandmother!'

She hadn't meant to confide in Bobbie but when you worked with someone, you sometimes found yourself letting down your guard. Besides, she liked this young, hard-working, harassed mum whose children ran rings round her. It reminded Vanessa of herself at that age, even though she'd only had

186

one child and no husband. Mind you, from what Bobbie told her, this Rob wasn't much help. A workaholic husband who constantly criticised his wife's child-rearing skills was more of a liability than an asset, in Vanessa's books. It almost made her glad she'd done it alone.

'Who've you got babysitting tonight, by the way?'

'My neighbour. She's a gran like me so I'm hoping she'll be able to cope if Sunshine wakes with one of her nightmares. What about you?' She couldn't resist making a joke. 'Presumably it's not your pot-smoking niece? Or even Dr Know. I saw an article about him the other day.'

'Don't!' Bobbie groaned. 'Mum must have lost her marbles.'

'In my experience the older you get, the less you care about what others think.' Vanessa gave her a little nudge. 'Here comes teacher. Wow! Look at her left hand. That's a whopper, isn't it!'

'Sorry I'm late!' Judith Davies was beaming even more than usual. 'I got a bit held up on the way.'

'She must have got engaged since last week!' whispered Vanessa with excitement. Funny really. Even though she couldn't help feeling jaded about men and marriage, she still got that frisson whenever anyone got a ring on their finger. Maybe, despite everything, she was an old romantic after all.

That got her thinking about Brian. Warm, cuddly, funny Brian who always had something interesting to talk about, yet also listened to what she had to say.

'What do you think, Vanessa?'

She gave a little start. 'I'm sorry. Could you repeat that?'

'How do *you* set boundaries with your daughter?'

'Granddaughter, actually.'

'Of course. I'm sorry.'

Vanessa thought back to dinner that night when Sunshine had announced that Van Van really ought to stop eating meat because it wasn't kind to animals. She'd found herself tucking into one of those bean things she'd been buying for her granddaughter and finding, rather to her surprise, that she liked it.

187

'Actually, she seems to be setting boundaries for *me*! She's turned me vegetarian. Well, almost.'

There was a ripple of laughter although Judith didn't seem so amused. 'Compromise is important when it comes to bringing up children. But it's important that as parents – sorry, carers – we take the lead. Now I'd like us to do some role play on house rules. Bobbie, can you be the adult?'

'I don't feel like one at the moment,' she muttered.

Vanessa resisted the urge to giggle. What had got into her tonight? She was here to learn, and she was picking up some good tips, but in fact it was the friendship she'd made with Bobbie that was really helping. It was so nice to run things past a younger mother: someone who was still in the thick of it, unlike her contemporaries who were well past the bringing-up-little-children stage.

'See you on Wednesday in the shop,' she said as the evening finished.

Bobbie glowed. 'I'm looking forward to it.'

It took Vanessa a bit longer than usual to get home that night. One of the roads was closed because of maintenance works and then her own road was chock-a-block with cars. It would be nice to have a home that had its own parking, she mused as she walked up to her door. One day maybe. But not unless – no, *until*! – she was reunited with Brigid. It was imperative her daughter knew where to find her, just in case she turned up one day.

It was a dream, however foolish, that Vanessa couldn't dismiss from her heart.

'Hello,' she called out softly. 'I'm back.'

That was odd! There were voices coming from the lounge. Adult voices. Rather cross ones. What on earth? Vanessa stared in disbelief at the thin, weasel-faced youth with plug earrings lounging on the sofa with his feet up. Jason! Next to him was her granddaughter. Fast asleep, thumb in mouth.

'I'm so sorry,' said her neighbour nervously. 'He insisted on coming in and waiting for you. Said he was Sunshine's father.'

The youth grinned, making no attempt to move. 'Hiya, Vanessa! Nice place you've got here. Thought I'd pay a visit to my daughter.' He looked tenderly down at her. 'Had to wake her up, I did. But she's dropped off again.'

How dare he! Vanessa flew across to the sofa and scooped Sunshine into her arms. If she'd been bigger, she'd have thrown this youth out of the door. 'You've no right to walk in like this. Besides, Sunshine's not your daughter!'

There was a sneer. 'Thought you might say that. That's the other reason I dropped round. Wanted to give you this in person.'

Languidly, he got up, stretching himself, before thrusting an envelope into her hand: an official-looking envelope that made Vanessa's throat tighten again. 'It's from my solicitors.' He narrowed his eyes. 'It says I have a right to insist that Poppet here has a DNA test.' His face softened and for a moment, Vanessa could see a young man, keen – for some reason – to prove what he really felt was his right.

'You know, Vanessa, a kid needs two parents. My mother wouldn't let me see my old man when I was growing up and it wasn't right.'

He looked down at Sunshine again with the same tender look she'd noticed earlier. 'There's no way that a kid of mine is going to miss out like what I did.' Then his expression hardened. 'Get it?'

HOW TO BRING UP CHILDREN

Set a limit of £5 for Christmas/birthday presents.
Cut all extra-curricular activities. Kids need to get
   bored.
If they won't finish their meal, serve it up again and
   again. Nothing like a touch of botulism to teach
   them a lesson.
Ignore brother/sister punch-ups. How else will they
   learn to start wars?
Re-introduce National Service. From the age of ten.

Extracted from How to Bring up Kids Properly *by Dr
H. Know.*

Chapter 18

ANDY

It had been a week since Bobbie had told him about Mel smoking cannabis. Andy's first inclination had been to have it out immediately with his daughter. But she'd been asleep when he got back that night and the following morning, she'd left early for the school geography field trip.

No point, he told himself, in having a row before she went. It would be better, surely, to wait until she returned: next Monday evening, just after the next parenting session which was – ironically – about setting boundaries.

The session went quite well actually; mainly because Kieran wasn't there for some reason. The relief made him feel quite light-headed. So much so that he had to concentrate hard on what everyone was saying.

'Whenever I try to set boundaries, I end up by moving the goalposts,' confessed Bohemian Mum. 'The other day, I caught my daughter using my credit card. Turned out she'd run up a bill of over a grand.'

There was a collective gasp. 'What did you do?' asked someone.

'Well, I told her straight. You can't spend more than fifty pounds at a time. Otherwise I'll exceed my allowance.'

'You allowed her to continue using your card?' asked Audrey, aghast. 'Even though she stole it?'

'We share things in our house!' Bohemian Mum beamed. 'It works better that way.'

Jilly, sitting next to her, shook her head. 'One of my au pair girls got a caution for credit-card fraud. She said she didn't know what she was doing because she was drunk at the time. And high too. She was only seventeen.'

Andy listened, appalled. Credit-card theft? Drinking? Drugs? What happened to children during those teenage years? One minute, they were smiley, gappy-toothed eleven-year-olds and then suddenly – or so it seemed – they'd turned into potential criminals.

It wasn't as though they could even blame their background. Not in middle-class Corrywood. Andy drove back – after finishing an hour early because three of the mums were going on to a book club party – determined to have it out with Mel. He'd discuss the whole cannabis episode in a calm, reasonable fashion. Explain that he understood the pressures that teenagers were under today and that, believe it or not, he had gone through something similar himself. He knew what it was like to be pushed into doing something by friends. But that was part of growing up. You had to learn how to do the right thing, even if you made mistakes along the way.

When he put it like that to himself, it all sounded very reasonable. But as soon as Andy put the key in the lock and heard the music blasting out, all his good intentions went out of his head. 'Turn that down!' he called out.

No answer.

He went into the kitchen, and stopped in shock as, horrified, he took in the empty wine bottles on the kitchen table; some lying on their side and dripping on to the floor. The kitchen television was blaring out – even though no one was watching – showing a late-night panel show of earnest speakers, including a man with a goatee beard, knitted eyebrows and an extremely bossy manner.

'The trouble with teenagers', he was hissing, 'is that they just don't know where to stop. And whose fault is that? That's right. Their parents!'

Andy switched off the programme and shut the open fridge door, which was making a loud angry bleeping sound. Then he headed for the French windows, made at great expense in Lyons, which were banging against the outside wall in the breeze because no one had fastened them properly. Bloody hell. There were hordes of teenagers lying on the lawn. Laughing, drinking and smoking!

'Mel! Nattie!' He strode out, hardly believing his eyes. A group of large kids were sitting cross-legged on the giant trampoline that they'd bought the girls when they were younger. Instead of jumping on it, they now used it as a giant outdoor crash pad. Was that his youngest daughter? Swigging from a wine bottle? Next to a docking station.

'Mel asked everyone back after the geography trip, Dad!' Natasha's slurred voice indicated he should know that already.

'But you've got school tomorrow.'

'It's half-term!'

Was it? Why hadn't anyone told him? Dimly Andy remembered one of the mums asking at last week's session if there would still be a parenting class next week because if there was, she was going to have to miss it.

'That still doesn't explain this, young lady.' Andy pointed to the cigarette in Natasha's hand.

'Chill out, Dad.'

Chill out! He made to take it away from her but something stopped him. Something from the Perfect Parents' handbook for teenagers. *Try seeing the situation from their point of view.*

Bugger that. 'WHERE'S YOUR SISTER?'

'There's no need to shout, Dad. She's upstairs. And give me back my cigarette.' Natasha lay down again on the trampoline next to some kid in a leather jacket. Leaning forward, Andy grabbed the phone from its dock, cutting the music off. There was a mass groan of 'Who did that?'

'Right everyone. Party's over. Go back to your own homes. But clear up this mess first. Do you get me?'

Natasha's face was furious. 'Dad, you're embarrassing me!'

She spoke as though he'd just committed the biggest sin in the world. 'Too bad. When you've finished tidying, I want to talk to you. Both of you.' Then he strode back into the house to find Mel. Going up the stairs, he had to step around the clothes lying everywhere. It was like an assault course.

193

But nothing could have prepared him for the sight that greeted him when he went into Mel's room. Oh my God. Was that really his daughter? His little girl? Half-naked? With a boy?

Andy turned away, clutching the door for support.

'Dad!'

Mel's voice suggested she was as shocked as he was. But it wasn't just the bedroom scene that had thrown him. It was the smell. The sweet distinctive fragrance that indicated Bobbie's accusation had been right.

'GET OUT,' he snarled at the youth. 'As for you, Mel, I want you downstairs. Immediately. We need to talk.'

They hadn't been in any fit state to talk, of course, so it had had to wait until morning. Well, lunchtime actually because that was how long it took them to stumble down to the kitchen, bleary-eyed with messed-up hair and smudged mascara. They didn't look anything like the daughters he thought he knew.

'Sit down.' Andy indicated the kitchen table where he had put a large pot of coffee. The smell was calming. 'Croissants, anyone?'

They eyed him with suspicion. Exactly what he had hoped for. Andy hadn't sat up all night, mugging up on the Perfect Parents' handbook for nothing. *Change your pattern,* it suggested. *Instead of yelling, be their friend.*

Here goes!

'It must have been tempting to have a party when Mum was away and I was out for the evening,' he began, pouring out the coffee into one of Pamela's fine china mugs.

Mel snorted. 'I've told you, Dad. I didn't have sex. We just had a party. Mum never minds. You just didn't know before cos you were always away.'

That hurt.

'But she didn't let you smoke and drink, did she?'

Natasha giggled. 'She did it *with* us, Dad! My friends love her. They think she's cool.'

Were they speaking about the same woman?

'The thing is, Dad,' said Mel, talking as though she was the adult giving some advice to a kid, 'we have an arrangement, Mum and us.'

An *arrangement*?

'Sure,' Natasha piped up. 'We make sure everything's nice and calm for you when you're around but then we do what we want when you're away working.'

This didn't fit into the Perfect Parents' handbook. 'I don't understand.'

'It makes it easier.' Mel broke off a piece of croissant and stuffed it into her mouth. 'That's what Mum says. She hates arguments.'

That was true enough. Pamela was always cool and unflappable. Almost too much so. 'But what about the drugs?'

'Drugs?' Mel laughed. 'Cannabis is harmless.'

'No it's not.' He felt his voice rising. 'That's why it's illegal. It can tip some people over the edge; make them psychotic.'

'But Mum did it when she was younger.' Nattie's voice sliced through the air. 'She told us.'

Andy couldn't speak for a moment. Then he found his voice. 'Well, she shouldn't have.'

'Shouldn't have taken it or shouldn't have told us?'

He was still reeling. 'Both,' he managed to say.

Mel shrugged. 'It's why we get on, Mum and us. We're more like friends than mother and daughter.'

Exactly what the parenting handbook said you shouldn't be! *Parents need to be approachable without being best buddies.*

But this was on another level. This was dangerous. Drugs, in Andy's mind, had always been out of bounds, even when he'd been a teenager. He didn't care for anything that made him lose control; drink could be just as dangerous – that night with Kieran, all those years ago, had taught him that.

Sometimes it's best to discuss things later when everyone's calmed down. That was another tip from the handbook.

Andy took a deep breath. 'OK. But I don't want you smoking that stuff any more. Or drinking so much. I mean it, both of you. Otherwise I'll . . .'

He stopped, wondering exactly what he would do. Haul them down to the nearest police station? Withdraw their allowance? This was something he needed to discuss with Pamela; it was the kind of decision that both parents needed to make. 'Otherwise there'll be trouble,' he ended lamely. 'Now why don't you finish breakfast and I'll take you out somewhere. How about bowling?'

Mel snorted. 'We're not kids any more, Dad.' She stood up, stretching. 'I'm going back to bed.'

'Me too.' Nattie gave him a nervous look before planting a kiss on his cheek. 'Sorry, Dad.'

'I've got to speak to you,' he said when Pamela finally picked up her mobile phone. 'Something's happened.'

Her voice, as collected as ever, didn't seem unduly alarmed. 'What, Andy?' She gave a small laugh. 'Has the dishwasher broken down? Or couldn't you find your way to the supermarket?'

'Look.' He tried to stay calm. 'I can see why you're doing this. You've gone off to your mother's to show me that it's not easy being a parent and you're right. But did you know that Mel is smoking cannabis?'

She made a *so-what* noise. 'Don't make such a fuss. They all do it nowadays. It's better that they experiment in the open than behind their bedroom door.'

So it was true! She did know. 'What's got into you, Pamela?'

'I don't know what you mean. Coming, Mummy. I won't be long. Sorry, Andy. Got to go.'

'But . . .'

Too late. She'd put the phone down. Right. Andy's hands closed round his car keys. 'I'm going out,' he called up the stairs but the music coming from the girls' bedrooms was too loud for him to be heard. Maybe it was better they didn't know he was going or they might have another party. He'd

196

be back before nightfall, anyway. It wouldn't take that long to drive down to Sussex.

Andy hadn't banked on the half-term traffic. He got stuck for ages behind a huge black people carrier with a GRUMPY DAD ON BOARD sticker in the back. Then his mobile rang with an Unknown call but he didn't take it because he'd left his hands-free behind.

'Quite the model citizen now, aren't we?' he could just imagine Kieran jeering.

Finally he reached Camilla's village: a pretty leafy hamlet which had managed to hang on to its post office-cum-shop with ivy trailing up the front. Camilla's own home, a pink thatched-roofed cottage which she'd moved into after her husband's death, was deceptively large inside. If that was her idea of 'downsizing', it was a good thing she'd never seen the places he'd grown up in.

It was lunchtime, Andy realised as his stomach rumbled. Or was it making that noise because he was frightened? This was ridiculous! How could he be nervous of his own wife, just because she was beautiful and aloof and had so much more poise in the tip of her little finger than he could ever have?

'Andrew!' His mother-in-law's shocked expression gave him a certain amount of pleasure. Suspiciously, he glanced at her arm. It was indeed in a cast. So Pamela had been telling him the truth about that one.

'I've come to see Pamela,' he said firmly.

Her mouth, with that trademark pink glossy lipstick, tightened. 'Thought you might. You'd better come in.'

Honestly, after all this time, she could be a bit more civil, couldn't she?

'Pamela!' She was calling up the stairs; thick, heavy oak stairs that you couldn't get nowadays, with family photographs lining the walls. Pictures of his wife as a child on her pony. Pictures of Rob in his cricket whites, sitting very straight in a row of shiny-faced boys. Each one, no doubt, with a family behind them.

'Pamela!' called his mother-in-law again. 'You've got a visitor!'

A visitor! Is that what he'd become? How about husband? Then he stopped. Pamela was walking down, hanging on to the handrail. How pale she was! Thin too. And she was looking at him as though she was trying to work out who he was.

'Are you ill?' asked Andy, unable to hold back his shock.

Camilla's voice cut in. 'She's been over-doing it. If you'd been at home for years with two children, you'd understand that she needs a rest.'

'But I thought she was helping you!'

'There's no need to talk about me as though I wasn't here.' Pamela kissed Andy's cheek briefly before stepping back and linking her arm with her mother's. 'We're helping each other, aren't we, Mummy?'

Talk about feeling shut out! But that wasn't new. Whenever Pamela and her mother got together, they seemed to form an invincible unit against the rest of the world.

'Shall we go into the drawing room? Sit down, Andy. Now what's going on? It's all right, Mummy. You can stay.'

'Actually, Camilla,' retorted Andy, finally finding his voice. 'I'd like some time with my wife. Alone.'

His mother-in-law raised her eyebrows but rose up from her seat nevertheless, her back straight and erect despite that arm. 'I'll make some coffee,' she said tersely. 'One-handed. No, don't get up, Pamela, dear. I can manage.'

At last! 'If you found it so difficult with the girls, why didn't you say?' he asked when she'd gone.

Pamela moved away from him on the pale yellow sofa, just like their own at home. 'There's no need to be confrontational!'

Was he? Andy thought back to the role play they'd been doing at school. Empathise. Positive praise. 'You've done a great job with our daughters,' he added.

Pamela's face softened slightly. 'Really?'

He hesitated, wanting to be truthful without alienating her again. 'They're wonderful when people come round and

198

they always seemed very well behaved when I was home.'

Pamela laughed. 'That wasn't very often, was it?'

'We've been through that. If I didn't work, we wouldn't have the lifestyle we have now. That's another thing.' He had been dreading this bit. 'How can you owe ten thousand pounds?'

Immediately her face darkened. 'How did you know?'

'You had a final demand—'

'You've been opening my post?'

His chest began to pound. 'I thought it might be urgent.'

'You had no right.' Pamela stood up, her pale face taut. 'If you can't respect my privacy, Andy, perhaps we should have another think about our marriage. As for the girls, I brought them up *my* way.'

'By allowing them to put on a front and then letting them do what they wanted behind my back.'

'Exactly,' she snapped back. 'It was easier. Go on, criticise me if you want. But I'd like to see you do a better job. That's why I'm having a break. It's also why I couldn't do the parenting course. It would have made me feel like a fraud. And before you ask, I didn't volunteer to run it – I was invited because everyone thinks I'm perfect. Well I'm not, as you're about to find out.'

She gave him a little push. 'Now go. Back to teenage hell. And good luck. You'll need it. Go. GO, I SAID.'

This wasn't his Pamela! This wasn't his wife! What had got into her? And what on earth had she meant when she'd said that stuff about 'finding out'? Andy felt all his old insecurities flooding back. 'You're not going to leave me, are you?'

'Yes. No. I don't know.'

To his horror, his wife burst into tears. Pamela *never* cried.

'Shhhh.' Camilla came rushing in, taking her daughter in her arms. 'It's all right, darling. It's all right. Go and lie down and I'll see Andrew out.'

'It wasn't my fault,' he started to say as Camilla virtually frogmarched him to the door with her good arm.

Then she stopped to face him and to his surprise, he saw that her face looked oddly sympathetic. 'I know it's not. Well, not all of it. You've got to understand, Andrew. Pamela's going through a difficult time at the moment. She has some tricky choices to make.'

'What do you mean?'

For a moment, his mother-in-law looked as though she was going to say something but then thought better of it. 'Nothing. Please leave, Andrew. Please. You're making it worse. Give Pamela a few weeks with me and she'll be all right. I promise. She just needs a rest.'

Reluctantly, Andy went back to his car. Driving it round the corner, he stopped again, outside the post office, to gather his thoughts. Maybe Pamela was having a breakdown? That was it. The girls had got too much for her and instead of sharing with him (difficult, as he was never at home), she'd tried to sort it on her own. It was *his* fault.

BBRRM. Wow! Andy's car shook as a sleek black sports car shot past, driven by a man in sunglasses and a determined look on his face. Bloody hell, that was close. Something made Andy get out and walk round the corner, just in time to see the sports car screech to a halt in Camilla's drive. The man got out. Then the cottage's door opened. It was Pamela! My God. They were hugging, and then the door shut.

Andy felt nausea rising up into his throat. His wife had been telling him a pack of lies. Pamela hadn't come down to her mother's to get away from the children. She had a lover! A boyfriend! And Camilla was providing a little love nest for her; letting her daughter get away with it, just as Pamela had allowed Mel and Nattie to get away with smoking and drinking and boys.

Shaking, Andy went back to the car. He could march back up. Knock on the door. Demand what was going on. But would that really be the right way to win his wife back – if that's what he wanted to do?

Just then, his mobile vibrated in his jacket pocket. That Unknown caller again.

'Hiya, Barry! Or should I say Andy?'

Not now . . .

'Kieran, this isn't a great time.'

'Missed you too, mate! I would have been there last night but I had a job to do. Actually, there's summat I want to talk to you about. How about a pint at your local? Don't worry, I know where it is. I've found out where you live, you see!' There was a chuckle. 'That's the thing about a small town like Corrywood. Everyone's secrets come out in the end. Don't they?'

There was a young dad in his teens,
Whose children refused to eat greens.
He bribed them with sweets
And all kinds of treats
Before opening a can of baked beans.

Chapter 19

BOBBIE

'So how long is it since—'

'Mum! Look!'

'Sorry, Mrs Botting. There seems to be some interference on the line.' Bobbie glared at her daughter, gesticulated madly that she was on the phone, and tried again. 'How long is it since you—'

'MUM, I SAID, LOOK!'

'*I can't*,' Bobbie mouthed. 'I do apologise. As I was saying, how long is it since you had—'

'MUM!'

This was no good! When Vanessa had asked if she could possibly mind the shop today because it was half-term and she had to do 'some legal stuff' in London with Sunshine, Bobbie had almost said no. Not only did she have the children at home but she also had to finish this week's quota of market-research questions.

But then Vanessa gave her permission to take the kids into work with her (they could play at the back) and, privately, Bobbie had thought she might be able to fit in a few calls between clients. It was a bit quieter at the moment; lots of the regulars had gone off on skiing holidays. One woman announced that she'd paid for her trip to Verbier through saving up the year's proceeds from her sales to the shop. 'I intend to find a new man on the slopes who'll buy me some more clothes!' she'd informed Bobbie. It didn't sound as though she was joking.

'MUM, LOOK AT ME!' Daisy now demanded, twirling in front of her. At any other time, Bobbie would have seen the funny side. Her daughter was wearing a sparkly green dress from the size-8 rail which actually looked rather good on her, especially with the jaunty little hat.

'*I am. I am.* Sorry, Mrs Bottom. I mean Botting. I wasn't talking to you. No, please don't go! I've almost finished. All I need to know is how long it is since you and your husband had . . .'

Too late. 'Since you and your husband had a flu jab,' muttered Bobbie down the dead line (she'd had to use Vanessa's phone as she didn't get much reception in here). Blast! Thanks to the kids, she'd lost another one! And she still had twenty-two more to do before Friday.

'YOU WEREN'T LOOKING!' Daisy had whipped off the hat and now donned another. It was a huge black one with netting that completely hid her daughter's face. Perfect for a funeral. She spoke in a Dalek voice. 'WHAT . . . ABOUT . . . THIS . . . ONE?'

Bobbie wished she had time to giggle.

Enjoy your children, the perfect-parenting guide had informed her in the bath last night (one of the few places she could read in peace). *Try to take time out every day to give them your full attention. See it as a pleasure, not a chore! They grow up so fast that before you know it, they'll be adults and you'll never, ever, get that time again.*

Talk about trying to make you feel guilty.

'Only someone whose own kids have already grown up could write that,' Vanessa had commented quietly when Bobbie had shown her the offending paragraph this morning, before dashing off to the station.

Sometimes, Bobbie got the impression that Vanessa hadn't had an easy time of it when her daughter was at home. Or indeed now. It was certainly a strange business; Sunshine being deposited on her grandmother's doorstep like that. This rushing off to London on 'business' – as well as all that other time off – suggested things weren't quite right. But Bobbie didn't like to pry. It wasn't as though Vanessa was a best friend like Sarah.

'MUM, MUM!'

'Very nice.' Bobbie glanced up quickly. This time, Daisy was sporting a boater with a blue and white band round it. Where was she getting all these hats from? They were on the top shelf at the back of the shop above the size 18s.

Oh no.

'JACK!' Leaping up from her desk, she dashed across to her son who was leaning down perilously, handing the next little fashion number to his sister. 'You're going to fall. Hold my hand!'

'No. I like it up here.'

Try not to raise your voice at the children, no matter how difficult the situation. The parenting handbook's words drifted into her head.

'I SAID GET DOWN.'

And never, ever use words that you might regret.

'PLEASE!'

Jack shook his head. 'Can't. I'm stuck!'

Oh God. It was the phone again. 'Doesn't it bloody well stop?' she groaned.

'Mum!' gasped Daisy delightedly. 'You said the "b" word. *And* I can smell Pongo! It's you that's farted this time, isn't it?'

That's what happened when you'd had two kids and were under stress! She was busting for the loo, too! And the phone was still ringing. 'Answer it, will you?' she yelled, trying to help her son down.

'Only if you say "Please!" in Mandarin! Remember? It was in my vocab last week.'

'GET THE BLOODY PHONE!'

'Don't be rude, Mum.'

'HELP!'

'Jack!'

'It's Mrs Bottom,' Daisy called out imperiously. 'She had to answer the door but now she can do your survey if you want.'

'Tell her I'll . . . oh NO!'

Bobbie gasped with horror as Jack leaped from the top shelf. He was writhing on the floor now, clutching his ankle and yelling. Writhing in agony? Or writhing for effect? It was hard to tell with her son.

'MUM! Mrs Bottom's waiting!'

Bugger!

'I seem to have come at rather a bad moment!' A young, pretty woman with a double buggy hovered at the door. Bobbie recognised her from school. It was Gemma Balls, the primary head's wife. How much had she heard?

'Please, come in.' Bobbie had to raise her voice above Jack's yelling. It had moved down several decibels now which indicated that he was seeking attention rather than being mortally wounded.

'Hi.' Gemma knelt down beside him. 'My older boy is always jumping off things too. He's with his godmother this week otherwise he'd be tearing around like a bluebottle! Are you all right, Jack?'

So she knew his name! Then again, didn't everyone at Corrywood?

Her son sniffed. 'Sort of.'

'Does this hurt? No? That's good. And can you bend it this way? And that? Great.' Gemma looked up. She had a lovely smile! Just the kind Bobbie would like to have. *Had* had until she'd lost her sanity. 'Hope you don't mind but I've just done a first-aid course.'

'You have three kids *and* you have time to go on courses?' gasped Bobbie.

Gemma laughed. 'I need to keep up during my career break. Besides, it's one of the plusses about being married to a teacher. He's around in the holidays.'

Bobbie thought of Rob, who had hurried off to yet another conference. She wouldn't mind doing the same. Nice hotel bed. Unused bar of soap. Mini-bar. No one yelling at you. Someone else putting food in front of you. Heaven!

'Now let's see if you can stand up, Jack,' continued Gemma brightly. 'Can you walk?'

206

Looked like it. He could also run. Straight into his sister. 'HE'S HURT ME, MUM! HE'S HURT ME!'

What would Gemma Balls think? But she was laughing. 'You should hear our lot when they get going.' She glanced down at the buggy where a toddler and a baby were both fast asleep, thumbs in mouths. 'Mind if I leave them by the desk while I take a look?' She headed for the size-12 rails. 'I need something for my best friend's wedding. It's going to be rather smart. Lots of celebrities will be there. She's a singer, you know! We're terribly proud of her.'

Bobbie sprang into work mode. Already she was discovering that she had a flair for picking out the right colours and styles to suit customers. Just before Jack had got stuck and then the phone had gone, she had . . .

Oh my God! The phone! She dived past the buggy and grabbed the phone. 'Mrs Botting? Are you still there? I'm so sorry to have kept you waiting. Yes, it does sound like a zoo.' She sat down heavily. 'To be honest, it's half-term and I'm trying to work at the same time. Well, do two jobs actually. Thank you. It *isn't* easy. You've got lots of bored friends who would like to answer my questions? That's wonderful!'

Things were definitely looking up! By the end of the afternoon, Bobbie had several ticks on her survey list *and* she'd sold four outfits, including a lovely pink and grey one to Gemma Balls who was, she'd decided, absolutely delightful.

'I think your children are fantastic,' the young mum had said with a wink as she'd handed over her credit card. 'Jack's a real character and Daisy is so grown up, isn't she?' A rather wistful look came into her eyes. 'I'd love a little girl one day.'

She *was* lucky, Bobbie told herself. Wasn't that what the parenting book had said, more or less? Enjoy them. Perhaps it had a point after all. Meanwhile, there was just time to tidy up the rails before they went home.

'What about these, Mummy?' Daisy pointed to a large bag of waiting-to-be-looked-at stock under the desk. 'Didn't

Vanessa ask you to go through those and see which ones might sell?'

She had too! Bobbie had felt quite flattered that Vanessa trusted her. 'Would you like to help me?'

Daisy's eyes lit up. 'Cool!'

Find things to do together. That was another thing they'd been talking about in parenting class. And no, Judith Davies had said swiftly, arguing didn't count.

'What about this one?'

Daisy cast her eye on the orange pair of trousers and frowned. 'No way, Mum.'

On second thoughts, she was right. Kids often were, unfortunately.

'Look!' Daisy was examining an elegant pair of cream trousers. Now *they* were really beautiful. Bobbie stroked the fabric, astonished that someone didn't want them. If only she could squeeze into them herself! But after the kids, she'd got stuck between a 12 and a 14.

'They're Auntie Pamela's,' announced her daughter.

'Really?'

'Don't you remember, Mum? She wore them last Christmas and Jack spilt wine on them. Look, here's the pink stain. It's very faint but you can still see it.'

Her daughter had eyes like a hawk! Bobbie wavered. Vanessa was adamant about not having soiled stock in her shop but maybe she'd make an exception for these trousers. After all, if you didn't know the stain was there, you might not notice it. She'd give them a chance! Better go through the pockets first, though, as Vanessa had taught her. Mind you, Pamela was organised. Not the kind of person who would leave something behind.

Gosh! What was this? Bobbie stared at the piece of paper in her hands before tucking it away in her bag. She hadn't expected *that*!

'JACK!' Daisy bellowed. 'JACK, GET OUT!'

Not again. Her son was strutting around the window display in a long dress with that big black hat over his head, revelling in the attention from the open-mouthed crowd gathering outside.

'If you get out,' hissed Bobbie, 'I'll buy you a skateboard.'

Her son stopped. 'Promise?'

'Promise.'

Sometimes bribery was the only way. Even if she was meant to be saving money.

It took ages to calm down the kids that evening.

'Get off your skateboard, Jack! It's not for inside. And have you cleaned your teeth?'

'No he hasn't!' Daisy sounded like a mother herself. 'Did you know that when a crocodile loses his, he just grows them back again?'

Fascinating. But not just now. Eventually, Bobbie managed to coax them into bed, before pouring herself a glass of wine – just one! – and putting her legs up on the sofa. She was dying to tell her husband about the receipt in his sister's pocket but Rob's phone was still off. Surely he could make time during this team-talk conference thing in Northumberland to contact his family?

Suddenly Bobbie had an overwhelming desire to talk to her mother. Tell her about her day and how much she'd enjoyed the shop. Tell her too about that other thing that she didn't even dare voice in her own head.

'Hello. This is Phyllis! Sorry I'm not here!'

Bobbie waited for the greeting to end before adding her message. 'Mum, it's me. Hope you're having a good time. Just rang for a chat. Bye!'

Purposefully, Bobbie made her voice sound bright. She might not approve of Dr Know but as Vanessa said the other day, children didn't have a right to dictate who their parents fell in love with. Besides, what if (this was another of Vanessa's ideas) that tough-guy approach was just a cover and Dr Know turned out to be a real pussy cat? She only hoped so for all of their sakes.

Yes! Her phone was ringing!

Was it Mum?

Sarah?

No. Rob.

'You've missed the children. They're asleep now.' The resentment zapped out of Bobbie's mouth before she had a chance to take it back.

'Sorry.' She could hardly hear her husband's voice over the noise. 'We've been busy.'

'Sounds like it.'

Why had she said that? She was going to tell him about her day; make it interesting for once. But already she'd blown it.

'We've been power-threshing.'

'Power-threshing? What's that?'

'It's this new— Sorry, Araminta. I'm just coming.'

'Araminta?' Bobbie stiffened. 'Who's she?'

'My new secretary.' Rob was hissing down the phone. 'I told you.'

Not her name, he hadn't. What kind of secretary was called Araminta? Bobbie's mind flew back to that poor woman in the changing room whose husband had abandoned her. A posh girl, that's what kind! One who spoke with marbles in her mouth. She'd be a size 8 but would still have massive boobs that didn't droop. She'd be funny and never lose her rag. She wouldn't have a car that was littered with sweet wrappers. And she wouldn't have stretch marks. She'd be the type who was only working until she could find a husband.

Someone else's.

'Look, Bobbie, I'm sorry.' Her husband sounded rushed. 'I've got to go to the next session.'

'At this time of night?'

'They're working us flat out.'

'Obviously.'

There was a sigh. 'I'll call tomorrow. Oh, and give my love to the kids.'

Bobbie switched off the phone with a sinking heart. She hadn't exactly been the welcoming wife, she told herself ruefully. Nor had she told him about Pamela. But what was the point? Rob was obviously too taken up with more important matters. Like Araminta.

She should feel angry, but instead, she was frightened. In need of reassurance and a friendly voice to talk to. Her fingers began to punch in Sarah's number. The answer phone! *Still.* Disappointed, Bobbie found herself dialling another number. The only other person who would understand. After all, he was family, wasn't he? He knew how that lot worked.

'Andy? It's me. Bobbie. Look, I know it's late but there's something I'd really like your advice on. Do you have time for a coffee this week?'

'MUM! MUM! JACK'S BEEN SICK OVER HIS SKATEBOARD AND IT'S ALL RED. I THINK HE'S HAD SOME OF YOUR BEETROOT JUICE!'

There once was a mum from Poole,
Who was always late for school.
Her kids got detention
For flouting convention –
But she simply thought she was cool.

Chapter 20

VANESSA

'I want the sky, Van Van! I want the sky!'

Sure, Vanessa felt like retorting as they walked down the high street towards the station. But 'I want' doesn't get! How was it possible for a child to have changed so much in such a short space of time, she wondered, looking down at Sunshine, skipping along beside her wearing blue spotty leggings and a matching top. She was almost unrecognisable from the ragged bundle that had been dumped into her arms.

It wasn't just her appearance either. It was the alacrity with which Sunshine had adjusted to her different life, coming back from school every day with new words, not all of which were appropriate. Always wanting this and that. Making a fuss when Vanessa said she had to turn off the television for tea. Not chanting as often as she used to. Declaring that she didn't want to wear the outfit Vanessa had put out and insisting on wearing something else. In other words, she'd become a normal child.

Vanessa too had been thrown into another world. One that consisted of things called Moshi Monsters and DS games and other toys that she'd never heard of before. It didn't surprise Vanessa that Sunshine now wanted the sky! Those adverts on television were nothing short of blackmail. If parents didn't give in, their children created merry hell. Everyone said so in parenting class. It had been a bit like that when Brigid had been young, she told them all, but not nearly as bad.

Brigid! Her daughter was never out of her mind. But the Foreign Office still hadn't come up with anything. What else could she do but carry on and try to be a good grandparent? 'You can't have the sky, silly,' she said, holding Sunshine's hand tightly as they crossed the road.

'WHY?'

Another word that she'd picked up from Jack and Daisy, along with the loud speech that sounded as though it was in capital letters.

'Because, well, because if you did, the world would fall down.'

'WHY?'

Oh, for goodness' sake! Vanessa could feel herself getting exasperated, which wasn't like her at all. 'Please, Sunshine. Stop asking so many questions!'

If they didn't hurry, they would miss the train. Vanessa felt a sick feeling inside as she thought of the letter inside her bag that told them where to find the DNA clinic. It had to be done. At least, that's what the lawyer had advised. But Sunshine was standing stock-still now, in the middle of the pavement, refusing to move on.

'Distract the little buggers.' Wasn't that what one of the mothers had advised the other week? The one who wasn't really pregnant and had it in for poor Bobbie. 'Give them something else to do so they stop whining.'

Not a bad idea.

'Look, Sunshine, there's your favourite programme!' She pointed to a large television screen in the window of a shop they were passing. It showed a large pink pig called Mollie who spoke in unintelligible grunts, just like most of the children's presenters nowadays. Or maybe she was just old-fashioned. There was a notice next to it with the words: GREAT OFFER FOR SKY SUBSCRIBERS.

'YES!' Sunshine stopped crying and began jumping up and down again, this time with excitement, her plaits flying. 'That's what I said I wanted!'

Oh! Her granddaughter didn't want 'the' sky. She wanted Sky! That's what came of going to Jack and Daisy's for tea. 'We can't, I'm afraid,' she said, glancing at the package offer

214

next to the screen where Mollie the pig was dancing, trotters raised. 'It's too expensive.'

Sunshine's face crumpled. 'I want it,' she began to cry. 'I want it.'

'Too bad,' Vanessa felt like saying. But right at this moment, she needed to pacify her, stop her yelling. Get away from that older passer-by who was clucking disapprovingly. 'Come on!' she said, tugging Sunshine's hand. 'Or we'll miss our train.'

'Don't want to get the stupid train!' Sunshine's face was streaming with tears and her words were coming out with huge sobs. 'Want the Sky.'

'Not now.'

'WHY NOT NOW?'

Because we have to do a test to see who your father is!

Not that she could say that, of course. There were some things an adult should never tell a child. And some things that a child really ought to tell an adult. 'I'll have a think about Sky *after* we've been to London,' she heard herself saying.

'Promise?' Sunshine was eyeing her suspiciously. How had she learned so much, so fast? Bobbie's kids were lethal teachers. They'd certainly give Dr Know a run for his money! How she'd like to be a fly on the wall when *he* came to visit.

'Promise,' Vanessa heard herself saying, just as she used to promise Brigid all those years ago.

I promise I won't read your diary. I promise I won't talk to the teachers about you. I promise I won't be angry. All promises that she had broken.

But this time, she vowed as they held hands and ran towards the station, she really would try to do better.

It was much easier than she had realised to get a DNA test done, even though she was deeply reluctant to agree. 'You can fight it,' advised the lawyer, 'but that would mean going to court, which could be expensive and involve social services and all kinds of complications.'

Social services! Vanessa didn't want that. One of the women

215

in their class – the breastfeeding one from Ohio whom she and Bobbie had nicknamed American Express – had told them a horrendous story about social services 'removing' her neighbour's child because the mother had allowed it to get too fat. There didn't seem to be much rhyme or reason about how they operated nowadays.

'All a DNA test involves', the lawyer had continued, 'is a swab from the inside of the cheek. You can get DIY kits or you could go to a clinic. One of my clients recently used one in London. I'll find you the details if you like.'

What if this awful weasel-faced ex-boyfriend of Brigid's (whose ears had looked a bit like her granddaughter's, come to think of it) turned out to be Sunshine's father? Did he then have a right to her?

'Not necessarily.' The lawyer sounded sympathetic. 'The court always takes the decision that is best for the child.'

Vanessa was gripped with fear. 'But what if they think it's best that Sunshine has someone younger to look after her?'

'Age won't decide the issue, although it might play a part. However, you must prepare yourself for the possibility that if paternity is proved, this, er, gentleman might well be entitled to partial custody.'

Partial custody! The very thought of that horrible creep looking after her Sunshine for half a week was so awful that Vanessa felt like picking up her granddaughter and making a bolt for it.

'Don't be daft, love,' Brian had said worriedly on the phone when she'd run it past him. 'That would just lead to more trouble. Besides, if it was me, I'd want to know the facts. Then you can decide what to do. I really miss you, by the way.'

She missed him too! Still, there was no time to think of that now. Grabbing their train tickets she flew down one set of stairs and up another. Good thing she was fit for her age. 'Come on, Sunshine! That's right. You can sit by the window.'

But Sunshine wasn't happy. 'I want to sit on the roof.'

A young girl giggled, nudging her mother, who gave them

an odd look. 'The roof?' Vanessa had a sudden picture of the crowded trains from the documentary about India she'd seen. There had been hordes of passengers, she remembered, all clinging to the top of the train. 'We don't do that here.' Vanessa patted a seat further down the aisle from the giggling girl and staring mother. 'We sit inside.'

'BUT I WANT TO SIT ON THE ROOF!,

'Sunshine! You can't. Now please sit down. I've got some crayons with me. Look!'

Reluctantly, her granddaughter did as she was told. Vanessa settled back with her favourite magazine but couldn't concentrate. Every time she looked at Sunshine, she saw Brigid. Why? she kept asking herself. Why did you send your daughter away? Are you really in trouble? Or did you get frustrated because she stopped you doing your own thing, whatever that was? Was it possible that Brigid could be so selfish?

Her thoughts and fears occupied her all the way into town. As they got out at Marylebone, Vanessa hung on to Sunshine's hand tightly. The half-term crowds were claustrophobic with heads bobbing, parents shouting and children whining. It was like a discordant orchestra. That was the thing about family trips, she remembered. They always seemed a good thing in theory. 'Stay close or you'll get lost,' she called out to Sunshine. 'And please don't wave and smile like that at everyone! We don't do that here.'

'Why?'

'Just because we don't, poppet. Remember what I told you about not talking to that man with the rings in his nose?'

'The one who knew Mummy?'

'Exactly.'

Sunshine's eyes widened. 'But *why* can't I talk to him?'

'Just because.'

'But *why* because?'

Vanessa shepherded Sunshine through the crowds. 'Because I said so. That's why.'

Sometimes there were no easy answers.

*

The clinic that the lawyer had directed them to was a short walk from the station. It was very clean, Vanessa noted with approval. Friendly too. And, incredibly, there were quite a lot of children and anxious adults sitting in reception.

'So I told him, it's your son and I can prove it,' a rather well-spoken woman was saying to her neighbour. 'It's not his money I want. It's the recognition.'

Vanessa put her arm around Sunshine protectively. 'So,' she began, 'remember what I told you? It's like going to see the doctor, the way you did when you first arrived.'

Sunshine was playing with a hand-held battery game that Jack had lent her. 'To have a check-up?' she said without looking up.

'Sort of. It's rather like seeing the dentist too. All you have to do is open your mouth and the doctor will put a stick inside. It won't hurt. I promise.'

Sunshine shrugged. 'OK.'

It was indeed as simple as that. 'How long will it take for the results to come through?' Vanessa asked when it was over.

The receptionist gave her a glossy smile. 'Difficult to tell. We're rather busy at the moment.'

There was a persistent tug at her hand. 'Where are we going now, Van Van? You said we'd have a treat afterwards if I was good.'

So she had. After all, they might as well do something here now they were in London. How about Madame Tussauds?

The queue went on for ages but it was worth it just to see Sunshine's face. 'I know her, I know her!' she squealed, jumping up and down. 'It's our queen! Mummy's school has a picture of her on the wall!'

Vanessa still couldn't get used to the idea of her rebellious daughter being a teacher.

'And that's Princess Kate! We've got a picture of her too!'

In fact, Sunshine seemed to know nearly all the royals, as well as some other faces like Daniel Radcliffe. 'Harry. Harry Potter,' she called out. 'I saw him at the cinema with Mummy.'

So they had a cinema? Maybe this place that her daughter lived in wasn't so remote after all.

After that, they went to the zoo at Regent's Park. 'Look at those monkeys!' Sunshine was in her element. 'We've got those at home.' But the funny thing was that none of these memories seemed to upset Sunshine. If anything, they appeared to comfort her.

'Time to go back, I think,' said Vanessa after they'd had a bean burger at a café nearby. Heavens, she realised, half an hour later, when they were fighting their way on to the tube, she'd left it rather late. It was packed!

'Hold on to me,' she called out in the crush. But then someone elbowed his way past them and somehow that little hand came adrift from hers. 'SUNSHINE!' she gasped. But the doors were closing.

Desperately, Vanessa hammered on the glass. 'OPEN THEM, SOMEONE, PLEASE!' But to her horror, the train lurched and then moved off, leaving her behind on the platform, heart in her mouth.

'Just jump on the next one,' urged a woman next to her with a pushchair, who'd noticed her distress. 'With any luck, someone will realise she's lost and get off with her to wait at the next stop. It's what I've taught my lot to do.'

Too late, Vanessa realised she should have given the same advice to Sunshine. Oh my God. Tears pricked her eyes and she found herself blubbing just like her granddaughter had over Sky. If she found her now, she'd give her anything. The moon and the stars if necessary. Just let her be safe. Please! Thank God. Here was another train! Vanessa fought her way on with a determination that surprised even herself. 'Watch out,' said someone. 'That's my foot you've just trodden on.'

'Sorry.' The tears were gushing down now. 'I've lost my granddaughter! We got separated when the doors closed just now.'

But the man whose foot she had hurt just shrugged. 'Should have held on tighter, then, shouldn't you?'

He was right. How could she have been so negligent? What

would Brigid say? How would she, Vanessa, ever cope again if something happened? Why was the train stopping like this? Thank heavens. It was on its way again. Here they were! At the next station. But where was Sunshine?

Vanessa leaped out of the train, searching up and down the crowded platform. She wasn't here. She must have stayed on the train! '*Sunshine,*' she wept, crouching down on the ground, her head in her hands. The irrational thought came into her head that if she screamed loudly enough it would make it all right again. Was that why toddlers had tantrums? 'SUNSHINE!'

'Are you looking for a little girl?' Looking up through her tears, Vanessa saw a man in London Underground uniform. Unable to speak, she made a choking sound and tried to nod at the same time. 'It's OK, love. She's safe. Someone saw she was lost and brought her to us. She's in the office, right now.' He smiled. 'Right little charmer, isn't she? This way.'

Vanessa had never, ever, been so relieved in her life. Not even when the hospital had given her the five-year all-clear. 'You're safe,' she wept, flinging her arms around Sunshine. 'You're safe.'

The little face beamed up at her with that toothy gap. 'A nice lady on the train looked after me! She has Sky too, like Jack and Daisy. She was telling me all about it. And so does Stan.'

Stan? The other man in this small office shrugged apologetically. 'The wife made me get it. Little Miss Chatterbox here has been telling me all about the waxworks and the zoo and the dentist.'

'I told you, Stan!' Sunshine stamped her foot imperiously. 'It wasn't the dentist. It was the Dee En A lady.'

Vanessa didn't know where to look! Stan's expression wasn't quite so friendly now.

'Thank you so much for everything.' She delved in her purse but Stan put up his hand. 'Please. We were just doing our job.'

Of course he was. Still, she'd have paid anything to get her

220

granddaughter back safely. Never, she told herself as Sunshine cuddled up to her on the way home, would she let her out of her sight again.

'Mrs Thomas?'

A friendly voice cut in from the seat behind. Vanessa turned round. It was Miss Davies! Strange to see her on the train instead of in the classroom. She was in jeans instead of her usual navy suit. And her hair was loose. It suited her. 'Hello, Sunshine! Have you been to London for the day?'

'Yes!' Sunshine nodded her head. 'I had a D—'

'Dentist appointment,' cut in Vanessa quickly.

There was an indignant squeal. 'No, I didn't!' Vanessa shot her a don't-say-anything look which, miraculously, Sunshine took notice of. 'And we went to the zoo and Madame Two Swords,' she added.

'Sounds wonderful!' Miss Davies beamed. 'You'll be able to write about it in your "What I did at half-term" project next week!'

Vanessa silently groaned at the thought. Now the Dee En A test would be all over school. She was sure teachers only got children to write 'What I dids' to mortify parents. Or grandparents. They were at a stop now and people were getting out. One of the seats in front of her became vacant.

'Shall I take that?' suggested Miss Davies brightly, and Vanessa nodded. She could hardly say no.

'What have you been doing in town?' she asked, trying to change the subject.

'Visiting my little sister. She's at university there.'

'Do you like her,' asked Sunshine solemnly, 'or do you kick her like my friend Daisy kicks her brother?'

Miss Davies – it seemed too familiar to call her Judith – laughed. 'I like her very much.' Then she lowered her voice a bit. 'I helped to bring her up after our parents died.' She didn't exactly say 'So I know what you're going through' to Vanessa but her face implied it. That was a surprise! Perhaps she and Bobbie shouldn't have been so hasty in criticising a non-parent for running a parenting class.

'I like your ring!' cooed Sunshine shyly, putting out her finger to touch the stone. 'It's really pretty.'

'Thank you!' Miss Davies looked pleased.

'Are you getting married soon?' Vanessa couldn't help asking.

'Next summer.' She glanced down at Sunshine, who was still stroking her ring. 'We'd like to start a family as soon as we can.'

Good luck! Then she'd find out what it was really like! 'Nearly back, now,' Vanessa remarked as the familiar fields and church tower came into view. Not for the first time, she told herself how lucky she was to live in a semi-rural market town which was also close to London. 'Let's get our things together, shall we?'

Pulling out the tickets and her mobile from her bag, she checked for messages. A missed call from an Unknown and a message from Brian. Like her, he hated texts.

'*I think it's time for me to meet Sunshine properly, don't you?*' His kind deep voice gave her a lovely jolt. '*How about next week? I'll bring some fish and chips over. Let me know if that's all right. Oh, and I've got an idea!*' There was a chuckle. A lovely warm chuckle. '*Don't say no until you see it. OK?*'

There was an old granny from Herts,
Whose grandchildren loved to make tarts.
But they got IBS
So made quite a mess
When they let out enormous . . .

(Ed's note: Substitute offending word with 'smells'.)

PERFECT PARENTS: SESSION FIVE

LEARN TO LISTEN

BELOW ARE SOME COMMMON HOUSEHOLD PHRASES WHICH WE'RE ALL GUILTY OF IGNORING – WHATEVER OUR AGE!

SHUT THE DOOR.
WAIT.
HE DID IT FIRST!
TAKE OFF YOUR SHOES.
WHERE'S THE LOO ROLL?
SHE DID IT FIRST!
GET THE PHONE.
ANYONE SEEN MY GLASSES?
DINNER'S READY.
ARE YOU LISTENING?

Chapter 21

ANDY

'So you see,' said Bobbie, flicking back her mousy brown hair (he rather missed those pink streaks!) in that almost schoolgirl fashion, 'I really don't know if I'm being silly or not.'

They were sitting in the garden of a pretty thatched pub a few miles outside Corrywood: a place that Bobbie had suggested when she'd rung the other night to ask if she could 'run something past him'. And no, she didn't want to meet at a coffee shop in the high street. There were too many ears in this place.

She had said 'this place' as though she didn't like it much. Andy could understand that. Corrywood could get very insular with its small-town mentality. So different from the places he used to live in. At times, he felt protected by the security that came from the smart high-street shops and three-cars-in-the-drive houses. At other times, he felt like an outsider, waiting to be exposed. Today was one of them.

Now, as Bobbie sat opposite, twisting her thin gold wedding ring nervously and telling him about Rob who was 'never around', he felt really sorry for her. And, it had to be said, for his brother-in-law. Somehow, he had to explain that, without pushing her away.

'Rob has to deal with the States, doesn't he?' he pointed out. 'So he'll have to start taking their calls from afternoon to night, which makes it a sixteen-hour day.'

Bobbie nodded. 'That's what he says. But I wasn't sure if he was exaggerating.'

'Afraid not. It's only now that I'm having a break that I can see how crazy the whole thing is.' He put his hands out in a wide what-can-you-do? shrug. 'But it's the way the world works. If you want a nice lifestyle, you have to kill yourself for it.'

'I get that. I really do. But it's hard for the person who's bringing up the children. I don't know how Pamela manages! She's always so calm and your girls are amazing.' She flushed then, looking awkward. 'I mean, I know there was that trouble over Mel the other night with smoking but it was probably a one-off.' She glanced at him, more sharply this time. 'Wasn't it?'

He nodded, not wanting to burden her with his own worries. This was *her* time. Not his. 'What about the secretary?' he prompted gently. 'The one you mentioned on the phone.'

Bobbie bit her lip. She looked really sweet and vulnerable when she did that. He liked the fact that she wasn't plastered with make-up either, like so many women (including his wife). And that T-shirt suited her: casual but flattering. There was a lot to be said for women with curves. So much more feminine than a stick.

'She's called Araminta.' The very name seemed to stick in her throat.

He let out a snort. 'Sounds like that *Made in Chelsea* programme that the girls like.'

Bobbie giggled but there were tears in her eyes at the same time. 'He went on a three-day conference the other day and when he rang me, I could hear her in the background.'

Her hand was gripping the edge of the table now. It was all Andy could do not to stroke it in reassurance. 'I'm probably being a bit paranoid,' she continued in a wobbly voice, 'but I'm worried I'm going to end up like my best friend Sarah in London. Her husband went off with the MD and she says that Rob is showing all the classic signs of an affair. You know, distant, cold. Always critical. And then I got talking to a woman in the shop the other day, whose husband had just left her, and it's got me all worried.'

She ran her hands through her hair and Andy wondered if she realised how pretty she was, especially when vulnerable. 'In fact, I wanted to ask you something.' Then she stopped.

'Please, Bobbie. You can ask me anything!'

'All right.' She looked slightly more reassured. 'You're married to his sister. So I wondered if Rob has said anything to Pamela? I don't want you to break confidences but I have to know.'

'If he has, she hasn't told me. Pamela keeps her cards close to her chest. In fact, she's not at home any more than your husband. Made from the same stable, those two.' The anger flew out of his mouth before he could hold it back. Bobbie looked startled. 'Sorry.' Mentally he kicked himself. 'I didn't mean to tell you all my stuff too.'

'No.' Her hand rested on his, briefly. 'Please tell me, Andy.'

Then somehow it just all blurted out! How the girls weren't well behaved at all but had been bribed over the years by Pamela (with money and clothes and anything they wanted) to behave well when he was at home 'just so that Pamela could have a quiet life'. About Pamela going down to her mother's and the sports car. About the enormous loan which he had paid off for her, even though she wouldn't tell him what it was for.

It was so nice to tell someone who understood what this family was like.

'I would never have believed it,' she whispered.

'Nor me.' Andy took a deep breath. 'So tell me. What do you think about Pamela from a woman's point of view? Does this man in the sports car sound dodgy?' He tried to laugh. 'Do you think she's having an affair? I mean, I know I'm being silly. She wouldn't really do that to me.'

'Actually.' Bobbie's fingers began tapping the table. 'I wasn't going to tell you this but . . .'

A coldness wrapped itself round his chest as he leaned forwards. 'No, please. Do. I need to know everything. Just like you.'

Bobbie bit her lip. 'All right. You know I told you that I'd started working in that second-hand designer shop in town?'

He nodded. He'd been impressed by that. Somehow he couldn't see Pamela working in a shop if their finances ever

229

went tits up. 'Well, the other day I was sorting through some clothes and I found this pair of trousers that Pamela had asked my boss to sell.'

'My wife *sells* her clothes? Why? I thought she just gave them away when she didn't want them any more.'

Bobbie flushed. 'A lot of seemingly wealthy women need the pin money; you'd be surprised. Anyway, Vanessa – she's the one who owns the shop – told me to always check the pockets first.'

She stopped for a second. Andy's heart felt as though it was going to burst out of his body with apprehension.

'What did you find?' he asked slowly.

'A receipt. For drinks at a club.'

Was that all? He'd been expecting an incriminating note. Or another loan statement. Or a condom, even. No. That was ridiculous.

'The date,' Bobbie continued solemnly, 'was Rob's birthday. That's why it rang bells. I was having a family dinner: you couldn't make it because you were away in Singapore.'

He remembered that.

'Pamela said she couldn't come because of a migraine.' Her hands were twisting nervously in her lap now. 'It might be nothing but on the other hand . . .' Her voice tailed off.

'Thank you.' Andy felt surprisingly calm. Very quiet. Not angry the way he thought he might. Almost distant as though this wasn't happening to him at all.

'It's not proof of anything,' Bobbie was now saying quickly.

'No. No. Of course it's not.'

'What are we going to do?' She was looking at him as though expecting him to take the lead. Despite his churning chest, Andy rather liked the 'we'. It made him feel that he wasn't alone in this. 'I think,' he said, putting his elbows on the table and leaning towards her again, 'we should carry on as normal for the time being. But we need to be watchful.'

'You're not going to say anything to Pamela about the man in the sports car?'

He shook his head. 'Call it cowardly if you like but I don't want to rock the boat until I have proof. It's the way we work in the office if we suspect someone of fraud. I'd do the same with Araminta, if I were you.' He sighed. 'It's very easy to get too close to people you work with; I've seen several of my colleagues make mistakes like that. But if you accuse someone too soon, they can talk their way out of it and you look stupid. And you're not,' he added hastily. 'Anything but.'

Bobbie ran her hands through her hair again. 'Maybe you're right.' She glanced at her watch. 'I've got to get back now for the babysitter.'

'You definitely don't want to use Mel any more, then?'

There was an embarrassed look. 'I'm so sorry. Rob says that he can't allow the children to be . . .'

'To be in the company of a pot-smoking teenager,' he finished off the sentence for her. 'I understand.' This time his hand really did stretch out across the table to give hers a little squeeze. 'It's good to know we can talk, isn't it? Only we know what that family is really like. I blame our mutual mother-in-law. Camilla's an absolute cow.'

Bobbie laughed though her eyes were still wet. 'She is, isn't she?'

Then they left, going their separate ways. He would have liked to have told her about Kieran but enough was enough for one night. Besides, he needed to get back to see what the girls had been up to during his absence.

The house was impeccably tidy. He'd say that for his family. They were very good at covering up their tracks. If it weren't for the stubs in the bins outside and the giveaway smell of air freshener, he wouldn't have known. No wonder he had been fooled when he'd come back from one of his many long trips.

At least in the office he got things done! Here, he felt that hours – no, days – could go by when he didn't actually achieve anything.

'I'm back! Mel? Nattie?'

His elder daughter was sitting at her desk in her bedroom,

with an open textbook beside her. Her coursework? But as he approached, she quickly pressed a button so that the screen changed. Clearly she'd been looking at something else. 'Working hard?' he asked with a slight touch of sarcasm.

She nodded. 'I am, actually.'

'What are you doing then?'

'Researching the life of Matisse. Go away, Dad. You're putting me off.'

Matisse? Andy felt so inadequate when his wife and daughters came out with names and words that he wasn't familiar with. It all went back to education: something he hadn't had. The only thing that made sense to him was figures; a gift that neither of the girls had inherited.

'Where's Nattie?' he asked, looking around and nearly tripping over her telephone charger. He'd never seen her room in such a mess before! Clothes everywhere; mugs half-full with cold coffee; books all over the floor; nail varnish with the lid off . . . whoops, discarded lacy black pants. And the air was so stale! He made his way to the window to open it. It was like negotiating your way through a female minefield.

Mel shrugged. 'In the shower. She's just been to the gym.'

But there was giggling from Nattie's bedroom!

'Dad!' His younger daughter glared at him as he opened the door. 'What are you doing?'

'What are *you* doing, more like?' he said, taking in the youth who had jumped up from the bed wearing only a pair of boxers. At least his daughter had a dressing gown on but her hair was wet and so too was the boy's. She might well have been taking a shower, but not alone. The kid only looked about twelve!

'Get dressed,' he growled, 'and then get out.' Furiously he turned to Nattie. 'I want you downstairs to talk. Now.'

It was bad enough that he'd found Mel half-naked the other day, even though she swore it hadn't gone any further. But Nattie? His little girl?

'You're not listening to me,' yelled his daughter as she

perched on the kitchen surface, glaring at him as though he was the one who'd been caught virtually with his pants down. 'I've told you. Tyrone's a friend from the gym. The showers weren't working so we came back here. Nothing happened, Dad.'

Did she think he was born yesterday? 'I don't believe you.' His hands clenched inside his pockets. 'You're fifteen, Nattie. Too young to do that sort of thing.'

'What sort of thing, Dad?' Nattie's eyes were sparkling with fury. 'Go on. Say it. Sex. That's what you meant, wasn't it? Well, Tyrone and I don't do that. He's gay anyway.'

Good one. She was a clever liar. Just like his wife.

'I'm not talking about this any more!' She jumped down from the counter. 'What's the point of you running some stupid parenting course if you don't listen?'

'Come back,' Andy called out. Too late. His daughter had already run upstairs and slammed the door behind her.

After that, Nattie refused to speak to him. 'What do you think I should do?' he asked Pamela on the phone.

'I don't know!' She sounded amused; as though enjoying this. Quite chatty in fact. Almost over the top. Very different from their last meeting at her mother's house. 'You could always email Dr Know's problem page! Did you know he's going out with Bobbie's little mother? Rob told me. Now I must go. I've got to take Mummy to the physio.'

'You're not going out with your friend then?' he couldn't resist saying. 'Out to another club?'

'What on earth are you talking about?'

Andy could have kicked himself. Hadn't he decided not to say anything? To let it all blow over in the hope that it might be all right again? 'I don't know,' he mumbled. 'You must have friends down there from when you were growing up.'

'They're not here any more,' said Pamela sharply. 'What are you implying, Andy? I'm not here for a holiday, you know. I'm looking after Mummy.'

But Camilla had said she was looking after *her*. Couldn't anyone tell the truth any more? Including him?

233

'OK, everyone. Let's get into pairs.' Andy glanced at the tutor's notes to make sure he was getting this right. 'We're going to be doing a listening exercise. One of us is going to be a stroppy teenager and the other is going to be a parent. The idea is that the parent has to resist the temptation to butt in; instead, they have to listen to what the teenager is saying.'

If only they knew, thought Andy, what a hypocrite he was!

'I'll pair up with you,' purred Audrey.

Uh oh. Was he imagining it or did she have a crush on him? She'd been hanging on to his every word during the feedback session. And now she had pulled her chair right up close. 'Do you want to go first?' she trilled.

Andy took a deep breath. 'OK. I'm, er, a stroppy teenage daughter.'

She clapped her hands together. 'I love it already!'

'How dare you barge into my room like that!' Andy heard Nattie's voice coming out of his mouth. 'Aren't I entitled to any privacy?'

'Very realistic, if you don't mind me saying!'

'If I want to have a shower with a friend, that's up to me.'

Audrey's eyes were opening wide. 'Imaginative!'

'And yes, I *was* surfing the net when I should have been doing my homework just now. But sometimes I need a break, just like you need a break from the office.'

More nodding from Audrey. 'I get that. Sorry! I'll keep quiet. You've finished? Really? I don't know much about your girls even though I'm on the PTA with Pamela. Keeps her cards quite close to her chest, doesn't she? But if I didn't know better, I'd think you were basing it on real experience! Shall we swap places now?'

She stood up and managed to knock into him. 'Sorry! Mmm. You smell nice. Is that Hugo Boss cologne?'

Andy felt unsettled all through the post-exercise discussion. It wasn't just Audrey's open admiration; he'd had to bat away that sort of thing for years in the office. It was the way he had felt indignant on behalf of both his daughters during the role play. He could sort of see where they were coming from. They did need their privacy. Up to a point. And if they didn't make their own mistakes, without him interfering, how would they learn?

'Have I missed something?' The mother who flitted between his class and Judith's slid into the classroom. 'Sorry but I got caught up with this amazing role play. I was a screaming toddler!' She beamed. 'They couldn't stop me yelling! It was brilliant! Really therapeutic!'

'Actually, you're just in time for the relaxation exercise.' This bit, with its physical contact, really made him squirm, but the handbook said it was important. 'Let's hold hands, everyone, and visualise what it would be like to return home to a peaceful family without any arguments.'

Audrey didn't need asking twice. 'I loved the way you listened to me, Andy,' she gushed, squeezing his hand so tightly that his wedding ring cut into his flesh. 'No one else does that to me. I really enjoyed our session tonight! You've got a gift for teaching. An absolute gift!'

'Actually,' he tried to say, 'it's not teaching. It's simply facilitating.'

'Nonsense!' There was a shake of that red mane. 'Pamela is a lucky woman!' Her eyes flickered for a minute. 'A really lucky woman, under the circumstances.'

What circumstances? Andy went cold. 'I'm not sure what you mean.'

'Really?' Audrey smiled. 'Then I've said too much. After all, they're only rumours and you shouldn't believe gossip, should you?' Then she was gone in a waft of perfume and hair shaking before Andy could ask more.

'Finished talking to your admirer now, have you?' Kieran was smirking beside him. Thank goodness the classroom was empty now. 'Then you're ready for that chat, are you? Your local or mine? We agreed your local, didn't we?'

'Neither.' Andy couldn't risk being overheard. 'We'll go out of town.'

Kieran's eyes narrowed. 'Don't want to risk your reputation?

Frankly, I can't blame you. Come on then. I've always fancied a ride in a fancy car like yours.'

They ended up at the same place that he and Bobbie had gone to the other day. If only he was here with her now instead of this monster. Because that's what Kieran was. A monster! Every now and then, Andy allowed himself to think what had happened that night. When he did, the horrifying memories were always mixed up with that distinctive odour of urine and cabbage and Brussels sprouts; funnily enough that was exactly what he could smell now, sitting opposite Kieran.

'I reckon it's meant that our paths crossed again,' Kieran said, slurping the pint that Andy had bought him. It left a froth on his upper lip; something that Andy chose not to point out.

'Meant?'

'That's right. I found God a few years ago. When I got married to the missus.'

'You didn't tell her what happened, did you?' broke in Andy, appalled.

'Nah. She wouldn't get it. But she's Catholic, the missus. So she got me into going to church. It's great, Andy. You go, do you?'

Andy thought briefly of Midnight Mass, which he and Pamela always attended with the girls because it was the thing to do. A perfect family. Neatly dressed. Christmas lunch cooking slowly in the Aga for the next day. 'Not much, to be honest.'

'You ought to try it.' He took another enthusiastic slurp. 'Any road, the priest wiped my slate clean. Said God understood cos I said I was sorry.'

'Sorry!' Andy felt sick. 'You think that saying sorry is enough?'

Kieran's eyes grew even piggier. 'I know what you mean, mate. It's always on your conscience, isn't it? That's when I began to think of the alternative.'

That sick feeling got worse. 'What alternative?'

236

'Don't you see, mate? We've got to go to the police. Tell them what we did. Face up to our responsibilities.'

'What *we* did? What *they* did, you mean.'

Kieran's eyes narrowed even more. 'You were there, mate. Like me. We were up to our eyeballs. We could have stopped them.'

'I tried!'

'Yeah, well, blubbing wasn't enough, was it? Nah.' Kieran stood up. 'I reckon that if your missus and kids knew what you were like as a kid, they wouldn't have much to do with you.'

So that was it! He was blackmailing him. In a way, that was a relief. Frankly Andy would give away any amount of money to shut him up. 'How much do you want?'

Kieran laughed loudly; so much so that the drinkers at the table next to him turned round to stare. If he wasn't mistaken, they were the same people who had been there when he'd had a drink with Bobbie.

'I don't want money! I want justice. If I'm going to confess – and that's what the priest says I've got to do if my soul is going to get saved – I'm taking you down with me.'

He shook his head. 'Let's face it, mate. Murder is pretty serious. Isn't it?'

ALL TOO TRUE . . .

'Parents are the bones on which kids cut their teeth.'
Peter Ustinov

'A parent is allowed to embarrass the kids. It's a perk of the job. And one that you can't be taxed for.'
Anon

'Parenthood is the one job you can never get sacked from. But sometimes we should be.'
Anon

Chapter 22

BOBBIE

'Hi, everyone!'

Judith Davies looked a bit nervous. That usually bright smile of hers seemed to have dimmed, although when she saw Vanessa in the circle, she gave a little tilt of the head in recognition of their chat on the train.

It was weird meeting teachers outside school. Made them seem more normal; more like approachable human beings instead of kids in charge of your own kids.

'How did we get on with our half-term diaries, everyone?'

'Absolutely brilliantly, thanks!'

Bobbie and Vanessa rolled eyes. Perfect Dad, as they called him, had turned up at the second session and always announced that everything was brilliant. He and Perfect Mum took it in turns to come to the parenting classes because, as they announced smugly, they didn't like the idea of babysitters. She wasn't so bad but Bobbie had disliked *him* on the spot.

Mr P. was one of those five-foot-nothing men who seemed to think he needed to make up for his size with a very loud mouth. And he was always telling poor Judith Davies how to do it. Clearly he was here to *give* advice rather than receive it.

'My wife and I thought the diary was a great idea although I would like to make one small suggestion. We got the twins to write down *their* feelings too!' He was standing up on a chair, waving an open page at them. 'Like this entry last Thursday. We had a bit of a discussion about whether our youngest (he's the one who was born three minutes later if you remember) should have natural yoghurt or raspberry for supper. He wanted raspberry, you see, but the eldest had his eye on it too. So the wife divided both pots in half and gave them a mixture. She wrote down in the diary that she felt she'd reached a happy compromise. Then the kids wrote down their feelings.'

Boring! Boring!

Miss Davies's eyes were glazed too. 'Thank you for sharing this with us. I will certainly bear your adaptation of the exercise in mind for future classes. Anyone else like to read out their diaries?'

There was no way, thought Bobbie, that she was going to talk about the kids playing up in the shop; not with her new boss sitting next to her. Or about that other worry that had emerged recently and which she kept pushing to the back of her mind.

Vanessa had already told her on the way in that she certainly wasn't going to 'share' that awful experience about losing Sunshine on the Underground. There were some things, they both agreed, that had to be kept quiet. Looked as though the others felt the same, judging from the nervous shuffling around on seats.

'Is that all?' Judith looked disappointed. 'Let's start with role play. As usual, one of us is to be the child and the other, the parent. But I'd like you to choose a different partner from last time.'

Bobbie threw a look of sheer panic at Vanessa. Over the weeks, the two women had grown quite comfortable doing the exercises with each other; especially as Sunshine was now really quite good friends with Jack and Daisy. In fact, her two were over at Vanessa's house right now. She only hoped that Vanessa's neighbour was coping with Jack, who was on a sugar high, thanks to some disgusting sweets that Rob had brought home after work the other day. (If he thought that could make up for not being around enough, he was wrong!)

Now Vanessa was being teamed up with Too Many Kids Mum, while Bobbie was with Mr Perfect. This was going to be fun. Not.

'I'd like the "children" to act out a chore,' trilled Miss Davies. 'It might be homework or tidying their room or washing up.'

Bobbie laughed. 'My lot don't do any of those things.'

'Really?' Mr Perfect frowned.

'Are you all listening?' Judith shot her a disappointed look. At times, Bobbie felt this inexplicable urge to act up in parenting class and play the fool, just to lighten the atmosphere. Was this how Jack felt?

'The parent', continued Judith, 'has to find fault with everything that the "child" is doing. Feel free to be really critical!'

That shouldn't be difficult!

But Mr Perfect was scratching his head. 'My wife and I never criticise the kids. We don't need to.'

'Then why are you here?' demanded Bobbie irritably.

'We don't like to think we might be missing out on something.'

Another competitive parent!

'After you, Bobs.' He gave a mock bow. 'I'll be the adult. Time for homework! Have you started it yet?'

Bobs! No one called her that. Not even in role play. Grumpily sitting down at one of the child-sized tables, she pretended to write. Mr Perfect was hovering behind; she almost felt his breath on her shoulder.

'Why don't you hold your pencil this way, Bob! Then your writing will be neater.'

Was he acting yet or just interfering?

'And don't look so closely at your work, Bobs, or you'll give yourself eye strain.'

'But I don't understand what it says!' Even as she spoke, it came to her. Wasn't that what Jack had said the other night when struggling with geography homework?

'Why not?' snapped Mr Perfect.

Oh dear. Just what she'd said to her son. 'I wasn't listening properly.' Jack again.

Mr Perfect's voice was shocked. 'Then you should have been!'

That had been her answer too.

'OK, everyone,' trilled Judith. 'How did that make us all feel?'

Bobbie found herself putting up her hand, bashfully. 'I don't know about the rest of you but I felt rather demoralised.'

'Really?' asked Perfect Dad, frowning.

'Don't take it personally.' She looked away from him, suddenly feeling horribly embarrassed. 'But it did make me realise what it was like to be criticised.'

Judith clapped her hands as though Bobbie had just won the prize in pass the parcel. 'Criticism does make us feel down, doesn't it? And that's where positive praise comes in! Remember that from the first session? Great. Next week, we're going to look at . . .'

But Bobbie wasn't listening. Instead, all she wanted to do was to get back to Vanessa's and collect the kids. She'd try not to have a go at them tonight. She really would.

'What do you mean you didn't finish your homework?'

'You know you're not allowed to watch Adult Only films.' (She hadn't expected Vanessa to have *those* kind of DVDs.)

'Why did you tell the babysitter you were starving?'

'Don't undo your safety belt, Jack. We're not home yet.'

By the end of the evening, Bobbie's voice was sore with nagging. All her good intentions from class had faded in the battle to get the children home and to bed. Even though it was so late – gone ten o'clock! – both seemed to have found another rush of energy.

'No, Jack, you can't have chocolate spread on toast. There're only a few hours until breakfast. AND GET OFF YOUR SKATEBOARD!'

'Can we have pizza instead?' This was Daisy.

'No! It's too late.'

'So?' Her daughter pouted. 'Did you know that Americans eat three hundred and fifty slices of pizza every second? It says so on Google.'

Talking of pizza, Rob's dinner was all crisped up at the

bottom of the oven. Where on earth was he? Bobbie had a flash of Mr and Mrs Perfect sitting up and eating nicely together. She and Vanessa might take the mickey out of them but every now and then, she did wonder what it would be like to have a husband who was more hands-on. Like Andy for instance. She'd hoped to catch a word with him after the session but he'd rushed off with a wave and something that sounded like 'I'll give you a ring soon.'

Bobbie hoped so. She'd been flattered when he'd confided in her the other night and it had been nice to confide in him too. Meanwhile, the kids were actually asleep, unless they were pretending again, and there was still no sign of Rob.

She felt slightly sick. After all, if Pamela could play around, why not her brother?

'Any chance of you doing another day?' asked Vanessa the next day. 'Only I've got some important business to sort out.'

Something was definitely going on. Bobbie was sure of it. Her new friend seemed extremely distracted and not like her usual self. She'd even seen her snapping at little Sunshine the other day after school because the child had left her homework behind.

'Everything all right?' she'd asked but Vanessa had given her a cool look.

'Why shouldn't it be?'

Still, Bobbie wasn't complaining. She really loved working in the shop. It wasn't just the thrill of getting out of the house instead of being stuck on the phone at home. It was the clothes. Bobbie had loved fashion as a young girl but since the kids had come along, there was never much over at the end of the month for buying non-essentials – not with the price of children's shoes.

But here at Vanessa's, she could try things on when it was quiet and pretend that she was going out. Bobbie did a bit of a twirl in front of the mirror. The red suited her! She could be a different Bobbie. Someone who was about to go to the races, especially if she added this hat. She would stand in the hospitality tent (Rob was always talking about hospitality tents) with a glass of Pimm's in her hand.

By her side would be Andy – no! Where had that come from? By her side would be Rob. Not the always-tired, always-critical Rob but the old one, before the children had been born.

They would . . .

'Hello? Anyone there?'

Quickly, Bobbie slipped out of the sleek, chic red outfit and back into her own navy trousers. She had a customer! Two actually! Goodness, there was a crowd of them! Talk about three double-chins coming at once!

'I'm off to Marbella,' said one in a rather haughty voice that reminded her of Camilla. 'Someone told me that you have some rather nice outfits here. Not that I've ever bought anything second-hand before, of course.'

Everyone said that. It was a bit like parenting class. Most people felt rather awkward going but when they got there, they were surprised at what they could pick up.

For the next hour, Bobbie was up to her eyes. Many customers seemed to be preparing for an Easter break in the sun or going to the big fund-raising ball at the golf club. It was like being Cinderella but actually she was having a ball herself! She loved the challenge of persuading a woman to try on an outfit that had previously been ignored on the rail.

'This is perfect!' trilled one of the members of the PTA. 'You are clever!'

Bobbie flushed with pleasure. How nice it was to be appreciated!

'Good heavens!' said an older woman, taking down a very boring brown jumper from the size-14 rail. 'I swear this is the top I gave to my daughter-in-law last year. If it is, it's extremely rude of her. Can you give me the name of the seller?'

Bobbie had been warned about this by Vanessa. It wasn't the first time that unwanted gifts had been discovered by their original donors, just as *she'd* found that cardigan she'd bought Pamela. 'I'm afraid that's confidential.'

'Anyone seen a brown suede jacket?' demanded the haughty Marbella voice.

'Sorry.' Bobbie called up from the rails. 'I sold it half an hour ago.'

'SOLD!' The voice sliced through the surrounding chitter chatter, leaving a scared silence. 'But it's mine! I left it here on a rail while trying something on because the changing rooms were full.'

Shit. It hadn't had a price tag on, that was true, but Bobbie had presumed Vanessa had simply forgotten to label it and had used her 'discretion' in fixing a price.

'You'd better get it back right now!' thundered Lady Marbella. 'Who did you sell it to?'

'I'm not sure.' Bobbie could hardly believe this was happening to her. Her concentration – not to mention her memory – had been all over the place recently. And that Dr Know business didn't help. He was in the papers again today; this time about a provocative remark he'd made concerning ten-year-olds and straitjackets. 'She's not one of our regulars. At least I don't think she is.'

'Then find out her details from her card or cheque or however she paid you!'

'I can't,' quaked Bobbie, feeling a wave of nausea. 'She paid cash!'

There was a shocked silence again followed by urgent giggles and whispers from everyone else in the shop. 'This is outrageous!' Lady Marbella flung the dress she'd been about to buy on the ground and flashed her a furious look. 'Where is your boss?'

'She'll be in tomorrow.'

'Then so will I! Trust me. You haven't heard the last of this. And I shall tell everyone I know that this place is no more than an amateur second-hand place that sells the very clothes off your back!'

With that, she marched out. Bobbie quaked as she dialled Vanessa's mobile only to find that it went straight through to answerphone. Now she'd really done it.

Vanessa's phone still wasn't picking up by the time she got home. She'd have to go into the shop first thing to explain, Bobbie told herself. Meanwhile, the children were, for a change, behaving really well. Amazingly, they went to bed when she asked them.

Were they ill?

Still, it meant she had time to ring Mum. Even if Mum didn't have time to talk to her.

'Can't chat just now, darling! Herbert and I are on our way out. He's so looking forward to meeting you.'

Why can't you listen? she wanted to say. Is that so hard to do? But at least it gave her a bit longer to prepare dinner. A special dinner with candles in a bid to make a real effort.

'What's all this about?' asked Rob bemused when he got back dead on nine; just as he'd promised.

Bobbie gave a little twirl in the red dress she'd borrowed from the shop. It was only for one evening, she told herself. No one would notice. 'Just thought it would make a change,' she said nonchalantly, lifting her head up to him for a kiss.

He brushed her cheek. 'Something smells good. Nice dress. Have I seen it before?'

'I sort of borrowed it.'

'Borrowed?'

Bobbie was beginning to feel guilty now. 'I'm testing it out. For Vanessa's shop.'

'Oh. Right.' He seemed distracted. Fiddling with his BlackBerry rather than listening to her. 'Look, I've just got to take this. Won't be long.'

For the next twenty minutes, she could hear him talking urgently from the sitting room. Keep your voice down, she wanted to say. You'll wake the children. Eventually, he came back, hands shoved in his suit pockets, looking rather subdued. 'Sorry. That was urgent.'

It always is, she almost said, but then she reminded herself: Don't criticise! Don't criticise! But despite forcing herself to keep mum, the evening was a disaster. Even though Rob had declared the lukewarm salmon pie was 'very nice', he picked at it unenthusiastically. That would teach her to make it herself. Even worse, every time she tried to talk to him, Rob's head began to drop with exhaustion. 'Rob,' she started to say and then he'd give a little start and pretend that he hadn't fallen asleep.

In the end, he did just that, right there at the table. No, she told herself, she wouldn't wake him. Frankly it was easier to clear up around him. Whoops. His mobile had fallen out of his pocket as he sat there. Picking it up, she saw that there had been a message.

Andy's words came back to her. 'Only we know what that family is really like.' Her heart thumped so hard she could hear it in her chest. Should she open it? No. Yes.

Hope it's all sorted now! A x

Hope it's all sorted now? What was? Did 'A' stand for 'Araminta'? And if so, why the kiss?

Bobbie's first instinct was to shake Rob and demand an explanation. But that would only lead to another row and that was the last thing she needed right at this moment. Perhaps she should do what Sarah had suggested weeks ago. But that was risky and possibly illegal.

God, she felt sick. And not just from nerves. Usually she loved salmon but tonight it had left a horrible metallic taste in her mouth. Bobbie stood looking at her sleeping husband. He'd been right to suspect that this dinner wasn't just her making an effort. It was also to tell him something.

Something that she'd been in denial about for a couple of weeks now. Something she could hardly believe herself. Something she'd been wanting to tell Mum and had almost told Rob. The reason why she'd been feeling nauseous and kept needing to go to the loo and would never be able to fit into those lovely cast-offs from Pamela.

She was pregnant.

MAKES YOU THINK . . .

'Every beetle is a gazelle in the eyes of its mother.'
Arab proverb

'The one thing that children wear out faster than shoes is parents.'
John J. Plomp

'Insanity is hereditary – you get it from your kids.'
Sam Levenson

Chapter 23

VANESSA

It was like waiting for a pregnancy result! When she'd suspected, all those years ago, that she'd been up the duff, Vanessa had had to twiddle her thumbs for two days before she knew for certain. She could still recall how her heart had thumped – boom, boom, boom – as she'd sat in the surgery, before the doctor had broken the news.

Harry had gone all quiet when she'd told him and then gone out to the pub to celebrate. On his own. It would be all right when the baby was born, she told herself. But it wasn't. Harry had never really bonded with Brigid. He hadn't been what you'd call a hands-on dad.

Of course it had been a terrible shock when that woman had turned up on the doorstep, claiming she was his wife, but in a way it was also a relief. Her mother (bless her soul) had been right. Harry hadn't been the right man for her.

That's why she'd been so upset when Brigid had announced she was pregnant at sixteen. 'You're going to end up like me!' she'd cried. 'A single mother. You don't realise how hard that will be!'

They were going to be talking about that in the next parenting session. She'd already read up on it in the handbook. There was a lot of stuff about how you often repeated the mistakes that your own parents made, because the pattern made you feel comfortable. It didn't make sense, when you thought about it. Why repeat something that you knew wasn't right?

But somehow you did.

And now, here she was, her pulse racing every time the

post arrived, in case there was a letter from the DNA clinic with the results. How could she cope if that weasel-faced, multi-pierced youth was Sunshine's father? 'Even if he is,' the solicitor had reminded her, 'it doesn't necessarily mean that he will get custody. Remember how I said the court always puts the child's interests first?'

But he might well get access! The law was also, apparently, very keen for a child to have a 'suitable' male figure in his/her life. Surely Weasel Face wasn't suitable with his tattoos and piercings? The solicitor had smiled wryly. 'You'd be surprised. There's no rhyme or reason in this game.'

Game? Vanessa had bristled at that. This was no game! This was her granddaughter they were talking about! A child who was really blossoming now. Always telling the same joke, the way kids do.

'Van Van! Why did the banana go to the hospital?' Then, before Vanessa could reply, Sunshine would jump in and say: 'Because it wasn't peeling very well!' Each time, Vanessa had to laugh and pretend she hadn't heard it before.

'Sunshine's a popular little girl, isn't she?' Miss Davies often said.

She certainly was. Vanessa was always being asked in the playground if her 'daughter' could come round to tea. 'Goodness, you look too young to be a granny!' one mother said, which made Vanessa feel rather good about herself.

Naturally, all the guests had be invited back. She'd been worried about this at first; for a start, it meant closing the shop earlier unless Bobbie was able to help out. 'What will your friends want to do?' she'd asked Sunshine.

'Watch the Sky!' she'd retorted.

But Vanessa had got them to make fairy cakes instead in her little kitchen, which went down so well that the mothers all asked for the recipe. 'My au pair doesn't know how to make them and I haven't baked a cake for years,' said one woman, who was a stockbroker. 'Such a clever idea of yours. My son loved it!'

Yet still there was no letter. 'I'm sorry,' said the clinic

receptionist, when Vanessa rang yet again. 'We've got a real backlog at the moment: everyone's having them.'

She spoke as though having a DNA test was a fashionable thing to do. Had the world gone mad? Was it that hard to know who was the father nowadays? In the meantime, she had to sort out the problem of the suede jacket. Lady Marbella, as Bobbie called her, was understandably furious. 'What are you going to do about it? That jacket cost me an absolute fortune!'

Vanessa felt tempted to point out that she'd actually sold the jacket to her in the first place, at a very reasonable price, but it wasn't the point. 'I hope you're going to sack your assistant,' Lady Marbella had thundered.

Poor Bobbie feared the same thing and had even offered to pay for it out of her wages. But no, Vanessa told both of them, mistakes were made sometimes. It was extremely unfortunate but the shop *had* been very busy at the time. Perhaps Madam would like to choose something else instead. Anything. Yes, even that evening dress with the matching shoes and bag that was an original Zandra Rhodes. Of course, in return, Vanessa would be grateful if Madam didn't carry out her threat to 'badmouth' the shop. After all, that could be construed as slander, could it not?

It seemed to work. Trade was busier than ever. Perhaps rumour had spread about the jacket incident and everyone else was hoping for an original Zandra Rhodes dress? Certainly, she'd had to remind more than one customer that they'd 'accidentally' left the clothes that they'd come in with on the sale rail.

Despite that one cock-up, Bobbie had proved to be a dab hand in the shop. She had a great sense of colour even though she herself had been looking rather wan recently. 'Just tired,' she said, brushing Vanessa's concern away. But her own instinct told her it was more than that. She was genuinely worried and, from a selfish point of view, she needed her help. It meant Vanessa could reduce her own hours to do things with Sunshine, like go swimming.

That had been a real revelation. 'Where's the sea?' her granddaughter had been saying again and again, ever since she'd arrived.

'We don't have it here,' she'd replied, amused, but Sunshine hadn't been convinced.

'The sea, the sea!' she kept repeating wistfully.

Then one day, they'd passed a sign advertising the sports complex just outside town. There was a poster of some children sliding down a water chute. Vanessa loathed swimming: in fact, embarrassed as she was to admit it, she'd never learned as a child. But Sunshine was jumping up and down. 'Sunshine wants to go! Now, Van Van. *Please!*'

When she really wanted something, Vanessa had noticed, her granddaughter adopted baby language. Reluctantly, she had taken her there, loathing the smell of chlorine which reminded her of all the swimming lessons she'd had as a child; none of which had done the trick.

'Come back,' she called out to Sunshine as they stepped through the foot bowl. But she was off! Straight in, swimming like a little fish! Vanessa stood on the side, gobsmacked. She was incredible! Oh my God! There was a flash of red bathing suit haring off to the deep end. 'Sunshine, don't dive!'

But there she was! Poised on the edge of the springboard; so full of confidence. 'Practising for the next Olympics is she, your daughter?' demanded a clever-looking mother with steamed-up glasses whom Vanessa vaguely recognised from the teenage parenting class up the corridor.

'I wouldn't be surprised.' Vanessa didn't bother correcting her about their relationship.

'You swim too, Van Van,' urged Sunshine, who'd covered the entire length of the pool in the time it had taken Vanessa to catch her breath.

'I can't.' She stood in the water, shivering in her one piece, conscious of what was – or rather wasn't – underneath it. 'I'll just watch.'

Somehow she felt safer here within reach of her grand-daughter, rather than watching from the spectators' gallery.

Even if she couldn't swim herself, at least she was close.

'It's easy,' Sunshine urged. 'Look, Mummy showed me when I was little. You just put your right arm out like this and then your left. Kick your legs at the same time.'

Goodness! Brigid had taught her daughter something that she, Vanessa, hadn't been able to do. 'You did well,' she murmured. 'Very well. But for God's sake get in touch, will you?'

Yet still there was nothing, from either Brigid or the clinic. Sometimes, Vanessa would wake in the night in a pool of terror, convinced that something awful had happened. At other times, she felt furious with her daughter for going off on some jaunt with a boyfriend, abandoning her own child.

Meanwhile, it wasn't long until Brian was coming round.

'We won't be able to do anything, you know!' she said bluntly on the phone when they made arrangements. Best to make it plain from the start. 'Not with Sunshine here.'

'Hey!' He sounded offended. 'I'm not just after your stunning body, you know!'

Stunning? Was he taking the mickey?

'I mean it, Vanessa. You're gorgeous and it's about time you realised it. Besides, I told you. I need to come round to show you this idea of mine.'

However hard she pushed, he refused to tell her what it was all about. Vanessa felt quite excited; almost in a childlike way. 'I've got a friend coming to dinner,' she told Sunshine the following evening when she'd given up trying to get her to bed. Sky had a lot to answer for.

'Is it a man friend?' asked Sunshine without taking her eyes off the screen.

Might as well come clean. 'Yes it is. His name is Brian. He's the friend you saw before.'

'Mummy has a man friend too.'

Vanessa's heart skipped a beat. 'What's your mummy's friend called?'

'Simon,' said Sunshine, as though that was obvious.

Vanessa knelt down next to her. 'And does Simon live with you?'

'No, silly!' Sunshine giggled. 'He's married to someone else.'

She might have guessed it! 'Is that why Mummy sent you here?' Vanessa asked, her mouth dry.

Sunshine shrugged. 'Simon said it was best if I left.'

How awful. Yet wasn't this just what she'd feared? Vanessa put her arm around her grandchild and held her tightly, breathing in her smell.

'You're hurting me!' Sunshine pushed her away. Then she frowned. 'Will your friend want me to go away too?'

What a question! The poor kid, she must feel so insecure! 'Of course he won't,' retorted Vanessa indignantly. As she spoke, there was a knock on the door. 'There he is now.'

Sunshine's face had gone tight. Too late, Vanessa realised this wasn't a good idea. Maybe she'd explain the situation to Brian. Ask him to go home. He'd understand. She was sure he would. And if he didn't, well, that was too bad. Her granddaughter had to come first.

'I'm sorry . . .' she began, opening the door. Then she looked down and gasped. 'Are you mad, Brian?'

His eyes twinkled. 'I told you it was a surprise. I also asked you to think about it before you said no.'

He stopped at the rush of light footsteps behind her. 'A *dog*!' Sunshine's eyes were out on stalks. Throwing herself to the ground, she flung her arms around the little black puppy who had, Vanessa had to admit, the cutest face she had ever seen. 'Don't do that,' she squealed, pulling her granddaughter away. 'He might bite!'

'Nonsense.' Brian laughed. 'This one's got a heart of gold.'

'We can't possibly keep him! I'm at work all day. It wouldn't be fair!'

'I'm not suggesting you do.' Brian was more serious now. 'Bingo's mine, aren't you, lad? A mate of mine's dog had puppies and, call me soft, I've taken one on. But I also thought that you might like me to bring him round every now and then.' His eyes twinkled. 'Now he's had his jabs, we can go for walks. And he might be a pal for this little lady here. By the way, I don't think we've been introduced. Not properly.'

He held out his hand to Sunshine who was still sitting with her arms wrapped around the puppy. 'My name's Brian.'

'I'm Sunshine,' she answered gravely. 'Nice to meet you.'

Vanessa glowed at her granddaughter's good manners.

'Please come in.' Sunshine had jumped up now and was pulling Bingo by his little red lead inside the hall. 'He *can* come in too, can't he, Van Van?'

Vanessa had to admit that it was a brilliant idea after all. Sunshine had fallen asleep on the floor in front of the television, snuggled up against Bingo, after 'talking' to him all evening. 'Do you have brothers and sisters?' she asked. 'I don't. I just have my Van Van. Where do you sleep at night? Under the stars, like my dog at home with Mummy?'

'I didn't know you had a dog, Sunshine,' Vanessa had said.

'I had to leave him behind.'

She spoke in that voice that Vanessa had learned to recognise: it sounded as though she didn't mind but underneath, it was hurting. Now, as she carried her sleeping grandchild to bed, Vanessa felt a huge lump in her throat. 'It was good of you to think of us,' she said, returning to Brian in the lounge.

He looked pleased. 'Glad I've done something right. Thought I might have messed everything up when we almost got found out in bed.' He gave her a nudge. 'And don't look so worried. I'm not going to ravage you again, much as I'd like to. Not when Poppet is in the house, anyway.'

Then he kissed her. A lovely warm slow kiss that made her melt inside. 'You're a lovely woman, know that? But I'm going to go now before I do something I shouldn't, despite what I just said.'

How tempting it was to ask him to stay, but no. It was better that she saw him to the door. 'See you,' she said hopefully. Then she spotted a figure hovering by her little gate. No mistaking that weasel face and earrings. It was Jason!

What was he doing here? And how dare he walk right up to her as though she'd asked him in?

He grinned, showing his horrible teeth, a disgusting mixture of black and yellow. 'Thought I'd come round and see my daughter.'

What a bloody cheek! After last time too! 'We don't know she's your daughter until the results come. And besides, it's late. She's in bed. Stop harassing me like this.'

Brian laid a hand on her shoulder protectively. 'You heard the lady. Now clear off, Jason, or I'll call the police.'

The youth spat on the ground. 'Is that so? Maybe it's me as should call the cops. I don't like the idea of my daughter being in a house with an old woman and her bit of rough.'

'How dare you?' Brian pushed the boy away. Not hard but firmly enough to send him reeling on to the verge.

'Oy! You can't boss me around now!' He scowled. 'I could report you for this, you know!'

'Go ahead.' Brian tightened his arm around her. 'It's all right, Vanessa. He won't trouble you again. Not while I'm breathing.'

But somehow she wasn't so sure.

Later that night, Sunshine called out in her sleep.

'Shhh,' Vanessa soothed, lying next to her and holding her in her arms. 'It's all right, Van Van's here.' She lay there for some time, until certain that the child was breathing peacefully. Then she gently eased herself off the bed, taking care not to wake her. As she did so, she knocked her left breast on the side table. Ouch. That hurt.

Cupping it with her hand, she froze. There was something hard there! Something, she was certain, that hadn't been present the other week when she'd checked herself. It was only the size of a pea but it was definitely hard. With a rather uneven shape.

Oh God! she whispered as all the old fears came flooding back. Please. Not a lump. Not now.

MORE KIDS' STUFF

'Having a family is like having a bowling alley installed in your brain.'

Martin Mull

'The secret of dealing successfully with a child is not to be its parent.'

Mel Lazarus

'Always end the name of your child with a vowel, so that when you yell, the name will carry.'

Bill Cosby

PERFECT PARENTS: SESSION SIX

WHAT WERE *YOU* LIKE AS A CHILD?

HOW COULD YOUR PARENTS HAVE DONE IT BETTER?

LEARN HOW TO BREAK OLD PATTERNS – AND MAKE NEW ONES !

Chapter 24

ANDY

Murder! That's what Kieran had called it. Ever since that awful day, all those years ago, Andy had convinced himself that it hadn't been his fault. But would a jury see it in the same light? Quite possibly not.

All through his teens, Andy had been on tenterhooks in case the police got on to him; jumping every time the doorbell went or the phone rang. But as time passed, he learned to imagine a massive steel mental door coming down between him and his fears.

Now and then, however, a chink opened in that door, especially when Camilla was around. For some reason, Andy was convinced that his mother-in-law was suspicious of his past. Every time he saw her, he expected her to wave the newspaper cutting in front of his nose and declare that her daughter was far too good for a kid who had committed such a terrible crime.

Andy shook his head. Both at himself and this bloody vacuum cleaner which wouldn't turn itself on. It had been almost a week now since Kieran had threatened him. He had to do something about it. Had to nip it in the bud before Pamela got to know – or the kids.

'Dad! I can't believe you've been so stupid!'

Andy froze and then turned round slowly to face his younger daughter who had her arms folded and a disapproving look on her fifteen-year-old face. 'What do you mean?' he said faintly.

'Put the washing machine on sixty. You've ruined the top I was going to wear tonight.'

Andy breathed a sigh of relief.

'And as for the vacuum, you're going to break it if you do it that way! Mrs C. will kill you. Let me do it!'

Nattie yanked the handle away from him. 'Honestly, Dad. When are you going to go back to work? If you're going to hang around all day, can't you go to the golf club or something?'

'I've told you,' he faltered. 'I like being at home. And besides, it's good for us, isn't it?'

Nattie threw him a you-can't-fool me look. 'You just don't trust us on our own here, do you? Not like Mum does. She lets us get on with it because she remembers what it was like to be a teenager. She says we need to find our own way, instead of being told what to do like her own dad did with her and Uncle Rob.'

Really? Pamela had never explained that to him.

'She says that we're bound to make mistakes but that's how we're going to learn.' Nattie's voice rose over the sound of the vacuum cleaner. He had never heard her sound so passionate about anything before, unless it was about an increase in her allowance.

Then she turned it off and put her arms around him just as she used to do when she was little. 'I'm sorry about the other evening. But didn't you ever do stuff you regretted when you were my age?'

Andy nodded, not daring to say anything.

'What?' Nattie was looking at him with an amused expression in her eyes. 'Forget to hand your homework in on time?'

If only she knew!

'That's the thing, Dad.' Nattie was turning back to the vacuum cleaner. 'That's why it's so hard for us all, including Mum. You expect us to be perfect, just like her dad did. But we're not. And now you're at home all the time, we can't hide it like we used to.'

Andy found his voice. 'I'm glad. It's not right to hide things. And I *don't* expect you to be perfect.'

Nattie frowned. 'I think you do, Dad. Mum feels you do. That's why she's gone away; it's not just to look after Granny, or so that you can see what it's like. It's so she can have a break.'

So his girls were in on this too!

Does Mum have a boyfriend? That's what he really wanted to ask. But there were some things that a parent should never ask a child.

'Why didn't she tell me then?' Even as he spoke, Andy felt stupid. He shouldn't have to ask his daughter what his wife was thinking.

Nattie shrugged. 'Maybe she thought you wouldn't listen.'

Listen! Just what they'd been doing at school! Oh God. School. He'd promised to give Kieran an answer after parenting class tomorrow night. What the fuck was he going to say?

'Tonight, we're not going to follow the handbook,' said Andy, sitting on the edge of the desk in front of the horseshoe of chairs. 'We're going to do something a bit different.'

There was a ripple of excitement, which made him feel good about himself. In a funny way, he was glad to be here. It was refreshing to be out of the house. After years of that, he loved being at home. But he could see why women got bored. Could understand why Pamela had had enough.

'A bit different?' repeated Audrey, eyes shining with unadulterated admiration. 'I love a man who does the unexpected,' she whispered loudly to no one in particular.

'Those of you who have already read ahead—'

'I have!' chirped Audrey.

'Teacher's pet,' muttered someone.

Andy chose to ignore the interruption but felt himself sweat with embarrassment. 'Those of you who have already read ahead', he continued, 'will know that we are meant to be talking about our own experiences as teenagers and how our parents – or whoever looked after us – dealt with them.'

'I've got plenty to say about that one,' whispered Paula, who worked with Jilly from the au pair agency.

'But I've decided we're going to skip that bit.'

There was a loud murmur of dissent. 'I was looking forward to this,' pouted Audrey. 'It really got me thinking.'

'Me too,' said someone else.

Andy sneaked a look at Kieran. The man was grinning nastily. 'Don't want to go down memory lane, eh? Tell you what, mate, why don't we all get up, one after the other, and tell the whole class about our teenage experiences?'

'Brilliant!' trilled Bohemian Mum. 'I was talking to my daughter the other night – well, rowing actually – and she said I didn't understand what it was like to be a teenager.' She gave a nervous laugh. 'She has no idea!'

There was another ripple of excitement. 'I know what you mean!' The redhead nodded excitedly. 'They think we were born middle-aged.'

'Exactly,' said the woman with all the kids, ready to dash down to the junior section. 'My daughter still doesn't believe that I once saw the Clash!'

'Nor do I,' muttered someone else.

'All right.' Andy threw Kieran a challenging look. 'Who'd like to go first?'

'I will!' The redhead leaped up. 'When I was fourteen, I stole twenty quid from my mum's purse. That was a lot in those days.'

'Why?' asked the woman by the door.

'So I could go on a day out with my friends to Minehead. I'd saved some money from my summer job but it wasn't enough.'

Really? She seemed far too proper and upright to steal from her parents. 'What did your mother do when she found out?' asked Andy curiously.

'Told me to wait until my father got home.' She made a rueful face. 'I was sent to my bedroom for a week: they left my meals outside the door.'

'Did it work?' demanded Mum.

Audrey's eyes narrowed. 'No way. As soon as I could, I left home. I felt dirty, you see. Ashamed of myself. Even now,

I've still not forgotten it.' She flushed. 'I feel bad, telling you lot, but in a way, it's also cathartic.'

Several heads nodded. 'What would you have liked your parents to do?' asked Andy gently.

'Talk it through with me instead of yelling. My dad never wanted me to go to Minehead anyway. Didn't trust me, he said. Thought I'd get into bed with the first boy I met.' Her voice was rising in anger. 'Said I was no better than a tart. That's why I don't see anything of him any more.'

'That's sad,' said Jilly. She was right. Maybe, Andy wondered, that was why Audrey flirted. Perhaps her self-esteem was low and she needed constant approval. Bloody hell, what was coming over him! This course was turning him into a flipping psychologist. Perhaps he could make a living out of it, like Dr Know.

'So in a way, I lived up to my reputation. I'm on my third marriage now.' She smiled challengingly. 'If I hadn't nicked that twenty quid, life might have been very different.'

Wow! That made him see her in a totally different light. Out of the corner of his eye, Andy could see Kieran bursting to speak. There was no way he was letting that happen. Who knew what he might come out with? 'I need to confess,' Kieran had said. Well, not here, he wasn't.

'Let's throw it open for discussion, shall we?' suggested Andy. 'The handbook suggests that we tell our children what it was like when our parents brought us up.'

'Wait a bit, mate! What if we didn't have parents?' Kieran was standing up and looking around for mass effect. 'I was in a care home meself.'

There was a wave of 'poor you's. Sweat began to trickle down Andy's back.

'But it didn't harm me!'

Who was he kidding?

'I was a good lad.'

What?

Kieran now fixed Andy with a steady gaze, daring him to disagree. 'That's why I don't hold with all this psychological stuff you lot are coming out with. I reckon it depends on the kid's personality and not where they come from. My own lad's quite a good 'un, actually. Though my missus's son can be a bit of a handful. Just as well he lives with his dad.'

'Is that why you're here?' asked Jilly from the agency.

'In a way. My own lad's only thirteen but he might change when he's a bit older.' His eyes narrowed as he focused on Andy again. 'Did you find that with your girls? Mel and Natasha, isn't it?'

Andy bristled. How dare he talk like that? And how did he know their names?

The others could feel the tension; you could tell from the way Audrey was frowning. 'I think we're getting away from the subject,' she said, giving him a sympathetic look. 'Why don't you tell us about *your* childhood, Andy?'

'Yeah!' Kieran was grinning. 'Why don't you, Barry – sorry – Andy!'

Andy suddenly felt very calm. Very together, as though someone else had taken over. 'All right, I will.' He was looking straight back at Kieran now, hearing his own voice speak steadily. 'I wasn't brought up by my parents either. Someone else brought me up.' An image of himself as a young boy flashed into his head: crew cut; tough face to hide the fear inside. 'Unfortunately, I fell into the wrong crowd.'

As he spoke, he was aware of a weird sense of relief. The guilt began to fall away from him like well-cooked meat from the bone. 'When I was twelve, someone in my gang suggested that we—'

Kieran's face was white. 'Maybe you ought to stop here, mate. I was wrong just now. You're the leader, Andy. It's not right to expect you to tell us stuff.'

'No!' Audrey was sitting forward in her chair, mouth open in expectation. 'I think you're wonderful, Andy, to share this with us. Please. Go on.'

For a minute, Kieran's interruption had made him lose his

nerve but now Andy could see that this was the only way to feel right about himself again. Whatever the consequences.

'The gang wanted me to—'

'What the fuck was that?' Kieran jumped up as though he'd been shot.

'The alarm bell!' The woman at the door with all the kids – was she still here? – was nervously looking up and down the corridor as a loud persistent clang reverberated around them. 'I wonder what's happened?'

Everyone started to gather their things. 'I think we ought to evacuate the classroom,' said Andy, trying to remember Judith Davies's instructions 'in case of emergency'. 'It might just be a practice but you never know.'

As he made his way to the playground, Andy was aware of Kieran jostling along by his side. 'What the fuck was all that about?' the man hissed.

'Thought you wanted to tell the truth.'

'Not in a room full of strangers. What do you think this is? Bleeding Jerry Springer! 'Sides, I've changed my mind. The missus doesn't fancy having a husband in the nick.'

Andy looked at him with distaste. 'You never had any intention of going to the police, did you? You just wanted to make me feel uncomfortable.'

Kieran grinned. 'Succeeded, didn't I? But it still doesn't change the fact that you and I have a little secret.'

'So you *are* blackmailing me.'

Kieran sniffed. 'Well, someone like you ain't going to miss a few grand, are you?'

'Listen!' They were in the playground now, in a little huddle. The others were talking into their mobiles urgently. Hopefully they couldn't hear. Andy put his face close up against Kieran, forcing himself to eyeball him even though the proximity made him want to throw up. 'If you ever try to blackmail me or approach my wife and daughters, I'm going to make sure that the whole world knows about that night, even if it brings me down with you. Got it?'

Kieran smiled, his little piggy eyes glinting. 'Don't believe you, mate. You've got too much to lose. I want a couple of grand by next week or else. Got it?'

There was the sound of a whistle from the school buildings. It was Judith Davies. 'Sorry everyone, false alarm! Shall we go back and finish off?'

'Not me,' growled Kieran. 'I've had enough for one night. See you next week, mate. And by the way, cash will do nicely.'

Andy was walking back to his car when he felt someone touch his arm. For a split second he thought it was Kieran, waiting for him. Spinning round, he was about to seize the man by the scruff of his neck but then realised it was Bobbie.

'Sorry!' She looked pale. 'I didn't mean to startle you. You were miles away!'

She spoke lightly but it looked to Andy as though she was upset. 'Is everything all right?' he asked gently.

'Not really.' Her voice was shaky. 'I don't suppose you have time for a quick coffee, do you?'

They went to what she referred to as their 'usual' place even though they had only been there once before. The waitress gave Andy a funny look; she probably remembered him from that drink with Kieran. God, the thought of that man made his blood boil.

'It's very good of you to spare the time,' Bobbie began. Then, to his horror, she began to cry. Slow silent tears slid down her cheek.

'I've got a tissue here somewhere.' Awkwardly he began to search his pockets, hoping that the waitress wouldn't think he was responsible for her distress. 'It can't be that bad,' he said helplessly, ignoring his mobile which was vibrating in his pocket. Whoever it was could wait. There were some situations which had to come first and this was one of them.

'It is, believe me.' Bobbie shook her head. 'I'm pregnant.'

Great! The waitress chose exactly that moment to walk by! Her look said it all.

'But that's fantastic news!' he spluttered. 'Isn't it? I'd have loved three.' He stopped out of loyalty to Pamela, who had

268

declared she wasn't 'ruining' her figure any further. 'What does Rob say?'

'That's just it!' Bobbie began to weep again. 'He doesn't know.'

'Shouldn't you tell him?'

She shook her head again. 'I'm waiting for the right time but I know what he'll say. He doesn't want a third child. Never did. We can't afford it, for a start.'

'Then . . .'

'It was an accident.' She laughed hoarsely. 'Believe me, there was only one night when it could have happened. We'd both had a bit too much to drink.' Then she flushed as though she'd said more than enough.

'Surely he'll understand when you tell him.'

'I don't think so. Not from the way he's behaving at the moment.'

He couldn't bear to see her so upset. It seemed very natural to take her hand and stroke it comfortingly. 'You don't honestly think he's interested in his secretary?'

'Actually I do.' Bobbie's cheeks were bright red. 'I looked at his phone the other night and she'd sent him a text with a kiss after it.'

Stupid man! 'What did he say when you asked him about it?'

'I haven't.' Bobbie was beginning to shred her paper napkin. 'I was going to but there never seemed to be the right time. And besides, I don't want him to stay for the wrong reason.' She glanced down at her stomach. 'It wouldn't be right.'

'So what are you going to do?'

They were still holding hands, he realised, but Bobbie didn't seem to want to let go.

'That's what I wanted to ask you.'

'You've got to be honest,' he heard himself insist. 'Tell him everything. Marriage gets corroded when one of you has secrets.' He gave a short laugh. 'Trust me. I know.'

A sympathetic light went on in her eyes. 'You still think Pamela is having an affair?'

'Possibly.'

'Then you haven't asked her either?'

'No.' He let go of her hands then. Instantly he missed them. 'We make a right pair, don't we?'

She nodded, sniffing but smiling at the same time. 'Thanks, Andy. I still don't know what I'm going to do but I feel a lot better knowing I've got someone to talk to. I must go now but can I ring you if it all gets too much?'

He felt flattered. 'Of course.'

She gave him a quick hug. 'It goes without saying that you must do the same with me.'

Without meaning to, he moved towards her and gave her a brief kiss on her cheek. The sort of kiss, he told himself, that a man might give the woman who was married to his brother-in-law. But as he drew back, he saw a woman staring coldly at him. Not the disapproving waitress but Audrey from class, who'd been sitting, he suddenly realised, at the table right behind him. Close enough, possibly, to have heard every word.

Only later, when he returned to the house, did Andy find a missed call from George, his financial adviser, on his phone. It was too late to call him back.

Besides, right now, money was the last thing on his mind.

FUNNY BUT TRUE . . .

'Children seldom misquote you. In fact, they usually repeat word for word what you shouldn't have said.'

Anon

'The trouble with being a parent is that by the time you are experienced, you are unemployed.'

Anon

'Ask your child what he wants for dinner, only if he's buying.'

Fran Lebowitz

Chapter 25

'Mum! MUM!'

She shouldn't have told Andy she was pregnant, realised Bobbie as she nipped back into the house to fetch her purse, leaving the children in the car. Not before she'd told her own husband.

Honk! Honk!

But he'd been so kind and thoughtful. Far more so than Rob nowadays. Funny to think that she hadn't really known him until the last few weeks had brought them together.

Honk! Honk! Honk!

'Coming,' Bobbie called, making gestures through the kitchen window to indicate that she wouldn't be long.

'You must tell Rob about the baby,' Andy had urged.

He was right! But when she'd tried to broach the subject last night, her husband had virtually fallen asleep at the table before she'd even got to the 'Don't panic but . . .' sentence she had so carefully formed in her mind.

He was shattered. Too drained to talk after work. Just what Sarah's husband had been like, before going off with his boss. Then – and this was the awful bit! – when she finally got to bed, she found Rob talking in his sleep.

'Araminta,' he was murmuring.

Araminta!

'You and me,' he murmured again. 'You and me.'

You and me?

Bobbie felt sick. 'What do you mean?' she wanted to say. But if she had it out with him, he might go. And if she told him she was pregnant, he might feel obliged to stay. Just as her father had done.

HONK! HONK!

The sound of the kids on the horn brought Bobbie sharply back to the present. How could she handle a marriage crisis *and* an ordinary day's work of bringing up kids and missing purses?

Shit. How on earth had it got there? Bobbie stared through the door of the washing machine. She remembered now. Picking up her purse from downstairs to go out and then rushing upstairs when Jack had called out that the loo was overflowing. Then she'd put on the washing machine. But somehow she must have put the purse in at the same time and now, there it was, bobbing around merrily with a collection of credit cards and receipts and goodness knows what else that would, no doubt, bung up the filter.

Still, that was nothing, compared with her husband going off with his secretary.

HONK! HONK! HONK! HONK!

'I'm coming, I'm coming!'

Oh my God! A clown face beamed out at her from behind the wheel. With that daub of pink lipstick and heavy maroon eye shadow, Jack was almost unrecognisable. 'I've been practising my face painting,' announced Daisy, who had Bobbie's make-up bag open on the front seat. 'Miss Davies said I could help her at the school fête.'

Her new lipstick! Not only was it all over Jack's face but it was also smeared over the car seat. As for her mascara, it seemed to be everywhere apart from Jack's eyelashes: his cheeks; his ear; Daisy's hands, which were now leaving navy-blue handprints on every available surface.

Forget what she'd said earlier about not wanting Rob to stay out of guilt! Of course she did! How the hell was she going to manage with three children when she couldn't even cope with two? Maybe getting pregnant was exactly what she *did* need to keep their marriage together. She'd just have to work out a way of getting rid of Araminta, that's all.

Ugh! What was that smell?

'Pongo,' said Jack, putting his arms around her in contrition. 'He can't help it. Can he?'

'I've told you what to do,' Sarah said firmly when she came down to visit their new home, which after four months wasn't so new now.

Bobbie felt sick and not just because of the constant nausea. Her waistline was already thickening so that she now had to leave the top two buttons of her jeans undone. 'It's too much of a risk!'

'Nonsense!' Sarah was walking briskly alongside her while the children were racing along ahead, rather too close to the canal.

'Daisy! Jack! Tom!'

'They're all right,' said Sarah airily. 'I used to fuss like you but we've been learning to let go at parenting class. You should try it. You're awfully tense, if you don't mind me saying.'

Actually, she did! Either the class, or the new friend that she kept talking about, had changed Sarah.

'It can't go wrong!' Sarah was really pushing her now. 'Trust me. It's the perfect way to find out things about people.'

Bobbie gasped. 'You still do it?'

Sarah gave a wicked smile. 'Course I do. When I wanted to find out more about *her*, I simply masqueraded as a medical researcher. You'll never believe what I found out.'

Bobbie nudged her old friend in the ribs as a shortish man with a rather nice boyish face approached, holding a little girl's hand. 'Shhh. I know him. He's a widower in our parenting class.'

'Nice,' muttered Sarah approvingly.

Really? Bobbie wouldn't have thought Matthew was Sarah's type.

'Hi, Bobbie. Lottie thought she recognised you. Didn't you, princess? Whoops! She's off!'

The little figure in pink was belting towards the other three children who were feeding the ducks by the side of the canal.

'Kids always spot each other before the parents do,' laughed Sarah in a tinkly tone that Bobbie hadn't heard before.

'That's right!' Matthew laughed; the sort of laugh that men make when they are attracted to women. Good heavens! Did he fancy her too?

'Aren't you going to introduce us, Bobbie?'

Sarah was making it so obvious but, incredibly, Matthew didn't seem to mind.

'Sorry. Matthew, this is Sarah. She's an old friend from London.'

'We knew each other when I was married,' intercepted Sarah quickly. 'But I'm on my own now.'

Matthew's face softened. 'I'm sorry.'

'Don't be. He was a bastard.'

Sarah had blown it now! Matthew didn't approve of swearing: he always frowned when Not Really Pregnant Mum let rip. But surprisingly he was actually looking rather sympathetic. 'They say that anger is a great healer.'

Sarah shrugged. 'In that case, I need a whacking big tube of Savlon inside me.'

Heavens! Matthew actually seemed to think that was funny.

'MUM! MUM!'

Bobbie shot round. The cry for 'Mum' always made her do that – a constant reminder of being on duty. But it wasn't one of hers this time. It was another child, a few feet away. 'Look, Mum! That little boy is stuck in a tree.'

Jack. It just had to be.

'I'll go,' said Matthew.

'That's so kind of you!' Sarah's voice was sugar sweet. 'Bobbie shouldn't be rushing around in her condition.'

Matthew was already running but not before he'd glanced down at her stomach as if he could see the two undone buttons beneath her jumper. How could her friend be so indiscreet? Now the whole world was going to know before her husband!

*

In the event, Jack was already shinning down again – with a gash on his knee – just as Matthew got there. 'Please don't tell anyone I'm pregnant,' Bobbie managed to whisper after thanking him. 'It's meant to be a secret.'

Jack, of course, was totally unrepentant. 'Why do you always have to test my limits?' she demanded as they walked back home after saying goodbye to Matthew and Lottie.

He sniffed. 'I just wanted to see how high I could go.'

Sarah shook her head. 'You know, Bobbie, in our parenting class, we learn how to empathise with children when they step out of line.'

Bobbie groaned. 'OK, Jack. I know just how you feel. I want to climb a tree myself.'

Her son's eyes widened. 'Really?'

'No, *not* really. If fact, if you do that again, I'll confiscate your DS.'

Daisy tutted. 'And then we'll just find where you've hidden it, like we always do. Look! There's Sunshine over there. She's with a dog! Can *we* get one too?'

'Absolutely not.' Bobbie waved in the distance to Vanessa, who was helping her granddaughter to throw a ball along with an older man. Was he the 'gentleman friend' she'd been talking about ? They seemed really happy! A proper family, unlike them. What kind of husband had to work on Saturdays? The kind of husband who was having an affair, that's who.

'You know a lot of people here already, don't you?' commented Sarah. She sounded rather envious. 'It's really lovely, isn't it? All these green parks and fresh air and ducks and widowers.'

'Sarah!'

Her friend shrugged. 'Nice single men go fast. Didn't you read that survey in *Charisma* magazine? They have an average shelf life of ten days.' She gave Bobbie a sly look. 'Is Matthew with anyone yet?'

'I did hear that he'd just broken up with someone.'

'Fantastic! What can you invite me to? There must be a

party or a PTA barn dance or something. That's what people do in the country, isn't it? Apart from snogging cows, of course.'

'We've got our school fête soon!' piped up Daisy. 'I've been practising my face painting. We could introduce you to Lottie's dad then. She plays in our orchestra.'

Bobbie shot Sarah a look to say 'See! That's what comes of talking in front of the children.'

'Great!' Sarah beamed. 'Make sure you invite me.' Then she lowered her voice as Daisy ran ahead to join the others. 'Don't go all prudish on me, Bobbie. I've seen how you flush when you talk about your brother-in-law.'

'Andy's *not* my brother-in-law! He's my sister-in-law's husband. And I don't flush.'

'You can't hide it from me!' Sarah gave her a big wink. 'I know you too well. And good luck when you make that phone call. We'd better head back to the station now. But let me know what happens, won't you?'

Of course it was ridiculous: Sarah's plan was far too audacious to risk! But when Rob had come home at midnight again, muttering something about having to stay on to finish 'the campaign', Bobbie decided that enough was enough. She'd do it! But not until the afternoon as she'd promised to do the morning stint in the shop.

By lunchtime however, her resolve was weakening. What if she got caught? Then a pretty woman in her mid-thirties came in, clutching several designer carrier bags with a desperate air about her. 'I don't want to get rid of them,' she confided, 'but I need the money. My husband and I have just split up.'

Another abandoned-wife tale? Bobbie made a sympathetic noise as she sifted through some rather lovely outfits. Vanessa had warned her that she'd hear all kinds of stories in the shop and she wasn't wrong. The most common – and the hardest to hear right now – were those of the nouveau pauvre ex-wives of Corrywood. Bobbie listened with mounting dismay as the pretty woman (whose daughter, it turned out, was in the same class as Daisy) poured out her heart.

Slightly against her better judgement, Bobbie took all the clothes on offer, in the hope of making a few pounds for her. 'Thanks so much! Anything will help. Anything. He promised to pay my mortgage, you see, but now he's changed his mind. My solicitor says it often happens.'

Bobbie bit her lip. 'Does he have someone else?'

The pretty woman laughed bitterly. 'He said he didn't but now he's suddenly "met" someone. I was a fool to believe him. Looking back, I can see all the signs. In fact, I'm almost certain he started when I was pregnant with my third!'

That was it! If Bobbie had had her doubts, this was enough to make her throw them to one side. As Sarah said, her marketing-research job gave her the perfect cover. And she had at least half an hour before the kids got back from school. Surely it wouldn't matter if she shut shop just a little bit early? She couldn't risk being interrupted.

Racing back to the house, Bobbie dialled her husband's direct number, taking care to put 141 first so she couldn't be traced. He was going to be in a meeting, he had told her that morning. An all-day meeting. So, with any luck, this Araminta would pick up. No. Engaged. She dialled again. Yes!

'Good morning. Sorry, I mean afternoon!' trilled Bobbie in the high-pitched voice she'd been practising on the way home. 'I'm from Research Trivia and I just wondered if you had time to answer a couple of easy questions . . .'

'Yes, I *am* a market researcher and I appreciate that you are very busy but we're offering a free spa holiday weekend for every one hundredth person who answers our questions and – I shouldn't tell you this – but you are the lucky one!'

Bobbie said all this very quickly, terrified in case Araminta with her plummy accent put down the phone. OK, so she'd told a big whopper about the spa holiday but she'd had to do something to pin her down otherwise she'd have lost her.

'You will! That's wonderful. Thank you so much. We're doing a survey on employers. Yes, I promise it's confidential.

Right. Do you like your boss? You do? That's good.' Bobbie gave a nervous laugh. 'It would be awful to work for someone you don't like, wouldn't it? Exactly!'

Build a relationship up with the interviewee! That's what she'd been trained to do. Pretend you're on their wavelength.

'So, does your boss take you out? Yes, to meetings and, er, anywhere else. Nice! Lucky you! Conferences can be a lot of fun, can't they?'

Bobbie felt her nails digging into the palms of her hands. 'Do you find your boss attractive? Actually, yes, this *is* an important question. You *do*? I see. No, of course we're not mentioning names in the survey.'

She took a deep breath. 'So would you consider having a relationship with a married man? I'm sorry – I didn't quite catch that . . .'

'MUMMY, MUMMY!'

Shit. The children were back early! They must have taken the spare key from its hiding place and let themselves in.

'Vanessa's taking us swimming with Sunshine!' Daisy's little voice was feverish with excitement. 'Where did you put our costumes?'

Bobbie hadn't felt this hot since the day they'd gone to the Eden Project when Jack had shimmied across the rope bridge and then performed a handstand halfway along. 'Would you mind holding for a moment?'

'Why are you talking in that funny voice, Mummy?'

'I'm not! I'm . . .'

Too late! Snooty Araminta with her plummy voice had put the phone down but she'd got enough already. 'Would you consider having a relationship with your boss?' she had asked. And Bobbie was pretty sure she had started to say the 'Yes' word before putting the phone down.

Oh God. Her body began to shake. So all her suspicions were correct! Rob *was* having an affair. How *could* he ? And what on earth was she going to do now?

EXCLUSIVE INTERVIEW WITH DR KNOW!

'Parents might love to hate me! but they know I talk sense.'

Read about Dr Know's controversial campaign for introducing parent licences (like the old-style dog licences)

Chapter 26

VANESSA

Vanessa was reading an article about Dr Know in the doctor's waiting room, while Sunshine wriggled in her seat impatiently. 'Can't we go home now?'

A mother sitting opposite rolled her eyes sympathetically. The irony was that until a few weeks ago, Sunshine would have sat as good as gold without making any fuss. But now, thanks to school – or, more importantly, Jack and Daisy's influence – she was becoming much more difficult.

No, Vanessa corrected herself, as she tried to get Sunshine to read her book quietly. More like an ordinary six-year-old. 'It won't be long now,' she said, hoping that she was right. The waiting room was packed.

'Why are we here anyway?' demanded Sunshine. 'Is it because of my worms again?'

There was the muffled sound of laughter from the mother opposite, which encouraged her granddaughter even more. 'You said that tablet would get rid of them.'

'It did!' hissed Vanessa, embarrassed. When Sunshine had begun to complain of an itchy bottom, she had suddenly remembered how Brigid had done the same at her age. It had been a big thing then, she'd remembered, but now, or so the chemist had assured her, it was 'quite normal', along with head lice.

'Then why *are* we here?' Sunshine was aware now that the other patients were beginning to look. And no wonder! She was such a cute little thing with that mop of black hair, flashing green eyes and a very clear way of speaking: quite different from some of the kids she'd met at school. 'Is it because of my nits?'

The middle-aged man on the left of her shuffled away.

'You don't have nits!' declared Vanessa, horrified.

'I might! Everyone else in the class has them. We got a letter about it.'

A letter? 'I haven't seen it.'

Sunshine shrugged. 'It's in my satchel.' Then she took Vanessa's hand, twisting it gently and giving her a wheedling look. 'May I have a Mollie the Pig bag for school, Van Van? Like everyone else?'

Really? But the satchel had been Brigid's at that age. Vanessa had been so excited when she'd found it in the attic, marvelling at how the strong brown leather had lasted over the years. Initially, Sunshine had expressed a touching delight, marching up and down the hall, trying it out for size. But not now. Her granddaughter had become so aware of the latest trends.

'Mrs Thomas?' called out the receptionist.

Vanessa stood up quickly, her heart beating. To be honest, she'd been glad of her granddaughter's constant questions and demands. It had taken her mind off why she was really there.

'You stay here, poppet,' she said quickly. 'I won't be long.'

Vanessa trusted Dr Macdonald. She was the one who had picked up the lump the first time and said, yes, it really ought to be investigated 'just to be on the safe side'. She was also the one who had been monitoring Vanessa's check-ups at the hospital and who had celebrated, with a brief hug in the surgery, when Vanessa had had the five-year all clear.

Now as Vanessa lay on the couch with one arm behind her head, as instructed, she sensed a hesitation on the part of the middle-aged woman with the gold crucifix round her neck examining her. 'I think we'd better organise a mammogram. Just to make sure.'

Vanessa's heart began to pound so hard that she could feel it beating against her ribs. 'Do you think it is . . .you know?' She still couldn't bring herself to say the word 'cancer' even though there had been people on her ward who said that the only way to beat this thing was to face it square on.

'I don't know, Vanessa.' Dr Macdonald's voice was steady but sympathetic. 'I'm sorry. Wish I could be more certain.' She glanced at her notes. 'But even without your history, it's only sensible to check it out.'

'It's not me I'm worried about. It's Sunshine.'

'I can understand that.'

The doctor glanced at the wooden-framed photograph on her desk, showing two boys grinning; one quite a lot older than the other. 'It's every mother's fear that something will happen to her family,' she said softly.

Vanessa shook her head. 'You're wrong, actually.'

Dr Macdonald raised her eyebrows.

'It's every grandmother's fear too.' Vanessa felt her hands tighten. 'If something happens to me, I don't know who will look after Sunshine. You see there's literally no one else, unless . . .'

Unless the DNA test proved Jason was the father, she almost added. But that alternative was too horrific to contemplate.

'Don't think about that yet, Vanessa. Remember what we agreed before, five years ago? One step at a time. Meanwhile, I'll make sure you get put through on the fast track.' She smiled encouragingly. 'Then at least we'll know where we are, won't we?'

Vanessa's head reeled as she went back into the waiting room. Then again, what had she expected? As soon as she'd felt that lump, she knew the doctor couldn't tell her it was all right without any investigation. But somehow she'd hoped Dr Macdonald might just wave a magic wand and . . .

Sunshine! Vanessa did a quick sweep of the waiting room. Where was she?

'It's all right,' called out the girl at the desk. 'She's gone to the loo with her friend.'

Her friend? Only then did Vanessa see Bobbie sitting there, engrossed in a magazine. Thank heavens for that. She must be with Daisy.

'Hi,' she said, sitting next to her.

'Oh. Hi.'

Bobbie didn't look very thrilled to see her.

'How are you?'

Bobbie shrugged. 'Fine, thanks.'

'Are the kids poorly?'

They certainly didn't seem ill. Not from the way that Jack was ripping out pages from a magazine that had a *Please Don't Remove* sticker on the front. And there was Daisy now, coming back with Sunshine, both with their arms round each other and giggling. She didn't look poorly either – and if she was, Bobbie shouldn't have allowed her to be so close to Sunshine. Vanessa couldn't help feeling like a worried new mother when it came to 'catching things'.

Something didn't seem right. Not unless Bobbie was doing the usual thing that everyone did at the doctor's: saying you were fine because you didn't want to admit what you were in for.

'Are *you* all right?'

'Me?' Vanessa nodded as enthusiastically as her friend had done just now. 'Great, thanks. Absolutely great. Come on, poppet, we've got to go now. If we don't open the shop, I might miss some business.'

Bobbie shifted uneasily. 'No news on the missing suede jacket.'

'No, but I didn't expect there to be.' Vanessa shook her head. 'It's just one of those things, I'm afraid.'

She'd tried to sound reassuring but Bobbie's eyes were filling with tears. 'I'm so sorry.'

Vanessa patted her on the arm. 'Just forget it,' she said. 'Honestly. It's in the past now.'

That wasn't *quite* true! As she'd said to Brian on the phone the other night, she was still a bit annoyed. She'd had to pay the understandably aggrieved owner a handsome sum in compensation, as well as give her that Zandra Rhodes. It had wiped out her profit for the week.

'Thanks.' Bobbie really seemed really on edge. 'Actually, there was something I was going to tell you but . . .'

'CAN YOU STOP YOUR SON DESTROYING THESE

MAGAZINES?' thundered a very upright matronly woman sitting opposite. 'You've just been sitting there, nattering away, without even telling him off.'

Poor Bobbie! Vanessa felt for her friend, who'd flushed deep red.

'Mrs Wright!' called out the receptionist. 'Room Three please.'

Looking flustered, Bobbie jumped up. 'Sit still, you two. Or there'll be trouble.'

Vanessa hesitated. 'Sorry I can't stay and look after them.' She looked at Daisy, who was now helping Jack to make paper hats out of magazines.

There was a loud harrumph from the matronly patient. 'Children are allowed to get away with anything nowadays. It's the parents' fault.' She fixed an eye on Bobbie. 'They're far too weak.'

'Room Three, Mrs Wright!' repeated the receptionist sharply.

'Please stop doing that, you two,' Bobbie pleaded. 'I won't be long.'

It was only after she'd gone and Vanessa was trying to tidy up the mess on Bobbie's behalf while persuading Sunshine that no, she couldn't stay too and play with her friend, that she noticed the magazine that Bobbie had left under her chair. *Pregnancy For You.*

Of course! Suddenly it all made sense! The peakiness. The sudden aversion to coffee. The buttons on the back of Bobbie's skirt the other day that hadn't been done up. So *that* was why she was here!

By the time she got to the shop, two of her regulars were already waiting slightly crossly outside, looking at their watches. 'I'm so sorry,' Vanessa tried to explain. 'I had a doctor's appointment. In you go, poppet.'

But Sunshine didn't want to sit and play like she used to. Nor did Vanessa feel like being in the shop. All she wanted to do was go home and lie on the bed in a little ball until she could have a mammogram. It was the not knowing that was the worst. She remembered that all too well from last time, but over the last five years, she had managed to shut it out. Now all the worries were coming back. But at least last time, she had only herself to worry about. What would happen to Sunshine if the worst came to the worst?

Vanessa wasn't a particularly religious person but every now and then, she found herself talking to whoever was out there. 'Please make Brigid get in touch,' she murmured. 'Please.'

In the event, Vanessa shut up shop early, partly because she just couldn't concentrate – she'd already given one customer a ten-pound note in change instead of a fiver – and partly because Sunshine was so restless. 'We'll go back for our stuff and go swimming,' she said.

'Yeees!' Sunshine skipped along beside her and then stopped, pointing at an old man shuffling towards them, puffing away on a fag. 'Van Van? Is that old man going to die soon?'

How embarrassing! Vanessa didn't know where to look! He had heard too, judging from his startled expression.

'Of course not. Shhh,' she said quickly, trying to move Sunshine on.

But her granddaughter was standing fast, staring after him, still speaking in the same high-pitched indignant voice. 'But that's what it said on the poster at the doctor's. SMOKING KILLS. And that old man is smoking, isn't he?'

'Well, yes but . . .'

Sunshine was wagging her finger as though Vanessa was a naughty child. 'It's wrong to lie! Miss Davies says so. So is he going to die or not? If he does, is he going to come back as an ant? That's what bood ists do. Daisy says so.'

Vanessa briefly tried to imagine herself as an ant. If there was such a thing as reincarnation, she'd prefer something else. A tree maybe. Stretching out its branches towards the sun.

'There are a lot of things we don't understand in life, poppet,' she said, giving that little warm hand a gentle squeeze.

'Now let's get back, shall we? Brian said he'd be round with Bingo.'

That seemed to do the trick. Sunshine was running ahead now and Vanessa had to break out into a jog to try and keep up. 'Not so fast,' she called. 'Wait! Wait!'

'Look!' Sunshine was pointing across the road. 'There they are!'

'I said, WAIT!' Just in time, she grabbed her granddaughter's hand. 'OK, we can cross now.'

Immediately Sunshine belted over and flung herself down on the ground next to Bingo, kissing him all over and rubbing noses.

'Let's do the same!' whispered Brian, rubbing his nose against hers too, Eskimo-style.

'How's your day been?' asked Brian as they walked towards the park.

'Brilliant, thanks.'

'Van Van had to see the doctor,' chirruped Sunshine before grabbing the puppy's lead.

'Really?' Brian raised his eyebrows.

Vanessa waved her hand. 'It was only a small thing.'

'Promise?'

He was looking at her. Really looking. Sunshine's words from earlier rang in her head. 'It's wrong to lie!' Maybe. But sometimes, when you were a parent, you had to compromise.

'I promise. Look at Sunshine! She'll wear Bingo out!'

Suddenly she felt Brian take her hand. It was warm. Firmly reassuring. 'I was thinking that I might stay round for supper again if that's all right. I've taken the liberty of buying three of those rather upmarket supermarket meals. How does that sound?'

Vanessa felt a lovely glow inside, tempered only by that funny flutter of fear that had been there ever since she'd found the lump. 'Lovely. Absolutely lovely.'

At the school gate, Vanessa made them laugh about the old man smoking.

'How are you getting on with these weekly diaries that Miss Davies wants us to do?' asked American Express worriedly. 'I've written down that my son was sick during the night but I thought he was well enough to go to school. Then I got a call at work to collect him and when I got there, he was sitting on the receptionist's knee. Know what he said? "I told them I was sick last night, Mum." Now she'll think I'm really irresponsible.'

Everyone laughed, apart from Mr Perfect and Bobbie, who seemed rather quiet. How peaky she looked, noticed Vanessa, but it wasn't her place to pry. Bobbie obviously didn't want anyone to know about her pregnancy yet.

'Anyone want to hear my diary?' asked Too Many Kids Mum chummily. 'My Alfie emptied my handbag out in a shop the other day. Everything fell out of it – and I mean *everything*!'

The mind boggled! Vanessa's thoughts began to drift off towards Brian and the other evening. They hadn't meant to do anything but Sunshine had fallen asleep, exhausted by all that running around with Bingo. By mutual silent agreement, they had sneaked off into her bedroom.

'You're beautiful,' Brian had whispered, tracing her scar gently. 'Really beautiful, you know.'

She had almost told him then about the lump but something stopped her. Why spoil the moment? One step at a time. After all, that's what had got her through before.

The following day, as she was rushing round the house to find Sunshine's lost shoe (it turned out to be in the garden, thanks to Bingo, two pieces of post fluttered through the letterbox. Vanessa's heart pounded as she noticed the hospital frank. Her mammogram appointment.

There was a postcard too, half hanging through the letterbox.

Greetings from Goa!

Vanessa's head began to spin as she took in the picture of a sandy beach and an impossibly blue sea.

My darling Sunshine, hope you are having a lovely time
with Granny. Be a good girl. Love Mum.

It was dated four weeks ago.

So Brigid hadn't been kidnapped or hurt or been put in
prison or any of the other things she'd been worried about.
She was simply enjoying herself. Leaving others to handle her
responsibilities.

'This time, my girl,' Vanessa muttered, 'you've gone too
far.'

There once was a working mum,
Who said, 'It's all right for some!
I want family time
Before sixty-nine.
I need time to sit on my bum.'

PERFECT PARENTS: SESSION SEVEN

<u>HOW TO KEEP SANE AS A PARENT!</u>

(Ed's note: Is this really possible?)

Chapter 27

ANDY

Surely she ought to be back by now? Andy paced up and down the lounge or, as Pamela called it, 'the drawing room'. It was nearly ten o'clock! What was Mel playing at? She had school the next day.

'I'm just off to the gym!' That's what she'd said when she'd pushed her dinner to one side earlier in the evening (fish fingers that he'd cooked specially) and then announced that she wasn't very hungry.

He hadn't blamed her. His cooking repertoire was extremely limited and although he'd tried to tame the fish fingers, they had somehow got slightly singed in that extremely complicated cooker which Pamela usually presided over. Ridiculous thing! It looked more like an inbuilt sports car, set into the gleaming chrome complex that she'd had fitted at huge expense last year.

'The gym?' he'd repeated approvingly. 'Nattie, don't giggle. It's good to be healthy.'

Perhaps he ought to do the same. Since being at home, he had piled on the pounds himself. So easy when there wasn't anything to do but run the house and look after the girls. Then he'd discovered the store of Bourbon biscuits that Pamela kept at the back of a cupboard for Mrs C., their daily. Back in the days of the home, Andy remembered, you were given a Bourbon or a jam ring if you did something good. It was a very rare treat and the sweetness had been comforting. Very comforting. Especially when you were bored, as he was now.

Boredom was not something that Andy was used to. When he'd been working, he would come back exhausted at the end

293

of the day, feeling secretly envious of Pamela who had spent her days shopping or having lunch with friends or making their home into one of those places featured in the current issue of *Stunning House* magazine that sat on the coffee table.

'What did you do today?' she'd often ask him, but he would gloss over the deals he'd had to cut and the interminable meetings, because that was the last thing he wanted to talk about. Only now did he realise that Pamela's questions had been directed more from envy than curiosity. She had probably been as bored as he was! After all, you could only do so much home-making and shopping.

No wonder he was going stir-crazy! Perhaps, Andy asked himself, as he went to the window to see if his eldest daughter was coming up the drive, that's what had made him almost spill the beans on his past at parent class. Or maybe it was to call Kieran's bluff. Then again, perhaps it was due to this desperate need to unburden himself.

Over the years, he had learned to live with his secret; push it to one side, pretending that it had happened to someone else and not him. But meeting Kieran again so unexpectedly had opened up a whole new can of worms and now it just wouldn't go away.

Then there was the other thing. 'Are you sure you want to go ahead?' George had asked doubtfully when he'd told him what to do.

'I'm certain!'

Just saying the words gave him a buzz; rather like the one women were meant to get when they went shopping. It was just like the old days in the office when he'd taken huge gambles with other people's money. Gambles that usually paid off.

Where the hell was Mel? Andy began to feel a tight panic rising up his chest. Why was her mobile still going straight through to answerphone? And why was Nattie playing loud music from her room when she was meant to be asleep?

'Chill out, Dad,' said his youngest crossly when he went to investigate.

What? He could hardly hear her above the noise.

'Dad!' Nattie's furious little face glared at him as he headed for the off switch on the expensive stereo system that had been 'part of' her last Christmas present. Pamela had thought it was too much but Andy wanted the girls to have everything he hadn't had as a child. Now he was beginning to wonder if he was right.

'I was listening to that!' Her words were lashing out at him as though she was the angry parent and he was the child that had done something wrong. 'And knock next time, can you? Mum always does. She says we're all entitled to privacy. Now get out of my room, Dad. Please. I'm trying to do my homework.'

But . . . Yes! There was the sound of a key in the lock! 'Mel,' he called out, rushing down stairs. 'Where on earth have you been?'

His oldest daughter glared at him. 'To the gym, Dad. I told you!'

She was indeed wearing jogging bottoms and a cute little top. But she didn't look particularly sweaty or mussed up the way he had done when he'd attempted to do an hour on the power plates the other day.

'But it's so late!'

'Late!' She laughed. 'Get real, Dad. We're not babies any more.'

Something wasn't right. His instinct told him that. His daughter reeked of cigarettes. Ordinary cigarettes, thank God.

'Who were you with?' he demanded.

'What is this? Twenty questions?'

As she spoke, there was a sudden roar of a car revving up before shooting down the road. 'Did someone give you a lift?' he demanded, looking her straight in the eye.

'No, Dad.' She glared back brazenly. 'I walked.' Quickly, she grabbed her bag and shot up the stairs.

'Mel?' he yelled, hammering on her locked door. 'Were you in someone's car just now? You know the rules! You're not allowed to be driven by any of your friends unless they've had a full licence for at least six months.'

That was something that both he and Pamela felt strongly about. There were too many teenagers racing around in Corrywood: kids in their parents' cars who had more money than sense. 'Mel? Do you hear me?'

The music volume rose in response.

Choices, the parenting course said. Give them *choices*.

'I'm warning you, Mel. If you don't listen, I'll . . .'

He'd do *what*?

Why was it that parenting was recognised as the most important job in the world but no one could give you a manual for it? One that *really* worked.

If only he didn't have parenting class the next day. Andy knew he was doomed from the minute he walked in. It wasn't just yesterday's horrible argument with the girls which made him feel like a hopeless parent, let alone a hopeless teacher. It was the look that Audrey was shooting him right now. That withering, disappointed yet also sullen stare that said, 'I saw you. With that woman in the pub last week.'

He glanced at his notes, which he hadn't had time to absorb properly. Fail to prepare and prepare to fail. That's what he'd learned at work. And now here he was, heading for a fall.

'This session is about getting the kids to be polite,' he began, looking around for Kieran. Great! He wasn't here. Maybe working late again. That was something. 'Some of you may already know that I have two teenage daughters,' he continued. 'I've been looking after them full-time while my wife is away.'

There was a snort from Audrey followed by another loud whisper in which the words 'while the cat's away' could be heard quite clearly. Maybe this wasn't such a good idea. But they were all waiting expectantly! He couldn't stop now. Besides, at work, he'd been good at winging it. So he should be able to do that now.

'I have to say that my daughters aren't as polite to me as I would like them to be.'

There was an impatient sound from Paula. 'If *you* can't get it right, what are you doing in charge of the course?'

'Exactly my point! I'd like us to brainstorm our own situations. Give each other suggestions. Going back to my own predicament . . .'

'Me, me, me,' muttered Audrey, rolling her eyes.

He hurried on, ignoring her. '. . . last night, I found that one of my daughters had lied to me. She said she was going to the gym but in fact, I'm pretty certain she was in a friend's car.'

Audrey yawned. 'So what's the issue here, Andy?'

'She'd been lying! We have a rule that our girls can't go out in the car with friends who've only just passed.'

There was a mutter of 'good idea's. 'At least she isn't smoking dope,' mumbled Bohemian Mum sleepily. Andy only just stopped himself from correcting her.

'I would suggest a family conference,' sighed Intellectual Mum, wiping her glasses. 'We tried one the other day. But Julius refused to leave his laptop.'

'I know it's not easy,' he began unsteadily, 'but it's worth persevering.'

'Is it?' Audrey was rising to her feet. 'To be honest, Andy, I don't know if I'm getting much out of these sessions any more. They were OK when they started but it's not helping. Not with the kind of stuff I'm having to deal with.'

'What kind of stuff?' asked Andy desperately.

'It doesn't matter.' She slung her bag over her shoulder. 'I'm off. Anyone else coming with me?'

'It was awful,' said Andy over what had now become a regular weekly coffee with Bobbie after class. 'Two of the other parents went too. It was almost a mass walkout. I feel a real failure.'

'Of course you're not!' She gave him such a lovely kind sympathetic look that he wanted to take her hand and hold it.

No. Stop right there. Bobbie was his brother-in-law's wife.

And she was pregnant. Tonight, she looked particularly pale and vulnerable. His heart went out to her.

'I think it was very brave of you to share your own issues,' she continued. 'Miss Davies is sweet but she's not a parent so she can't possibly understand.'

Andy felt a flash of sympathy for the young teacher. 'I'm not sure that's entirely true.'

'Well I do. This woman you mentioned. You said she had red hair. Was she the one who was staring at us in the pub last week?'

He nodded.

'The one who had the hots for you?'

He wished he hadn't said anything now. 'Well, yes, but . . .'

'So that's why!' Bobbie let out an I-don't-believe-it laugh. 'She's jealous! She thinks you and I have got something going on together. How ridiculous!'

Was it really?

'I hope she doesn't start spreading rumours.' Bobbie's eyes were wide with apprehension. 'She's a terrible gossip.'

'You know her?'

'She came into the shop the other day with a friend of hers.' Bobbie shuddered. 'They were braying to each other through the curtains about a teacher having an affair with one of the fathers.'

Andy felt a tremor of apprehension. 'That's awful.'

Bobbie looked around the pub, which was packed. 'Maybe we ought not to meet up like this. People might take it the wrong way.'

'That's crazy!' The thought of not seeing her next week punched a hole in his stomach. 'We're family!'

Bobbie nodded. 'I know. But that woman is trouble, Andy.' She glanced down at her stomach. 'And things are difficult enough for me at the moment.'

Of course they were! He should have asked about the baby earlier, instead of being wrapped up in his own problems. 'What did Rob say? Was he all right in the end?'

She bit her lip. 'I still haven't told him. Don't look like that, Andy. I'm just waiting to find the right time.' Then she looked away. 'If you don't mind, I don't want to talk about it.'

Andy was about to leave the house – he could get down to Sussex and back in a day if he went right now – when Mrs C. stopped him by the door. From the look on her face, he was in trouble again. Last week, it had been the conservatory, where he had committed the ultimate crime of cleaning the floor with a tin of polish that he'd found under the sink. The wrong tin apparently.

Why was it that he'd had no trouble in holding his own at work but when it came to home, he felt like a kid? 'Please,' Mrs C. had told him in an exasperated tone that made him feel he was the employee instead of the other way round, 'leave the cleaning to me.'

But he had to do *something*. This house-husband stuff was driving him mad! He missed Pamela too: even a cold, icy, distant wife was better than no company at all. It was all very well giving her space. But how long did she need? As for the girls, they much preferred their laptops or phones or iPads or iPods. Anything but the company of a parent.

'What have I done wrong now?' he asked in a jokey way although deep down he felt quite resentful. Were all the women in this house against him?

'It's not you, Mr Gooding. It's . . . well, it's this.' She beckoned to him. 'Could you come and have a look?'

He followed her up the stairs and into Pamela's walk-in dressing room. Mrs C. shut the door behind them. What was going on?

'I've been wondering whether to show you this for some time,' she said quietly. 'I've tried to mind my own business but I can't keep mum any longer.'

'I don't understand,' Andy started to say but then stopped. Mrs C. was standing on a stool and taking down a large hat box from a top shelf.

'Open that,' she commanded.

Andy hesitated. 'I don't like to go through my wife's personal things.'

'Oh, for goodness' sake!' For a minute, he thought she was going to shake him. 'You steam open her post, don't you? Don't deny it. I've seen you.'

It was true! After that loan statement, he just didn't trust Pamela. But he hadn't realised he'd been spotted.

'If you won't open the lid, I will. There! Now look inside.'

Bloody hell. He hadn't expected that! Numbed, he stared at the contents.

'There's something else too.' Mrs C. beckoned him towards the laundry room. So? What was wrong with a line of cleaning fluids, neatly stacked in rows?

'Take the lid off one of those bottles.' Mrs C. had both hands on her waist, imperiously. 'That's right. Now taste it!'

Andy felt sick. It was just like that time at the home when one of the boys had taken him and Kieran by the scruffs of their necks and threatened to pour bleach down their throats if they so much as breathed a word about what had happened that night.

But he wasn't there now. He was in his own home. 'Don't be ridiculous, Mrs C.'

Aghast, he watched her pour out a capful, swig some of it herself and then hand it to him.

Only then did he realise.

'Your wife,' said Mrs C. shaking her head sadly, 'she is very clever.'

In a way, he'd been expecting something like this, Andy told himself as he roared down towards Sussex. It made sense even though nothing else did.

Two months ago, he'd been the perfect family man with two perfect teenage daughters and a perfect wife. Now he was being blackmailed by a con from his past and had three lying women in his house to boot. Maybe four if you counted

Mrs C. and that bottle of 'cleaning fluid' he'd spotted in her bag when she'd left.

By his side, in the well of the passenger seat, was the hat box. 'Take it with you,' Mrs C. had urged. 'Otherwise Mrs Gooding will try and talk her way out of it.' Her eyes had softened. 'I don't want you to think I'm being disloyal but someone has to help her.'

It was true. Yet now, as he pulled up outside Camilla's cottage, Andy felt sick with nerves. This would be it. His wife had been livid when he'd opened that loan statement. Goodness knows how she'd react when she saw the contents of the hat box. On the other hand, he had to do something.

Why are you so scared? he asked himself. Why can't you go in there like a man and tell her you knew the truth?

Because she might leave him. That's why. Leave him just as his parents had left him. Then his world would crumble down around him, all over again. It simply wasn't an option.

Slowly he walked up Camilla's front path, steeling himself, going over the carefully prepared words that he'd been finessing in the car.

'*Bonjour?*' An extremely tall, very handsome young man with a small black moustache opened the door, looking at him disdainfully up and down. 'You want sometheeng?'

So Camilla's new au pair had arrived. 'I'm Andy, Pamela's husband. May I come in?'

The small black moustache quivered. 'I 'ave to check with Meeses Camilla. Plis. Wait there.'

The man left him standing on the doorstep. Then he heard the sound of footsteps. 'Of course you can let him in, Pierre. He's my son-in-law!'

Heavens, she sounded almost friendly!

'Andrew!' The door was flung open and Camilla was standing there in front of him. Or was it her? He'd never seen his mother-in-law without make-up before. She looked vulnerable. Scared. Like a little girl. And if he wasn't mistaken, she'd been crying.

'I'm so glad you've come. I was just about to call you.'

'Why?' He felt a burst of alarm. 'What's happened?'

'You'd better come in,' she said, sniffing loudly. 'I'm sorry, Andrew. I should have told you a long time ago. And now I'm worried it might be too late.'

There was once a stay-at-home mum,
Whose kids had her under their thumb.
So she found a childminder –
'Twas really much kinder!
Then went back to work for some fun.

Chapter 28

BOBBIE

'But you've got to have it out with him!' insisted Sarah down the phone. 'You can't just let Rob get away with it! From what you've told me, this Araminta woman has virtually admitted to having an affair.'

In the past, Bobbie had never understood why women stayed with men who were unfaithful. But now it was happening to her, she was beginning to understand. How could she allow the children to grow up without a resident father? Wasn't it better to turn a blind eye, just as Mum had done, in the hope he would 'go off the other woman' and stay put? Or was that hypocritical, as Sarah was arguing?

The dilemma, plus the morning sickness that she was passing off as a 'bug' that was going around, made her nauseous.

'Mum! Jack's doing it again!'

'Sorry, Sarah, I've got to go.'

'But you haven't told me what the doctor said!'

Automatically, Bobbie put her hand down to her stomach. It was incredible that something was growing there. Something that had happened during 'a quiet night in' to celebrate her birthday. Rob in particular, she remembered, had had rather a lot to drink. Had he been fantasising about Araminta when he had done it? What a horrible thought.

'He's booked me in for a scan.' Bobbie gave a hoarse laugh. 'I suppose I'd better tell Rob by then.'

'MUM! Jack's doing it AGAIN!'

'You need to keep your powder dry!' Sarah spoke with the authority of the woman who had put a private detective on her husband's tail. 'Actually, there is one other thing you could do.'

Bobbie listened with incredulity to her friend's suggestion. 'I'm not sure about that.'

'Why not?' Sarah sounded offended. 'My last idea worked, didn't it? If you hadn't "interviewed" Araminta, you wouldn't have known the truth.'

Maybe it would have been better if she hadn't.

'MUM, MUM!'

'I'll ring back later this week.'

'Well, give it a go, will you?'

CRASH!

Oh my God! The glass coffee table was smashed. Jack was sitting beside it, surrounded by shards of glass. 'Are you hurt?' gasped Bobbie, kneeling beside her son.

'No!' He grinned up at her.

Relief turned to anger. 'What on earth were you doing?'

He shrugged. 'Just jumping.'

'You mean leaping off the sofa and on to the table without touching the ground.' Daisy had both hands on her waist in her best headmistress mode. 'I did tell you, Mum, but you were on the phone. Again!'

As if on cue, it rang once more. Forget it.

'Keep away, both of you.'

Bobbie grabbed a dustpan and brush and began to sweep up the mess. 'I don't want you to get cut.'

'But what about the phone?' Daisy was still poised importantly. 'I'll get it.'

'Ouch.' Bobbie sucked her finger where a tiny piece of glass had cut it. This could have been really nasty! Sometimes when she looked back at the scrapes her son had got into, she wondered how he'd survived.

'That was Vanessa!' Daisy announced, putting down the receiver. 'Her babysitter has let her down tonight so she wanted to know if she could bring Sunshine here. I said that was fine.'

'Did you?' Bobbie regarded her daughter with a mixture

of awe and irritation. She was so bossy – just like her sister in Australia – but at the same time, so in control. She could almost run the house! But how would she cope if she became one of those children that was passed like a parcel between two parents? Of course it happened all the time. But to other families. Not hers.

'I told her that Dad was babysitting tonight.' Daisy was nodding excitedly. 'I heard him promising he'd be back on time. Oh, and Granny texted me when you were on the phone to Sarah. She says her boyfriend is on television tonight and don't forget to watch him!'

'Sorry we're late!' whispered Bobbie as she and Vanessa crept into the classroom. The film had already started, which meant they'd missed the 'How did you get on' bit at the beginning. Shame! She and Vanessa rather enjoyed giggling at the 'Absolutely wonderful' feedback from Mr or Mrs Perfect.

'We're talking about how to keep calm when the kids are driving you crazy,' whispered Too Many Kids Mum, who was sitting right next to the door.

'Shhhh,' hissed Mr Perfect.

Bobbie tried to concentrate. But it was difficult. All she could think about was Rob, who'd made them late. 'I got here as fast as I could,' he had said defensively. 'Don't have another go at me. You don't understand what pressure I'm under with this campaign.' Then he saw the smashed coffee table. 'What on earth happened?'

'Ask Jack,' she retorted. Now as she sat uneasily in the classroom, feeling bloated in that early pregnancy way, she wished she hadn't given Vanessa a lift. It meant she couldn't have a coffee with Andy afterwards and run Sarah's idea past him to get a male point of view.

'So what do you think, Bobbie?' Judith was giving her a friendly but slightly concerned look as though she knew she hadn't been listening.

'I think I'd better go and see her,' replied Bobbie without thinking.

'See her?' Judith Davies looked puzzled. 'I don't understand.'

'Sorry!' Bobbie shook herself. 'I was miles away, I'm afraid.'

'Me too,' yawned American Express. 'I'm always dropping off. No offence, Miss Davies. But I love coming here. It's the only "me time" I get.'

A couple of others nodded. The young teacher looked uncertain. Just you wait, Bobbie thought. You'll find out what it's like before long: this impossible mixture of intense love for your children, coupled with the constant need to make sure that they survive each day. No wonder so many marriages sink in the process. Something has to give along the way.

'Bobbie!' She turned round as they were leaving at the sound of Matthew's voice. 'It was good to see you and your friend in the park. Was Jack's knee all right?'

She'd forgotten that one. 'Fine. Trust me. It's just one more normal incident in our life at the moment.'

Matthew gave her a funny glance. 'Right. I see.' His hands began to twist as though he was nervous. 'Actually, I was wondering if I could ask you a favour.'

'Do you need help with Lottie?' she asked.

His face cleared. 'Oh, no, I'm sorted now, thanks.' He looked around him swiftly as the classroom emptied. 'What I was really wondering was whether your friend in the park was coming along to the school fête.' He coloured. 'It's not important. Not really.'

So Matthew really did like Sarah! Wow! Bobbie couldn't wait to tell. And to say she was going to take up her advice after all.

Yes, Vanessa said slightly reluctantly when she got to work the next day. She could leave the shop just after lunch, if it was that urgent. And yes, Vanessa could pick up Daisy and Jack and give them tea until Bobbie was back.

The older woman had waited then, as if expecting Bobbie to reveal where she was going. How she wanted to confide in her! After all, Vanessa was one of those really interesting women who, despite not being more than forty-fivish, seemed to have a wealth of experience. Every now and then she referred to an ex-husband called Harry, but in such a way that suggested she didn't want to take the subject any further.

It was tempting to ask Vanessa's advice about Rob and Araminta. Then again, maybe the fewer who knew, the better. Meanwhile, Bobbie tried to fill in the next few hours by sorting out the new clothes that had come in and helping a pair of sisters (who must be sixty-five if they were a day) to find 'something glittery'.

'We go dancing,' they said, almost at the same time. 'Every Thursday afternoon at the town hall. Got our husbands to take it up after our children left home to fill in the gap. Mind if we practise? Vanessa always lets us. We have to make sure that the clothes don't restrict our movement, you see!'

And off they went: holding each other at arm's length, kicking their legs up this way and that and gliding across the shop floor! It almost took Bobbie's mind off the afternoon ahead. She and Rob used to love dancing before the children, although not the ballroom kind. What would *they* do to fill in the gap when the kids had left home? It seemed too far off to be believable. She couldn't imagine a home without Daisy and Jack. And what if she and Rob weren't together by then?

Bobbie pressed her nails into her palms. They *had* to be! Besides, she told herself as she agreed to a slight discount on the sequinned skirt, Rob was being much nicer suddenly. He'd been surprisingly understanding over the glass-table episode. 'These things happen,' he'd said after he'd calmed down. 'It's OK, son. I remember doing something similar myself. My father caned me for it.' His face darkened before adding, 'By the way, I've got to go to Scotland for a few days. With any luck, we'll have cracked the campaign then.'

'Are you going on your own?'

He gave her a strange look. 'Yes. Why?'

Oh God, she thought, returning to the present. She was going to be sick again. 'Sorry,' she blurted out to the surprised dancing sisters before dashing to the loo. Thank heavens! She had just got there in time. But – blast – there was a large sick stain on her beige trousers: one of the few pairs that fitted now. There wasn't time to go home and change; not if she was going to lock up at lunchtime and then get to the station. She'd have to borrow something from Vanessa. She wouldn't mind, surely! After all, she hadn't noticed the red dress the other week, which she'd had cleaned and then popped back on to the rail. In fact, this pair of suede trousers in a bigger size than she normally took would do nicely. So too would this jersey top. Since working at Vanessa's, she'd learned quite a lot about fashion!

It took ages to get to Rob's London office. Bobbie's heart began to rise towards her throat as she approached the revolving doors and clip-clopped across the shiny floor in the high heels borrowed from the shop to go with her new outfit. Then she caught sight of herself in the mirrored wall. Wow! She looked very different from the usual Bobbie who lived in jeans. This woman meant business!

Striding towards the desk, she held her head high, still not knowing exactly what she was going to say. But somehow she had to get hold of her rival. Had to appeal to her better nature, as Sarah had advised. Point out that she and Rob had two children – two and a bit actually – and that she simply had to let her husband go.

'Araminta Avon, please.'

Bobbie went rigid with shock. Was the oldish, rather tubby man in front of her at reception, asking for *her* Araminta?

'She'll be down in a minute, sir. Would you like to take a seat over there?' The crisp receptionist turned to her. 'May I help you?'

'Actually, I've just remembered. I need to make a phone call first.' She gave the girl a smile, trying to pretend she was the smart version of herself: the one in the mirror. 'I'll come back.' Smoothly, she headed for the seating area where the tubby man had made himself comfortable. Good! There was a pile of magazines there. Swiftly, Bobbie picked one up as camouflage.

'Minty! Not too late, am I?'

Bobbie peeped above her magazine. Aramintas with plummy voices were meant to be size 8s with beautifully cut hair and immaculately made-up faces in clothes to die for. Weren't they? This Araminta was a plump, short, squat girl with spots on her chin and a really boring skirt with flat ballet-style pumps. They were standing so close that she could hear every word, even though the posh voice was trying to be a whisper.

'I've missed you so much!' the man was saying.

'Me too!'

'How long have we got?'

'Half an hour at the most. Like I said, my boss is away in Scotland.'

They were walking together now towards the revolving doors. As she followed, Bobbie saw a flash of gold on the man's left hand. He was married! What a creep. His poor wife! Bobbie's heart soared. This awful husband-hunting Araminta wasn't after Rob after all! She was after someone *else's* husband!

All those fears about him working late and all that chat about his secretary were groundless, judging from the way the little squat man had his hand on her bottom as they walked along in front of her. As for that kiss after the message that she'd sent Rob, maybe Andy was right! Perhaps it *was* common nowadays. True, there were those ramblings in his sleep, but didn't she have the odd dream about Andy? It didn't mean anything. Did it?

Bobbie floated home on a cloud. Her marriage was safe! She would finally be able to tell Rob that she was pregnant. In fact, she'd do so as soon as they had a quiet second together. Somehow, they'd manage. After all, Daisy and Jack were getting older, weren't they? They might even like looking after a little one. 'Thanks for having the children!' she trilled when she reached Vanessa's maisonette. 'Everything all right?'

'Not really.' Vanessa's face was grim. 'Jack's wrecked my kitchen floor with his skateboard and now he's hidden Sunshine's flute and won't tell her where he's put it.'

Jack flew into her arms and burst into tears. 'IT WASN'T ME, MUM! HONEST!'

'Well, all I can say is that Sunshine had it in her hand when we got home and now it's gone. Come on, Bobbie. We all know what he's like.'

'You shouldn't label children! We talked about that at class. I'm sorry, but I think you're out of order here.'

'Like you, you mean?' Vanessa took in the suede trousers and the jersey top and the high heels. 'I don't remember giving you permission to borrow those.'

Shit. Bobbie reddened. 'I forgot to ask. I was sick. Think I've got this bug. There wasn't time to change so I thought I would just borrow something. I'm sorry.'

Vanessa's lips tightened.

'Would you like me to work in the shop this week?' asked Bobbie, suddenly feeling very small.

'I'll let you know.' Her voice was crisp and sharp. 'But I want those clothes back tomorrow. Dry-cleaned.'

It wasn't fair, Bobbie told herself, walking back a subdued Jack while Daisy skipped ahead. Just because her son had a reputation, it didn't mean he was responsible for everything that went wrong. On the other hand, she *had* been out of line with the clothes. How stupid! Just as she'd found a job she really enjoyed, too. Hopefully, she thought, checking her emails while the kids scooted off to argue over the remote control, they'd make it up tomorrow. Oh no . . .

Stunned, Bobbie read and reread the message from her online boss at Research Trivia; the words swam before her eyes.

Complaint . . . Miss Araminta Avon . . . traced back your number . . . inappropriate questions during medical survey . . . threatened to contact the standards authority . . . no longer in need of your services . . .

There was a young boy called Will,
Who simply wouldn't sit still,
So his au pair smeared glue
Between floor and his shoe
And then gave him a mild sleeping pill.*

*She got six months and it didn't work.

Chapter 29

VANESSA

'Not that way, Van Van. Like this!'

Vanessa tried to look up from the shallow end but her eyes were almost blinded by the water and that horrid stench of chlorine. No wonder she had loathed swimming as a child. How could she have let Sunshine talk her into this?

'Kick your legs this way. As though you're a frog! Watch me!'

It had started when they'd seen the poster, during one of Sunshine's own sessions: FREE SWIMMING LESSONS FOR ADULTS.

'You could do that, Van Van! I know you could!'

Vanessa had been torn between fear and admiration for her granddaughter's reading skills. 'I don't think that's for me,' she'd said uncertainly, although she'd learned that when Sunshine got a bee in her bonnet, there was no getting out of anything.

'But you *must* learn to swim,' the child insisted in a voice that sounded so like Brigid's as a teenager that Vanessa had had to look twice to check it wasn't her daughter.

Without quite knowing how, she had allowed herself to be dragged inside where she had signed up for a course of lessons. So far, she'd had just one but, as the instructor said, it was very important to practise, providing you did it in a 'safe environment under supervision'. That was why they were here, right now, with the rest of Corrywood splashing around them.

If nothing else, it was helping to keep Sunshine's mind off the postcard.

Vanessa had been so angry when she'd first received the

cheap, dog-eared picture of a sandy beach with the word Goa printed in the corner that she considered ripping it up and putting it in the bin. Didn't Brigid realise that a reminder of her absent mother might cause more harm than good? Sunshine was only just getting used to her new life and those nightmares when she had called out 'Mummy! Mummy!' in heartbreaking little cries were beginning to ease off.

If she now showed the postcard to her granddaughter, it might unsettle her again. Yet on the other hand, Vanessa couldn't bring herself to throw it away. 'I think you've got to come clean,' advised Brian. So she had.

Sunshine's face when she read it had been proof, if any was needed, that Brian had been right. 'Look! It's from Mummy.' Then she read the words out loud clearly as if in class. '*Hope you are having a lovely time with Granny. Be a good girl. Love Mum.*' Her little face was glowing. 'I knew she'd be all right!'

Oh, she was all right, thank you very much, thought Vanessa angrily. If she wasn't, she wouldn't have sent a card like that. She was probably *very* all right, in fact, living it up at all-night parties, no doubt, and having wild sex on a beach like the one in the picture. Maybe smoking some kind of weird drug too and completely forgetting that she was a mother with responsibilities.

Sunshine had insisted on taking the postcard into school with her to show her teacher. 'Miss Davies says we're going to do a project on India and I'm going to help her,' Sunshine had announced. But then the nightmares started again. Worse than before, with loud terrified cries that startled Vanessa in her sleep and sent her running in. 'MUMMY, MUMMY, MUMMY!' screamed Sunshine over and over again.

'It's all right, it's all right,' Vanessa soothed repeatedly but it was impossible to calm her. All she could do was sit by her side and hold her tight while those little limbs thrashed out around her. Yet during the day, she was fine! Happy as Larry, as her own mother used to say, especially now she'd got her flute back.

Vanessa was still furious about that. 'I'm afraid Daisy was to blame this time,' Bobbie had admitted shamefacedly. 'I found it in the bottom of her bag. But I'm sure it was a mistake.'

Really? Those kids were uncontrollable and frankly, she was beginning to think that it was Bobbie's fault for not being firm enough. Vanessa was also cross about the 'borrowed clothes'. She wouldn't have minded if she'd asked permission first. She was in two minds whether to sack her or not. But she needed an extra pair of hands in the shop.

'That's right, Van Van! You've got it! You're kicking the right way now!'

Her granddaughter's voice brought her back to the present. 'Nice to see you practising, Mrs Thomas,' said a young man in Speedos, striding by. 'Got your helper with you, I see! Looking forward to the next lesson!'

Sunshine giggled. 'Is that your swimming teacher, Granny?'

Vanessa nodded, conscious, as she went up the steps of the shallow end, of her body. Protectively she wrapped her towel around her chest.

'He likes you, Granny!' Sunshine was grinning toothily. Another baby tooth had fallen out last week – one more milestone that Brigid had missed out on, silly girl – and it made her look different. 'Yes he does! I saw him looking!'

Vanessa felt uneasy. A child of Sunshine's age wouldn't be so aware of a man looking at a woman unless she'd grown up in the wrong kind of environment. 'Come on now,' she said briskly, taking Sunshine's hand. 'Let's go and change, shall we?'

Her granddaughter now nodded seriously, taking in the way that Vanessa was holding her towel. 'Is your scar sore, Van Van?'

There were times when this mixture of maturity and childlike sweetness brought a lump to her throat. Her granddaughter could be frighteningly intuitive for her age. 'A bit.'

It was too. Ever since she'd found that pea-sized lump, the

scar had started to ache as though saying: 'I'm here. Don't ignore me.' She wasn't sure if that was a good thing or not.

Still, she'd find out soon enough. After all, the mammogram was tomorrow.

'Anything in particular that you'd like me to do today?' Bobbie asked when Vanessa had reluctantly left her in charge the following afternoon.

'You could sort out the sizing,' replied Vanessa coolly.

Bobbie nodded eagerly. 'Sure. They seem to have got rather muddled up, haven't they?'

Normally they would have had a little laugh at this point; maybe talk about one particular customer who was always pulling armfuls of stuff off the rails in her eagerness to 'secure a bargain' and then putting them back in the wrong order. But Vanessa didn't feel like joking. It wasn't just because of Daisy stealing Sunshine's flute out of spite (there was no other reason for it, was there?). It was because she was scared. Very scared.

'I'll come with you, lass,' Brian had offered when she'd finally told him what was up, but she'd said no, thank you. Secretly, she was worried about making a fool of herself by breaking down in tears. If she was going to do that, she'd do it on her own. Like last time.

Bobbie of course, didn't know where she was going. 'I have an appointment,' she'd said briskly. Yet now, as she walked down the high street to queue up at the bus stop for the hospital, she began to think that maybe she'd been a bit hard on her assistant. Bobbie *was* pregnant, after all. And she wasn't totally to blame for those kids being such live wires. Of all people, she should know that. Just look at Brigid! When she got back to the shop, Vanessa decided, she'd be a bit friendlier.

'Anyone want a lift?'

Vanessa was about to ignore the man in the white van who had pulled up next to the bus stop and was now leaning across through the open window. 'Not from strangers,' she started to say haughtily but then stopped. 'Brian!'

316

'Something told me that you might have changed your mind about wanting some company.' He patted the passenger seat. 'Go on, lass. Do me a favour.'

'Do *you* a favour?' she repeated, getting in.

'That's right. It will put me out of my agony to be there instead of fretting at home.' Then he gave her a kiss. A lovely warm kiss in full view of the others standing at the bus stop. And then he winked as he started up the engine. 'Makes a change to be able to have a snog without being spied on, doesn't it! How is the little one? Still having nightmares?'

Vanessa thought back to last night when Sunshine had, miraculously, slept through the night without waking. 'I think we might be getting there, with any luck.'

'Great!' He shot her a smile and patted her on the knee. 'Now all we need to do is to get you there, don't we?'

We. Despite her earlier protestations to herself that she could do this on her own, the word was comforting. Two small letters. But with so much meaning. 'Thanks for coming, Brian,' she said quietly.

'Wouldn't miss it for all the world, lass.'

Her feelings were reinforced when they got to the waiting room and found that nearly everyone there had someone with them. Not necessarily a partner, from the looks of things, but a friend or even, in some cases, a parent. The oncology breast clinic wasn't limited to the middle-aged, thought Vanessa ruefully as she looked around and took in a couple of young women with toddlers.

'Would you like to come in with your wife?' asked the nurse when it was her turn.

Vanessa felt a little thrill closely followed by embarrassment. 'We're not married—' she began to say but Brian cut in.

'What would you like me to do, lass?'

'I don't mind the company,' she heard herself saying.

In the event, it turned out that Brian wasn't allowed in the actual room 'because of the radiation', as the nurse explained. But he was invited to wait by the little cubicle where she got into a gown.

317

To her amusement, he gave a wolf whistle as she emerged. 'Very fetching!'

The nurse giggled. 'It's our new style. The old ones had a gap at the back and were a bit too revealing, if you know what I mean.'

Brian put on a silly face. 'I've no idea!'

It all helped to relax her so that by the time she was standing by the machine with that horrible heavy plate that came down and crushed her remaining breast, Vanessa wasn't as scared as she thought she'd be.

'Just because you've had cancer once doesn't mean you'll have it again,' said the nurse sympathetically.

Vanessa tried to explain that she understood that but the right words wouldn't come out of her mouth. 'I just want to know,' she managed to say.

'Course you do!' The heavy plate was rising now, allowing her breast to breathe. 'The results will go to the consultant and you'll be seen as soon as possible.'

'How long?'

'Within ten days to a fortnight, I should think. Earlier if . . .'

She stopped but Vanessa knew what she had been about to say. Earlier if the results weren't good. That's exactly what had happened last time.

'But it's not last time, is it, lass?' reassured Brian as they drove back. 'No two things in life are ever the same. I know Mavis and I had our ups and downs but when she died, I thought I'd never find anyone else like her. And I was right.' Then he reached across and took her hand briefly. 'She was special in one way. But you're special in another, Nessie.'

Nessie! He'd never called her that before. It was what they'd called her at school, years ago. Nessie the Loch Ness monster! How she'd hated it! But the way Brian said it was touching. Loving.

'You know what we need to do now?'

'What?' sniffled Vanessa.

'Pick up that granddaughter of yours from school and take

318

her on a nice long walk with my Bingo! By the way, we've signed up for dog training. Fancy coming?'

It was hysterical! Vanessa had never seen anything like it. Nor, it seemed, had Sunshine.

'Sit, Bingo. SIT!'

Brian had allowed Sunshine to take his place, holding the lead, while he and Vanessa watched from the side of the field as a dozen or so dog owners and their 'hounds' (as Brian called them), walked briskly round. Every now and then, they'd stop to do an exercise, like now.

'Isn't that cheating?' asked Vanessa as the group leader, wearing jodhpurs as though she was running a riding stable, announced it was time for a 'treat'. 'Dogs will do anything if they're bribed, won't they? Just like children.'

'Nothing wrong with that,' twinkled Brian. He nudged her gently. 'Works on elderly boyfriends too.'

The distraction was certainly working for her; well, up to a point. Vanessa's insides glowed as she watched Sunshine walk round the ring, holding the lead in her right hand but also clutching it half way down with the left as she'd been taught to do.

'Right!' barked Jodhpur Woman. 'Time for the emergency stop!'

'You've got to see this,' said Brian. 'Bingo wasn't bad last week. Let's see what he's like with the little lass.'

Vanessa watched, mesmerised, as each owner took turns to walk to the edge of the field, instructing their dog to 'Sit, stay' and then walking back again to the original position. Then they had to call their dogs and yell out 'STOP' halfway across the field. The idea, apparently, was to make your dog screech to a halt in an emergency situation, like a busy road.

'STOP!' yelled Sunshine in a voice that was louder than any of the others. But Bingo, his ears flapping in the wind, completely ignored her and shot right up to Brian, leaping up and covering him with kisses.

'You daft dog,' said Brian but not in a cross way. 'Go back

to the class now. Don't worry, Sunshine. It wasn't your fault.'

Luckily, Sunshine didn't seem too upset as they drove back. Instead, she was rabbiting on, ten to the dozen, in the back of the car. Not to her or Brian but to Bingo who was sitting erect, listening to everything she was saying. 'You'll have to do better next time! I always stop before I cross the road. It's safer that way.'

'Best thing I ever did was to get a dog,' remarked Brian as he pulled up outside her house. He looked her straight in the eye. 'Stops me feeling lonely.'

Vanessa couldn't help it. Sunshine might be in the back of the car but so what? A hug was all right, wasn't it? 'You'll never be that,' she whispered. And then she broke off. Because that's just what he might be – and Sunshine too – if her results weren't good.

'Walked into that one all right, didn't I?' sighed Brian. 'Come on, Nessie. Let's go out tomorrow night, shall we? All of us. We could try out that pizza place round the corner.'

She shook her head reluctantly. 'I promised to meet up with Bobbie and some of the other girls from the parenting class.'

'Any good?'

'A bit. I've made new friends.'

Then she thought of Bobbie. The mammogram had helped her to focus. Had reminded her that life was too short to fall out with anyone.

If only her own daughter understood that.

They all met up in the new pasta place to have an 'informal gathering' in between classes. 'The handbook recommends it,' Judith had chirped enthusiastically. Most of them were there, including American Express, Too Many Kids Mum, Not Really Pregnant Mum and Matthew as well as her and Bobbie. Judith had suggested they talked about arguments and how they started in the family. 'You might be more comfortable doing that outside one of the usual sessions,' she had said. 'It's one of the tips in the handbook. Anyway, give it a go!'

It was quite nice, actually. American Express talked about

how her husband thought it was time she stopped breastfeeding but that she didn't feel ready.

'If you ask me,' said Not Really Pregnant Mum, 'it's time you did.' She patted her stomach. 'I've finally decided to have me fibroids out. I was a bit scared, to be honest.' For a minute she looked like a little girl. 'Don't really care for operations. But my own son asked me if I was up the duff the other day. So I'm going ahead.'

There was a murmur of 'well done's but Vanessa remained silent during the ensuing discussion on fibroids and breast-feeding. Who had the right to tell anyone what to do? Bobbie was quiet too. One of them had to make up, she thought.

'I didn't mean . . .' she began

'I had a terrible . . .' said Bobbie at the same time.

They both stopped. 'You first.'

'No. Please you.'

'OK.' Bobbie looked away. 'I had a terrible row with Daisy over the flute,' she said, shamefacedly. 'I told her it was totally unacceptable and I've stopped her pocket money.'

Vanessa looked uncertain. 'Why did she do it?'

'Attention-seeking, I think. She and Jack have always been fiercely competitive. And now . . .'

She stopped.

'. . . and now you're pregnant?'

Bobbie gave her a startled glance. 'How did you know?'

Vanessa took the younger woman's hand. It felt so good to be friends again! 'The big giveaway was the pregnancy magazine you were reading at the doctor's. But then I saw your buttons don't do up and you were sick the other morning.'

'I'm so sorry about borrowing those clothes.'

'Forget it.'

But Bobbie still looked troubled.

'There's something else, isn't there?'

She nodded. 'I've done something really silly, Vanessa. Dug myself into a real hole. Now I don't know what to do about it.'

Vanessa looked around. The breastfeeding argument was

getting heated: no one would hear them. 'Why don't you tell me?' she said kindly.

By the time Bobbie had finished doing exactly that, Vanessa didn't know whether to laugh or cry. 'I'm not saying that you were wrong to suspect your husband of having an affair,' she said. 'In my experience, it's often the ones you least expect. But it's not the end of the world if you end up on your own, you know. As for Araminta's complaint, there's one very easy way out.'

'Is there?'

Vanessa nodded. 'Absolutely.' She beckoned Bobbie to come nearer. 'If I were you, this is what I would do . . .'

Vanessa felt quite light-hearted when she let herself in. There was nothing like making up. She'd always hated arguments anyway.

Sunshine was fast asleep, her neighbour (who'd been babysitting) reassured her. The phone had rung a couple of times but she hadn't got to it in time, she was afraid. Still, Vanessa had an answerphone, didn't she? And thanks for leaving out the chocolate biscuits. They were delicious!

Vanessa first checked Sunshine, who was breathing evenly, before playing back the messages. It would be Brian. Warm, wonderful Brian who always rang her in the evening but must have thought she was back already.

The first message had been left at 6 p.m., just after she'd gone to pick up Bobbie.

'This is a message for Mrs Thomas. It's the breast clinic at St Nicholas' Hospital speaking. Please could you ring back as soon as possible to make a further appointment.'

But she'd only just had her mammogram! That meant there was something wrong. No. No. Please, not again. Not now she had Sunshine. And Brian. It wasn't fair!

Numbly, she pressed the button for the second message. 'It's me. It's—'

And then the message cut off before the speaker could say any more.

WHAT KIND OF PARENT ARE YOU?

When they won't pick up their clothes from the floor, do you:

1. Insert pins in boxer crotches.
2. Let them dig a path.
3. Send the lot to Oxfam (the kids, not the clothes).
4. Go through all pockets. The consequent discovery of condoms and police cautions will teach the owners to hang up their jeans.
5. Give up.

Answer: A hopeless parent (If this is too small to read, it means the kids have destroyed your eyesight along with your sanity).

(Note from editor of I Can't Cope With My Kids magazine. This is the last in the series. Author is pregnant again . . . see back issue on foolproof contraception.)

Chapter 30

ANDY

Too late? Andy stood on Camilla's doorstep, taking in his mother-in-law's distressed face. What did she mean?

'Where's Pamela?' he demanded, following her in. Despite the situation, he couldn't help admiring the paintings on the wall, the polished mahogany hall table and the spacious sitting room with oak beams that led to a pair of French windows with beautiful gardens beyond. He'd seen it all before, of course. But every time it reminded him of how different his own background had been from his wife's.

'She's in trouble.'

Andy glanced down at the box under his arm. 'I think I know what you're talking about,' he said slowly.

'I doubt it.' Camilla sat down on the edge of the sofa in her usual erect posture but with fear in her eyes that he had never seen before.

Andy was really beginning to get nervous now. 'Just tell me where she is.'

Camilla's voice was almost inaudible. 'Somewhere safe.'

'For God's sake, stop playing games!' He was getting angry now. 'She's with *him*, isn't she? The man in the sports car. Don't deny it. I saw them on the doorstep, all over each other.'

Standing up with her usual erect poise, Camilla walked briskly over to the drinks cabinet. Pouring herself a large glass of gin, without offering one to Andy, she slugged it back. 'He wasn't any good for her. I told Pamela that.'

Andy took the glass out of the older woman's hand just as she began to refill it. 'That's not going to help, is it?'

To his amazement, she didn't resist. Instead, she clutched

his arms, as though drowning. 'I don't know how to tell you the rest, dear. I really don't.'

Dear? Never, ever, had Camilla referred to him in anything other than the most scathing of terms. Something was seriously wrong. Andy heard his voice come out like a twelve-year-old Barry: tough, to mask the fear. 'I want to know where my wife is. Tell me, Camilla. Tell me.'

'Please don't shout at me. If you must know, I made her go to one of those places.'

'What do you mean?'

She was walking towards the French windows now, lighting up a cigarette. Andy, who hadn't smoked for years, suddenly felt a desperate urge to join her. 'When she came down here to help me, I realised how bad things had become. She tried to hide it of course – addicts can be very cunning – but I'd had practice with her father.'

Addict? Of course! How stupid he had been. How daft to think Pamela would have honoured her promise when they'd got married. The signs were all too clear now. Tense one minute. Hyper the next. The demand from the loan company. Her abandonment of the family.

It wasn't just the drink. Or the contents of the hat case, which he could hardly bear to reveal to anyone else. It was far worse. 'She's taking drugs again? Like she did before?'

Camilla's eyes widened. 'You knew about that?'

Oh yes, he had known all right. Pamela had been a complete cokehead when they'd first met. Not that it was immediately obvious: she'd been good at concealing it from some but not good enough to hide it from a streetwise kid like him. On their third date, to his amazement, she'd confessed that she'd 'had enough' and wanted to stop. She wanted to get out of modelling, too. The fact that her agent was about to drop her over the drug rumours that were already circulating the industry didn't come out until later.

Not that it had mattered to him. The young Andy Gooding had been hook, line and sinker in love with this fascinating creature who agreed to spend the rest of her life with him.

So what if it was his money that had attracted her? He loved her and, besides, he believed her when she said she wanted to wipe the slate clean, even though many wouldn't have.

He'd been proved right, or so he'd thought. From the day they had exchanged their vows, Pamela had been a perfect mother. A clean mother. Until now. No wonder Mel had thought it was acceptable to smoke joints. 'What's she on?' Andy felt his throat tighten as he spoke. 'Drink? Heroin? Cannabis?'

'A bit of everything.' Camilla's eyes wouldn't meet his. 'Soon after she came down, I rang the rehab centre in town – it's really quite famous – and she started off with one of their support groups. That was run by the young man in the sports car whom you saw.'

'So they weren't having an affair?'

'Don't be silly. Anyway, he was hopeless, so then I persuaded her to go in full-time. It's expensive, naturally.'

'Ten thousand pounds?'

'More, by the time she's finished. But they're helping her to work it out. Of course, it all started with self-esteem. When that went, she turned to something else that gave her a buzz.'

'Her self-esteem?' repeated Andy.

'Are you deaf?' Camilla was back to her old dismissive self. 'You must have noticed – oh, of course, I forgot. You were never at home, were you? When she gave up modelling to have the girls, she lost herself. Her sense of worth.'

Andy looked down at the hat box was sitting by his side. 'I need you to look at this,' he began tentatively. Removing the lid, he took out a photograph, a large black-and-white glossy, and handed it to his mother-in-law.

She smiled through her tears. 'That's exactly what I meant.'

Together they stared at it. The photograph showed Pamela, head thrown back in an exaggerated pose as she held out her hands on both sides. She was wearing a Bruce Oldfield dress; it had been taken during London Fashion Week some twenty-odd years ago when she had been the toast of the fashion pages.

But there was a big black cross through it and a word scrawled in black pen, in Pamela's own handwriting, over the picture.

Useless.

'There are piles of them in here,' said Andy, showing her. 'Each with the same word.' He rubbed his eyes. 'At first I didn't understand but now, I think, I get it. At least part of it.'

He thought back to his own feelings. That sense of frustration and uselessness now he wasn't doing anything any more, apart from running around after the girls and making sure they were doing what they should be. When it came to teenagers, it was like trying to fill a bucket with a hole. You could never win.

'Why didn't she tell me she felt like this?'

Camilla gave another little sarcastic laugh. 'Don't you see? She was frightened of losing you.'

Pamela? Frightened of losing *him*? But it was *he* who was frightened of losing *her*!

'She knew you wanted a secure family life after your aunt died. She also knew that you'd saved her. No. Don't deny it.' Camilla's eyes narrowed. 'We both understand why she married you. It wasn't just because of the drugs or because her career was over, was it?'

Andy gulped, thinking back to the night that he had proposed. 'You don't want to marry me,' a drunken Pamela had laughed in that high tinkly voice that used to come out when she'd had far too much to drink. 'I'm pregnant! Pregnant with someone else's child. A man who doesn't want anything to do with me. If you knew who it was, you'd understand!'

He'd been shocked, of course. Taken aback. But at the same time, her words had given him hope. He would never have had a chance of gaining such a glittering prize unless it had been 'damaged'. A top model who was pregnant by someone in the public eye; a man whom Pamela absolutely refused to name. He would only deny it, she kept saying.

Everyone would be too scared to believe her. He didn't understand the world she lived in.

This beautiful woman needed someone to look after her. And he was there. 'I'll bring the child up as mine. I promise.' Anything to have the woman of his dreams!

Each had, or so he'd thought, fulfilled their part of the bargain. He gave her security. She gave him a family. By mutual agreement, they had never told Mel. It would only lead to awkward questions, Pamela had insisted. For his part, he honestly saw Mel as his own; had felt that way from the minute she was born all wriggly and wet with a cry that had pierced his heart. Hadn't he known what it was like to be unwanted? He'd be damned if another child was going to feel that way.

'But why now?' he asked Camilla. 'Why has Pamela suddenly flipped?'

'You silly boy! It's not sudden. It's been a slow burn, although there was a trigger, I'll admit.'

'And Pamela's trigger was?'

'Nattie, of course! Well, part of it, anyway.'

Nattie? Andy thought back to when she'd been born, barely two years after Mel. Such a beautiful little thing who looked so like her older half-sister that for a moment, Andy had wondered if Pamela had been seeing that man again; the man whose name she still refused to reveal. But then he'd seen her ears, which were so like his with that little kink in the earlobes, and he had felt reassured.

'Two months ago, she told Pamela that she wanted to be a model! Didn't you know?'

'No!' A flash of Nattie's bedroom wall adorned with posters of beautiful girls came into his head. Her pickiness with food. The way she walked, so erectly. The way she drank; maybe to lose her inhibitions. Just as Pamela had done.

'Pamela said that she wasn't going to let her daughter make the same mistakes as her.' Camilla sighed. 'I told her it's what all parents fear; their children making identical errors. But you have to let them do it or they won't learn.'

An overpowering aroma of cabbage and urine and Brussels sprouts suddenly came into his head. 'I'm glad you've told me, Camilla.' Then he remembered. That earlier hesitation. The 'part of it' bit. He grabbed the older woman's hands. 'Was there something else, too? Something else that made Pamela flip?'

Camilla edged away. 'No.'

She was lying. He was sure of it.

'But I will tell you this, Andrew. She might hide her feelings' – his mother-in-law was straining as though having to push every word out of her mouth – 'but she does love you.'

Did she? Does she? Or had he just been a convenience all these years? A safe harbour to bring up her illegitimate daughter. A harbour that she'd now wearied of.

Andy stood up. He'd had enough of this. Enough of these secrets and games.

'Give me the number of the centre, please.'

'They won't let you see her.' His mother-in-law almost sounded sorry for him. 'She's told them she doesn't want you there. Not at the moment. Not even for their family-group sessions.'

His eyes hardened. He was Barry all over again. 'Then if I can't see her, I want to talk to whoever is treating her.'

He rang from the car but the centre said that someone would ring him back. Andy drummed his fingers on the wheel in frustration. He didn't want to wait. He wanted to know now! So when the mobile rang again on his hands free, his heart leaped.

'Andy? It's me, George.'

George! He'd forgotten to call him back with everything else that had been going on. 'Look, I've made the transfers and I moved the shares as we discussed. We'll just have to wait and see what happens now.'

George's voice didn't sound like his old confident self. Twitchy even. Andy felt a slight give in his chest. His financial adviser hadn't been very keen on the gamble that Andy had

329

suggested but he knew he was right. Always had been. He might have got his family life wrong over the years but when it came to money, he had the golden touch. Even in today's climate.

Anyway, he was nearly home now. Time to concentrate on what really mattered. His poor girls! It was up to him to provide as much stability as he could until Pamela got back. But then what? Andy felt a nasty feeling at the pit of his stomach.

'Hi, Dad!' Mel sauntered down the stairs. How could he ever have thought of her as another man's child? She was his! She even had his gung-ho, I-can-do-this approach to life. Who said personality was genetic? Mel was living proof that nurture played its part too.

Then he did a double-take. What was she wearing? Or rather, not wearing. Shorts with heavily laddered black tights?

'You're not going out dressed like that!'

She gave him a bemused look. 'Chill out. It's the fashion.'

'Where are you going and who with?'

'You sound like the Gestapo! It's Nattie you should be worried about. Look, Dad, I shouldn't tell you this but she won't be back until tomorrow. I promised to cover but I can't lie any more.'

'Where's she gone?'

'London, for a studio shot session. We didn't tell you 'cos we thought you'd go mad like Mum did when Nattie won the last competition.'

'What last competition?'

Mel waved her hand dismissively. 'For a model! There was this really big row. Mum wouldn't let Nattie take the prize – that was a studio session too. She also said we weren't to tell you about it. So when Nattie won this one, she said nothing was going to stop her.' His daughter made a daddy's-little-girl face. 'You won't tell her any of this, will you? Or she'll kill me.'

No, he wouldn't, Andy assured her. Yet at the same time, he couldn't help feeling that Mel was taking a certain pleasure in getting her little sister into trouble.

'By the way, Dad. Are you out tonight?'

'No. My parenting group is having a get-together on its own for a change.' Her disappointment was all too obvious. 'Why? Thinking of having a party?'

Mel pouted. 'Why do you and Mum keep treating me like a kid?'

'Because you *are* one.'

'No I'm not. Jason says that when his daughter is older, he's going to understand when she wants to do stuff.'

'Who's Jason?'

'My boyfriend, course.'

'That bloke with huge plug earrings I saw in your room? He's got a *child*?'

Mel looked a bit awkward. 'Well, he thinks it's his daughter but he's having some tests done to prove it.'

This was awful! 'I don't want you going out with someone who's . . .' His voice faded away. What he really meant was that he didn't want her going out with anyone who had 'done it'. His Mel! His beautiful Mel who was only seventeen. How dare some oikish bloke with a kid in tow get his hands on his daughter?

Mel grabbed her bag at the splutter of tyres on the gravel outside. Looking through the window, Andy spotted a beaten-up old Corsa creaking to a halt. 'You're going out in that?'

'Keep your hair on, Dad.'

'But it's got L-plates!'

'That's for me!' Mel grabbed her bag. 'He's giving me practice, Dad. See you!'

And she was off before Andy could stop her.

EMAIL FROM JUDITH DAVIES TO ANDY GOODING

Hope you don't mind me asking but the Perfect Parents' handbook suggests that we end the course with a weekend retreat! This will help the group to consolidate

331

what they have learned! The book also suggests that they bring partners and children. Someone mentioned that you have a house in Devon. We wondered if it would be possible for us to go there in the holidays? Perhaps you could let me know what you think?

There was a young Jock, who wouldn't say please –
Not even when mum went down on her knees.
But she got her own back
For him giving her flack
By taking away his house keys.

PERFECT PARENTS: SESSION EIGHT

LEARNING TO LET GO!

ONE OF THE ~~EASIEST~~ HARDEST JOBS AS A
PARENT IS TO GIVE YOUR KIDS THEIR
INDEPENDENCE.

PLUS! WHAT HAVE WE GOT OUT OF THIS
COURSE?

(Ed's note: Why is there a blank space here?)

Chapter 31

BOBBIE

'So,' chirruped Miss Davies, 'this is our last session!'

There was a murmur of 'we'll miss it' amidst a few embarrassed smiles. They'd all felt so awkward at the beginning. Now it seemed impossible that they wouldn't carry on meeting every Monday night. The teacher's table was already piled with thank-you gifts. Bobbie had brought a lavender sachet. It was meant to be calming, according to the label. Maybe she should keep it for herself. Ever since that email, she'd been a nervous wreck.

'Complaint . . . Miss Araminta Avon . . . traced back your number . . . inappropriate questions during medical survey . . . threatened to contact the standards authority . . . no longer in need of your services . . .'

She knew every word off by heart now. At first, Bobbie hadn't understood how Araminta had traced her number and given it to her boss at Research Trivia. Hadn't she dialled 1471? Then she'd remembered with a cold jolt. It had been engaged. So she'd dialled it again – without the prefix!

And now she'd not only lost her job but was also, as her line manager had informed her, guilty of breaching their code of conduct. 'If Miss Avon chooses to press charges, you could be facing a stiff fine or even a sentence,' he'd informed her icily.

Prison? Her legs had turned to jelly. What would happen to Jack and Daisy? What about the child inside her? And what on earth would Rob say?

'The good news', continued Judith chirpily, 'is that Andy Gooding, who runs the teenage group up the corridor, has kindly offered his holiday home in Devon as a weekend retreat.'

Andy's name caught Bobbie's attention. How she wanted to tell him about this awful mess she'd got herself into! Then again, she'd already confided in Vanessa.

'Please let me know by the end of the evening if you're interested. Meanwhile, would anyone like to give us all some feedback on the course – has it helped at all?'

Everyone began to shuffle. No one wanted to speak first, least of all Bobbie. It would be so nice to say, if only to please Judith, that Daisy and Jack had turned over a new leaf between them. But they hadn't. Maybe her kids were in a class of their own when it came to bad behaviour. It wasn't long now until Mum's visit, so Dr Know would just have to take them as he found them. Even if she was behind bars by then.

'It's helped me to understand my granddaughter a bit better,' piped up Vanessa. 'Thanks for that. *And* I've made new friends.'

Sitting down, she exchanged a small smile with Bobbie. If nothing else, it looked as though she really had been forgiven.

Battered Mum had her hand up. 'The other day, my son tried to push me. But I caught his hand before he could hurt me and told him that he had a choice. Either he stopped this violent stuff or else I put him up for that programme on telly. The one where they send bad kids to strict parents in America. It's called *The World's Strictest Parents*. Have you seen it? It's brill.'

Judith looked as though this wasn't the answer she'd been expecting.

'What did he say to that?' asked Not Really Pregnant Mum.

'We're waiting to hear if they'll accept him.'

Vanessa caught her eye and they both tried not to giggle. Then Bobbie stopped. How could she laugh when things were so serious?

'I've learned that you can't get it all from books,' offered Too Many Kids Mum. 'It also seems there are no magic answers. It's a question of trying out different alternatives and

338

seeing what works, without expecting a miraculous turn-round.'

Miss Davies beamed. 'Wonderful! Anyone else?'

Bobbie took a deep breath. 'I asked Daisy to explain why she had stolen something – a flute that belonged to someone else – and allowed her brother to take the blame. She said she didn't know.'

Not Really Pregnant Mum bristled. 'Stealing again! Someone ought to report you. And your kids.'

She should have kept quiet! This was turning into a witch hunt.

'Actually,' said a voice behind her, 'my Lottie went through a period of stealing money a couple of years ago.'

Bobbie turned round gratefully. 'Really?'

Matthew was standing up now, with a go-on-then-criticise-me-too look on his face. 'I was cross at the time but then I realised it was attention-seeking.'

How complicated kids could be! You needed a degree in psychology to be a parent.

'My wife had recently died,' continued Matthew, 'and my daughter didn't like having au pairs in those days.'

'Understandable,' snorted Not Really Pregnant Mum. 'But what's *your* excuse, Bobbie?'

'Well,' she began, voice wobbling, 'we've got family issues at the moment. I think my two are picking up on the vibes and doing things that they wouldn't normally do.'

Bobbie sat down heavily, aware of Vanessa's hand reaching out for hers. 'Well done,' she whispered. 'That was very brave.'

Was it? Or had she simply dented her family's reputation even further? Meanwhile, Miss Davies was handing out feedback forms and they all settled down to watch the final DVD, optimistically entitled *Looking Forward to the Future*.

The prospect of the future filled her with dread. Maybe Vanessa was right. Her only option was to pay another visit to Araminta.

But it was a gamble. A huge one.

*

339

'I've got a tummy ache!'

Oh no. Every parent hated 'tummy-ache days'. You had to put your own judgement on the line. Work out if it merited a long wait at the doctor's or whether it was just plain skiving. Usually, with Jack, it was the latter. She eyed him sceptically. 'This wouldn't have anything to do with the maths test today, would it?'

'No.' He shook his head dramatically. Too dramatically.

Mmmm. He was well enough to be playing with his computer game under the covers, but even so, she couldn't risk it. Not after the last time when the school secretary had told her off for sending him in when he was under the weather. Blast! What was she going to do now? This was her last chance! Rob was away at another conference and Araminta would, or so she hoped, be in the office.

'Bobbie?' It was Rob on the mobile. 'Listen, I'm sorry to do this to you, darling, but I've left something at home.'

Darling? It had been years since he'd called her that. Unusual endearments and unexpected bunches of flowers were all signs of affairs, weren't they? But Araminta was seeing another man, and besides, recently Rob seemed to have been making a real effort – for some unknown reason. She couldn't imagine now how she could ever have suspected her husband of anything.

'I know you're really busy with the children.'

What had come over him? Rob was always telling her how easy she had it at home, compared with 'the real world'.

'But I wondered if you could possibly take some papers into the office. Stupidly, I've left them behind and they're too confidential for me to send a courier.'

'MUM! MUM! I WANT TO SPEAK TO DAD! CAN YOU PUT HIM ON SKYPE?'

'He's too busy, Jack. Later.'

'No,' interrupted Rob. 'It's all right. Put him on.'

He'd never, ever said that before!

'DAD! My tummy hurts. Mum says it's nuffing and—'

'That's enough!' Bobbie grabbed the phone. Rob had given

340

her the perfect excuse to have a face-to-face with Araminta. Her Research Trivia line manager had let slip that Araminta hadn't realised it was her – Bobbie – who had made that call, only that it was one of the company's freelance employees. Maybe if she told her what had really happened, as Vanessa had advised, Araminta might withdraw her complaint. It was her only hope if she was going to hide this from her husband.

'It's all right,' she added, down the line. 'I don't think Jack's really ill so I'll take him with me. Just tell me where these papers are and we'll be there as soon as we can!'

Maybe life really had turned the corner! Bobbie felt a sense of optimism inside as she waited on the station platform with Jack who was actually – miracle of miracles! – sitting next to her quietly on the bench. Usually she was having to hang on to him to make sure he didn't go near the track or run off down the stairs to the car park. But she'd used that tip Not Really Pregnant Mum had mentioned in class: the one where you pre-empted the situation and then offered them something that they really, really wanted.

'I know you're going to be bored stiff sitting here while we wait for the train,' she'd said when Jack began to whine because she wouldn't let him skateboard on the platform (he'd insisted on bringing the darned thing). 'I'm going to be bored too. But you can have my iPad to play with for a whole hour!'

So what if it was bribery! Incredibly, they had a virtually pain-free journey to London. 'What a well-behaved little lad,' said an older woman as they got off.

Bobbie looked around to see whom she was talking to. 'My son? Gosh. Thanks.'

Then she took Jack's hand. 'Leave me alone,' he whined. 'You're messing up my game.'

The older woman looked disappointed. Oh well, illusions never lasted. For a moment there, Bobbie's mind had been taken off the job in hand. Now she was beginning to feel butterflies just like the last time she had come to Rob's office.

'Araminta Avon, please,' she said, standing at the smart

reception desk. 'Can you say that it's Mrs Wright. Yes, I believe she is expecting me. Jack. Come here!'

Oh God. He was off. Scooting across the marble floor on his flipping skateboard, flicking bogeys as he went.

'Mrs Wright!'

The squeaky little-girl voice shrilled across the lobby. 'I'm sorry to keep you waiting.' She glanced nervously at Jack, who was now zooming back towards them. Araminta nipped out of the way just in time. 'You must be the little man that your daddy's always talking about! Very proud he is of you.'

Could this really be the woman that she'd seen as a threat? Close up, she seemed quite nice. And even spottier. That brace was really obvious. Fantastic!

'I've brought the papers.'

'Great!' Araminta made to take them.

'Actually, I wondered if we could have five minutes to talk.' Bobbie scoured the busy foyer for Jack, who was now scooting off in another direction 'Somewhere more private. There's a playground over the road, I noticed, with a skateboard park. My little boy could let off steam there.'

Araminta glanced at her watch. 'I'm very busy. Your husband is a real workaholic, you know. Keeps my nose to the grindstone.'

'Please.' Bobbie fought to keep the desperation out of her voice and lost. 'It's about your complaint. The one to Research Trivia.'

'It was *you*? You were the one who asked me all those questions about my personal life?'

Araminta's expression had changed from 'being friendly to the boss's wife' to one of outright hostility.

'No, wait. Listen. JACK, COME BACK. Don't go, Araminga. I mean, Araminta. I thought you were having an affair with my husband, you see.'

'Your *husband*!' There was a loud laugh and a flash of expensive braces.

'It's not that funny.' Bobbie felt quite defensive. 'He's very

342

good-looking and he talked about you once in his sleep.' She felt herself turn puce red just as she remembered something else. 'One night, he came back reeking of perfume – unless, oh God, he's having an affair with someone else.'

'Of course not! He wouldn't have time!' Araminta clutched her hand. It felt surprisingly comforting. 'The thing about advertising – and not everyone gets this – is that it's utterly consuming. When you're running a campaign like we are at the moment, it's twenty-four/seven. You and Me is one of the biggest projects we've ever had. There's a lot at stake.'

'Sorry,' said Bobbie interrupting. 'You and Me? That's a *project*?'

'Shhh.' Araminta looked around. 'It's actually a code name for this really big lingerie company that we're rebranding. No one's allowed to discuss it. Not even in our sleep!'

'I see! JACK! COME BACK!'

'Your husband is a *very* attractive man, I grant you that. But there's nothing going on between us.'

Bobbie still felt a bit unsure. That 'very attractive' bit had been said with great enthusiasm. This woman might be plump and spotty with braces but, as Sarah was always saying, there was no accounting for taste. (Her friend's ex-husband's new bit had extremely thick white puffy ankles.)

'I have to say though, you had a nerve, pretending to interview me. Not bad. Not bad at all.' Araminta sounded almost impressed. In fact, she was getting out her notepad. 'We might be able to use that one in a campaign. We're pitching for a tracking-device account at this very moment.'

This was her life they were talking about! Not work! 'Didn't you recognise our home number when you did 1471 after my call?'

Araminta was still writing. 'Sorry? What? No, of course not. I always use Rob's mobile when I need to get hold of him. Not your landline.'

Bobbie thought back to the text with the kiss. 'So I gather.'

'Trouble is,' continued Araminta chummily, putting her pad away, 'a lot of marriages in advertising break up under the strain. It's usually the wives who can't cope. We have to work as a team and sometimes that includes eating, drinking and sleeping together – well, not like that although I won't pretend it doesn't happen.' She made a wry face. 'I've made that mistake myself.'

Bobbie was beginning to panic again now. 'But not with Rob?'

'Course not. I never have affairs with men who have kids under ten.' She touched Bobbie's hand again. 'I do have morals, you know. In fact, I'm always telling your husband not to stay so late in the office.'

'You do? JACK! I'M NOT GOING TO TELL YOU AGAIN!'

'Absolutely. I had a real go at him the other day. Your kids need to see you, I said. They might be asleep when you get home but they still need to know that you've got that last train.' Araminta looked slightly smug. 'He may be my boss but we have a very good relationship.'

Clearly!

'As for the perfume, I'm afraid you are right on that one. Every now and then, he gives me a big cuddle.'

Bobbie felt nauseous. 'So there *is* something between you? JACK!'

'Definitely!' Araminta was nodding. The crop of spots on her chin was close to eruption. 'He's been helping me through a rather difficult time: listening and giving the odd comfort hug. You see, I'm having a relationship with someone who isn't available. Well, not at the moment.' She looked around, as if worried someone might hear. 'I know it's wrong. In fact, your phone call did me a favour. It spooked me out and I tried to break it off with Duncan.' Tears came into her eyes. 'But then he kept ringing; insisting that his marriage was over anyway.'

That old chestnut! 'Does he have children?' interrupted Bobbie, recalling Araminta's rather dubious not-under-ten rule.

'No.'

That was something. Bobbie didn't like the idea of anyone

having an affair but if two people were terribly unhappy, who was to decree that they had to stay together forever? 'The thing is that Rob and I *do* have kids, as you probably know. Two.' She glanced down at her stomach. 'And I would do anything, anything, to keep my marriage together. Even if it meant making crazy phone calls. Now I can't think what got into me.'

A misty look came into Araminta's little piggy eyes. 'Love! That's what it is. Look, I didn't realise it was you making that call, obviously. So I'll withdraw my complaint. Rob doesn't have to know. He's been so good to me that I wouldn't want to hurt him.'

Bobbie was still unsure. 'They might still take action.'

'Not if they don't have me to give evidence.' Araminta looked smug again. 'I used to be an employment lawyer until I switched to advertising, you know.'

'Thank you! Thank you! Oh my God. JACK! That's too high! Stop right there! And where's your helmet?'

Both women stared as Jack, poised at the top of the half-pipe, grinned before launching himself down and then up the next slope. He was really rather good!

'Goodness,' gasped Araminta. 'You need nerves of steel to be a parent, don't you? Your little boy reminds me of my brother. He was always doing naughty things. Drove my mum mad. It's why I don't want kids myself, to be honest. I don't want to end up like her.' Then she glanced down at Bobbie's stomach. 'Hope you don't mind me asking, but are you expecting again?'

Of course she wouldn't spill the beans about her pregnancy, Araminta had assured her with a bracey smile. Instead, she'd persuade Rob to get back early from his conference so Bobbie could talk to him about it before he fell asleep at the kitchen table again.

She and Rob certainly had a strange relationship, thought Bobbie. The secretary getting her boss to leave early? Maybe it was like that nowadays. It had been so long since Bobbie had worked in an office that she'd forgotten. Either way, she had to hand it to Araminta. Rob *was* back early and, amazingly, both children were settled in bed by the time they tucked into the salmon en croûte which she'd 'made' from the local supermarket.

'That was really nice.' Rob gave her a little kiss on her cheek. It had been ages since he'd done that. Rather guiltily, Bobbie thought of Andy and how he touched her hand every now and then. That had been dangerous, she could see now. Too much blurring of boundaries. Not that she would have let it go any further, of course. But it had been tempting at times.

'Is this for a special occasion?'

'Sort of.'

It was no good. She could feel the flush rising up her neck. Bobbie had never been able to lie, apart from the odd fib about ready-made meals, but that was different, wasn't it? To hide her confusion, she began to clear the table.

'Hey. Leave that.'

This was unbelievable. Rob never took the plates! Well, he was rarely home long enough to eat off one.

'Tell you what.' Gently he pulled her down on to his knee. 'Let's just sit here for a bit and have a chat, shall we?' His hand began to stroke her stomach. 'When were you planning on telling me about this?'

Bobbie gave a little start. 'You know?'

'I haven't watched you go through two pregnancies for nothing.' His voice was soft as he now stroked her hair, just as he used to in the old days. 'I know the signs. The sickness. The buttons that don't do up. The mood swings – dare I say it? I just don't know why you didn't tell me before.'

Because I thought you were having an affair, she almost said. 'Because I wasn't sure how you'd react. I mean, we didn't intend this to happen, did we?'

'No, but it's great news!' He gave her a cuddle – just a brief one, but a cuddle nevertheless. 'I know it's not easy with me working such long hours but I'll try and do my best. I

346

really will.' Then he looked away. 'In fact, I'm afraid I've got a confession to make too.'

No. Please no. Not an affair.

'Matthew Evans let it slip the other day.'

Matthew? From parenting class? 'How do you know him?'

'We started getting the same train recently and fell into conversation. Then we found we both had children at Corrywood.' Rob placed a little kiss on her forehead. 'He was telling me about the parenting course and how he admires you for working *and* bringing up the kids. It made me think. I'm sorry if I haven't always . . .'

'Mum! Dad! I can't sleep.'

Jack was standing in front of them, rubbing his eyes. He looked so soft and warm. So unthreatening. Not at all like the human bullet that zoomed around during the day, wreaking havoc. Bobbie's heart fluttered as she breathed her son in. Why was it that no two children ever smelt the same?

'It's OK. I'll sort it.' Rob lifted his son up.

'But how will we manage?' Bobbie whispered. 'How will we cope with three?'

Rob gave her a look. The kind of loving, warm look he used to give her. 'We just will. Talking to Matthew has made me realise how lucky we are to be a family. Now come on, little man. Time for bed, I think!'

There once was a teen called Giles,
Who was always out on the tiles.
One night he missed his train –
Moaned mum, 'Oh not again!'
So he walked home – all twenty-five miles.

(Author's note: The true story behind this one is that Mum paid £100 to get Giles back by taxi from Northamptonshire when he slept through his station.)

Chapter 32

VANESSA

'Granny!'

Sunshine flew out of school, pigtails flying, with the lovely gappy smile that Vanessa was getting used to now. It would seem strange when that new front tooth actually came through. 'I'm Reader of the Week again!' She grabbed Vanessa's hand excitedly and did a little pirouette, à la Daisy. 'Miss Davies says I'm the bestest she's ever had.'

One of the mothers standing near muttered something about competition not being healthy any more but Vanessa didn't care. Nor did she try to correct her granddaughter's grammar. The great thing about being an older mother (or rather a younger granny) was that you rose above the competition and the jealousies and the friendships and the fallings-out. The only important thing was to make sure your child was happy and healthy.

And from the look of things, Sunshine *was*. No one would have guessed that this little bubbly girl was the same introvert scrap who had arrived on her doorstep barely two months ago. They said children were resilient and they were right! Even the nightmares were easing off now.

Instead, it was Vanessa who was getting them. Ever since that strange broken-off phone message, she'd felt distinctly uneasy. What if it had been Brigid? She'd rung the Foreign Office again and spoken to a really nice woman, who was very understanding but still had no news. 'We're trying to trace her,' she'd been assured. What else could she do?

'It will be all right, lass,' Brian had said, wrapping his arms around her. But he had said it in the way that a parent spoke to a child when the situation was in fact, uncertain. Meanwhile, she had to carry on as best as she could, looking after her granddaughter and bracing herself for the hospital appointment tomorrow morning.

'VAN VAN! I SAID DO WE HAVE A PICTURE?'

'Sorry?' Vanessa looked down at the little girl skipping along beside her as they made their way home.

'Do we have a picture of Mummy when she was growing up?' Sunshine waggled her finger at Vanessa. It was a habit she'd developed recently, she'd noticed. Maybe the teacher did it. Children were such great mimics. 'You haven't been listening to me, have you? We're doing a project on families – it's going on the classroom wall for the fête! I need a picture of Mummy.' She gave another little skip past a cluster of spring daffodils sprouting up by the side of the road. 'They said we needed pictures of Daddy too but I told them that I didn't have one. Mummy and I are quite enough. That's what Mummy always said.' Then she slipped her hand into Vanessa's. 'But I love you too.'

The lump in Vanessa's throat was so big that she could hardly speak. 'Pictures of your mummy? I'm sure we can find them somewhere.' Inside, she was cross. Didn't teachers realise, in this day and age, that there were lots of children out there who only had one parent? A project like this was really insensitive. She'd have to have a word with Miss Davies.

'Where's Jack?' Sunshine had ground to a halt, looking back with a frown on her little face. 'And where's Daisy?'

Heavens above! She'd forgotten. Bobbie was managing the shop this afternoon. And she, Vanessa, had promised to pick up the children. 'Quick!' She grabbed Sunshine's hand and started running back towards school.

'Faster, Van Van, faster!'

'Practising for the mothers' race, are you?' laughed one of the mums from Sunshine's year as she tried to keep up. Very funny. She might be a young gran but there were times, like this, when Vanessa really understood how older mums felt. She breathed a sigh of relief when she saw that Sunshine had found Daisy by the new hopscotch mat in the playground. But where was Jack?

'He went to look for you,' said Daisy disapprovingly. 'We thought you'd forgotten us.'

'We did!' chirruped Sunshine, jumping up and down.

Where on earth *was* the child? And why wasn't there a teacher in sight? 'Wait there, you two. And don't move.'

She rushed into the school building. It had that undressed air that schools wear when they are empty of children. Weren't there any adults here, for heaven's sake? Mr Balls, that nice new head of primary, was still in his office.

'Mrs Thomas. Good to see you.' Then he frowned. 'Anything wrong?'

'I've lost a child! I was meant to be picking up Jack Wright and he's not here.'

The words came out in such a rush that it was amazing he could understand. But immediately, Mr Balls swung into action. 'No one is allowed to leave until they're ticked off the list.' He gesticulated to a chair. 'I'll be back in a sec. I'm sure we'll sort this out.'

They had to, Vanessa told herself, her heart hammering against her chest. How could she go back and tell Bobbie that she'd mislaid her son? But Mr Balls seemed to know what he was doing.

'Mrs Thomas?' The head's voice was tight. 'I'm sorry but I'm afraid the duty teacher hasn't ticked Jack's name off and yet he doesn't appear to be in school.'

Vanessa closed her eyes briefly as if shutting out the world for a second might change things.

'But the teacher in question did happen to notice that Jack was messing about on his skateboard.'

She nodded. 'He's addicted to it.'

'Then I'm just wondering if he might have decided to take himself off and try out the new skate park.'

Of course! Vanessa remembered now. It had caused quite a row, this skate park, in the local paper. Some parents were for it – claiming their kids needed something to do – and lots of others, who were probably non-parents, said it would attract the wrong kind of crowd.

'Shall we go there first, before we call the police?' suggested Mr Balls briskly.

They ran, all four of them, including Sunshine and Daisy, who seemed to think it was a game. The effort gave Vanessa a pain in her stomach but she had to keep going. How could she have been so negligent? What was she going to tell Bobbie?

'There he is!' yelled Sunshine and Daisy at the same time. 'Look!'

Open-mouthed, they watched Jack flying down the slope – just like a very wide slide! – his hands out on either side as though he was flying. 'Good, isn't he?' observed Mr Balls.

But Vanessa was marching up to the child, tempted to shake him by the scruff of his neck. 'How could you just go off like that? You worried the life out of me.'

Jack shrugged as he picked up his board and proceeded to go back up the steps towards the slope. 'You weren't there and I was bored.'

'That's no excuse!' she snapped. 'If you were my child, I'd . . .'

Then she stopped. What right had she to criticise someone else's kid when her own parenting skills were so sorely lacking? And to think she'd hoped to get it right the second time round with Sunshine. 'I'm sorry,' she said after Jack had whizzed down the slope again with incredible poise and balance. 'It was partly my fault for not being there. But if anyone is late picking you up next time, then you must wait.'

'OK.'

Mr Balls nodded approvingly. 'Glad we've got it sorted.' Then he spoke in a quiet voice to Vanessa. 'I will, of course, have a word with the teacher concerned; we take these security breaches very seriously.'

'Someone could have taken him,' said Daisy sharply, putting her arm around her little brother. Vanessa had never seen such affection between them. Maybe the kid was milking it.

Mr Balls coughed awkwardly. 'Well, it's all sorted now.

Changing the subject, I heard that the parenting course has been quite a success! My wife's going to sign up for the next one, in fact. And I gather you're all going off for a "bonding" weekend in Devon. What a good idea!'

Was it, wondered Vanessa as she walked the children back through town. What with the not-knowing about Brigid and the hospital wanting to extract fluid out of her lump *and* the DNA result which *still* hadn't come through, a weekend with a load of parents – including some she'd never met – was the last thing she wanted to do.

But Sunshine was so excited! 'It's near the sea, Van Van,' she sang, linking arms with Daisy. 'We're all going exploring, aren't we?'

'I think we've done quite enough of that today,' said Vanessa. Here they were now, at the shop. Ready to face the music.

'Vanessa was late, Mummy!' Daisy's little face was puffed up with self-importance. 'And Jack went missing but we found him in the skate park. Mr Balls said he could have been taken by a stranger!'

What a little turncoat – and that wasn't quite true, either! Vanessa listened in horror as Daisy spouted it all out in front of Bobbie, whose expression was becoming ever more grim. 'I'm so sorry,' she started to say. 'I forgot them. But it was only for a few minutes.'

'That's all it takes,' Bobbie replied, shaking her head.

Vanessa had thought she'd understand! Everyone knew Jack was a nightmare. Didn't they? Always running off. Never waiting. 'Well at least we're quits,' she tried to say, partly as a joke. 'I mean, you borrowed my clothes and your Daisy pinched Sunshine's flute.'

Bobbie gave her a disappointed look. 'I hardly think that equates to losing my son,' she retorted.

'I didn't exactly lose him,' Vanessa began but then stopped. Bobbie was right. What she had done was unforgiveable. Her friend had entrusted her with the most important job in the world – looking after her child – and she'd let her down. What kind of a grandmother was she? What kind of a mother?

'Remember. This test is only precautionary,' said Brian, squeezing her knee as they drove to the hospital. He had insisted on coming and this time, she didn't try to change his mind.

'Yes.' She looked out of the window to distract herself. That mother from the parenting class – the one who'd been cross with Bobbie over some incident involving a packed lunch – was walking past, ear glued to her mobile while her son was jumping up and down next to her, trying to get her attention. Time, Miss Davies had said earnestly, at their last session, was the most precious gift that you could give a child. But what if your own time was running out?

'It is, isn't it? Brian glanced briefly across at her as they stopped at the lights. 'A precaution, I mean?'

'In a way. They want to extract some liquid out of the lump to see if it should come out.' Vanessa was still looking out of the window, trying to fool herself that she wasn't really going to the hospital. There was the school where Sunshine would be having lessons right now. There was the skate park. And there was Weasel Face! Brigid's ex! The boy who insisted he was Sunshine's father. He was snogging a beautiful tall blonde girl who was far too young to be with him, surely! She almost felt like asking Brian to stop so she could leap out and warn her.

Reaching into her bag, she brought out her phone.

'Who are you ringing?' asked Brian.

'The DNA clinic.' When Vanessa was upset, she found herself snapping, just as she used to with Brigid. But Brian seemed to understand. Pulling into the hospital car park, he gave her a hug. 'You've got a lot going on, haven't you, Nessie? But it's OK. I'm here for you. I mean it.'

That was nice. But not nice enough to compensate for the DNA clinic receptionist telling her that the results weren't available yet due to the backlog. Or for the pain of the biopsy.

It hurt like mad. Then again, Vanessa had known it would. She'd been through it before, hadn't she? It was what had happened last time, five years ago: the beginning of a long haul of treatment.

'But you're still here, aren't you?' insisted Brian as he drove her back home again. 'It goes to show that they can do so much nowadays. You've got to be positive, lass! Now, how do you fancy coming to the races tomorrow? Upper Cut is running at lunchtime and they reckon he's in with a chance!'

He was so sweet! 'I can't, I'm afraid. It's the school fête. And I've still got to look out some old family photographs for Sunshine to take into a "Guess Who's My Mum or Dad?" competition. I should have done it ages ago.'

'Putting it off, eh?'

She nodded. How well he was beginning to know her.

'I couldn't look at pictures of my wife for ages.' His face took on a faraway look. 'Thing is, Nessie, once you start to face the past, you can then go on with the future!'

Very true, Vanessa told herself as he kissed her goodbye. (Wow – it got her every time!) She'd get down to it right now: sort through those albums, which were neatly stacked under the stairs. If nothing else, it might serve as a distraction.

'Is that really my mummy?' giggled Sunshine as Vanessa showed her the pictures. 'She looks just like me!'

She did too. Vanessa had forgotten how her daughter had had the same toothy gap at this age. The rest of her – the nose and the eyes and even the hairstyle – was identical. 'Look at this one!' urged Vanessa, caught up in Sunshine's excitement. It was almost (but not quite) enough to make her forget the ache in her chest from where the needle had gone in earlier. 'She's older here.'

Her granddaughter's eyes widened. 'How old?'

'Sixteen.' Vanessa's voice caught in her throat as she recalled the time all too well. It had been around the time of that pregnancy test.

'And who are the other people in the photograph?'

'Her friends. Remember how I told you that she went to Corrywood too? She was at the big school then.'

'Will I go there? After Mummy comes back?'

The question threw Vanessa. 'I'm not sure. Probably. We'll have to wait and see.'

Sunshine pouted. 'I don't like it when you say "wait and see". It always means "no".'

Vanessa laughed. She could remember thinking exactly the same at that age. Maybe some things never changed from one generation to the next. In one way, it was reassuring. In another, alarming.

She had to shut the shop early the next day. 'I'm so sorry,' she explained to one of her regulars who arrived just as she was locking up. 'It's my granddaughter's school fête.'

The woman looked distinctly put out. 'I've driven into town especially. Can't I come in for just a few minutes?'

Oh dear. If only Bobbie were here. But, as she'd rather coolly informed Vanessa, she needed to go to the fête too. It was one heck of a black mark if you didn't! Besides, it was the last day of term before the Easter holidays. Most parents, even the ones who worked in London, made a big effort to be seen.

'I'm afraid I'm really going to have to go now,' said Vanessa, looking pointedly at the clock after her customer had been rifling through the rails for a good fifteen minutes without even trying anything on. 'I'm open tomorrow at the normal time, if that's any good.'

Judging from the muttering, it clearly wasn't. Too bad. Sunshine was more important. She'd been so excited about the fête with the face painting and the guess-the-mummy-or-daddy competition that Vanessa owed it to her to be there.

'Van Van!' Sunshine, who'd been holding Miss Davies's hand in the playground where all the stalls were set up, broke off and came hurtling towards her. Vanessa almost didn't recognise her granddaughter with the blue and pink butterfly markings all over her face. Did these enthusiastic face painters ever stop to think how long it took to get that stuff off?

'Sorry I'm late, poppet. I had to shut my shop up.'

'Ah yes, your shop!' Miss Davies had an enthusiastic ring to her voice. 'I must come in sometime. Everyone says it's brilliant.'

'Look!' Sunshine was pulling her towards a table manned by a horsey-looking woman with red hair. She'd seen her before, hadn't she?

'I'm in the other parenting class up the corridor,' the woman announced in a rather posh voice. 'I meant to come and say hello before.' She spoke as though they were already familiar. 'It's a long time since your Brigid and my Mark were friends.'

'Your Mark?' questioned Vanessa, confused.

'Yes. Look!' The horsey redhead pointed to the photograph on the board behind her. Sunshine had chosen to take in the one of her mother as a teenager. 'That's my son standing right next to your Brigid in the picture. Then someone said you were looking after her little girl.' She lowered her voice. 'What happened there exactly, then?'

How indiscreet! Couldn't she see that Sunshine was listening? 'My daughter went travelling,' said Vanessa smoothly. 'She's still abroad at the moment so that's why I'm caring for my granddaughter.'

Sunshine had skipped off now, towards Jack who was at the next stall. 'Stay still,' Bobbie was saying. 'No, you can't go off on your own. We've had quite enough of that.'

She had to talk to Bobbie – try and make up again. But the horsey redhead wasn't letting up. 'My Mark graduated from Oxford last year. He's a lawyer now, working in the City.' Her face shone with pride. 'We're hoping that his little brother is going to follow in his footsteps.' Her voice dropped again. 'Mind you, Sebastian's not proving as easy to bring up as Mark. He's from my second marriage, you know. Between you and me—'

A sharp voice interrupted her. 'I don't want to spoil your conversation but could I have a go at this please? No, not

357

the "Guess Who's My Mum or Dad" competition. The "Guess If It's Home-Made" one.'

My goodness! Vanessa stared at the narrow-faced woman with the elfin haircut who had just pushed in so rudely. She was wearing the jacket! The suede jacket that had been 'sold' from the shop when Bobbie had first started. She was certain of it. 'Excuse me!'

Her voice was drowned by a shout. 'JACK! JACK! COME BACK HERE NOW! AND GET OFF YOUR SKATEBOARD!'

'That child is an utter nightmare,' muttered horsey redhead. 'His mother simply can't control him.'

'It's not her fault,' snapped Vanessa.

'It's all right!' Sunshine called out. 'I'll catch him!'

'WAIT!' Vanessa began running after her. The two of them were heading for the road. But someone was at the gate, surely? No! The teacher who had been in charge was now rounding everyone up for the mothers' race.

'GOT HIM!' Sunshine was hanging on to Jack triumphantly. For a little thing, she was very feisty. Just like her mother.

'GERROFF.' Jack wrenched his way free and sulkily made his way back to his mother.

'Thank you,' Bobbie began to say. 'Look, I'm sorry about the other day.'

'BINGO!' Sunshine's little voice broke through Bobbie's apology as she began to wave furiously across the road. 'Look, Granny! It's Brian with Bingo. He's come to meet us like he promised.'

'COME BACK!' For the second time in five minutes, Vanessa tried to run but this time her legs were glued to the ground in fear. As if in slow motion, she tried to force herself forwards. For a second there, she thought she'd done it. Almost grabbed her little granddaughter by the hem of her school skirt. But it was too late. She'd pulled away.

'SUNSHINE!,

There was the flash of a car. Brian shouting 'STOP' in the same emergency voice they'd learned at dog training. A screech of brakes. And then a horrible, empty silence.

There was a little girl who wouldn't get dressed.
'I beseech you,' said mum, but daughter knew best!
She made such a din
That both parents gave in –
So she went to school in a vest.

Chapter 33

ANDY

'How is Pamela?'

'Your wife still away, is she?'

'Seems odd not to see Mrs Gooding! She's usually the one in charge here!'

'How nice that you've stepped in!'

Andy spent most of the afternoon at the fête, batting away questions with a smooth smile, while manning the face-painting stall with Natasha. Both had been roped in by the ever-persuasive Miss Davies because the original volunteers had been struck down by a virus that was doing the rounds. There was no way he could tell them what was really going on. Again and again, he played over the conversation with the psychologist in his head. 'Your wife is suffering from low self-esteem. It's a common trigger for addictions.'

Andy hadn't cared for the psychologist's silky voice. All this psycho-twaddle! If these people had grown up in a home, they'd know what it was like to be in the real world. 'Low self-esteem?' Andy had repeated. 'But she always acts as though she's better than anyone else! Pamela is cool, distant and . . . well, superior. She doesn't suffer fools gladly. And that applies to anyone who isn't her.'

'You sound very angry,' the psychologist had said.

Angry? No. Betrayed, yes.

'Pamela wouldn't allow me to contact you before,' she continued, 'but now, I'm glad to say, she's happy for you to come down for a family session.'

'With the girls?'

'No. Not yet. Just you.'

'SUNSHINE!'

Andy's thoughts were sharply interrupted by a woman's scream. Dropping the cash box, he spotted a little scrap of a girl rushing over the road at the far side of the playground. As if in slow motion, a car came along (not fast, thank God) and there was a terrible squeal of brakes.

'Shit, Dad,' breathed Nattie next to him, brush in hand.

There was a horrible silence: the kind you read about when a disaster happens. Andy was hardly able to look. And then, to his relief – and disbelief – he spotted the little girl sitting on the other side of the road, next to a man with a dog.

'Are they all right?' gasped someone.

'I don't know,' said another.

That small blonde woman whom Bobbie worked with was now belting across the road. Bobbie was by the entrance gate, her arms round Jack. She looked distressed. Andy found himself abandoning his stall and running over. 'What happened?'

She was shaking as he put his arm around her comfortingly. 'Sunshine ran over the road to see Brian. The car swerved and Brian managed to scoop her up just in time. Can you look after Jack? I just need to make sure they're all right.'

She was so unlike Pamela. If his wife had been here, she would have made some disdainful comment about parents who didn't keep their children under control.

Bobbie was coming back across the road now, holding hands with the little girl who had so nearly been run over. The child was chattering away, seemingly oblivious to her scrape with death in the way that only children could be. 'I just wanted to stroke Bingo,' she was chirping.

The woman who owned the shop was hanging on to the older man, who had a nasty cut on his arm.

'Who's in charge of First Aid?' someone called out.

'Sure you don't need an ambulance?' asked someone else.

'Definitely not,' said the older man cheerfully. 'Please don't make a fuss. Down, Bingo, down.'

'I still think we ought to get you checked out at Casualty,' said the small woman.

Andy turned away. Some injuries were only skin deep. Pamela's was different. Mental illness, the psychologist had said after they'd made the appointment, couldn't be sorted overnight.

'Thanks for looking after Jack.' Bobbie gave him a lovely warm smile that made him melt. She shook her head as her son ran off to help his sister on the 'Guess How Many Additives' table. 'He ran off first, you know. If Sunshine hadn't tried to stop him, she wouldn't have seen Brian on the other side of the road.'

She began to shake again. How he wanted to put his arm around her once more, but twice in one day might be too obvious. Instead, he steered her away to a slightly quieter spot, near the Friendship Stones, where children who didn't have anyone to play with could meet up with others. Maybe there should be something like that for adults, he thought.

'Look, this probably isn't the right time, but there's something I've got to ask you. Has Rob said anything about Pamela?'

'No. Why?'

'Oh, it's nothing.' She hadn't even told her own brother!

'Come on, you've got to tell me now.'

So he did. After he'd finished, she stared at him in disbelief. 'But that's awful. Poor Pamela! And you're going down to see her tomorrow? To this rehab place?'

He nodded. 'I'm dreading it, to be honest. I've got a feeling, from what the psychologist said, that they all blame me.'

'How can they? You've given her everything she could ever want.'

'I thought so too.' He smiled wryly. 'Clearly it wasn't enough.'

'Listen, Andy.' This time, it was Bobbie who put a hand on his arm. Her touch made his whole body tingle. 'You're one of the nicest men I've ever met. No one can blame you for this.'

He shrugged, looking across to Nattie, who was waving at him crossly, indicating she needed his help at the face-painting stall. There was a queue of parents waiting to hand over their money to turn their kids into Spider-Man, still an old favourite apparently, along with the butterfly. 'We'll see, after tomorrow.'

Her eyes widened. 'So presumably, with all this, you're cancelling the parenting weekend in Devon?'

Andy shook his head. 'No. I don't want to let everyone down. And it will do the girls good to get away for a weekend. They've both agreed to come, amazingly.'

'What do they think about Pamela?'

'That's the thing.' He couldn't quite meet her eye. 'They think their mother is just having a break. She doesn't want me to tell them about the drugs. Or the drink. And the psychologist says I have to honour her wishes.' He glanced across at Nattie again, who was still waving furiously. 'It's one of the things we need to talk about.'

Then he remembered. How selfish of him! Unable to stop himself, he glanced down at Bobbie's stomach, which was gently bulging. 'What about you? How are things going?'

'Wonderful!' Bobbie took away her hand and he felt a sudden sense of loss. 'I've told Rob about the baby and he was really excited! As for the secretary, she's seeing someone else. I can't believe I got the wrong end of the stick. Must be all those hormones flying around!'

'Great. Great.' Andy had to force the words out of his mouth. 'I'm so pleased for you.' And so he was, he told himself, making his way back to Nattie's stall. So why did he still have that silly idea in his head? The one that kept imagining what life would have been like if he'd married someone like Bobbie?

'Andy, mate!' A hot sweaty hand grabbed his sleeve in the crowd. 'Glad I've bumped into you.' There was a wheeze followed by a hacking cough. Ugh! The man was actually spitting on to the ground; some of the other parents – understandably – were regarding him with disdain. Andy felt defiled by his company, just as he had felt all those years ago

363

in the home. 'I've been sick, mate. My kid passed on that virus that's going round. But I'm back now.' There was another bout of coughing, followed by a hoarse whisper. 'Got that money for me, have you?'

'I'm not being blackmailed,' hissed Andy. 'And certainly not here.'

'So you don't mind everyone finding out about your past?' Kieran threw back his head and laughed, revealing a gold tooth at the back. 'Reckon you're calling my bluff. Tell you what, Barry – or Andy as you call yourself now. I heard about this little weekend away you've got planned for our group. Somehow I slipped off the group email but I'm sure you can send me another. We can settle up there. OK?'

'I've got a meeting today,' said Andy briefly over breakfast; a quick affair which you might miss if you blinked. Natasha was on her new 'no food' diet, sipping hot water with lemon. Mel, meanwhile, was texting furiously, sitting on the kitchen counter in shorts and laddered tights again.

'Is anyone listening?' he added. 'I've got a meeting today.'

'But you don't work any more,' said Mel, without looking up.

He thought of George. When he sold the company to Harry Screws, he'd expected the money to last a good year or so. But he hadn't reckoned on the bills for Pamela's place or the sudden dive in the stock market that had taken a severe chunk of his savings. 'Actually, I'm just having some time off until I find something else. What are you two doing now?'

'I'm going to be having wild sex and Nattie's going to keep on starving herself. Don't look like that, Dad. I'm only kidding.'

Was she? Andy wasn't so sure as he set off for Sussex in the Porsche which used to give him so much pleasure but which now did nothing for him. Just as well. If George's latest email was right, the car would have to go, along with everything else. Turning on the radio, he caught the tail end of a heated discussion about children and smacking.

'In my view, it should be encouraged.' The speaker spoke in a no-nonsense military manner. 'It's a necessary deterrent. Just like capital punishment.'

Bit harsh, wasn't it?

'Thank you, Dr Know,' said the interviewer uncertainly. 'I'm sure we will get plenty of feedback on that one!'

Dr Know? That was Bobbie's mother's boyfriend, wasn't it? What would this so-called expert have to say, wondered Andy, about an addict mother? Or a father trying to make up for lost family time?

The thought almost distracted him from the road. Only when he got on to the motorway and set cruise control did he allow himself to think. Andy had never been to a rehab centre before. He'd once seen a documentary about a really smart one in London; a programme which, he remembered now, Pamela had taken a keen interest in. How long ago had that been? A year perhaps. Maybe two. Was she on drugs then? Or taking those tranquillisers? If so, she'd hidden the signs pretty well.

Maybe the coldness was actually a symptom? A clue that his wife was doped up to her eyeballs. And what about those times when she had been really edgy and twitchy: had she been waiting for the next fix? There had been some kids in the home like that. He'd wanted none of it. But then again, it might have been better than the terrible thing that *he* had done.

No. He wouldn't think about that now. He needed to concentrate on Pamela. Andy stared up at the huge grey stone building with its porticoed entrance and neatly tended gardens all around. No wonder this place cost a bomb.

'Don't be surprised when you see her,' his mother-in-law had warned. 'She's not quite her usual self.'

He was feeling nervous now; he didn't mind admitting it. Making his way through the courtyard, he strode past a fountain and up the steps. It was like a hotel with these plush carpets and chandeliers. 'Mr Gooding,' he said quietly to the receptionist. 'I'm here to see my wife.'

She nodded as though he was expected. 'Please, take a seat.' She indicated a glass-topped coffee table laden with magazines. Andy tried to read but thoughts kept spinning round in his head. How many other stressed parents ended up here? Grown-up kids whose parents had mucked them up. Adults who couldn't cope with the impossible hoops that children put them through. And yet he couldn't imagine life without his girls. How sorry he felt for people who couldn't have them.

'Mr Gooding?' A slightly tanned, rather mannish woman with short blonde hair was standing in front of him. 'I'm Dr Banks. Nice to meet you. Would you like to follow me?'

He went through a pair of doors, followed by another. He half expected them to be locked to prevent the patients from escaping but it all seemed quite normal. Then Dr Banks opened a third door. Andy stopped. A tall, very pale woman was sitting on a sofa, looking listlessly out of the window. She was much thinner than when he'd last seen her, and her hair was hanging loosely instead of being twisted into that smart knot she usually wore. 'Pamela?' he said doubtfully.

The woman looked up at him. 'You came then.'

He sat down beside her. Her proximity made him feel uncomfortable. 'Of course I did.' Overcome with pity, he made to hold her hand but she took it away. He was aware of Dr Banks's eyes on him. 'Do you mind if we have some time on our own?'

The doctor looked at Pamela. 'What would you like?'

There was a silence. 'Yes. But not here.' Her eyes went out to the garden again. 'I can talk better outside. I can breathe there.'

'But you hate going outside!' Andy couldn't resist saying. 'Unless you've got your sunscreen and sunglasses on!'

The doctor made a noise in her throat. 'Actually, Mr Gooding, we find it helpful not to make too many assumptions here. Labelling people can do more harm than we realise.' She glanced at her watch. 'Can you come back in half an hour, please? It will be time for Mrs Gooding's next therapy session then.'

At first, it was hard to know what to talk about. The biggies, like 'How could you be so stupid as to take drugs?' seemed too huge to start with. So he began with mundane conversation such as what the food was like and what she did. Initially, she seemed to take a while to respond to his words; digesting each sentence before replying.

'We discuss things,' she said, sitting down on a bench by a rose bed. 'Everything. Our childhoods. What we like doing. What we don't like doing.' She gave a little laugh. He couldn't work out if it was a proper laugh or a sarcastic one. 'And we do practical things like housework and dusting and ironing. We all muck in.'

Ironing? Dusting? It seemed so banal!

'The rhythm is soothing. I take turns in the garden too.' She smiled at the rose bed in front of them. 'I've even learned how to prune.'

Her voice was different, he noticed. Softer. As though she was almost amused with herself. 'What did it, Pamela?' He moved closer. 'What tipped you over the edge? Surely it wasn't just Nattie and this modelling business?'

She jumped up. 'What do you mean "just"?' She glared at him now, like the old Pamela. 'What do you know about being at home all day? Did you honestly think that I was going to be happy, giving it all up to be a little home-maker?'

'You seemed happy enough at the time,' he flashed back.

'That was because I was scared! I was nineteen years old, Andy! I'd only been in the business for a year but already I was terrified! Everyone wanted a bit of me. The magazines. The photographers. My agent. I saw other models go under if they did something wrong or got too old. I thought I'd get out while I was still on top.'

'No you didn't.' He could tell she was lying. It was like that role play they'd done in parent class where the child (Audrey) had hidden something. 'You were scared, yes. But it wasn't by the drugs. Or because you were pregnant. It was something else.'

The look of pure panic that swept her face told him he was right.

'I can't tell you.' She began tearing up a rose leaf into tiny bits. 'If I do, you'll never forgive me.'

He began to sweat. 'Of course I will.'

'Very well.' She was back to the cool, distant Pamela again. It was as though she was two people. 'I told you I was pregnant. But what I *didn't* tell you was that I was raped.'

'*What?*'

She looked away. 'It was a photographer. Just before I met you. He said . . . he said I'd been asking for it but I hadn't . . . I hadn't . . .'

Now she was weeping into his arms. Huge juddering sobs. Andy held her but inside he felt violently sick. 'You said it was someone in the public eye who got you pregnant. That he didn't want anything to do with you.'

She pulled away and looked at him wildly. 'He was! It was . . .' She began to shudder. Then she began to retch. 'I can't . . . I can't even say his name. I don't want it in my mouth.'

Fucking hell! Andy suddenly thought of the headline in the paper on the day he had sold the company. That article. The one above the piece about the teenage gang. It had been a report on the lavish funeral of a world-famous photographer. *He* was the one!

Finally, Andy understood.

'His death brought it all back,' he said slowly. Just as, he added silently to himself, the report on the teenage gang had done to him.

Pamela nodded, tears still streaming down her face. 'For years I managed to blank him out. But when he died, he was everywhere! On the radio. On the television. In every magazine I opened. In . . . in Mel's face.'

Andy held out his arms again and she buried her face in his chest.

'Why didn't you tell me?' he whispered into her hair. 'Why didn't you tell me it was rape?' His fists clenched. 'I'd have bloody well killed him.'

'I wasn't sure if you'd believe me.' Her voice came out like a child's. The child that she had been, more or less, at the time.

'Of course I would have done.'

Or would he? There were girls at the home who'd got pregnant. Girls who claimed they had been raped. No one believed them. It was an excuse, designed to make them look like victims. So unfair, he could see now. But at the time, that's what they'd all thought. Including him.

'I felt so dirty!' She was lifting her tear-stained face to look at him. Never had he seen her like this before, with mascara streaked down her cheeks. She looked more beautiful than ever. Real. Natural.

'Dirty?' he repeated. He could understand that too. Hadn't he felt the same, in the home when the boys had made him do their stuff?

'At first, when we got married,' she continued, 'it was all right. I felt safe. I liked playing house. But I needed it all to be perfect to make up for what had happened before. I thought that if it wasn't, everything would go wrong again.'

His poor Pamela!

'It was easy at first because the girls were so good, but then they became teenagers and they began to argue back. They started to drink, like I used to. And go out with boys. I started to worry too, about Mel. Began to think that we should have told her the truth, years ago. Should have told her you weren't her dad.' She stared at him, distraught. 'How can we do that now, Andy? Answer me that?'

He couldn't.

'In the end, I got so stressed that I went to the doctor for some tranquillisers.'

It was like listening to someone else's life story. 'Why didn't you tell me?'

'Because you weren't around enough. And when you were,

369

I couldn't bear to think that I was letting you down. You were so proud of us. My perfect family, you used to call us. You worshipped me, Andy, admit it! Do you realise how terrifying that was? All I needed to do was to slip up and then I'd have lost you.'

He wanted to deny it but there were bits that were all too true.

'But what really got me' – Pamela shivered – 'was when Nattie won a modelling competition. What if she became as successful as me? I was jealous – terrible, isn't it? – but I was also scared in case the same thing happened to her. In case she got hurt too. That world, Andy, it can be evil. No one can understand unless they've been in it themselves.'

She was biting her nails. Pamela *never* bit her nails. 'That's why I started using again. I thought it might help me relax. One of the other mothers at school was my dealer.' Pamela gave a half-smile. 'You wouldn't believe how much undercover dealing goes on at the school gates. It helped a bit. But I couldn't get off it. When . . . when *he* died, I just couldn't cope any more. And then you sold the company! It seemed a brilliant opportunity to go down to Mummy's. Get away. After she broke her arm, it was an excuse to stay longer.'

Her eyes grew distant as though she was somewhere else. 'I felt safe at home. Like a little girl again.'

Andy felt a pang of jealousy. She should have gone to *him*. Not her mother.

'Mummy realised I needed help. A friend of hers suggested this place. Said it was expensive but that it worked for someone she knew.'

Andy didn't know what to say. It was all too much to take in at one sitting. His wife had just rewritten their entire family history. 'And is it working?'

'Maybe.' She smiled wanly. 'It's helped me tell you my story after all these years.'

That was true. Her courage, her honesty, had given him strength. It was time to tell *his* story now. 'Actually, Pamela, there's something I need to tell you.'

A clanging bell from the house cut him off, dammit. As if she was a robot, Pamela rose to her feet. 'I've got to go.' She was calmer now, yet still there was something not quite right.

'Are you still on that stuff?' he asked, willing her to say no.

'No. I had to go cold turkey. It's why I didn't want you to see me then.' She shivered and tucked her arm into his as they walked back towards the house. An onlooker, he thought wryly, might think she was perfectly well. 'What about you, Andy? How are you getting on? Are the girls all right?'

He'd expected her to ask him that earlier. Maybe the drugs made you self-centred. 'It's not easy, being a full-time parent,' he began awkwardly.

Pamela laughed, which made her seem more awake. Less dreamy. 'I know that. Is Mel still going out with that awful boy: the one that looks like a weasel?'

'You knew?'

She sighed. 'Oh yes, I knew. And is Nattie drinking? And not eating properly?'

This wasn't good enough! He rounded on her. Angry now. 'Why didn't you try to do something?'

'*Do* something?' she repeated with a little cry. 'Have you tried?'

'Well, yes.'

'And did you get anywhere?'

'No.'

All right, she'd proved the point.

'I've told them.' Pamela gave a small hysterical laugh. 'They'll only learn through their mistakes. That's why classes can't help. By the way, how is your little parenting group doing?'

'OK, thanks.' He took his arm away. Her touch made him feel awkward. It was too much. Too soon. 'We've finished the course now but we're having a weekend away. Down at Seabridge.'

'Seabridge?'

371

'Yes. You don't mind, do you? It's about time someone went down there anyway, to give the place an airing.'

'Is Bobbie going?'

'Bobbie?' He felt himself redden. 'Yes, she is actually. Why?'

Her eyes narrowed but she shrugged. 'No reason. Well, I hope it goes well.' She put out her hand as though he was a guest. 'Lovely to see you, Andy. Do come again when you have time.'

This was weird! 'Do you want to see the girls?'

'The girls,' she repeated as though she'd forgotten them. 'No. I don't think so. Not until I'm better. I'd hate them to see me like this. Don't you think?'

But what if she didn't get better? Where did that leave him? And Nattie and Mel? he thought as he made his way back to the Porsche. Troubled, he began to start the engine but as he did so, remembered he'd left his mobile under the front seat. Three missed calls from his financial adviser. He felt misgiving in his chest. Then the handset began to vibrate in his hand. George again.

'Andy?' He sounded tense. On edge. Excited? Or apprehensive? 'I've got some news. Are you sitting down?'

OF COURSE I'M NOT LYING!

Fibs that parents tell their kids:

Father Christmas is coming.
I'm not crying – it's something in my eye.
Daddy and I are just talking.
I haven't got any money.
If you don't eat that up, you'll starve.
Of course I'm not lying.

Chapter 34

BOBBIE

'Mummy! Mummy! Do goldfish float when they're asleep? Cos Daisy says so and I think she's lying again.'

Where did they get their questions from? Last week, Bobbie would have dismissed it with an impatient 'I don't know'. But she felt so much better! More able to deal with anything now that she and Rob were back on track.

Thank heavens Araminta had asked Research Trivia not to take further action. She could only hope they'd agree. Of course, they didn't want to use her any more but Vanessa had given her a few more shifts after all, which would just about cover the loss of income. Meanwhile, Rob – who didn't know anything about this, thankfully – was being so nice! Always asking how she was feeling as well as getting home at a reasonable time. If she didn't know better, she'd think he'd been on a parenting course himself!

In fact, it was almost like BK (Before Kids) as she and Sarah called it. Talking of Sarah, she and Matthew had got on really well at the school fête. Her old friend had needed no persuading when Bobbie had asked her down. 'It will be lovely to see you,' she'd gushed but then, as soon as they'd got there, she'd made a beeline for Matthew, offering to assist him on the "Guess the Teacher's Age" stand.

Who would have thought that Judith Davies was actually twenty-eight? She looked more like nineteen. They'd announced that one (rather brave of her, as everyone said), soon after the near-accident. Bobbie still got the shivers when she thought about it. But what she didn't admit to anyone was her relief when those brakes had screeched and she'd realised that it wasn't Jack: that he was safe on the school side of the road. It was every parent's fear that something would happen to their child.

'Mum!' Jack was tugging at her hand impatiently. 'Will you answer my question! Do goldfish float when they're asleep?'

Ah yes. She'd forgotten that one. Bobbie handed him her iPad. 'Why don't you ask Jeeves?'

'Don't want to.'

Oh dear. Jack was being bolshie again! In fact, they'd both been playing up ever since she and Rob had sat the children down and told them that they were going to be having another brother or sister. 'Which?' Daisy had demanded. 'Girl or boy?'

'We don't know yet,' Bobbie began.

'Why not?'

Rob had shot her a what-do-we-say-now look.

'Because it's a surprise,' Bobbie had said brightly.

Daisy had pouted. 'I hate surprises.'

From then on, she had been acting up even more than usual; bossing her little brother around and being really difficult. 'It's perfectly normal,' Not Really Pregnant Mum had said reassuringly when she'd commented on the bump at the school fête. 'My Wayne was a right little bugger when I was expecting his sister. Your kid will get over it. They don't have much option, do they? Mind you, I'm bloody impressed that you're up the duff.' She nudged her meaningfully. 'My hubby and I are too sodding knackered to have sex any more.'

Bobbie wasn't sure whether to be comforted or not by this. Even so, it was nice that Not Really Pregnant Mum finally seemed to be offering an olive branch. Perhaps it was because they'd just had the last class. Now they'd have the weekend in Devon to 'reinforce everything they'd learned' as Judith Davies had earnestly put it.

'Can you imagine what it's going to be like?' Vanessa kept saying. 'Everyone bringing their partners and kids? These relatives of yours must have a really big house.'

'They do.' Bobbie had been down there a few times and,

on every visit, had felt quite overwhelmed. It would have housed at least five families in London.

Only a few days now until they went! It might help to get through the first bit of the school holiday. That was never easy. The coming to terms with the arguments over the remote control and the skateboard-helmet nagging and the 'He hit me firsts' and the plasters which were never where they should be. Then, just as you'd got used to twenty-four-hour chaos, it was time to go back to the manic 'Get up now!' for a new school term.

But maybe these holidays would be a bit different. Vanessa had asked her to work three afternoons in the shop while she looked after Daisy and Jack at her house. 'It will give Sunshine someone to play with. We could do a swap on the other days.'

The brilliant thing about Vanessa was that she'd already brought up one child so she knew what to do. OK, so she'd lost Jack. Once. (So far Bobbie had done this at least twenty-three times although she'd rather no one else knew about that.) But even so, she was good at calming Jack down and had a real knack for giving Daisy jobs so she felt 'useful' rather than being bossy. Why didn't it work when *she* tried that?

Maybe there should be some government scheme where everyone had to bring up someone else's kid for a week or two. A sort of short-term foster arrangement. It would work both ways. You'd have to be nicer to the visiting kids because you couldn't scream at them like your own. And your own kids would learn to behave because, as every parent knew, children were usually nicer to anyone who wasn't their mother.

'MUM! MUM!' Jack's persistent voice brought her back to the present. 'Ask Jeeves says the goldfish floats when it's dead.'

Oh shit.

Vanessa was ready and waiting at the shop, rota sheet in hand. 'Ah! At last!'

'Sorry we're late,' whispered Bobbie, 'but I had to replace a goldfish.'

'Never mind. You're here now.'

Wow! Vanessa was in business mode! Maybe she was still upset after that horrible business with the car but at least Sunshine was all right, judging by the way she was prancing round Daisy, pretending to be on *Strictly Come Dancing*.

'Right. Let's go over this, shall we?' Vanessa had new purple glasses. They made her look even trendier. She pointed to a date in her diary. 'Can you do that day?'

'Actually, I've got my scan then. I was hoping you might be able to have the children.'

'No can do. I've got an appointment.'

Wow! Talk about being abrupt! What had bitten *her*?

'We'll just have to shut the shop early.' Vanessa sniffed. 'That's a nuisance. Can you do Thursday instead? Good. I'll take the children swimming. Then I'll do the Friday and then that takes us up to this weekend away.' There was a sigh. 'Thought I was going to have to cancel the trip to Devon but Kim's daughter has offered to step in as a one-off. By the way, she's just had an email from her mum in Peru!'

Vanessa seemed friendlier now. That was good. 'There's something else I want to run past you,' said Bobbie quickly. 'Have you ever thought about introducing a Just Pregnant rail? I'm finding it really hard to get clothes, especially at this stage when nothing does up and I'm not ready to wear tents.' She made a wry face. 'Stupidly, I gave away all my maternity stuff after Jack.'

'It could work,' mused Vanessa, putting her head on one side, just like little Sunshine did when considering something. It wasn't, Bobbie observed, the only mannerism they shared. They laughed in the same way when something amused them and they screwed up their noses when they didn't like something. Did Brigid do the same, she wondered? Poor Vanessa! No wonder she was edgy at times. She couldn't imagine not knowing where her daughter was.

Vanessa's eyes hardened. 'By the way, I'm sure I saw someone wearing that jacket at the fête.'

'Really? Who?' Bobbie still felt dreadful about inadvertently selling the jacket.

'Someone I didn't recognise. I was about to say something when Sunshine ran into the road.'

Bobbie gave her a brief comfort hug. 'It must have been such a shock for you. But going back to the jacket, we must be able to find the owner somehow. Someone at school must know her if she was at the fête.'

'Where's Jack, Mummy?' asked Daisy, interrupting.

Oh God. All it took was for her to think of something else for a few seconds and he was gone. It was like childminding a mosquito. 'The door's locked,' said Vanessa quickly. 'So he can't have escaped.'

Don't you believe it! Bobbie ran her eye over the top shelves. No. He wasn't hiding there amongst the hats like last time. Nor was he hiding in the shoe racks like the time before.

'I've found him! I've found him!' sang out Sunshine from the back of the shop. 'You'll never guess what he's doing!'

Taking the kettle plug to bits to see how it worked? Skateboarding through the stockroom? Trying on some of the clothes out the back and leaving muddy hand marks on them?

Or . . . *what*? Surely he couldn't be doing *that*?

'Are you ill?' asked Bobbie, rushing towards her son. Quickly she felt his forehead. Cool.

'He's *reading*!' Daisy's voice could have been her own. 'Look, Mum. Look!'

But Jack never read! He only *watched*! 'Well done,' Bobbie said faintly but Jack didn't even look up from the pile of Sunshine's books that were around him. Wow! Was it possible that they had finally turned a corner?

It actually gave them a bit of time to finish off the staff rota. 'Listen,' said Vanessa when they'd finished. 'I'm sorry I was a bit terse earlier. The truth is that someone at school went and contacted social services after Sunshine nearly got run over.'

'No!' Bobbie gasped. 'Who?'

'I don't know. But somehow they seemed to have heard about that time I lost Jack – you know, when I was meant to be picking him up. So it must be someone we know.'

How awful! Bobbie racked her brains. Mr Perfect? Someone else from the group? One of the teachers? It could be anyone. Parents could be such busybodies. Always trying to score points.

'Now one of the social workers wants to see us.' Vanessa looked worried. 'I feel like a criminal!'

'But they can't take Sunshine away from you, surely?'

'They can do almost anything they want nowadays.' Vanessa's voice was shaky. 'After Baby P. and those other awful cases, they're in a difficult situation. They can't afford to get anything wrong. There's another thing too. I haven't got any official right to look after Sunshine. I don't have the right paperwork. There's a good chance they might get me on that.'

'But you're a brilliant mum. I mean, gran.'

'Am I?' Vanessa sniffed. 'I didn't do very well with Brigid, did I?'

'Do you think that *was* her on the phone?'

'If it was, she hasn't rung again.' Vanessa shook herself as though wanting to change the subject. 'You know, your idea for a Just Pregnant rail is a good one. We'll put up some notices in the shop and maybe in the local paper. After that, you can be in charge. Make it your baby, if you like!'

Bobbie felt a lovely warm glow. 'That's wonderful! Thank you so much. I won't let you down, I promise!'

'MUM! MUM! Jack's got chocolate over this lovely dress in the back and we can't get the stain out.'

Talk about a short attention span. Did it ever end? Then she thought of Sunshine and the car. It made you count your blessings. It really did.

'Coming!' she called out.

*

It looked as though there was nothing for it but to take both Daisy and Jack with them to the scan. 'Isn't there anyone else at school you could ask?' Rob had said the night before.

'Not really.' Thanks to Jack's behaviour, it was still difficult to make friends with the other mums although, it had to be said, Angie, alias Not Really Pregnant Mum, had actually waved at her across the car park the other day. It would be interesting to see how they all got on in Devon. 'You could always give your niece a second chance.'

'No way.' Rob's mouth tightened. 'When it comes to drugs, I've got zero tolerance.' He dropped his voice even though, miraculously, both children were in bed. Jack was actually reading again; encouraged by the challenge which Mr Balls had set for the Easter holidays. 'I've never told you before – we tried to keep it in the family – but when Pamela was modelling, she took—'

'Mum! Jack's stolen one of my Moshi Monsters again!'

'I'll go.' Rob jumped to his feet. Usually it was always her who got up first. But this time, Bobbie had the distinct feeling that her husband was glad to be interrupted.

'No, wait! You were about to say something. About Pamela when she was modelling.'

'MUM! MUM!'

'Forget I said anything. It's private. And I was sworn to secrecy.'

'But I'm your wife!'

Too late. He was gone. Despite Rob's 'new leaf', Bobbie still felt as though she was a complete outsider when it came to her husband's close-knit family. Andy felt the same, he said. It would be good to catch up with him during this weekend. She'd missed their chats.

The following day they were on their way to the antenatal clinic with Jack tearing along the corridors making loud buzzing noises – 'ZZZZZZZZZZZZZZZZZZZZ!', – and

Daisy marching bossily behind him. 'I've told you before, Jack. Don't run or you'll hurt someone.'

'Just imagine what she's going to be like when the baby arrives,' said Rob, putting his arm around her.

'You know, I was really worried about telling you.' She lowered her voice so the children couldn't hear. 'You've always said that two was enough.'

'That was before—' Rob stopped.

'Before what?'

He made a face as though unsure whether to tell her. 'To be honest, Matthew and I have been sitting on the train next to the husband of a woman in your parenting class. The one with lots of children; apparently she's always running between your session and Andy's. The three of us have become quite good friends. Too Many Kids Dad, as we call him, is always telling us about the things his children get up to. It sounds mad but it's also, or so he says, a lot of fun.'

Rob looked more solemn. 'He lent me a book too. It's the one you've been using in class actually. I was quite upset by the bit about dads losing touch with their kids.' They paused in the corridor, just outside the antenatal sign. Jack had already steamed ahead and was inside – she could hear him. And Daisy too, asking questions already. 'It made me realise that maybe I haven't been as much of a hands-on dad as I'd meant to be. I'm sorry, Bobbie.'

Was this really her husband talking?

'I see this baby – our baby – as a clean slate.' His eyes were shining. 'Let's go in and see what it looks like, shall we?'

'MUM! What's an antenatal scam?'

'It's scan, not scam.'

'MUM! Will we able to talk to the baby like we talk to Aunty Jeannie on Skype in Australia?'

'Sort of.'

'MUM! Will the baby talk back to us? Cos if so, I'm going to tell it that it can't have my bedroom. It can share with Jack.'

So many questions! Bobbie did her best to field them as she lay, all jellied up on the bed, trying to make sense of the squiggles on the monitor.

'MUM!' demanded Jack, staring at the screen with a where-is-it? expression. 'How does the baby jump out of the television screen?'

'It doesn't, silly.' Daisy's voice was laden with scorn. 'It comes out of Mummy's vadge ina. We've been learning about it in biology.'

The radiologist giggled. She was about Judith Davies's age (why were they so young nowadays – or was it just that she was getting older?) and had said yes, of course the children could come in, provided they didn't touch anything. It was a new policy, apparently: part of a campaign to bring families together and reduce sibling rivalry. Some hope.

Then she wrinkled her pretty little nose. 'Goodness – what's that smell?'

'Pongo,' chirped Daisy, flushing. (Why was it that your kids inherited the traits you *didn't* like about yourself?) 'He's our dog.'

The radiologist looked around. 'I'm afraid we don't allow animals in here.'

'He's only pretend,' cut in Bobbie. 'JACK! DON'T TOUCH THOSE WIRES. STOP FIDGETING, WILL YOU?'

'There's no need to shout,' said Jack. He was staring at the screen. 'Is it a boy or a girl, Mum?'

The radiologist looked at him and then Bobbie and then Rob again. 'Do you want to know?'

'No,' she said, glaring at her husband. They'd talked about this quite a bit at parenting class. American Express said she spent most of her pregnancy wishing she wasn't having a boy and then as soon as the baby was put in her arms, she fell in love with him. 'You think you know what you want but you want what you get,' she'd said. Bobbie had been rather moved by that.

'WE WANT TO KNOW! WE WANT TO KNOW!' chanted the children.

'Actually,' said the radiologist slowly, 'it's not easy to tell because one of them has got its hand on the other.'

'What did you say?' breathed Rob next to her.

'Please tell me you're joking,' Bobbie squeaked. Everyone joked about having twins before a scan. Still, it had happened to the Perfects and to Jilly who ran the au pair agency.

'There's no doubt!' The radiologist now sounded as excited as if it was happening to her. 'Do you see! There's one head. And there's the other!'

Both Rob and Bobbie were still reeling with shock as they stumbled back to the car. Daisy and Jack, on the other hand, were racing ahead, each trying to beat the other into the prized back seat behind the driver. The kicking seat, as it was known. 'When the babies come, I'm going to strap them in,' announced Daisy.

'No. I am.'

Bobbie glanced at Rob. 'It will be all right, won't it?'

'Of course it will.' He didn't sound sure. 'People manage, don't they?'

But not if they worked twenty-four/seven! Already, her husband was checking his BlackBerry to see what office calls he'd missed. 'That's odd.' He was frowning. 'I seem to have your phone.'

Jack must have swapped their covers again! Yes, he had! Little monkey.

'What's this?' He pushed her screen under her nose.

Dn't worry abt mkt research people. Hve withdrawn complaint and told them u are pregnant and under severe mental stress. So they're not taking it any further. Won't tell Rob. Gd luck with scan! Araminta.

Her husband's eyes had gone cold. Hard. Distrustful. As though he didn't know her. 'Do you want to tell me what this is all about, Bobbie?'

LIES THAT KIDS TELL THEIR PARENTS

I've done my homework.
He hit me first.
Mum says I can.
Dad says I can.
I passed my maths exam.
I've cleaned my teeth.
We only kissed.
I've lost my school report.

PERFECT PARENTS' RETREAT WEEKEND

SUMMING UP AND MOVING FORWARD!

Chapter 35

VANESSA

'But I want to go swimming!' Sunshine tugged at her hand as they walked through town towards the building with the Social Services sign. 'You promised!'

Vanessa tried to sound bright and reassuring. 'I know I did! But first we have to visit someone and then we'll go.'

When children didn't want to do something, offer them a choice, or at least a softener. That's what the parenting course had suggested. But that kind of advice was surely intended for ordinary everyday situations. Not a visit to the social worker who had called for a meeting to 'discuss Sunshine's future'.

'Promise? We'll go to the pool as soon as we've seen this awful woman?'

'Please! Don't call her that.'

'Well *you* did.'

She'd forgotten that children were like parrots! They repeated everything they heard – well, anything that could be awkward or embarrassing, anyway. Jack and Daisy were just the same. It must be something they learned at school. Probably on the national curriculum.

'Sunshine, please listen.' Vanessa stopped in the street, causing a youth with a pushchair to bump into her. Apologising profusely (Heavens, in her day, boys wouldn't have been seen dead with a baby!), she bent down to get on to the same eye level as her granddaughter; another useful tip she'd picked up from class. 'Look at me. It's really important that we don't argue in front of this lady.'

'Why?'

Vanessa hesitated. How could she tell Sunshine that someone was questioning her suitability as a carer? She wasn't by nature an angry person but if she ever got her hands on whoever who had complained, she'd really give them a piece of her mind. And more.

'Because', she continued, 'I'm older than some of the other mummies.'

Sunshine wrinkled her nose, the way Brigid always used to when she didn't understand something. 'That's because you're my Van Van, silly!'

Vanessa gave her a cuddle. They were almost here now. It was too late to practise any more of those 'don't say this' and 'remember to say that'. They'd just have to hope that the social worker would see their point of view.

'Can you tell me what happened, Sunshine?' asked the young girl earnestly. She was wearing, Vanessa observed disapprovingly, an A-line grey skirt that didn't suit her with those clumpy ugly flat shoes that were so fashionable nowadays. But this young girl made her nervous. So too did all these rules and unspoken assumptions.

Of course she understood that these people had to be careful. There had been yet another case in the paper the previous week: a child who had been found half-naked and hungry in his grandfather's care. The social worker had been blamed for failing to 'conduct proper checks'. They didn't have an easy job. But surely anyone could see that Sunshine was being looked after!

Vanessa couldn't help feeling a rush of pride as she took in her granddaughter's neatly plaited hair, her little blue leggings with the matching sweatshirt and her brand-new Start-Rite shoes. The expense of having another mouth to feed (not to mention the clothes) meant that Vanessa had to go without herself. But it was worth it!

'I need to know what happened at the school fête, Sunshine,' repeated the girl brightly. 'Would you like to draw a picture instead of telling me?'

Not that art therapy again!

'OK!' Sunshine's face brightened.

'We love to draw together,' said Vanessa, suddenly spotting an opportunity. 'In fact, she likes it much more than watching television, don't you poppet?

'NO!' Sunshine burst out laughing as though Vanessa had just said something very stupid. She began to pick through the box of wax crayons the girl had given her. 'My favourite thing is Arctic Penguin.'

'Is that a book?' asked the social worker encouragingly.

'NO!' Sunshine scoffed. 'It's a game on my laptop.'

The girl began to make notes. 'You have your own laptop?'

'It's just second-hand,' said Vanessa quickly. 'We bought it from a friend.'

More notes. 'Are you allowed on the net, Sunshine?'

'No. Not without my supervision.'

'Please, Mrs Thomas, I'm asking your granddaughter.'

'I email my friend Daisy sometimes. And I check my spelling homework with Google even though we're not meant to.'

This was getting worse.

'What about swimming, Sunshine? We go every week, don't we?'

'That's cos Van Van's still learning! No one taught her, you see.'

There was a sharp intake of breath. 'Presumably you take someone who's a competent swimmer with you, Mrs Thomas?'

This wasn't going well. 'Sunshine swims like a fish! She's better than most children who are much older than she is. And besides, there are lifeguards there.'

More notes. 'Let's see, Sunshine. What are we drawing now? Is that a road?'

There was a nod; her little tongue poking out with concentration.

'And who's that next to you?'

'My friend Jack.' Sunshine beamed. 'He tried to run across first but I stopped him.'

The girl's face was rigid. 'And where was Granny?'

'Talking to someone.'

'Actually, I . . .'

'Please, Mrs Thomas. And who's that on the other side of the road?'

'That's Van Van's boyfriend and Bingo.'

There was a sucking in of breath. 'I see. And what's Granny's boyfriend called?'

'Actually—'

'Please don't interrupt, Mrs Thomas. As I was saying, Sunshine, what's Granny's boyfriend called?'

'Brian, of course.'

'Right. Brian.' She said it in the same way that she might have said 'child molester'. 'Would that be Brian Hughes?'

Vanessa stared at her. 'How do you know?'

The girl looked smug. 'We have to make it our business to know these things.'

'How? Have you been watching us? Has someone said something to you?'

The girl's lips tightened. 'I'm afraid I'm not at liberty to say.'

'But he's a retired headmaster!'

'Mrs Thomas! I am sure you must be aware that a respected occupation isn't an automatic defence. Now, you mentioned Bingo just then, Sunshine. Who is he?'

Sunshine gave her a patronising stare. 'He's just a puppy!'

'Ah! So he's not a little boy, holding hands with Granny's boyfriend?'

'That's Bingo's lead in Brian's hand, silly!'

'Sunshine, that's rude!'

'Well, she is silly! You said she was yourself!'

Vanessa stared at the floor, unable to meet the woman's eyes. 'And does Granny's boyfriend live with you?'

Her head jerked up. 'No he doesn't, although I don't see the relevance.'

'Mrs Thomas, I'm not asking you. Sunshine, can you tell me if Granny's boyfriend lives with you?'

There was a toothy, shy grin. 'He stays the night sometimes.'

'That's not true!' Vanessa jumped to her feet. 'He always leaves after you've gone to bed.'

'But I've seen him!' Sunshine was laughing. 'I've seen him in your room, Van Van, when you thought I was asleep.'

Could it get any worse?

'Van Van?' questioned the girl.

'It's what she calls me.'

'So she doesn't call you "Nanny" or "Gran"?'

'Or any of the other so-called politically correct terms that you've doubtless got in that book of yours,' cut in Vanessa. 'No. She doesn't. But I can assure you that what she does have is a loving, warm, safe home.'

'Brian likes Van Van!' piped up Sunshine suddenly. 'And I think the man at the swimming pool fancies her too!'

'That's not quite true.'

'I think we've had enough for today.' The girl put down her pen. Very neatly in line with her notepad. 'Would you like to wait outside in the corridor, Sunshine, with June from reception? That's right. Off you go. May I have that picture please? We need that for our records. Thank you!'

Then she turned to Vanessa. 'I have to say that I'm not happy about Sunshine witnessing inappropriate behaviour in the home.'

'If you mean Brian, we've been very careful!' Vanessa felt herself going hot like a teenager justifying herself. 'Lots of single carers have relationships. It doesn't mean that Brian is going to . . .' She couldn't even bring herself to say the word 'abuse'. But that's what the girl was thinking, she knew it. After all, wasn't that what had happened in that awful case last week?

'However, I gather that a complaint has been launched against him for violence.'

What? 'Who by?' asked Vanessa, stunned.

'I'm afraid we're not at liberty to say.'

Instinctively, Vanessa glanced at the girl's open notes. There was a name. Written clearly on the form in front of her. Even though it was upside down, she could still read it.

Jason Wood. Aged 24. No fixed address. Handyman.

Brigid's weaselly faced ex-boyfriend! Vanessa felt her legs weaken as she remembered that argument outside her place. Brian had pushed Jason away when he'd been harassing her over Sunshine. Not hard, but just enough to make a point.

The social worker was gathering up her papers. There was a book poking out of her denim bag, she could see. *Dr Know's No-Nonsense Guide to Parenting.* It didn't surprise her. 'If I were you, Mrs Thomas, I would make sure that you don't put yourself in any more compromising situations.'

Compromising situations! 'But wait. I haven't had a chance to tell you about everything else!' Vanessa whipped out the file that she'd brought with her. 'This is Sunshine's homework diary. It's full of stars and wonderful comments about her reading skills. She's streets ahead of the others.'

'You'll have a chance to put your side forward at the conference.'

Vanessa's blood chilled. 'What conference?'

'Mrs Thomas! Your granddaughter nearly got run over through negligence. You are fraternising with a man who has been accused of attacking someone. And there is still no sign of her real mother.' She glanced at her notes. 'I believe we are also waiting for the results of a DNA test.'

It didn't look good: even she had to admit that. 'In addition to that, your doctor's report states that your own health isn't particularly good. We have to think long-term here, I'm afraid.' For one fleeting moment, the girl sounded sympathetic. Then her lips pursed. 'I need to see you both again.' She glanced at her diary. 'I don't normally work weekends but I'm a bit pushed at the moment. Is this Saturday suitable?'

'Actually we're going on a parenting retreat then. It's part of a programme we've been doing at school: learning how to be better parents.' Vanessa gave a nervous laugh, desperate to curry favour. 'Or in my case, a better grandmother.'

The girl gave a grudging nod of approval. 'I heard about that from Mr Balls. We'll see you in a week's time then.' She made a note. 'I have to say that if it wasn't for the glowing report we've received from Corrywood Primary about your capabilities, Mrs Thomas, we might have taken Sunshine into care immediately.'

'But you can't!' This was her worst nightmare come true!

'Mrs Thomas, I'm sure you appreciate that a child's wellbeing has to come first. We have to follow up complaints.'

So it wasn't Mr Balls who had set them on to her, then. Not that she would have expected that. He was always so friendly and supportive. She wouldn't have thought it was Judith Davies either. Maybe it was someone from the class: someone who'd been there when she'd finally felt comfortable enough to discuss the difficulties of being a gran and a mum at the same time. Someone who had flouted the rules about confidentiality that Judith Davies had set at the start.

Not that that was important, right now. Her priority, Vanessa told herself, as she took Sunshine's warm little hand and assured her that yes, they would go swimming now, was to make sure that no one took her granddaughter away from her.

'I'm sorry,' she whispered into Brian's shoulder, 'but I can't see you any more. Not for a while, anyway.'

His stricken face stared down at her. 'But these people can't go round saying things that aren't true! It's disgraceful. I could have them for slander.'

'They haven't actually said anything.'

'Implied it then.'

She moved away from him. Sunshine was in the room next door, chasing penguins on screen with Bingo curled up next to her. It wouldn't do if she came in and found them cuddling up. She couldn't chance any more observations that might get passed on to the social worker. 'I can't risk it, Brian.'

It was so difficult! Every bone in her body wanted to snuggle up against him again, feel his big bear arms around her. 'I understand really.' The pain in his voice was almost unbearable. 'It's me or the little one, isn't it?'

Silently, she nodded, feeling a sick feeling in the pit of her stomach.

'Then there's no contest.' He scratched the back of his neck in the way she'd come to recognise as a sign that he was deep in thought. 'Nor should there be. If I'd been lucky enough to have kids, I wouldn't have let anyone come between me and them, either.'

Vanessa couldn't help it now. She had to feel his skin; had to have his arms around her one last time. 'I'm so sorry.'

Brian's eyes were wet. 'Give me a ring, lass, after this conference. Let me know what happens. And I want to know about your result too. That goes without saying.'

'You will. I'll keep in touch.' The words sounded so inadequate. Keep in touch? Was that all there was to mark the end of a passion which she had never, ever experienced before?

'I need to say goodbye to the little one,' he said quietly.

Vanessa nodded. 'Sunshine,' she called out. 'Brian's off now and so is Bingo.'

'Have they got to go?' Her granddaughter had developed a really demanding Daisy whine, she'd noticed.

'Just for a bit, poppet,' said Brian slowly.

Sunshine hung on to to Bingo. 'But you'll be back tomorrow, won't you?'

Vanessa made an involuntary noise in her throat.

'Not tomorrow or the day after that, I'm afraid.' Brian spoke steadily. 'Granny – I mean Van Van – will let you know when I'm allowed to come back.'

When, thought Vanessa sadly. Not if but when. It was all very well Brian being optimistic but what if she was only allowed to keep Sunshine if she didn't have a 'gentleman friend'? The thought of his arms not being around her any more was impossible. But so, too, was life without her granddaughter.

Sunshine buried her face in Bingo's fur. 'I'm going to miss you, little doggie. I'm really going to miss you!'

*

Maybe the long weekend was a good idea after all. It would help to distract both of them.

'It sounds as though this social worker gave you a hard time,' sniffed Bobbie when they rang to make arrangements about travelling down to Devon. They agreed to travel in Vanessa's car because Bobbie's ancient Volvo had started making weird noises and she didn't want to chance a long journey.

Vanessa shivered. 'She did. Have you got a cold?'

'Sort of.' She lowered her voice. 'Actually I'm feeling a bit upset. Rob and I have had a row.'

'Not over the scan?'

Vanessa still couldn't believe her friend was expecting twins. Was that why they'd had an argument? Or was it over the sexes? Bobbie had said they didn't know what they were but perhaps she was keeping it quiet. Maybe Rob was hoping for another son. Men could be funny like that. Harry hadn't bothered to hide his disappointment when Brigid had been born.

'Not exactly. It's a long story. The thing is that he isn't coming down to the weekend after all.'

Poor Bobbie! What a shame. Vanessa had been looking forward to meeting this man: putting a face to a name. Not that she'd liked the sound of him from everything she'd heard over the previous months. 'So I'll come over and we'll transfer to your car. Is that all right?'

By then, both she and Sunshine were more than ready to go. They had both been uncharacteristically tetchy with each other. 'Why can't Brian and Bingo come round?' her granddaughter kept whining.

Because of you, Vanessa wanted to say. But somehow she managed to bite her tongue, concentrating instead on briefing Kim and getting their cases packed. *We're five minutes from the sea*, the email from Andy had said. *So do pack beach clothes in case the weather is good, besides walking shoes. We plan to have plenty of outdoor activities as well as talking sessions.*

HONK! HONK! 'They're here!' Sunshine ran to the door before Vanessa could get there.

'You know you're not allowed to do that,' Vanessa began. Too late! Her granddaughter was already flying down the path, leaving Vanessa to carry the cases. It was amazing how much you needed to take a six-year-old away, even for two days!

'Just caught you, have I?' said the postman, coming up the path at the same time.

'Thanks.' Vanessa took the two envelopes he handed her – and froze. One had a hospital stamp on it. Her biopsy result! It had to be.

And the second had a London postmark. With the DNA clinic's name franked on the front.

There was a little girl called Lucy,
Who loved to eat all things juicy.
Her favourite was worms –
Oh, how her mum squirmed!
It made her feel all faint and woozy.

(Author's note: the real story behind this one is that Lucy
preferred yew berries and had to be pumped out at A
& E.)

Chapter 36

ANDY

'Why have we got to come to Devon with you?' whined Nattie. She was sitting in front of her dressing table, hair done up in a white towel turban while applying eyeliner in what looked like an extremely skilled manner. If only you could buy such confidence in bottles. If only more parents dished it out. If only he'd had it himself as a kid.

'I've told you.' Andy looked away. It was odd how you suddenly reached a point as a father when it didn't seem right to see your own daughter scantily dressed in her underwear any more. Yet it didn't seem very long ago that they'd all had Sunday-morning family cuddles together in bed.

Who was responsible for puncturing such innocence? Those awful abuse cases you read about in the paper? Social workers who could never do right? Evil people like that bastard of a photographer who had raped Pamela all those years ago? How had the world got to this state? And was it really possible to get back to good old-fashioned family values?

'I've told you,' he repeated. 'We're having a Perfect Parents' weekend and children are invited too.'

There was a snort of laughter from Mel at the door. 'Perfect Parents? That's a joke. 'Sides, we're not kids any more.'

Andy did a double-take. She'd dyed her hair black since breakfast! That beautiful blonde hair that other girls would surely give their eyeteeth for. He started to say something but then bit his tongue. Don't sweat the small stuff.

'I know. I know.' He tried to laugh. 'But we need you girls to help out with the little ones and take part in discussions. Some of the other teenagers are coming too.'

Nattie paused, mid-mascara flick. 'Who?'

Mel sniggered. 'You're hoping that Nick's going, aren't you? His mum's been coming to your sessions, Dad. She runs an au pair agency. I might ask her about a job abroad. Anything to travel and get out of this hole.'

'You haven't embarrassed us, Dad, have you?' asked Nattie sharply. 'If you've told Nick's mother anything confidential, I'll never talk to you again.'

Andy cringed, recalling some of the you-won't-believe-what-my-two-have-done-now confessions he had made along with the others. Was this really a good idea? A weekend away with all the parents and their partners and their kids, not to mention Judith Davies? 'I'm really looking forward to it,' she had trilled yesterday when they'd been going over the arrangements. 'The handbook says it's a wonderful way to sum up everything we've learned and to help us bond even more.'

The thought of bonding with Audrey the redhead was so improbable, given those icy looks at the school fête, that Andy almost laughed. Still, it was too late to get out of it now. They were meant to be setting off after his meeting with George. Andy wasn't sure whether to feel sick or relieved about that. As for Kieran, he still hadn't sent that email. He'd work out what to do about the man when he got back.

He turned back to the girls. 'I can't force you both to come,' he began to say, recalling that stuff in class about choices and empathy and non-confrontation with a dash of healthy bribery, 'but if you do, it would really help. And you can go to bed as late as you like. Just for the weekend, that is.'

'OK,' said Nattie coolly. 'If you think Nick really will be there.'

Mel sniffed. 'Go on then. Suppose I'll help out.'

Bloody hell. It worked! 'By the way.' Andy paused at the doorway. 'I went to see Mum the other day.' He stopped, working out how to say this carefully. 'The girls mustn't know I'm in this place,' Pamela had insisted. Yet at the same time, he didn't want to tell lies. 'She's staying with some friends now, not far from Granny.'

'Dad—' began Nattie.

'We know,' Mel interrupted.

A shot of fear went through him. 'You know?'

'Sure.' Mel bent over her sister to check her own reflection in the mirror. 'Granny told us.'

Interfering old bat!

'Mum needs some time to herself, apparently.' There was a shrug. A hurt shrug, he could tell. 'We're too much for her.'

'It's not that!'

'We're not stupid, Dad.' Nattie gave him a wounded look. 'It's great that you've taken time off work to look after us instead.'

Andy began to feel even more uncomfortable. 'Actually, that's the thing. It's not really like that.' But just as he was about to go on, his phone began to hum in his pocket. It was a text from George. *I tht we were meeting. Where R U?*

George again! If his middle-aged financial adviser was talking teen-text style, things must be wrong.

'Look, I'm sorry but I've got to go somewhere. I won't be long. It would be really great if you two could clear up the kitchen while I'm gone.'

'OK.'

Great! Positive expectation, as the handbook called it. It worked! Well, sometimes.

'And you do promise that you'll both be ready for Devon then, won't you? It could be your last chance.'

Shit. He hadn't meant to say that.

Mel's eyes narrowed. 'What do you mean?'

He was tempted to fudge. But hadn't he learned that lies always caught up with you? 'We might have to sell Seabridge, I'm afraid.'

'Why?' Nattie's eyes looked frightened. 'It's going to stay in the family for ever. You always said that. We'll be able to take our own children down there when we have them.'

Andy thought back to the telephone call he'd had with

George; the one that was going to change all their lives. 'Look, we'll talk about it another time, maybe when Mum's back. Meanwhile, let's enjoy this weekend, shall we?'

The meeting with George didn't take long. There wasn't much to say and what there was didn't make nice listening. Andy felt just as he used to in the home when being told off for something. So he did now what he had done then. Pretend he was somewhere else. Imagine it wasn't happening to him. Get the hell out as soon as he could. Blame someone else.

No, he wouldn't do that.

'I did advise you not to do it, Andy. Said it was too much of a gamble.' Poor George, with his thinning grey hair, tweed jacket, stiff manner and posh way of speaking. His financial adviser looked as distressed as if he had just lost all that money himself.

'It's OK.' Awkwardly Andy patted him on the back, even though he wasn't the kind of bloke you did that to. 'You were right.' He scratched his head and smiled ruefully. 'Guess I thought I was still wonder boy; that nothing could go wrong.'

George made a wry expression. 'You've been very lucky in the past. In fact, you're one of my few clients who made a killing out of this recession. I'm still not quite sure how you did it, to be honest.'

'Nor me.' All this was so unreal that it was as though he was discussing someone else. 'When I first started work, I thought hedge funds were what you got paid if you did a Bob-a-Job, trimming someone's garden.'

George managed a weak smile. 'I suppose this puts an end to your sabbatical, then. Any thoughts on where you'll go next?'

'Not sure.' Andy considered telling his financial adviser about Pamela being in rehab: a place they couldn't afford now. No. There were some things you had to keep to yourself. 'But I'd like to do something that lets me spend more time with my family. I'm not going back to that insane life when I never saw them.'

George nodded. 'Know what you mean. In fact, my wife's been itching to get back to work for years. Now the boys are out of nappies, we've decided it's time for a career swap.' He looked a bit embarrassed. 'I'm going to work from home while Julia's going back to the City.'

Andy tried to imagine George as one of the older dads on the school run and failed. His financial adviser hadn't got married until he was fifty, he'd once told him, and could easily be mistaken for his boys' grandfather. 'Good luck. Maybe you ought to do a parenting class.'

'Interesting!' George scratched his chin. 'I've been reading about them in the *Telegraph*. Bit of a growing trend, aren't they?'

'You could say that.'

'Ever been tempted to do one yourself?'

'I have, actually.'

There was no way Andy was admitting to actually running one. Not when he was so clearly a hopeless example himself.

'Any good?'

No, Andy was about to say. But then he thought of Paula, who worked with Jilly at the au pair agency. The woman who always wore gym kit and who had come up to him at the fête, telling him that the role play about teenagers and clothes had 'really helped to smooth things over with my lot'.

'Not bad at all. In fact, we're just off for a bonding weekend.'

George's eyebrows rose.

'Not that kind of bonding! A summing-up session, down at our place in Devon.'

'Great! Pamela going too?'

'No. She's busy.' Mention of his wife's name gave him a bit of a jolt. Reminded him why he was here in George's smart office with the mahogany desk and photograph of a family with expensive public-school smiles. He'd need to tell Pamela at some point. Tell her that he'd lost their money. That they were, more or less, broke.

*

'Call this a "holiday place"?' gasped Sandra, the woman with all the kids, whose husband turned out to be a very quiet, meek man. 'It's a flipping mansion.'

Andy tried to look as though he wasn't listening although he'd heard similar comments, phrased in different ways, from quite a few of his guests as they arrived in a straggle of cars and (in one case) by train.

He'd felt the same when Pamela had, some years ago, dragged him down to this small seaside town not far from Exeter. Bloody hell, he'd thought, gawping at the huge white 1920s place sprawling in front of him. This could have housed the entire boys' home! It even had a hot tub in the garden, despite the fact it was a stone's throw from the sea. 'Going cheap,' Pamela had assured him eagerly. The footballer who had owned it had gone broke. They could afford it, couldn't they?

That hadn't been an issue although Andy still had doubts even after he'd allowed his wife to have her way. It didn't seem morally right to him that they should have such a huge second home when they already had a lovely house in Corrywood. 'You work so hard,' Pamela had sulked. 'The least you can do is to make sure we have family weekends in the country. Proper country; not the suburbs.'

In the end, she'd been right. They'd had some great times down here, especially when the girls had been too little to object to 'nice healthy walks'. They'd also had Rob and Bobbie and the kids down too, although not as often as they should have done, perhaps. 'Those children could wreck a barn,' Pamela would say crossly after they'd gone, leaving a trail of handprints on the walls behind them.

Goodness knows what she would say if she saw the place now! Within a few hours of arriving, there was a pile of haversacks in the hall (scratching the paint) and sleeping bags strewn all over the bedrooms. Outside, families from Judith's session, some of whom he didn't even recognise, were putting up tents on the lawn. Too late, he realised that the grass would be ruined. And some kid had left the top off a lemonade bottle so it was dripping on to the floor in the kitchen . . .

He might have guessed. Jack! 'Hi there.' He ruffled the small boy's head affectionately. If someone didn't know better, they might have thought they were related by blood instead of marriage. The kid's boyish smile and those freckles reminded him of the only photograph he had of himself as a child. Faded and dog-eared, it was a copy of the one stapled to his notes in the home. 'Is Mum around?'

Jack was busy polishing off a tub of chocolate ice cream; part of some supplies that had been left in the freezer from when Pamela and the girls had been down last. Little pickle! 'Dunno.'

Andy looked around. There she was! Chatting to that small blonde woman who was a grandmother, according to Judith, even though she looked much younger than Camilla. They were on the other side of the kitchen by the French windows that led out to the hot tub. Andy felt a tremor of misgiving. He hoped everyone would be careful. He'd warned them all about the tub and the cliff path and the tides in the group email; explained that each parent needed to be responsible for their children's safety. Then Bobbie looked up, noticed him and gave a friendly wave.

His heart beating hard, he walked towards her. 'It's very kind of you to have us,' said the older woman, hooped gold earrings swinging.

'Not at all.' He turned to Bobbie, who was wearing a loose pale blue shirt outside her jeans. She must be what, twelve weeks or maybe thirteen now? Pregnancy really suited her! Pamela had loathed getting big, describing it as an invasion of her body. 'Did you find your room? I put you in the usual one.'

'It's great. Thanks.' Something in her eyes made him suspect that all wasn't right.

'Where's Rob?'

'He's not coming.'

Diplomatically, Vanessa moved away into the crowd of guests, all oohing and aahing over the Aga and the flat-screen television on the kitchen wall. 'We had a row.' Bobbie bit her lip. 'He found out that I'd rung his secretary.'

'So what?'

Bobbie coloured. 'The problem is that I pretended to be someone else.'

Andy caught his breath, gesturing that they should move round the corner for a bit of privacy. When Bobbie finished telling him the whole story about ringing up Rob's secretary and pretending to do a survey, he couldn't help being frank. 'You were lucky that no one pressed charges.'

'I know.' She hung her head. It was all he could do not to put his arms around her in comfort. Dammit. He couldn't *not*. Briefly he gave her a quick hug. To his relief, she didn't move away: instead, she spoke into his shoulder so her voice came out all muffled. 'But it was as though I was someone else! I was so scared he was having an affair that I just had to know.'

Then she stepped away as though she had said too much. 'I understand; I really do,' he replied quietly as they went back into the kitchen where Jack was ploughing through a second tub of ice cream. 'It's the not knowing, isn't it? It makes your imagination runs riot.'

'Exactly!' Bobbie caught his hand. 'How's Pamela getting on?'

'She seems to be doing well, although she still has issues too, from her past. Things she did that she now regrets. Other things too that she had no control over.'

'Don't we all, mate?'

Horrified, Andy heard an all-too-familiar voice beside him. What was *he* doing here? 'Kieran? I didn't think you were coming.'

'Why? Cos you didn't send the email?' There was a nasty little grin. That man's breath was disgusting! And he was still hacking away with that awful cough, right in everyone's face. No wonder Bobbie was taking a step back. 'Luckily one of the other parents told me how to get here.' He whacked Andy on the arm in a mock playful fashion. 'Nice pad you've got here, mate, I must say. Pity the wife couldn't make it. But she's on call.'

'On call?'

'Yeah. She's a doctor, you know.'

Sure she was. Kieran was a pathological liar. Andy didn't trust him as far as he could have thrown him. He didn't like the way he was looking Bobbie up and down, either.

'Aren't you going to introduce me then?'

There was nothing for it. 'This is my brother-in-law's wife. Bobbie Wright.'

'Brother-in-law's wife? Bloody hell, that's a bit of a mouthful, innit! Nice to meet you. Funny name, Bobbie. Isn't that a bloke's?'

Bobbie flushed. How he loved it when she did that! Andy ached once more to put his arm around her protectively. Bugger Rob. His wife was pregnant, for God's sake. He should be down here looking after her.

'It's short for Roberta.'

'Right posh! Must say, Andy, you've done well for yourself, haven't you? All these smart relatives and a place like this. Long way from the home, isn't it?'

Andy froze.

'See you around then.' Kieran winked. 'Just going to help myself to that food over there. Then after that, I'd like a little chat, if you don't mind. About that business venture of ours.' He nudged Andy hard in the ribs. 'By the way, hope you're not giving us Brussels sprouts for dinner, are you?'

Andy felt sick, recalling the argument he and Kieran had had in the home. Kieran had claimed Andy had been given one more sprout than him, so had leaned over and pinched his. Food battles had been two a penny but that incident had always stood out in his mind because that had been THE night. The night of the robbery.

Bobbie, he could see, was waiting courteously until Kieran had moved on before speaking. 'I've seen him around at school,' she said quietly. 'What did he mean about being a long way from the home?'

406

'*His* home,' said Andy quickly. 'We grew up near each other in Essex. One of those coincidences.'

Bobbie's face cleared. 'Amazing! Did you know that the woman over there – the one with the dangly earrings and arty scarf – used to go out with the very quiet chap who's married to the mother with all the kids? They haven't seen each other for years until today. Small world, isn't it?'

Andy tried to smile. 'Kieran wasn't a friend then and isn't now. To be honest, I wish he wasn't here.'

There was a light touch on his hand. 'I can understand how you feel, Andy, but you did the right thing to invite him.'

Hah!

'That's what this weekend is all about, isn't it? Getting to know each other better and working out how to be good parents. I only wish Rob was here. Oh no. JACK! DON'T MOVE! I'LL GET YOU!'

'What is it?'

'Look!'

Bloody hell. How did that little monkey climb on top of the freezer? Surely he wasn't really going to jump down on to his skateboard?

Oh my God . . .

ONE IN FIVE PARENTS DRINK 'TOO MUCH' AFTER THEIR KIDS HAVE GONE TO BED

Extracted from a news item in the Daily Wail.

(Ed's note: Check statistic. Office straw poll suggests figure much higher.)

Chapter 37

BOBBIE

Bobbie still felt hot under the collar when she thought of that awful row in the hospital car park after the scan. If only Jack hadn't swapped her mobile phone cover with Rob's! Then he'd never have got Araminta's message about dropping her complaint.

Rob's eyes had gone cold and hard with suspicion. '*You* were the one who made that call to Araminta?'

'Well, yes. Sort of.'

'Excuse me.' The receptionist from radiology had come running out into the car park at that point. 'You left your baby picture behind!'

'Do you realise how upset you made her!'

'So, er, would you like the picture now?'

'You realise it's probably illegal?' Rob had run a hand across his brow. 'I'm sure there's a law against obtaining information through deception.'

'MUM, DAD, DON'T ROW!'

It was the cardinal sin to row in front of the children, especially if there was a stranger present. But she had to explain herself if Rob was going to understand. 'I thought', Bobbie hissed quietly, 'you were having an affair.'

'Maybe I'll just post it.'

'How could you think that?'

'How could Mummy think what, Daddy?'

Bobbie tried to speak but all she could think of was the baby waving at her from the photograph. 'Hello!' it seemed to say. 'Please don't ruin my life before I get here.'

'You don't trust me, do you?' Rob shook his head

indignantly. The disappointment in his eyes was horrible. 'How can we honestly have another baby – babies! – together?'

'Are we sending them back, Daddy?' asked Daisy hopefully.

Bobbie's stomach began to heave. Had her husband really just said what she thought he'd said? That bit about not having another baby together?

'Do you realise what a difficult position you've put me in at work?' he added, holding open the car door for her.

'I'm so sorry.' She could see now how stupid she had been. Yet at the time, Sarah's idea had seemed quite a good one.

Rob was staring straight ahead. 'Just drop me at the station, would you?' he said flatly. And when she did, he just got out with a quiet goodbye to the children and nothing at all to her.

Since then, he had hardly spoken to her. Not even when she'd begged him to accompany her on the parenting weekend. Now, as she sat on the huge circular bed in Pamela's guest room, with its pale blue silk cover, listening to the screams of laughter outside in the garden, she was actually glad he hadn't come to Devon. Cold empty silences were no way to bring up children.

Suddenly there was a bleep indicating a text. Mum! As a teenager, and also in her twenties, Bobbie could remember thinking that her mother didn't understand anything about her life. In the last few years, however, she'd begun to realise that Mum was more in tune than she'd realised. Maybe she could talk to her. Tell her what a mess she'd got herself into. See if she had any solutions.

Hi, Bobbie! In New York for Herbert's pilot show! So exciting! Have just been up to the top of the Empire State Building for a reception! Canapés and champagne. Are we still on for Mothering Sunday? Herbert's diary is UNBELIEVABLY busy so he's asked me to check. Can't wait to see you! Don't ring or text back – just going to another party. Love Mum x

Maybe not.

'Right, Daisy! Are you sitting comfortably?'

Through the screen, Bobbie could hear her daughter giggling. In front of her was the audience, lounging on the carpet and on Pamela's now not-so-white sofas. Expectant faces whom she'd grown to know so well over the previous weeks. Not Really Pregnant Mum, Too Many Kids Mum, American Express (looking rather full), Matthew and parents from the other class whom she didn't know, like that chap with the bald head and tattoos who had grown up near Andy.

'Don't I know you from somewhere?' he kept saying. Did he? wondered Bobbie. It was true that he did look vaguely familiar. Now he was staring at her. Along with all the others. When Miss Davies had suggested, with that sweet earnest expression, that they played the Parent and Child question game (a form of Mr and Mrs), everyone else seemed to think that was a great idea.

Everyone apart from her, that was. It would be easier if she had some support. She felt quite envious of Jilly from the au pair agency who was holding hands with her husband in the front row. That loving, understanding glance between them just then had given her a little kick in the stomach. What was Rob doing now? Probably on the phone to his mother, telling her about 'poor' Araminta who'd been hoodwinked by his wife into revealing details about her personal life. Or having a team meeting with some attractive advertising executive. Someone who wasn't insecure. Someone who wasn't frazzled out with kids.

'Are you ready, Bobbie and Daisy!' Miss Davies's voice trilled out. 'The idea behind this game is to see how well you know each other. We're going to ask you some questions. Then you write down your answer in capital letters on the sheet and hold it up for the audience to see. Let's get going, shall we? Bobbie, what's Daisy's favourite colour?'

Easy! It had always been blue. When she'd been little, it was all she would wear.

411

'YELLOW!'

Miss Davies's voice rose above the roar of excitement. 'Sorry, Bobbie. That's one to Daisy.'

'But she's always loved blue!'

'That was ages ago!' sang out her daughter's indignant voice – so like Rob's. 'If you listened to me, you'd know I'd gone off it.'

There was a wave of laughter from the audience followed by mock tutting from Judith. 'No answering back! Not yet anyway. Right, Daisy, what is Mum's favourite colour?'

'Red! Cos that's what her face does when she's yelling at us.'

Another wave of laughter mixed with a few sympathetic looks from the crowd in front, including Andy.

'Your turn now, Bobbie. What's Daisy's favourite subject?'

No problem: 'English! She loves reading and telling stories.'

'You're meant to write it down, Mum, not shout it out,' giggled Daisy from the other side of the screen. 'Anyway, you're wrong! It's art.'

'Since when?'

'Children, children!' called out a woman with red hair. 'Don't squabble!'

'Right, Daisy. What was Mum's favourite subject when she was at school?'

There was a brief silence. 'I don't know. Mum's never told us. But she's awful at maths. She got me a D in my homework last week.'

Another wave of laughter. Maybe Miss Davies would see the funny side, thought Bobbie hopefully. No? Oh well.

'Right, last question then. Bobbie, your turn. Who's Daisy's best friend?'

This was a real minefield. Children changed their best friends from one day to the next. Besides, Daisy was still finding her feet at her new school. Aware that a sea of faces was staring at her, many of whom had been round to their house for play dates, Bobbie hesitated. This was the kind of question that could destroy Daisy's social life for ever if she got the answer wrong.

Then she saw Vanessa sitting at the back. Of course! 'Daisy has lots of friends,' she said carefully, 'but she loves to hang out with Sunshine. She might be younger but the two of them get on really well.'

'YES!' Daisy's bossy little voice came thudding through the screen. 'You've got it right, Mum!'

'Now what about you, Daisy?' asked Miss Davies. 'Who's Mum's best friend?'

'It's Sarah! We used to live near her.'

'No it's not!' piped up a little voice from the front. Jack? 'It's Uncle Andy! I saw them this morning, giving each other a cuddle!'

Oh my God! Had her son really just said that? Andy too looked horror-stricken. Even worse, no one laughed. Instead, there was a hushed silence.

'That's ridiculous,' she began. 'Andy's my brother-in-law,' she added for the benefit of those who might not know. 'We were just . . . just talking about family stuff.'

Miss Davies appeared flustered, undoing her ponytail and then putting it up again. 'Let's have a changeover now, shall we? How about you, Matthew and Lottie?'

Bobbie didn't know where to look. Forget the disapproving stares from the audience – especially Audrey who was whispering loudly – it was her children who mattered. Less Jack, who didn't seem to realise the significance of what he had just said, but Daisy, who was rushing out of the house, down through the garden and out of the back gate.

It wasn't easy to run when you were three months pregnant with twins. 'Daisy! Stop. Please!'

Reluctantly her daughter slowed to a halt. She was crying! With a pang, Bobbie remembered how sick she'd felt as a teenager when overhearing her mother accusing Dad of seeing someone else. Hadn't she vowed to herself then that she would never ever put her own children through that? Yet here she was again, repeating the same pattern.

'Daisy?' she began, sitting down beside her on a bench overlooking the sea. The gentle splash of the waves below made her feel slightly calmer. 'I love Daddy very much, you know.'

There was an accusing glare. 'Then why did you cuddle Uncle Andy?'

Life was always so black and white in children's heads!

'It was a comfort cuddle. I was a bit upset and Uncle Andy was making me feel better.'

There was a sniff. 'So you're not going to get divorced like Aunty Sarah?'

'No. No, we're not.' Bobbie heard her voice sounding stronger. That toe-curling scene just now had made her realise something. Yes, Andy was kind and understanding, but it was Rob she loved. That was why she had been so upset when she'd thought he was having an affair with Araminta. Besides, he was the father of her children: no one else could take that place.

I love him. Wasn't that what her mother had always said when explaining why she stayed with her father?

'In fact, I'm going to ring Daddy and ask him to come down.' Actually she'd *tell* him. Point out that they had to start behaving like grown-ups for the sake of the kids. Admit that she had faults too.

'OK.' Daisy set her little jaw. For a minute, Bobbie saw a flash of Camilla. Heaven help them. 'Do it then, Mum. Make up. Just like you're always saying to me and Jack.'

Right now? Bobbie's resolve began to weaken. Rob had been so mad at her!

'You shouldn't go to bed on an argument!' Daisy was virtually waggling her finger. 'That's what you tell us!'

She'd have liked more time to work out what she was going to say but there was nothing for it. Nervously, Bobbie pressed Rob's number.

'Hi, this is Rob Wright. Sorry I'm not . . .'

'Try the home phone.' Daisy's voice was dictatorial.

'Hi, this is the Wright family . . .'

414

Daisy's face crumpled. 'Where is he then?'

Bobbie drew her daughter to her. 'Probably in a meeting.'

Daisy broke away from her. 'I don't believe you. In fact, I don't believe either of you. You're going to get divorced, aren't you? It's that thing's fault!' She pointed to Bobbie's stomach. 'I don't want a stupid brother or sister. Send it back and then it will be all right again.'

'How are you doing?'

It was Andy. She'd been dreading this. The very sound of his voice filled her with so many different emotions that Bobbie didn't know which one to pick.

'I'm all right, thanks,' she replied neutrally, trying to camouflage her distress by unloading the dishwasher. Ever since they'd arrived, there had been a posse of well-meaning adults, each keen to outdo the others in the kitchen. In the end, at Miss Davies's suggestion, they'd drawn up a list of parent and child helpers. 'Not your own children,' the young teacher had urged. 'The handbook says it can be useful to mix and match.' Bobbie had ended up with the twins who belonged to Mr and Mrs Perfect. They were identical (as were Jilly's) which made it hard to know who was meant to be doing what. Right now, however, they were both laying the huge table in the dining room next door.

'I need to talk to you,' Andy said urgently. 'Please. The coast is clear. Honest.'

Turning round, she watched him take in her tear-stained face.

'You're not all right,' he said softly.

'Of course I'm not! My reputation – what little there was of it – has been completely ripped to shreds. And I've been trying to get hold of Rob but there's no answer.'

He nodded, his eyes sympathetic. 'I can't contact Pamela either.'

'NOT THERE, YOU MORON. YOU PUT THE FORKS THERE!'

'NO, YOU DON'T.'

415

'YES, YOU DO!'

There was the sound of healthy tussling from next door.

'NOW LOOK. YOU'VE MADE A MARK ON THE TABLE.'

Sounded like the twins weren't as easy-going as their parents made out.

'But I don't care,' added Andy. 'In fact, I'm beginning not to care about quite a lot of things.'

Help! He was moving towards her. Hadn't she guiltily daydreamed about this? Yet now it was happening, it didn't feel right. Not right at all.

'Excuse me, but I was looking for Sunshine.'

They both jumped as Vanessa came in through the back door, wearing a pair of dashing blue and white culottes that one of her regulars had brought in last week. It was one of those really bright spring days that was so warm, it could almost be June. Outside, the children had stripped off and were dashing around in T-shirts and, in some cases, just their underwear. 'Have you seen her anywhere?'

'No.' Bobbie peeled off her National Trust apron. 'But I'll come and help you find her. Andy, can you take over for me please?' Grabbing Vanessa's arm, she almost ran on to the patio. 'I'm so glad you came in just then!'

Vanessa gave her an odd look. 'I don't want to pry, Bobbie, but the two of you seemed to be getting rather close there.'

'I know!' Bobbie looked wildly around but the kids were all leaping on the trampoline or in the hot tub, under the guidance of Mr and Mrs Perfect who were sitting awkwardly on the edge, matching jeans rolled up, dipping their legs in the water. It was intriguing to see both the Perfects together. They hardly seemed to speak to each other.

'I think Andy's got a crush on me,' she whispered. 'Now I'm wondering if it's my fault. I mean, I have confided in him. Quite a lot. Perhaps I shouldn't have done. Maybe he thought I was leading him on.'

'Possibly,' said Vanessa quietly as they walked towards the little gate that led down to the sea. 'It can be so easy to give

416

the wrong impression in life, can't it? Look, I hope you don't mind me changing the subject but there's something I need to run past you.'

She'd known something wasn't right. Vanessa had been really quiet and withdrawn, not just on the way down but ever since they'd been here. Bobbie had presumed it was because the older woman was still cross with her. Now, looking at her pale face and shaking hands, she wondered if it was something else.

'I won't tell anyone,' she said, patting the space on the bench next to her. 'Not unless they make me play another party game.'

Actually, that wasn't funny.

'I got two letters this morning, just before we left. One was the result of the DNA.'

Bobbie frowned. 'What DNA?'

'Some awful boy in the town claims he's Sunshine's father so I agreed to a test.'

No!

'It's all right. She's not his. So he can't claim any rights.'

The significance began to sink in. 'Thank goodness for that.'

'The second letter was from the hospital.'

'To do with the DNA?'

'No.' Vanessa looked away. 'To do with me. Five years ago, I had cancer.'

Cancer? But Vanessa always looked so well. Bobbie's blood froze. 'And you've got it again?'

Vanessa shrugged. 'Possibly. I found a lump. In the "good" breast. The tests so far have proved inconclusive. But they've suggested I have it out.'

That was awful! Hadn't her friend got enough on her plate already? 'If there's anything I can do, please tell me, won't you?'

'That's the thing.' Vanessa's voice was tight. As though she was trying not to cry. 'I'm worried that social services might try and take Sunshine away when I go into hospital to have the lump removed. If it proves malignant, I could be there for quite a while.'

'She can stay with us.' Bobbie pulled the older woman towards her, wrapping her arms around her. 'If necessary, I'll hide her. Well, not seriously, obviously. But I promise you, Vanessa. No one will take Sunshine away from you. I won't let them.'

Vanessa smiled thinly. 'That's what Brian said. But let's be honest, Bobbie. If they want to do that, they can. My lawyer says it might be difficult to stop them.'

'I'M NOT GOING TO TELL YOU AGAIN, JULIUS! YOU HAVE TO WAIT YOUR TURN BEFORE GOING ON THE TRAMPOLINE!'

They both looked up at the noise from across the lawn. A mother with thick glasses was getting quite cross. 'Maybe', Bobbie said slowly, 'it's worth getting a second opinion. Did you know that woman over there is a lawyer?'

Impressed, Vanessa tried to get a better look. The woman who was losing her rag?

'*There* you are!'

Bobbie jumped at the sound of the cross, angry voice. Was it directed at *her*? She took in the rough man with the bald head and neck tattoos who was heading straight for her. 'Just remembered where I've seen you! Knew it would come to me in the end.' His piggy eyes were red with fury. 'You're the silly bitch what left her kids in the car, wasn't you? On that hill. If it hadn't been for me, they could have got killed when they let off the handbrake.'

Oh God. So that's why his face had been familiar. 'It wasn't as bad as it sounds,' she started to say, turning to Vanessa. 'And Sunshine wasn't in the car. I promise. I only dashed into a shop for a minute. I thought they'd be all right.'

But her friend just gave her a disappointed look. And then walked away, shaking her head ruefully. Bobbie sighed; sometimes Vanessa could be very irritating. Then again, no doubt she was the same at times. Perhaps adults were no wiser than kids . . .

By the time it came to supper, everyone seemed to have fallen into little groups. Audrey from the older class was flirting loudly, gin in hand, with the Greg Wise lookalike in a leather jacket, who turned out to be married to American Express. The latter was openly breastfeeding on the sofa opposite.

'I wish she wouldn't do that,' snapped the woman who always wore gym kit and a sweat band. 'Nigel can't take his eyes off her. It's not as though my husband needs any encouragement. I'm going to complain to Andy.'

'Me too.' Battered Mum was looking upset. 'I thought we'd agreed that everything we said in class was confidential.'

'It was,' nodded Jilly.

'Then how come everyone from your group seems to know that my children hit me? How do they know I haven't just fallen over?'

'You'd need to be pretty clumsy to do it all the time,' shrugged Sweat Band Mum. 'By the way, I heard a bit of gossip just now. Mrs Perfect, as I call her, was having a quiet word with the mum in our group who's a lawyer. She was asking for a definition of unreasonable behaviour. What do you think of that?'

There was enough here to write a novel! But this was real life. Complicated. Confusing.

If only Vanessa would understand about Jack and the handbrake, but her friend still had a disapproving air about her. Frankly, Bobbie didn't blame her. Why was it that you did stuff as a parent that seemed acceptable at the time but then, when something went wrong, you realised you'd made the wrong decision? It wasn't like making a mistake at work. There were little people at stake here. If you messed them up, as Larkin had pointed out, you mucked them up for ever. Affected the way that *they* would be parents. On and on it would go, a pattern that would last throughout the generations.

'Nothing like the sea air,' commented Matthew wistfully,

taking a seat beside her. 'Lottie and I have often thought about moving down to the coast. But it's a big step, isn't it?'

Meanwhile, the teenagers had cooked dinner: there were quite a few of them, including Rob's nieces who were being really sweet with the younger children. 'Who'd like to give me a hand?' Mel was saying. 'Well done, Daisy and Jack! That's brilliant.'

But both girls were ignoring Bobbie. They were being cool with their father too, she noticed.

Finally supper was ready, and they all gathered in the dining room.

'Wow! This is good,' said Bohemian Mum as they all tucked in. It *was* too. Mushroom stroganoff for the veggies and chicken supreme for the others.

'Ugh! Who's made a smell?' piped up Lottie.

'It's Pongo.'

'No it's not, Jack!' Nattie tickled him. 'It's *you*!'

Not Really Pregnant Mum nudged Bobbie in the ribs. 'Ever thought of putting him on a gluten-free diet? I can give you some tips if you like.'

Mr and Mrs Perfect and Mel were almost as loud as the other side of the table.

'Don't let him put salt on his food!'

'You try and stop him!'

So much for Mr and Mrs Perfect!

'Stop kicking your mother like that!'

This was Mel, talking to one of Battered Mum's kids.

'I'm not.'

'Yes you are. I've seen the bruises. If you don't stop right now, you little squirt, I'm going to tell my boyfriend. He'll sort you out.'

Wow! Nothing like peer pressure!

After dinner, someone suggested a 'good old-fashioned board game'. There was a general consensus of moaning at this from the adults, who crashed out in front of a Tom Hanks DVD that someone had brought. But to Bobbie's surprise, Mel and Nattie, along with the other teens, got the kids round a

Monopoly board and turned up the volume on Andy and Pamela's high-tech music system.

'Let's have teams!' called out a rather good-looking boy who belonged to Too Many Kids Mum.

Instantly, Daisy and Sunshine clung to Nattie. 'We three want to be together!'

So sweet! Yet heart-breaking at the same time. Poor Vanessa, not knowing what was going to happen to Sunshine. And what about her *own* family? What would happen to them if she and Rob couldn't make it work?

'Where's Jack? We need him!'

Oh my God. How could she have taken her eyes off him! It was being somewhere new, that's what it was. Too easy to get distracted. 'Jack? JACK?'

'He's at the front door,' someone sang out.

Probably trying to escape! Or skateboarding on the road again. Forcing herself up – she'd forgotten how tired pregnancy made you feel – Bobbie wandered out into the hall. There was the sound of voices. A woman's voice. So familiar that, for a moment, she could hardly believe it.

'Sarah!' How wonderful! Just who she needed when life was crumbling down around her. She flung her arms around her. There was nothing like an old friend at times like this. 'But I don't get it! What are you doing here?'

'I've brought someone.' Sarah stepped to one side. Coming up the path with an overnight bag was a man. A tall, good-looking man with blond hair, just like the children. Swinging from his arm was Jack.

Her son grinned. 'I saw Dad out of the window!'

'DAD,' yelled Daisy, who'd come running up to see what was going on. 'You've arrived at last.'

Bobbie turned to Sarah with a what's-going-on? look. 'I rang to have a chat with you and got Rob instead,' said her friend in a low voice. 'I could tell something wasn't right so I made him tell me. Then I persuaded him that he owed it to you and his kids – including the two you're expecting – to join you.'

She nudged Bobbie just as Matthew came into the hall to find out what the commotion was about. 'Besides, I thought it might be a good excuse to see a certain person again! Don't you think?'

I LOVE MY MUM BECAUSE . . .

She smells nice.
She cooks great Pot Noodles.
She loves me more than anyone in the world.
She says I'm her favourite although I mustn't
    tell the others.
She doesn't charge interest.
She pays my phone bill.
She's my mum.

With thanks to Corrywood Primary (see Mothers' Day
wall exhibition in class 1A)

Chapter 38

VANESSA

Vanessa woke early on the Sunday morning, wondering for a moment where she was. Then she took in the elegant dressing table with the curved legs along with the line of oyster-coloured wardrobes with mirrored doors and remembered. Andy had put her and Sunshine in the main bedroom: her granddaughter was sleeping next to her, thumb in mouth as usual while the other little hand clutched the small clay flute.

Snoring loudly in a second huge bed on the far side of the room (did Pamela and Andy sleep separately when they were down here?) was Audrey. She had a teenage son but he was bunked up with all the other adolescents in the summer house. 'I would have brought my husband,' she had declared last night with a toss of the head, 'but he's still on the rig.'

She said this in a way designed to make it clear that she wasn't on her own in life, as though there was still a stigma to it.

It was intriguing, thought Vanessa as she stretched out in bed, making sure she didn't wake Sunshine, to match the people she'd got to know over the previous few weeks with their partners. Couples weren't always what you expected. Take Mr and Mrs Perfect, who either ignored each other or snapped; even their kids fought tooth and nail.

Andy Gooding, too, was different from Pamela. More ordinary and laid-back than his posh, tense wife who had made Vanessa collect her cast-offs from home instead of actually coming to the shop.

Then there were Rob and Bobbie. She hadn't been prepared for that rather good-looking man with very blond hair (just like his sister Pamela) and a serious look on his face. He hadn't hugged his wife when he'd arrived, Vanessa had observed, merely given her a brush on the cheek. Nor had he swung the children into the air, as Brian did with Sunshine. Just sort of ruffled their hair as though they belonged to someone else.

Brian! The very thought made Vanessa lurch inside with emptiness. When it came to choosing between him and Sunshine, there was no contest. Yet she missed him so much! Missed his kisses; missed his cuddles; missed the touch of his hand on her breast. Automatically, her hand went up to the lump – which seemed to have got slightly bigger, unless that was her imagination.

It will be all right, he'd texted her last night after her message to say she and Sunshine had arrived safely in Devon. That was all they had now. Short texts and brief phone calls. She wouldn't blame him if he dropped her. Not many men could cope with a secret relationship; not at their age. Yet there was a new message now, this morning. *Miss you*, it said simply. Followed by a kiss.

'I miss you too,' she whispered out loud. Sunshine stirred at the sound and Vanessa held her breath. She didn't want her granddaughter to wake yet; she needed her sleep after all that running around yesterday. Besides, it also gave her time to think: to work out what on earth she was going to do about the social worker's veiled threat.

'No one will take Sunshine away from you. I won't let them,' Bobbie had said. Her friend had meant well but she knew – as did Bobbie – that there was nothing anyone could do about it. Even the very bright mother in Andy's group, who turned out to be a family lawyer, had tightened her lips. 'Come and see me when we're back home and I'll look into it,' she'd promised when they spoke briefly after dinner. Vanessa had wanted to ask how much she'd charge but was too embarrassed.

Still, she'd do anything to keep Sunshine, whatever it cost, thought Vanessa as she tossed and turned in the early hours of the morning. Sell the shop if necessary. It was only leasehold (with less than a year before the lease expired) but she'd had various offers over the last year from bored Corrywood mothers who wanted to buy the 'goodwill'. Frankly, she'd flog the clothes off her body to keep Sunshine. But it wasn't just a question of finding money for a second legal opinion. It was finding a way of persuading the social workers that Sunshine was better off where she was: with a grandmother who had suspected recurring breast cancer.

Enough! Vanessa had learned the first time that the only way to cope was to be positive. Wasn't that why she had thrown so much energy into her shop? Wasn't that why she loved clothes so much? It was one of the few things that calmed her. Now, Vanessa found herself getting out of bed (she knew she wouldn't get back to sleep anyway), padding across the soft, deep carpet and opening those inviting wardrobe doors in Pamela's room to run her practised eye over the row after row of beautiful clothes that belonged to their absent hostess.

Clothes always told you so much about the owner . . . Heavens. These were icons! Real vintage stuff going back to the eighties. And they all had original designer labels on them. Imagine what they would be worth! If she wasn't mistaken, they were samples; each one in a size eight. They must have been from Pamela's modelling days. Must have been pretty successful, looking at this lot. Ossie Clark. Zandra Rhodes. David Emanuel. The names were endless. In a different league from the other clothes that Pamela had sold to her.

What kind of woman wore this? wondered Vanessa as she held a beautiful glittery emerald-green sequinned dress up against herself in the mirror. Was Pamela really the cold fish that Bobbie made her out to be? There was something about these clothes and the way they had been so carefully preserved in their polythene bags with heavy hangers that suggested a different kind of owner. A woman who had once been Someone. A woman, perhaps, who found it difficult to leave all that behind her, otherwise she would have got rid of this stuff. A woman who still yearned for the past.

Vanessa shivered. It was all very well Bobbie declaring that she was 'just friends' with Andy but she'd seen the man's face when Rob had arrived last night and pecked his wife's cheek. It was jealousy. Pure, utter jealousy. Bobbie might not have the hots for her sister-in-law's husband but Andy Gooding sure as hell had the hots for her. She only hoped her friend didn't make a big mistake. At times, Bobbie did some daft things: like that secretary business and leaving the children in the car alone.

Vanessa wasn't too keen on her chum Sarah either. Not that she'd had a chance to get to know her. But Vanessa hadn't warmed to those rather sharp features, which somehow seemed familiar.

'Van Van!'

Hastily, she put back a slinky black dress, which she'd have loved to try on. Sunshine, who had been sound asleep a few minutes ago, had now leaped out of bed. (Why was it that kids could wake so easily?) 'Can we go in the hot tub before breakfast?' she demanded, slipping into the red swimming costume that Vanessa had dried last night.

'Sure,' she whispered brightly, glancing at Audrey, who was still breathing noisily. 'Sounds like a great idea.' Automatically, Vanessa put her hand to her chest. The uncertain side. The part that didn't know if it was malignant or not. That was the other thing about having kids, something she'd forgotten after years of being on your own: however uncertain life was, or however much your heart was breaking inside, you had to pretend that everything was all right.

'Go on, Van Van! You can do it!'

Sunshine was sitting on the edge of the hot tub, encouraging her on. It was a huge one, the kind where you could actually swim a width. If you could swim, that was. Vanessa had let her lessons slide recently with everything that had been going on but now her granddaughter seemed determined to make up for lost time.

'Remember what the instructor told you? Kick your leg out at the same time as your arms!'

There was a dark chuckle from the side. 'Keeping you on your toes, isn't she?'

Vanessa pushed back her floral rubber cap. It was that bald-headed chap with tattoos down his neck; the one whom she'd spotted having an argument one night with Andy after parenting class. She didn't like the look of him. His voice might sound jolly but there was a steeliness in his piggy eyes, and she didn't care for the way he was standing there, arms folded, as though eyeing her up.

'You could say that,' she replied out of courtesy.

'Time to get out, if you don't mind me saying.' He coughed and then spat on the ground. 'I've been sent down here to round up the troops. We've got some of that role play to get through.'

Vanessa got herself to the side. 'Right then. Thanks.'

The man was still standing there, looking. She hadn't seen him with a wife at dinner last night, only a skinny kid with the same pointed ears as his dad.

'Don't stare! It's rude!' Sunshine's angry little voice took her by surprise but it seemed to amuse the man.

'You're an outspoken little thing, aren't you? Is that why your mum is at parenting school?'

'She's not my mum. She's my Van Van.'

The man scratched his neck. 'Is she now? Well, we'll have to be entering her for the glamorous-granny competition, won't we?'

Sleazebag! Vanessa was about to make a cutting comment when there was the sound of a bell ringing from the house. 'We're about to start,' someone called out.

The man made to move away, thank goodness. 'See you later then.'

Not if she had anything to do with it, he wouldn't! Certainly not alone, anyway.

'I don't like him,' said Sunshine quietly as they quickly got dressed in the changing hut, which was bigger than her kitchen. 'He's like the men who told off Mummy.'

Vanessa's mouth went dry. 'What men?'

'The men who talked in loud voices.'

'What happened after that?' breathed Vanessa.

The child shrugged. 'She said she had to go away and that I had to be a good girl.'

Vanessa could hardly breathe. 'Did this have anything to do with Mummy's scar?'

A look of fear flitted over her face. 'I can't tell anyone. Mummy said I mustn't.'

'There you are!' The mother from the other group who always wore gym stuff and wanted everything done 'right now' was marching in, without so much as a knock on the hut door. 'We can't start without you and everyone's waiting. Do hurry up!'

Vanessa couldn't concentrate on the role play. Sunshine had just been on the verge of telling her something that she instinctively knew was important, and then that stupid woman had ruined it. When she had tried to find out more, Sunshine had just said she couldn't remember. Vanessa could have screamed with frustration.

'It's our turn! It's our turn!' Sunshine was jumping up and down.

'Not quite yet, I'm afraid!' Intellectual Mum was checking her list. 'It's Daisy and her mother.'

Bobbie stood up. She was wearing, Vanessa noticed, the soft blue floaty top she'd pressed on the young woman last week. Perfect, she'd told her, for hiding your bump and yet looking good at the same time. 'Actually, I'd like to suggest my husband does it instead.'

Good on you, girl, whispered Vanessa as Rob went into the circle, looking extremely uncomfortable. Intellectual Mum gave her a steely look before returning her attention to Rob. 'I'd like you to pretend that you are Jack and that you want some sweets from the checkout counter. Jack, you're pretending to be Dad. It's your job to explain that he can't have it. Got it?'

'Er, Dad,' ventured Rob awkwardly. 'I'd like these sweets.'

'You need to say it louder!' It was Daisy, calling out from the side. 'And you've got to scream and shout.'

Rob looked terrified. 'ER, I'D LIKE THESE SWEETS.'

'You've got to throw yourself on the ground and hit it with your fists, Dad!' sniggered Jack.

Vanessa almost felt sorry for the man. But then Rob whipped off his jacket (very formal for a casual weekend) and got down on all fours, and started throwing his head up and down and yelling. 'I WANT SOME SWEETS! I WANT SOME SWEETS!'

There was a burst of clapping until Intellectual Mum silenced it. 'All right, Jack. It's your turn.'

'YOU CAN'T HAVE ANY! THEY'RE BAD FOR YOU!'

'BUT I WANT THEM.'

'I'M NOT GOING TO TELL YOU AGAIN! STOP RIGHT NOW OR I'LL TELL YOUR DAD WHEN HE COMES HOME.'

'YOU CAN'T. HE'S IN THE STATES FOR THREE WEEKS. AND HE'S TOO EXHAUSTED WHEN HE GETS BACK TO BE THE BAD PARENT.'

There was a gasp. Was Rob being funny? Or simply stating the truth?

'I GIVE UP!' retorted Jack. 'HOW AM I GOING TO MANAGE WHEN I HAVE FOUR KIDS INSTEAD OF TWO?'

Oh my God! Bobbie was going beetroot red, poor thing. Everyone was staring; from their expressions, no one else had known she was pregnant – let alone expecting twins!

Rob was sitting back on his haunches now, staring at his wife as though no one else was there. 'We'll all have to make some changes,' he said in a quiet voice. Then he looked up at the audience and gave a small bow. 'Now do you think I could have some chocolate, please? I feel as though I deserve it.'

There was a loud burst of clapping, followed by a wolf

whistle. It was Sarah, Bobbie's friend, who was sitting rather close to Matthew, that nice widower. NO! Vanessa could hardly believe it. Sarah was wearing a jacket. THE suede jacket! It was HER! Vanessa recognised her now from the fête. She'd been wearing it just before Sunshine had nearly been run over.

'A customer took it off,' Bobbie had said when the jacket had originally gone missing. 'I must have sold it by mistake.'

But it hadn't been a mistake – she must have sold it to her friend. After all, hadn't Bobbie borrowed an outfit to wear to her husband's office that time? And hadn't she lied to the secretary, claiming to be doing a market-research survey? Like child, like mother! Look at Jack, who had eaten that chocolate egg in the supermarket. And Daisy who had stolen Sunshine's flute.

'Bobbie—' she began.

But her voice was drowned by Andy's voice from the door. 'Vanessa! There's someone at the door to see you!'

To see her? To see *her*? Something leaped inside her breast. A hope that she hadn't allowed herself to entertain but which she had been dreaming of. Her daughter! Miraculously returned. Explaining that she'd been kidnapped or taken away but had managed to escape. Brigid, who had come back at last to reclaim her daughter so she couldn't be swallowed up into the care system after all.

'Brian?' Astonished, she stared at the kindly faced man in front of her with those clear-framed wire specs, rather large nose and wispy grey hair which had, she knew, been combed carefully over the bald patch. By his side sat Bingo, although you could hardly see him. Sunshine had already charged through and had her arms around him, covering him with little kisses.

'You shouldn't have come,' she whispered. 'It's not allowed. How did you know where I was, anyway?'

'I'm afraid I texted your friend Bobbie: you gave me her number for an emergency before, remember?' He looked rather shamefaced.

'Bobbie had a word with me too and explained the situation.' Andy's voice was warm and welcoming. 'Surely no one can object to your friend staying just for the day? Not if we're all here. Besides, there's enough lunch to feed an army. Come on in and have a bite.'

Sunshine was already leading Bingo off into the kitchen to give him a bowl of water. Vanessa was left next to Brian, alone in the hall. 'I can go if you want,' he said quietly.

'No.' Vanessa was torn. 'It's just that I'm worried, that's all. Someone at the fête reported me to social services. I don't know who it was. Supposing they're here?'

'So what? Like Andy said, we're in a crowd, aren't we? It's not as though I'm staying overnight.' Then he drew her to him. 'I've missed you, lass. I can't tell you how much.'

It was so lovely to be kissed! So warm and exciting and comforting, all at the same time. She could have gone on for ever if it weren't for the fact that she needed to check up on Sunshine – and that the doorbell was ringing.

'Another unexpected guest?' joked Brian as she opened the door.

Good heavens! Vanessa stared at the two women in front of her. One was an older version of the first but there was no mistaking the resemblance. Mother and daughter! Both had the same sleek golden looks with immaculately cut blonde bobs and the same distinctive way of carrying themselves. As for their clothes, they bore the hallmark of elegant simplicity: the type which came at a price.

Instantly, Vanessa thought of the clothes in the wardrobe and recognised the client who wouldn't be seen in a second-hand shop.

'Hi,' she said apprehensively, addressing the younger woman. 'Nice to see you again, Pamela.'

432

Meet the mother-in-law from hell!
She tracks any household smell.
If your loo isn't clean,
She'll be oh so keen
To whip out her bleach and Jeyes gel.

Chapter 39

ANDY

'Pamela? Camilla?'

Andy looked from his wife to his mother-in-law and then back to his wife again. The others were crowding into the hall, wondering who had turned up when the weekend had virtually finished. Kieran, damn him, was breathing over his shoulder.

'What a lovely surprise,' Andy managed to say. 'You're just in time for lunch. This is my mother-in-law, everyone. And of course you know Pamela, my wife.'

'*Who*', snorted Camilla, glaring around, 'are these people?'

'Mummy, I told you!' Pamela had her hand on Camilla's plaster cast protectively. 'They're part of Andy's little parenting group.'

Andy stared at his wife. Why wasn't she going nuts? Demanding that everyone should leave? There was something different about her physical appearance too. For a start, she'd put on weight since his visit, even though it wasn't that long ago. It suited her; made her look less severe. As for Camilla, she looked exactly the same with those high cheekbones and sour expression, suggesting grave disappointment that the rest of the world didn't meet her exacting standards.

'We need to talk,' his mother-in-law muttered as a small child tore past, almost crashing into her legs. '*If* we can hear ourselves over this noise. It's like a zoo!'

'No.' Andy heard his voice coming out firmly. 'My wife and I need to talk. We'll see you later. Come on, Pamela.' Cupping his hand under her elbow, he steered her up the stairs, which were littered with sleeping bags. To his astonishment, she didn't even comment.

'It's a bit of a mess, I'm afraid,' he couldn't help saying. Pamela shrugged as he closed their bedroom door behind them.

'It doesn't matter.'

Was this really his wife speaking? He looked around at the clothes strewn on the floor and the open suitcases. 'I put two of the mums in here. One's a grandmother actually. She's looking after her six-year-old at the moment – doing a fantastic job.'

Pamela sat on the edge of the bed and looked at him as though for the first time. 'You've really got into this parenting stuff, haven't you?' She laughed. A strangely natural laugh. Then he realised what else was different about her. It wasn't just the extra pounds. She wasn't wearing lipstick! Never, ever, had he seen Pamela without lipstick. Not even in bed. 'I knew you'd be better at it than me.' She looked away. 'I was always a hopeless mother.'

'No.' His heart softened slightly. 'You did your best. But you had issues.'

She made an odd sound. 'You could say that.'

'I've got them too. Issues, that is.' He wondered where to begin. 'Have you run away,' he heard himself asking, 'or have they let you out?'

It was meant to be a joke but it came out too seriously. There was a brief silence. Then, to his relief, she visibly relaxed. 'My doctor felt I was ready to face the world again. For a few days. Then she wants to see me again to assess where to go from here. Besides, I needed to see the girls. Where are they?'

'Cooking.'

Her eyebrows raised. 'Really?'

'You know,' said Andy, searching her face, 'I didn't realise they were such hard work until you left.'

Pamela gave him a sad smile. 'There were a lot of things you didn't know about us. It was my fault; I know that now. We hid too much from you.' Her fingers slotted into his.

435

Pamela rarely made the first move. 'It was because I wanted to keep the peace, whatever it took.' She shuddered. 'The alternative was too awful. I was terrified you might find out I was using drugs again.'

She stood up and walked away to the window. Outside, it was beginning to rain. The children were scattering in different directions: from the hot tub; from the beach; from the croquet lawn. 'You've turned this place into a real family home with all this lot!' She turned back to him with a slow smile. 'And what about Bobbie? Is she here too?'

Andy nodded, not daring to say more in case his expression gave him away.

'And my brother?'

'He wasn't going to come but then he turned up unexpectedly.'

'Things still tricky between those two?' She sat down at her dressing table, pulled out a drawer and began to brush her hair. 'Poor kid. Rob could never cope when things didn't go his way. Just like our father.'

Andy watched her slow rhythmic actions, recalling at the same time what Camilla had said to him back in her cottage. 'I don't really understand.'

'Nor did I, until they explained it to me at the centre.' Her cool blue eyes met his in the mirror. 'Our parents were always arguing. You never knew my father, thank God, or you wouldn't be sitting there. You'd have either killed him or been crushed by him.'

Andy thought of Kieran. 'He was a bully?'

She gave a short laugh. 'That's one way of putting it. My mother has been a different woman since he died. But when he was alive, we had to do exactly what he said and, if we didn't, well, we got punished. When I was growing up, it was my job to protect my brother. It's why we're so close.'

It was all beginning to make sense now, along with their previous conversations in Sussex. Gently taking the brush out of her hand, he led her back to the bed. 'Sit down. Please. In fact, let's get under the covers.'

'What?'

'I don't mean *that*. I just want to talk. That's right.'

She began to giggle as he tucked the duvet around them. What had got into her? Pamela never giggled in case it gave her lines around her mouth. Nor did she get into sheets that someone else had been sleeping in.

Tentatively, he put his arm around her, expecting her to turn away as usual but, to his surprise, she snuggled in. 'I want to tell you something,' he began. 'Something about me.' He took a deep breath. 'You're not the only one with secrets. When I've finished telling you this, you might decide you don't want to stay with me any more. And I'll understand if you do.' His chest lurched with apprehension. Pamela's eyes were on him.

'Go on.'

Andy clenched his hands under the covers. 'I wasn't brought up by an aunt at all. My parents didn't die in a crash. My mother left when I was ten and then my stepfather. I was fostered.'

There was a small gasp beside him, which he ignored. If he didn't keep going, he would stop. 'But it didn't work out so they put me in a children's home.' He stopped briefly. 'It stank of cabbage and urine and Brussels sprouts.'

'My poor Andy!' She stroked his forehead. He was used to an emotionless Pamela. This new one made him feel uneasy.

'No. I don't want sympathy. I just need you to listen. I fell into the wrong crowd.' He laughed hoarsely. 'Most of them were wrong 'uns anyway, as the staff used to call us. In fact, so bad that they then sent me to another home that specialised in troubled kids.'

He waited for the reaction. 'Go on,' she whispered.

'But when I was twelve, something happened.'

There was a silence punctuated by a knocking on the door. 'Mum? Dad?' It was Nattie. In unspoken agreement, they lay there, silently, until she went away. This was too important to stop.

'We used to nick things from shops. Sweets. Pencils. Tennis

437

balls. Anything we thought we could get away with. We thought we were entitled to it, you see. To make up for not having proper families.'

'What *happened*?' prompted Pamela.

OK. Here goes. 'One night, we sneaked out of the home and went into a part of town we didn't normally go to. We'd had a few beers. More than a few, to be honest. The others started to take stuff off the shelves of this supermarket but for some reason, I didn't join them. I got scared. Just stood and watched.'

This was the difficult bit.

'Then the shopkeeper saw us. He ran after us, but tripped over one of his stands that was sticking out.'

'Oh God,' breathed Pamela.

'The others ran on.' Andy could see it now. The bright shop lights. The scattered tins on the floor. The pool of blood. 'But I couldn't move. My legs had turned to jelly. The shopkeeper was lying on the floor and I knew the police wouldn't believe us. They'd think it was us. Then the others yelled at me to beat it and I found my legs. We scarpered and climbed back into the home through one of the windows.'

Pamela's face was rigid. 'And did you get caught?'

He shook his head. 'No.'

'And the shopkeeper?'

It would be so easy to lie. So easy to say he was all right. To brush all this back under the lino where it had lain for years.

'He died.' Andy's words came out as though they belonged to someone else. Suddenly there was a massive crack in that steel wall he'd erected in his mind to separate the bloodied mess on the floor and the present.

Pamela gasped. 'That's awful! But didn't you get caught? Or call for help?'

Andy thought back to the big boys: the older ones who had grabbed him and Kieran by the scruff of their necks, swearing that if they so much as breathed a word to the staff, they'd be dead. 'Just be grateful we didn't leave you behind to face the music,' sneered one, 'or you'd be in for life.'

There was a pay-off, naturally. There always was in these places. Kieran and Andy had to give various favours to the older boys. 'Not *those* kind of favours?' shuddered Pamela.

'Not sexual, if that's what you mean. But we had to give them our food and run around for them.'

'Just like Rob's school.' Pamela was massaging his shoulders tenderly. 'It sounds to me as though it wasn't your fault. Not really.'

'Yes it was! If he hadn't chased us, he wouldn't have fallen.'

'But you didn't hit him.'

'How can I prove that?'

'You don't need to, darling.'

Darling? It had been years since she'd called him that!

'Actually, I might.' Andy took another breath. 'There's a man here. Kieran. Another parent. One of the gang from the home. And now he's blackmailing me.'

'That's outrageous.' Pamela leaped out of bed.

'I know but I have to pay him off.'

'No you don't! You have to stand up for what you know is right. I've learned that now.'

'The thing is', he continued, sitting up against the pillows now, feeling like a small boy, 'that even if I wanted to pay him off, I couldn't. We've lost our money, Pamela. Not all of it but a good chunk. It's my fault. I thought something was a good investment and . . . why are you laughing?'

Oh God. Maybe this was some kind of hysterical attack.

'Because I'm glad! Don't you see, Andy? We always had too much money. It was one of our problems. Now we can be normal again. Like any other family.'

'It's not that simple,' he tried to say but there was another hammering at the door. Louder this time.

'Mum? Dad! I've been calling you. Lunch is ready.'

Nattie again. 'Just coming,' called out Pamela coolly. 'Give me one minute.' Then, to Andy's utter amazement, she turned and gave him a kiss. Not just a brush on the cheek but a proper kiss. 'I think this could be the beginning for both of us,' she murmured. 'It wasn't until I had time away that I realised how much I missed you. How much I needed you. And now, after what you've told me, I want to be here for you. Just like you were for me.'

She cupped her hand behind his head, pulling him towards her. 'You do still love me. Don't you?'

If Pamela didn't look the same (apart from the weight), he might have thought that someone had planted a different kind of wife on him. 'Did she talk to you?' whispered Camilla, pulling up a chair next to him at the dining table.

'Yes.' He was loath to say more with all these people around them. It was so noisy with the 'Don't start eating yet' and 'Turn off your mobiles' and 'Eat that up!' that it was almost impossible to hear anyway.

'She's changed, hasn't she?' hissed Camilla in his ear.

'Too much,' he retorted drily. 'I hardly recognise her.'

'Give her a chance, Andy!' Camilla was bellowing down his ear now with the authority of those who believed they had the right to tell others what to do. 'She's scared of losing you. Her time in that place showed her what she really needs.'

Andy looked across the table to Bobbie, who was trying to persuade Daisy to eat what was on her plate and instructing Jack not to eat what was on everyone else's. Rob, he noticed, was deep in conversation with a rather kind-looking man from the other class; someone said he was a widower with a little girl.

Pamela was actually stroking Brian's dog even though she'd claimed to be allergic to animals. Probably an excuse for not having hair all over the carpets. Heaven knew what that treatment had done to her. But she couldn't expect him to accept these changes overnight. *He'd* changed too.

Just then, Bobbie looked up and caught his eye. 'Are you all right?' he mouthed. She gave a small shrug. Sometimes he thought that she was the only one who understood him. But Bobbie was his brother-in-law's wife; he couldn't possibly think along those lines. Could he?

After lunch Andy tried to seek out Bobbie to talk to her. Now that his wife knew his secret, it seemed even more important than ever to come clean with Bobbie too.

'Wotcha, mate! Been looking for you!' Kieran's black beady eyes bore into his. 'Reckon you've been trying to avoid me in this mansion of yours.'

The man made him feel sick. 'Actually, I've had more important things on my mind.'

Kieran sniffed, wiping his nose with his shirt sleeve. Ugh! And he still had his hacking cough. 'So I see. I recognise your missus, you know. She used to be a regular at one of my watering holes.'

'Pamela!' Andy laughed out loud. 'Don't be ridiculous.'

Kieran grinned again, nastily. 'That's what alkies do! They drink and snort in places where they don't think their own kind will find them.'

A vision of the receipt came into his head: the club receipt that Bobbie had told him about. 'How dare you call my wife an alkie!'

'It's true,' muttered Audrey, sidling past. 'She used to turn up at PTA meetings drunk as a skunk. And she does drugs. Reckon Miss Davies didn't know that when she asked her to run the parenting class.'

'Not any more,' he called out desperately.

Audrey laughed. 'If you believe that, Andy, you'll believe anything. People never change. They just pretend to.'

Was she right? Part of him wanted to run after her and yell at her for supplying his wife. Wasn't that what Pamela had implied, back in the centre? But he had no proof and Audrey would just deny it.

'MOVE OUT OF THE WAY!' yelled some children as they shot past, followed by Miss Davies, clutching a bundle of raincoats.

'We're doing an Easter-egg hunt,' called out Jack excitedly. 'Want to join us, Uncle Andy?'

'*Want to join us?*' Just what the boys in the home had asked all those years ago before raiding the shop.

'Tell you what!' Kieran had his face close up now. Andy could smell his fishy breath. See every open pore. Watch the spit in his mouth as he coughed. 'I'll let you off that money you owe me if you give me this place instead.' Those piggy eyes looked around. 'Taken quite a fancy to it, I have. It's either that or telling everyone the truth.'

'Then do it!' Andy grabbed the man's shirt collar. 'My wife knows everything. I don't care if you go to the police because . . .'

My God! Kieran was going a really strange colour! He was gasping for breath and clutching his throat. 'C-c-cough sweet,' he spluttered. 'Stuck.'

Was he pulling a fast one? They used to do this in the home when they didn't want to eat something. It had really scared the staff.

'That man's choking!' screamed Bohemian Mum. 'Thump him someone. Quick!'

'MUM, MUM. UNCLE ANDY'S HITTING SOMEONE!'

He was too. Belting him on the back; taking out all his anger on this bastard who was trying to wreck his life. It would be so easy to kill Kieran. A life for a life! Maybe throttle him into the bargain. Or beat the bloke into a pulp. Put an end to him. Hadn't he, Andy, done just that to someone else by doing nothing all those years ago?

NO! What was he thinking of? He couldn't hurt someone. There was no way his conscience would allow him to make the same mistake again.

Kieran was making a terrified noise like the chickens that his foster father had kept. A peculiar squawking noise. His eyes were bulging in terror. Linking both his arms around Kieran's back from behind, Andy brought his hands in sharply under his ribs.

Bloody hell! A small black object shot out of his mouth in an arc and landed smack on Camilla's chest as she came into the room. 'What on earth is this?' Wrinkling her nose, she picked up the offending sticky sweet and dropped it on to a passing drinks tray. 'How absolutely disgusting!'

Kieran was slumped on the ground, gasping for air. His face was returning to his normal colour. He'd done it, Andy thought. Bloody hell, he'd done it.

'DID UNCLE ANDY WIN, MUM? IS THERE ANOTHER ROUND?'

'You saved me, mate!' Kieran looked up at him with a mixture of shock and gratitude. 'You saved my fucking life!'

'Dad!' A small boy with an urchin haircut flew up and landed in Kieran's lap. 'Are you OK?' He glared up at Andy and put up his little fists. 'Don't you dare hurt my dad or I'll kill yer.'

'It's OK, son!' Kieran tenderly pressed his lips to his son's cheek. 'This bloke here was looking after your old dad.' He lumbered to his feet. 'Shit, I was scared. You hear of bleeders dying that way, don't yer? Thought I was a gonner then.'

Pity you hadn't been, Andy felt like saying. But Kieran was thrusting out his hand. 'Never thought I'd say this, mate, but we'll forget about all that other stuff. I owe you one now. Yes I do. Remember what we used to say in the home? A life for a life.' He was pumping his hand harder now. 'I don't have much but I can be on your side. Trust me, Andy, if you ever need anything, all you have to do is ask.'

443

TV REVIEW GUIDE

Dr Know is back! With a new series that is guaranteed to shock!

Plenty of tears and tantrums – and that's just from the parents as they're forced to clean up their act!

Unmissable viewing. Five-star rating.

Extracted from the Daily Wail.

Chapter 40

BOBBIE

The new arrivals completely changed the dynamics. First Rob and Sarah – who had dyed her hair orange. Wacky, but it suited her. Then Brian. And now Camilla along with Pamela. It was funny how only Brian seemed to fit in, merging into the crowd as though he had been one of them from the beginning.

Perhaps it was his headmaster side coming out, she thought, watching him chat easily to a group of parents in the beautiful conservatory overlooking the lawn. 'I know I push my kids too much but my mother pushed me,' Intellectual Mum was saying. 'That's how I ended up at Oxford. But if I push my own daughter, she'll end up by being torn between work and motherhood. And if I don't, she won't be fulfilling her own potential. It's so difficult!'

'MUM! MUM!'

It was Jack, charging in with yet another demand (where had she put his skateboard?) so Bobbie wasn't able to catch Brian's answer. But shortly afterwards, the two of them went for a walk, and when they returned, Intellectual Mum seemed much more at peace with herself.

Actually, a walk was a really good idea. Thirty-odd people under one roof was getting distinctly claustrophobic. 'How about some fresh air?' she suggested, perching on the sofa next to her husband and deliberately ignoring the that's-my-Moshi-Monster battle in the next room.

Rob made a face. 'It's drizzling,' he mumbled, glancing briefly up from his BlackBerry. Couldn't he *ever* stop working?

'Matthew and Sarah have just gone out,' she pointed out.

They had too! All togged up in borrowed rainwear, laughing under a shared umbrella.

'That's because they fancy each other.'

'Thanks very much!'

'Sorry.' Rob put down his BlackBerry. 'I just meant that . . .'

'That we don't have to bother any more?' Bobbie stood up disappointedly. 'That's where you're wrong, Rob. Look at your sister. She stopped bothering and now she's furiously backpedalling to make it all right with poor Andy.'

Rob frowned. '*Poor* Andy? What do you mean?'

'Nothing.' She began walking out of the room so he couldn't see her blushes. 'If you don't want a family walk, I'll take the kids on my own. Jack? Daisy? Tom?'

Flipping heck! Her two had stopped squabbling over Moshi Monsters and skateboards and were actually taking it in turns on Minecraft, while Sunshine – how sweet! – had that adorable puppy on her lap. Let sleeping kids lie! (Not the fib variety, obviously.)

Grabbing a spare raincoat by the door, Bobbie went out into the garden, bracing herself. Wow! The wind had really whipped up since yesterday: incredible to think they'd actually been in the hot tub then. Still, that was British weather for you. Baking one minute – even though it was almost Easter – and then showers the next.

Almost as unpredictable as kids and husbands.

She must have been mad, Bobbie told herself as she slipped through the side gate and down to the beach, to think that Rob would change overnight. No amount of role plays in the world would do that. The only way to make him realise just how difficult it was to bring up kids was to put him in charge. Go away for a few weeks like her sister-in-law.

But then who would earn the real money? Maybe there were no happy compromises. Not in real life. Unless you were as rich as Andy and could afford to take time off.

Still, it looked as though there might be one happy story out there! In the distance, beyond the beach huts, she could see two figures under one umbrella who might, or might not,

446

be kissing. Matthew and Sarah. The tide was going out now, leaving tracts of shining, virgin sand. Above her, the sun was shining through the rain. Bobbie never had understood how the tides were connected with the sun – or was it the earth? Maybe she ought to ask Daisy. Wow! There was a rainbow!

'Rather splendid, isn't it?' called out a voice behind her in the wind.

Whipping round, Bobbie took in a vision of grey Dannimac. That impeccable blonde hairdo was carefully concealed by a matching souwester-style hat, stylishly perched over her eyes so the face was half hidden. But even without that very clear, crisp, almost monotonous voice, Bobbie would have recognised her mother-in-law anywhere.

Camilla, as she and Andy had agreed over their post-parent-course coffees, was impossible. 'No one will ever be good enough for her children,' Andy pointed out. 'And if she doesn't like *you*, what hope is there for me?'

'I'll walk with you,' her mother-in-law now announced as though she was doing her a great favour. 'I like to take exercise in all weathers at home, especially after a meal.'

Her one chance to have some time alone and her mother-in-law had scuppered it!

'So,' announced Camilla grandly, raising her voice to speak even more loudly than usual. The wind might be whipping up but it was no match for her mother-in-law. 'That was some scene after lunch, wasn't it?'

What was she talking about?

'Didn't you notice?'

'I was washing up,' said Bobbie meaningfully.

'Ah yes. I let other people do that nowadays. So you didn't hear about it then?'

The rain was running into Bobbie's eyes now: she should have borrowed a hat or brought an umbrella. 'No. What?' Too late, she realised she sounded like Daisy. 'I mean, what happened exactly?'

Camilla's voice rang out against the wind. 'Your Andy saved that horrible little bald man from choking. He did one of

447

those clever things you do when something is stuck in the throat. I saw it once on television. A Heimlich, I think they call it. Or is that the beer? I can never remember.'

My Andy! Did she really say *my* Andy?

'Come on, dear! A little redheaded bird has been telling me about you two. Whispering and sending each other little glances.'

Bobbie began to sweat. 'You've got it all wrong!'

'Have I?' They'd reached a part of the beach where the cliffs hung over them, like an old-fashioned parasol made of rock. Instinctively, they stood under it to shelter from the rain. It was a small space so there was no option but to look straight into each other's faces. Why did she always go red even when she was innocent?

'Andy and I are just friends.' Even to her ears, Bobbie was horribly aware that her voice sounded like Jack's when accused of something. 'We might have met up a few times for coffee. But that's because we've both been involved in this parenting course; the one that Pamela bailed from.' She couldn't stop herself making that dig. 'But there's nothing in it: I can assure you of that.' Suddenly, Bobbie felt bolder. 'Nor should I have to justify myself, Camilla. It's none of your business.'

Something gave in the older woman's eyes. 'Ah but it is, dear.'

Dear? Camilla had never, ever, called her 'dear'. Or any other kind of endearment, come to that.

'You'll understand that, when Jack and Daisy are older. You never stop being a mother, you see. Never stop wanting to protect your children.' She gave a little sigh. 'I know my daughter isn't easy.'

'You're not kidding!'

Camilla looked sad for a moment. 'Imagine how you'd feel if Daisy became an alcoholic and a drug addict because she didn't feel she'd achieved her full potential.'

So that was the problem, was it? Poor Andy. 'I don't feel I've achieved mine either, Camilla. But I haven't taken to drink

– well, not much anyway. And definitely not drugs. Self-sacrifice comes with being a parent. It's part of the job description. Something that your son doesn't seem to have taken on board.'

Camilla smiled. 'Ah yes. Rob. I'm with you there. He's not around enough for the children; just like his father. I keep telling him but he won't listen.' She patted Bobbie's arm. 'I'm on your side, you see.'

Right. Of course she was.

'As for that little game you played on his secretary, I thought that was rather clever!' Another pat on the arm. 'I told him so in no uncertain terms. That's why he's here.'

Now she knew she was lying! 'But Sarah persuaded Rob to come down.'

Camilla smirked. 'I think you'll find that we both helped. I rather like your friend Sarah, by the way. She looks out for herself. An essential quality for women nowadays, providing it isn't at the expense of someone else's happiness.'

Her eyes grew steely. 'I believe you when you say that you are just friends with Andy. But I'm no fool, Bobbie. I spent years observing my own husband flirting with other women. I know the signs. And if I'm not mistaken, Andy is rather sweet on you. I wouldn't want anything to interfere with this rather long, complicated making-up process that you all have to do. Don't you agree?'

Then she turned to look at the sea. 'Goodness me!' Her voice was bright as if they hadn't had this conversation. 'It looks as though there's a really nasty storm on the other side of the bay. Look at that lightning! Better be getting back.' She held out her arm, inviting Bobbie to link hers.

'That's right,' said the older woman brightly. 'Family has to stick together. It's the only way forward! Now tell me. How is your mother getting on with that famous doctor boyfriend of hers? I'm one of his biggest fans, you know!'

Camilla was right; a storm was whipping up. Some of them were due to leave on the Sunday night (others were staying

449

an extra day) but it was clearly out of the question for any of them to go back now. Including Brian.

'Bingo can sleep with us, can't he, Granny!' sang out Sunshine when they'd had dinner: a rather strong curry which the men had prepared, complete with poppadums. Delicious! She could get a craving for these, Bobbie told herself, along with marshmallows and sardines.

'I'm not sure that's such a great idea,' said Brian nervously. Bobbie could see why. She glanced round the table. If Vanessa was right and it had been someone from the fête who had reported her to social services, that same person might well be right here. But who? Audrey? American Express, who had taken umbrage at Vanessa's advice about coming off the breast? Too Many Kids Mum who seemed mild but had, she'd observed, a difficult streak?

'The AA has advised against non-essential travel,' added Matthew.

'I could kip down in the van,' suggested Brian, clipping Bingo's lead on to him. 'I always keep a sleeping bag there.'

'Cool!' Jack's face lit up. 'Can I sleep there too?'

'And me!' said the kid whom Jack had tackled in football but who now seemed to be his best friend. Incredible how children could swap sides.

Some of the adults shifted uncomfortably. In their day, no one would have thought twice about a scoutmaster and kids sleeping over in a caravan. But now they all had to be so careful! Brian seemed to be aware of it too. 'There's only room for one,' he said quickly. 'But I'm sure Bingo would love to sleep with Sunshine.'

Bobbie waited for Pamela or Camilla to make some disparaging remark about dogs and beds and fleas. But no. Nothing. Her sister-in-law was sitting next to Andy on the sofa, her hand in his. He had a blank expression as though he wasn't there. Then he looked up at Bobbie. Really looked at her, in a way that a man shouldn't look at someone he wasn't with.

Quickly, she pretended to check her mobile messages. If

Camilla was right and Andy did have a crush on her, she mustn't encourage him. And if she, by any chance, had a crush on him, she had to get rid of it. Fast.

'I've had an idea!' announced Judith brightly. 'How about a game of Ask Mum.' She glanced at Matthew, who was sitting close to Sarah. 'And Dad too, of course! The idea is that the children – teenagers too! – can ask the adults anything they like about their childhood.'

There was a uniform groan from the adults and a cheer from the kids. 'Yeah, go on, Mum,' said one boy with huge white plug earrings who belonged, somewhat surprisingly, to Jilly from the au pair agency. 'Tell us what you got up to!'

Bobbie searched around for a seat. The sitting room was vast but with so many of them, it was a bit tight for space. She might just about be able to squeeze next to Vanessa. 'There's not much room,' said her friend coolly.

'Is something wrong?'

Vanessa shrugged. 'Ask Sarah.'

'What are you talking about?'

'Quiet everyone, please!' Judith's clear voice rang out, silencing even the adolescents, lounging on scatter cushions with a crate of cider. Goodness knows where they'd got that from. 'Who'd like to go first?'

The squat bald tattooed man from Andy's class – the same one who had apparently almost choked earlier on – shouted out, 'I think teacher ought to do it!'

'Yeah, go on, Miss Davies!' yelled Nattie.

Surely Pamela would reprimand her daughter for being cheeky. But no. Her sister-in-law was just sitting there with a scarily serene expression on her face and her head on Andy's shoulder. She was even ignoring Nattie who was painting her nails and – whoops! – knocking over a bottle of black varnish.

'Very well.' Miss Davies flushed.

'How old were you when you had your first boyfriend?' demanded the plug-earring kid.

'Nick!' His mother gasped. 'That's rather personal.'

'No. It's all right.' Poor Miss Davies was puce red. 'I was

451

fourteen. My dad didn't like him because he wore scruffy trainers and wanted me to go out during the week.'

'Did you do what you were told?'

This was Mel.

'Yes, apart from one night when I sneaked out to meet him.'

There was a sharp intake of breath from the adults and an enthusiastic 'Go for it!' from the teens.

'How did he punish you?' asked Bohemian Mum faintly.

'He didn't. The look on his face was enough to make me realise I'd let him down. I also failed the French exam I had to take the next day.'

'Are you making this up?'

For a minute, Bobbie thought it was her younger niece speaking but then realised it was Daisy. Two days of being with her older cousins, whom she adored, had made her daughter sound almost as grown up.

'No. I'm not. Honest.' Miss Davies blushed again.

'What about your mum? What did she say?'

'Actually, my stepdad brought me up.' Miss Davies spoke lightly as though this was unimportant. 'Right, now it's someone else's turn. Nattie, you pick.'

'I choose Dad!'

Bobbie's heart went out to Andy. He wouldn't like this. When they'd had those lovely heart-to-hearts before the row, they had touched briefly on their individual childhoods. 'Mine wasn't great,' was all he would say and she hadn't liked to press further.

'I'd rather not,' he faltered.

'*I'll* do it.'

To everyone's astonishment, Pamela rose graciously to her feet. The look on Camilla's face was priceless. Bobbie almost felt sorry for her. She would hate it if Daisy described her own childhood in years to come. A psychologist would have a field day.

'Right!' Pamela was sitting – on her knees! – waiting expectantly. Maybe she was used to this, thought Bobbie.

Perhaps that's what they did in that rehab place.

'Did you get on with your parents?' asked a boy with spiky hair.

'Not always.' Pamela looked straight at Camilla. 'My father sent me to boarding school.'

'Lucky you!' gasped one of the children. 'Was it like Harry Potter?'

Pamela smiled. Bobbie suddenly realised she'd never seen her sister-in-law do that before. Not a genuine, amused smile. 'Not really, although we did have quite a lot of fun.'

'What happened after that?' called out one of the Perfect twins.

'Well, my mother wanted me to be a model because she hadn't been one herself, even though she could have been.'

Camilla might have been preening or cringing. Hard to tell.

'What was your favourite colour?' sang out Sunshine.

Pamela was looking really excited: almost like a child. 'It used to be blue but then it changed to black when I was eighteen. We all thought it made us look slim.'

'What was your favourite number?' yelled out Jack.

'Three,' replied Pamela promptly. 'Always has been.' She looked at her girls and then up at Andy. 'Always will be.'

'Cool,' called out Nattie. 'I never knew that, Mum.'

Miss Davies clapped her hands. 'Wonderful! That's exactly what's so great about this game. It's discovering things about each other. Pamela, can you choose someone else now please?'

No. Please don't. No.

'Bobbie.' Pamela's eyes fixed on her; her smile faded. Her gaze was cool. She knows about Andy, thought Bobbie. Not that there was anything to know. Not really. But her sister-in-law thought there was. Which was even worse.

Pamela's voice was hard, attracting attention as she butted in. 'What kind of child were you?'

Bobbie resisted the temptation to point out that it was the children who were meant to ask the questions. 'Well, I'm the eldest of two although my sister lives in Australia now. When you're the first-born, you're meant to be "good".' Her voice tailed away as she looked at Daisy, who was sitting so neatly, cross-legged style. Yet she could see her daughter's hand reaching out to pinch her brother even as she spoke. 'You're expected to do what you're told.'

'What was your favourite subject?' called out Jack. 'OUCH, DAISY. DON'T DO THAT!'

'I DIDN'T!'

'YES, YOU DID!'

'Daisy,' said Rob firmly. 'You did. I saw you. Now listen to Mum.'

'Favourite subject?' She felt a sudden longing and sense of regret. 'Art! But at my school, that wasn't considered academic enough. So I wasn't allowed to go on with it in the sixth form.'

'Shame,' muttered Bohemian Mum, twisting her tie-dyed neckscarf.

'Do you miss it?' asked Rob curiously. Bobbie suddenly realised she'd never told him that.

'Yes.' Then she glanced at Vanessa. 'But some of you know that I help out at the second-hand designer clothes shop in town. I love the colours there and the designs.'

'Clearly,' sniffed Vanessa.

What on earth had she done to upset her?

'Excellent. Now can you pick someone?'

There was only one way to find out.

'I'd like to choose Vanessa, please.'

The older woman reluctantly got to her feet.

'Who was your best friend when you were six?' called out one of Too Many Kids.

'Why, Angela! Angela Miller!' Vanessa's face broke out into a wreath of smiles. 'I'd forgotten all about her. We used to go everywhere together. We'd play shops too. Even in those days, I liked the idea of being behind a till.' Then she looked stony again. 'Next question?'

Everyone was looking now. It was obvious that Vanessa was furious about something.

'Where did you go on holiday as a child?'

'The back yard.' Vanessa's voice was laden with sarcasm. 'We couldn't afford anything else.'

'Last question now, I think,' chirped Miss Davies. 'Then we'll have a break.'

'What did you want to do when you were grown up?'

'That's easy.' Vanessa was looking at Sunshine, curled up next to Bingo, thumb in mouth, and then at Brian. It was clear he was nuts about her. 'Have a family. When I eventually gave birth to my daughter, Brigid, I thought – still do – that she was the most wonderful thing in the world, apart from my granddaughter of course.'

She had tears in her eyes: tears she was impatiently wiping away. Brian was blowing his nose. Was he hurt at not being mentioned?

'Finished now?' glared Vanessa.

'Please,' whispered Bobbie urgently as they sat down, 'tell me what's wrong.'

The older woman gave her a chilling glance. 'I trusted you. And you betrayed me.'

'I don't understand!'

But Vanessa was getting up and flouncing out of the room. Everyone else was beginning to dribble out too, with cries of 'Time for bed' from the yawning adults and 'Not yet!' from the teens. There was a general sense of excitement; several families were putting down duvets on the floor. It looked as though you had to sleep wherever you could find a space. That rain outside was really crashing down now and, according to Matthew's iPad, the main roads back to London were closed owing to flooding.

'Shall we go to bed?' Bobbie felt exhausted. Maybe she shouldn't have walked quite so far along the beach. 'Andy put us in the guest room,' she added.

Rob gave her a strange look. 'Was that before or after you were seen kissing my brother-in-law? Don't deny it. Pamela knows too. The girls told her.'

Oh God. So he'd heard. 'It wasn't like that!'

'Wasn't it?'

455

'No.' Bobbie pulled him into the downstairs loo (the nearest place to get away from prying eyes) and bolted the door behind them. 'I'm fed up with being blamed for everything. Andy has been a good friend. No more. I swear it.'

'On our children's lives?'

What an awful thing to say! 'If you insist. I'll be honest: for a time, his attention – and yes, he did show me a bit of that – was flattering. But it's you I love, Rob. You're the father of my children. And even if you weren't, it would still be you.'

Something flickered in his eyes. 'Really?'

She paused. 'Actually, no. The person I really love is the old you. The Rob who had time for me. And for the kids. So let's move.' As she said it, Bobbie realised this was what she had been wanting all along. 'Change jobs. Buy a house in a cheaper area, where neither of us have to work so hard to pay the mortgage. I'm exhausted too, you know. That marketing job was awful. Working from home is very stressful – you can't shut the door on the job, like you can in the office.'

Rob nodded. 'That's what my mother said.'

Camilla really *had* been pressing her case then. Wonders would never cease. 'So what are we going to do?' She stared at him. 'Are you up for it? Because if you're not, I'm not sure I want to go on.'

'Do you really mean that?' whispered Rob, shocked.

'Hey! Are you going to be long?' The door handle was rattling. That clipped accent sounded as though it belonged to Audrey.

'Yes. I do.'

What had got into her? It was as though another Bobbie was speaking. The one who had to speak the truth instead of papering over any more cracks. But it was true. Enough was enough. Other women, like the redhead, might be prepared to put up with being a Married Single, but not her. Not any more.

Bobbie unlocked the door and stepped out, closely followed

by her husband. 'Actually, we've finished.'

'Finished?' repeated Rob, with a panicky edge to his voice. 'Is that it?'

'Well!' The woman gave his arm a playful flick. 'It's not often you catch a married couple having it off in the cloakroom! What's your secret?'

REAL QUOTES FROM KIDS

I love my sister but I wish she wasn't here sometimes.
I know Mum loves my brother more cos he goes to
  bed later.
I always get told off cos I'm the eldest.
My sister says I'm adopted.
Sharing is for saddos. My brother says so.
Would you all, please, stop treating me like a
  grown-up?

Extracted from siblingrivalry.co.uk

Chapter 41

VANESSA

Vanessa woke early the next morning and couldn't get back to sleep. She touched her lump – she always did when she woke in the hope that it might somehow have disappeared – before swinging her legs over the side of the bed and padding to the window in her slippers. Brian's van was parked in the driveway as clear as day; Bingo was curled up at Sunshine's feet.

She hadn't been able to resist slipping on her jeans and sneaking out into the crisp cool spring dawn air to knock gently on the van door. It was so lovely to nestle into Brian's arms and feel his warm breath on her. Was this what teenagers felt when they sneaked off to be with their boyfriends? Was this how Brigid had felt? Convinced that she was in love and that no one else, least of all her mother, could understand?

It was so lovely having Brian here even though they'd agreed to spend some time apart! In a way it scared her. She'd managed alone for so long, before him, that she'd got used to her own company. Rather enjoyed it really. She could go to bed when she liked; eat what she wanted; watch television if she chose to and switch it off without having to consult someone else.

But then, in the space of a few months, two of the most important people in her life had come along, just like that. And then, in a cruel twist, she'd had to choose between them. It was like a weird fairy tale except that until Brian had turned up last night (wearing the navy blue jumper she'd given him to replace his maroon disaster), she hadn't thought there'd be a happy ending.

And now here she was, lying in Brian's arms in his little white van, which had some strangely feminine touches about it, like that china teapot with the rose pattern. His wife's perhaps, bless her soul. The strange thing was that she had this weird feeling Mavis might approve.

'I shouldn't really be here,' she whispered even though no one could hear them. 'What if Sunshine wakes up?'

Brian held her to him, stroking the back of her shoulders in the way that always made her melt. 'She's got Bingo and besides, it's not as though you've been here all night.'

But responsible grandmothers didn't play hookey. Not when there was so much at stake.

'I must go now,' she said reluctantly, disentangling herself from Brian's warm body. 'But you will come in for breakfast, won't you, later on? With the others?'

Brian ran a hand ruefully round his chin, which already needed shaving. She loved the fact that he was one of those men whose growth started every evening and which, if he didn't tame it, made him look like Russell Crowe in a day or so. 'I'd like to, but only if you don't mind me using your bathroom.'

But before she could reply, Brian's mouth came down on hers. Every time he kissed her like this, she felt as though she had never been kissed before. Why had no one told her it could be like this? And how horribly, horribly ironic that she wasn't allowed to have both him *and* Sunshine.

'There's something I need to tell you,' he said afterwards.

Her heart fluttered.

'It's about Andy's wife. That glamorous blonde. I've seen her before. A few times.'

Vanessa hadn't been expecting this. 'Where?'

'At Ascot. Goodwood too. Had quite a reputation, she did.'

He was avoiding her eyes. 'What for, Brian?'

'Drinking too much.' He sighed. 'And for being rather close, shall we say, to men. Different men. Every time.' He was looking upset now. 'I didn't know whether to say anything to you.'

Vanessa thought quickly. 'Have you told anyone else?'

He shook his head.

She touched his lips with her finger. 'Let's keep it that way, shall we?'

He nodded, understanding immediately. Pamela Gooding had a husband and two daughters. Neither of them would want to be responsible for destroying a family by blowing the whistle. Besides, maybe the woman had put all that behind her. Vanessa could only hope so. Her husband seemed a nice man and the girls, good kids.

Brian was holding the van door open for her now, giving a little wolf whistle as she made her way across the dewy garden towards the house. The rain had stopped now although the garden was littered with branches as proof of the deluge the night before. Turning round, Vanessa gave Brian a little wave; turning back again, she bumped straight into someone. 'Gosh! Sorry! I didn't see you.'

It was Mr Perfect. 'Been for an early walk, have you?' His eyes went from Brian's van to her and then back to the van again.

'Just a quick one.' She flushed again, regretting her choice of words. 'I couldn't sleep.'

'Really?' His eyes narrowed, looking her up and down, as if he knew she was naked under her jeans. 'I always get up at this time. You can get so much done before the children are awake.'

Like spying on other people, she thought, bidding him goodbye before returning to the house. She'd never really liked that man.

Oh my God. Mr Perfect! Was he the one who had reported them at the fête? And now he'd seen her leave Brian's van. How stupid had she been!

Vanessa slid nervously back into bed next to Sunshine. Bingo raised his head as if to say 'Back, are you?' and then snuggled back down on the duvet. Closing her eyes, Vanessa drifted into an uneasy sleep in which Mr Perfect was hammering on her door, demanding to see her.

Heavens. It really *was* someone.

'It's me, Matthew,' called out a voice. 'May I ask you something?'

Was it already eight o'clock? Sunshine, who had usually woken by now, was still fast asleep, flute in one hand and the other wrapped around Bingo who had somehow managed to sneak right up on to the pillow like a human. Opening the door, she found a furrowed-browed Matthew with a rather pale-faced Lottie standing next to him. Matthew always looked worried. It was understandable, given that his wife had died of cancer. Every lump, every twinge could be the sign of something. Or nothing. Vanessa knew that all too well.

'I'm really sorry to bother you but Lottie isn't well. You've got more experience than me; well, than most of us. Do you mind taking a look?'

Gently, Vanessa got down on her knees so she was the same height as this pretty little girl. 'What's wrong, sweetheart?'

The child made an exaggerated face. 'I've got a tummy ache.'

Sunshine was beginning to get a few of those. Usually when she didn't want to do something. Brigid had been the same. Still, you never knew. 'Whereabouts is the pain?'

'Here.' Lottie touched the middle.

'Probably not your appendix then,' said Vanessa reassuringly.

Lottie twisted her face again. 'It's here too.' She touched the left. 'And sometimes here.' She touched the right.

Was that so? Lottie had a reputation for making up stories. Hadn't Matthew often said that you could never quite believe what she said? 'Is she upset about something?' asked Vanessa quietly, getting up again and feeling her knees creak.

'She doesn't want to go home.' Matthew gave her a what-do-I-do? look. 'She's really enjoyed being with all the other kids; it's pretty lonely for her in the holidays, even though we've got a lovely neighbour who looks after her.'

'Then she must come over and play with us.'

'That would be lovely. Thanks.'

462

But even as she spoke, Vanessa remembered with a jolt that she might not have Sunshine much longer herself. Not if social services got their way.

'Why can't I wear shorts?' Sunshine glared at her.

'Because it's cold.'

'But the sun is shining!'

She was getting used to these arguments. In a way, they showed that her granddaughter was really getting used to her new life. It was more natural, surely, than her almost-too-polite behaviour when she'd first arrived.

Even so, they were going to be late for breakfast. Vanessa tried to remember some advice from the group about the I-don't-want-to-wear-that battle. Give them a choice, Judith Davies had chirped. OK. 'You can wear shorts and get a chill or wear jeans and not get a chill.'

Sunshine pouted. 'You can't get a cold just from being cold. Daisy says so.'

Vanessa's mouth twitched. She'd much rather have a child like this than a boring one. Maybe that had been her problem with Brigid. Instead of admiring her daughter's ability to speak her mind, she'd seen it as a stumbling block. Well, she wouldn't make the same mistake this time round. Provided, that was, she was allowed to keep Sunshine.

Oh God. The thought of life without her granddaughter was unbearable. How she'd like to tell Mr Perfect exactly what she thought of him! If, indeed, it was him. Vanessa looked around for Brian, seeking reassurance. He was sitting at the far end of the huge refectory table, next to Camilla; both were bent over the *Racing Post*. Briefly he looked up to give her a wink, before returning to the paper. 'If I were you,' she heard him saying, 'I'd go both ways on the 3.40. Upper Cut. A real cert.'

'I don't want you to get the wrong idea, Mr Hughes,' Camilla was saying in that clear-clipped authoritative tone of hers. 'I'm not a serious gambler. Not like my dear late husband. But I do like to have a little flutter now and again.'

'Vanessa!' A sharp voice cut in. 'I've been meaning to have a proper word with you.'

It was Audrey, wearing her trademark low-cut top. 'I've been thinking about your Brigid, ever since the school fête, when you brought along that picture of her.' Audrey's voice had an edge to it, suggesting she had something else on her agenda. 'You said she was abroad, I believe?'

Sunshine looked up from her toast. 'She's in a place called Go Er.'

Why did children always listen when they shouldn't? And *not* listen when they should?

'Really?' The woman drew up a chair. 'My son – the one who was in her crowd at school – was very sweet on her, you know. In fact, she broke my Mark's heart.'

Where was this going? 'I'm sorry but I can't be responsible for that.'

'I'm not saying that you can but you might like to mention to Brigid that we met. Prick her conscience, perhaps.'

Vanessa glanced nervously down the table, concerned Sunshine was listening, but she was chattering now to the child on her left. 'I'm afraid we don't talk much at the moment.'

Audrey shrugged. 'My son's never really got over her, to be honest. Still, it's part of life, I suppose. Watching your children suffer and knowing you can't do anything for them.'

Vanessa's heart lurched. That was true enough. Those words were pretty heartfelt. Maybe the two of them had more in common than she'd realised.

'Just one more thing.' Audrey was staring rather fiercely at her now. 'I did hear through the grapevine that you might not be allowed to keep Sunshine with you any more.'

What! 'Keep your voice down,' Vanessa hissed. Dragging the woman by the hand, she took her into the conservatory. 'What exactly do you mean?'

The redhead looked a bit nervous now. 'It's nothing really. Just a whisper. Someone said that social workers got involved after Sunshine nearly got run over. There was something too about you having a boyfriend.'

'So it was *you*! It was you who reported us!'

'Don't be daft!' The woman stepped back, readjusting her top. 'Why don't you ask Bobbie? She seems to know rather a lot around here, if you ask me.'

What did she mean by that? Shaking, Vanessa went back to her room to pack. It was enough to stop you trusting anyone. Everyone seemed a suspect now. Friends from class. Bobbie. It almost made her doubt Brian. After all, how well did she really know him?

It was time to ask some serious questions.

'Do you know where Mummy is?'

'No,' said Jack, nodding at the same time as though he meant yes. Incredibly, he was sitting still, in one of the many bedrooms upstairs. Even more amazing, he was playing a game with his sister and Sunshine. Something was up. None of them was arguing.

'Are you sure you don't know?' asked Vanessa sharply.

'Mummy doesn't want to be disturbed,' announced Daisy bossily. 'She and Daddy are having a rest.'

Was that so? Vanessa knew she shouldn't interrupt them. But this couldn't wait. 'Bobbie?' She hammered on a door further down the corridor. 'Are you there? It's me, Vanessa.'

It took a while for Bobbie to open it; when she did, she was wearing one of the white guest dressing gowns and pretending to look confused.

Vanessa wasn't having that. 'You know why I'm here, don't you?'

'Something going on?' Rob loomed up behind his wife. He had his hand protectively on her shoulder: just as Brian used to do to her.

'Yes,' snapped Vanessa. 'There is.'

Bobbie was flushing deep red. That woman was guilty. She just knew it. 'Tell me straight. Did you ring social services?'

Bobbie took a step back. 'Of course not.'

'Are you sure? I know that you had something to do with that suede jacket. Don't deny it! I saw Sarah wearing it

465

yesterday. Not that that's important compared with Sunshine.' Vanessa had never seen herself as a violent woman but it was all she could do not to seize Bobbie by the lapels of that dressing gown. 'Do you realise the damage you've done!'

Rob was looking at his wife aghast. 'Please don't tell me you've done something silly again.'

'No. NO!' Bobbie was shaking her head. 'I promise you. It was nothing to do with me. I wouldn't do that to you, Vanessa.'

'I'd like to believe you, Bobbie, but I don't know if I can.' She turned round, feeling a horrible heaviness in her chest. 'You've told lies before. Just like your children. And to be honest . . .'

'CAN SOMEONE HELP ME?' Matthew came dashing out of the room next door. 'Lottie's in absolute agony. Something's wrong this time. I know it is. Call an ambulance. Quick!'

After they'd gone, complete with siren and flashing blue lights, it didn't seem right to stay on any more. Brian was the first to leave. Quite a lot of guests were still outside from when the ambulance had gone off, so she couldn't even have a proper goodbye kiss.

'How awful,' said Mrs Perfect as they gathered around, still not quite believing what had just happened. 'Mind you, I did think Matthew should have taken his daughter straight to the doctor when it first started.'

'No you didn't!' snapped her husband. 'Your exact words were: There goes that man making a fuss again.'

Vanessa was too upset to talk. Matthew had brought Lottie to her that very morning for advice. 'You've got more experience than me.' Those were his exact words. But she'd got it wrong. It was so easy to do that with kids. *Too* easy when the consequences could be fatal. That was one of the scariest things about being a parent. Making these huge decisions, often on your own.

Now all they could do was hope. Maybe say a little prayer too. No harm in that, surely?

'I'm going back with Rob,' said Bobbie, not looking Vanessa in the face. Sign of a guilty conscience if ever there was one.

'Yes. Of course.' Vanessa turned away.

'Presumably you won't want me in the shop tomorrow.' Despite her words, Bobbie's voice sounded hopeful.

'You presume right.'

'I didn't do it, you know!'

As she spoke, there was the sound of the horn honking from Rob's car outside. 'If you say so.'

Bobbie tried to kiss Vanessa on her cheek but she moved away. 'Please go, Bobbie. I've nothing more to say to you.' How, she wondered, watching Daisy waving madly at Sunshine from the back seat, could she have got Bobbie so wrong?

The journey back took ages. One of the junctions was still closed owing to the bad weather and there was an accident a few miles after that. She only hoped it wasn't one of their party. Then again, that was selfish. It didn't matter who it was, as long as they were all right.

'Do you think Lottie is better now?' asked Sunshine from the back.

'I hope so.'

'If Mummy was here, she'd be able to help. Like she helps the other women in our village.'

'Really?' Vanessa's hands tightened on the steering wheel. 'How does she do that?'

'She puts her hand on them and then they're better.'

Like a faith healer? Someone who laid on hands? But Brigid had always been so sharp. So angry. So abrupt. The picture didn't really fit.

Maybe it was just Sunshine's imagination. Kids came up with some amazing stories, as someone had said at the parenting class. If only you knew which ones to believe. They were nearly coming into Corrywood now; past the rich part where Pamela and Andy lived (fancy having two amazing homes!); then the middle-priced bit like Bobbie and Rob; and then their part, on the other side of the railway line. The wrong side. Maybe that had been another point against them in the social worker's books.

She'd find out this week, at the meeting. Vanessa felt a huge wave of apprehension. Devon had distracted her from all her problems: the hospital appointment as well as social services. But now they were back in the real world. Maybe she ought to prepare Sunshine, just in case.

'Poppet,' she began, her mouth dry. 'Remember the woman we went to see? The woman who you said smelt funny?'

'LOOK!' Sunshine's voice rose into such a shriek that Vanessa wanted to put her hands over her ears. 'LOOK!'

She was undoing her belt! Trying to scramble out of the car before it had even stopped; before she could find a parking space. For a minute, Vanessa thought she was referring to Brian. There was indeed a white van in the road. But it was bigger with gaudy psychedelic squirls on it.

'IT'S MUMMY!'

No. No. It couldn't be. But then Vanessa saw the girl running towards them. The tall, nut-brown girl with the startling blue eyes and jet black hair just like Harry.

'MUMMY!' cried Sunshine, running up and throwing herself into her mother's arms. Vanessa sat there, rigid, the engine still running.

Brigid? Brigid!

Was it *really* her?

PARENTS! SIX THINGS YOU SHOULD NEVER DO

Wear teen-type clothes.
Attempt to talk cool.
Ring another child's mum to ask why you didn't get
    an invitation to the class party.
Put a tracer on your mobile.
Snoop in their Trash box.
Give up.

Extracted from I Can't Cope With My Kids *magazine.*

PERFECT PARENTING AFRESH!

PUTTING EVERYTHING INTO PRACTICE!

Chapter 42

ANDY

Andy steeled himself for Pamela's disapproval as soon as they stepped in through the door after the drive back from Devon.

'I'm afraid I didn't get a chance to tidy up before we left,' he started to say, wishing he had at least emptied the kitchen bin or sorted out that unsavoury smell from under the sink.

She shrugged. 'Don't fuss. I'm just glad to be home.'

Mel exchanged worried looks with her sister. 'Are you OK, Mum?'

'I'll be better, darling, when I've had a drink.'

Oh God. Camilla had warned him about this; had pointed out that alcoholics rarely changed and that if Pamela was anything like her father, she'd revert to her old ways within minutes.

Bloody hell! His wife was putting on the kettle!

'Tea or coffee?' She wrapped one arm around Mel and another round Nattie. 'Your father and I have been talking about the drinking and smoking. All I can say is that I'm not going to get all heavy or ignore it like I did before. But you'll learn one day that it isn't the way to deal with your problems.'

Blimey! Andy stared at his wife. Was this really the uptight woman who had gone away shortly after that awful birthday party?

'From now on,' continued Pamela, stirring sugar into her tea – Pamela *never* took sugar! – 'we're not going to have any secrets from each other. In fact, I suggest we have regular weekly conferences.'

The girls groaned. 'Dad tried to make us do that and it was crap.'

'Well, I suggest we give it another go.' Pamela slipped her arm through his. 'We used to do it at the centre.' She looked rather coy. 'Even this rather famous actress, whom I can't possibly name, took part. What do you say, Andy?'

He didn't know what to think. This woman looked like his wife. Walked like his wife. Smelt like his wife. But she was coming out with stuff that belonged to a Pamela he'd never met. To make it more complicated, *he* had changed too. Being alone with the girls had made him see things differently. So had Bobbie. And, although he didn't really like to say so because it sounded a bit naff, the parenting course had given him a different perspective too.

'I reckon', he said steadily, 'that Mum's right. We do need to be more honest with each other. In fact, maybe we'll have a conference right now.'

Mel groaned. 'But I'm going out!'

'Then you'll just have to text your boyfriend and tell him you're going to be late,' retorted Andy. 'Sit down, everyone.' He gestured to the kitchen table, which still needed wiping down. 'I've got something to tell you.'

Nattie's voice trembled. 'You're not getting divorced, are you?'

'Of course we're not.' Pamela shot Andy a questioning look. 'Dad and I are fine, aren't we?'

Wistfully, Andy thought of Bobbie. 'Of course we are.' He felt embarrassed even saying so. Why should parents have to justify their personal relationship to their children, especially if they couldn't even explain it to themselves? 'I'm talking about something else.'

By the time he'd finished explaining about the investments that hadn't worked out, the girls were actually listening. Not surprising really. They were clones of Pamela, weren't they? Anything that involved money would attract their attention.

'I'm glad we're skint.' Mel stood up, pushing her chair so that it banged against the wall. Normally Pamela would have snapped – she had got extremely agitated last year when Jack had made a mark on the paint by doing exactly the same thing – but now she was just ignoring it. 'Jason says it's selfish to be rich. It's not fair on everyone else.'

'Then why do you keep lending him money?' Nattie snorted. 'Yes, you do, Mel. Don't try to pretend to Mum and Dad that you don't.'

'Shut up.' Mel scowled at her sister. 'Have you told them that you're not going back to school?'

'*What?*'

His youngest daughter pursed her mouth sulkily. 'I've been offered a contract and I'm nearly sixteen. Before you say anything, either of you, I'm taking it. You can't stop me. Cos if you do, I'll just run away.'

'But . . .'

'No, Andy, she's right.' Pamela's fingers were tapping on the dirty table; her nails were bitten, he noticed. Unpainted too. Usually they were a glossy red. 'We've got to let her do this or she'll always resent us.'

Talk about a change of attitude!

'But there have to be some rules, Nattie. Don't you agree, Andy? You continue living with us until you're at least eighteen. And—'

'I don't think any of you realise,' he cut in exasperatedly. 'When I say that I've lost a lot of money, I mean it. We're going to have to sell the house. I don't know where we're going to be living – we might have to leave Corrywood!'

Pamela shrugged. 'That's OK. Isn't it, girls?'

Mel was already halfway out of the room. 'I'm going out.'

He leaped to his feet. 'Not with that boy, you're not!'

'Andy.' Pamela laid a hand on his arm. 'She's got to learn for herself. Now come on, Nattie. Let's sit down in the conservatory together. Just you and me. Mother-and-daughter time! I want to know which agency has offered you a contract. You have to be careful, you know. Some are much better than others.'

He needed to get out of this place. Snatch some air. Find a bit of sanity. Taking his coat, Andy slammed the front door behind him, just in time to see an old banger with L plates revving up before noisily making its way down the road. There was a flash of his older daughter in the driving seat and that lout, damn him, next to her. How dare he? But then a small voice came into his head. 'That could have been you!'

It was true. If he hadn't been given that chance at fourteen, might not he, Andy, have ended up as a loser? No job. No house. No family. It was a sobering thought. One that he would have liked to have shared with Bobbie.

Unable to stop himself, Andy walked across town to the part which, Pamela always said, wasn't the sort of area that she would choose to live in. He took a right and then a left. There it was. A modest Victorian three-storey terrace with a rather pretty plant climbing up the front. She was in there somewhere. Bobbie with her sweet smile. In another place and at another time, things might have been so different.

Andy's heart began to thump as he walked past, taking a detour back into the high street and up towards the police station. Pamela hadn't been keen when he'd told her back in Devon what he planned to do. 'It's in the past,' she'd said dismissively. 'Leave it alone.'

Impossible. Kieran might have let him off the hook, but Andy couldn't pretend any more. It was time to face up to his own shortcomings, just as Pamela had faced up to hers in the centre.

It had been a long time since he'd spoken to a policeman. In fact, part of him was rather hoping the station might be shut. After all, it was evening. But no. Lights were spilling out on to the street and the glass doors opened automatically. There was a woman at the desk, dealing with a group of kids; something about one of them having lost a phone.

Andy stood there sweating. Maybe this was a mistake. Perhaps he'd just go home after all. But then the kids left, pushing past him rudely, and now he was in front of the desk.

'May I help you?' The woman looked young. Clear face. Clear eyes. Clear conscience. What he'd give for one of those.

'I'd like to report a crime.' The words were out of his

476

mouth now. There was no taking them back. 'Something that happened twenty-five years ago.'

BOBBIE

Bobbie had been trying to corner Jack for bathtime but he'd shot under his bed: one of his favourite hiding places. Apart from the Reduced Bread shelf, that was. Now she was getting bigger, it was more difficult to retrieve him.

'Please come out,' she pleaded.

'No.' He growled. 'It's my den.'

OK. Time for the choice technique. 'You can either come out and have extra time after your bath before going to bed. Or you can stay there and go to bed earlier tomorrow night.'

'Stay here!'

It was hopeless! What on earth would happen when her mother turned up with Dr Know? The Perfect Parents' course had been all very well. In fact, it had taught her a few good tips. But it didn't have all the magic answers. Not when you had a child like Jack. 'He's got a personality,' Vanessa used to say encouragingly after class.

Vanessa! Bobbie's thoughts turned to all those awful accusations her friend had hurled at her. She'd already tried to ring Sarah – there had to be a simple explanation for the jacket – but she wasn't picking up. Maybe she was at the hospital with Matthew. Poor little Lottie.

Moving across Jack's bedroom, she made to close the curtains. How odd! Wasn't that Andy? Just standing there on the pavement. Staring at the downstairs sitting-room window. Bobbie's heart did a funny little flip. Part of her wanted to rush out and talk to him. Tell him that things were better now with Rob; quite a lot better, in fact. Tell him about their plans to downsize and for Rob to find a job that gave him more time with the children.

But at the same time, she was too scared to go out. Scared in case they both did something that one day they might regret.

'Do I hear trouble going on here?'

Bobbie shut the curtains quickly as her husband came in. Don't get cross with Jack, she wanted to say. Don't spoil everything by telling me that I'm too soft on him.

'Playing lions, are we?' Rob was actually getting down on all fours. 'Can I come in too?'

Jack giggled from under the bed. 'You're too big!'

'Want to bet?'

'MUM! MUM! I CAN'T TURN OFF THE BATH TAPS AND THE WATER'S GOING OVER THE SIDE!'

'I'll go,' said Bobbie automatically.

'Let me!' Rob had already jumped to his feet. 'We'll sort out those taps, together, won't we, Jack? I hear lions are very good at that sort of thing.'

He was trying. She'd give him that. 'By the way, that was your mother on the phone just now.' Rob dropped a kiss on top of her head. 'That boyfriend of hers is going to be on Channel 4 tonight. She says to make sure we don't miss it.'

VANESSA

The three of them were still sitting on the sofa, holding each other tightly in case Brigid disappeared again. Sunshine was on her mother's knee, arms round her neck. Vanessa was clutching her daughter's arm as though she was the child and her daughter, the parent.

'I don't understand,' she kept saying. This was where your age crept in. This awful inability to absorb stuff, especially when you were still in shock.

Brigid glanced down at her child. Sunshine's eyes were shut. Was she asleep? Or just pretending to be? 'I got into trouble, Mum.'

That's no surprise, she almost said but managed to stop herself in time.

'You know I've always been a bit outspoken?'

You don't say!

'I caused a bit of a fuss by standing up for a local woman.

She was being persecuted because she wanted her kids to go to school. Her husband insisted they should work.' Brigid's eyes shone with indignation. 'They were only ten and eight. Really bright too!'

Vanessa tried to imagine her daughter as a teacher in a school in India; a school that had been set up by a group of British and American parents to educate their own kids and also to encourage local learning. It seemed so responsible! Such a far cry from the angry Goth who had slammed the door on her all those years ago.

Brigid, however, had changed. She might look like a hippy with tattoos on her arm and the little silver nose ring. But she was so earnest now, talking with passion about women's rights in a place Vanessa knew nothing about. A place that her daughter had ended up in, apparently, after 'hooking up' with some other travellers.

'Some of the local men got rather nasty.' Brigid looked down at Sunshine whose eyes were still shut, arms still firmly entwined around her mother's neck. 'They didn't like me anyway because I'd been doing some healing.'

Healing? So Sunshine had been right.

'Someone in Thailand taught me.' Brigid sounded a bit abashed. 'Sounds a bit weird, I know, but it works, Mum. It really does. Yet it scared some of the locals, who said I was a witch. Things got really difficult when one of them threatened me with a knife.'

Vanessa gasped.

'He didn't hurt me badly. It was just a small cut.' Brigid's voice dropped. 'But then they began to threaten Sunshine.'

Instinctively, Vanessa bent down and kissed that little soft cheek. She'd kill anyone who tried to hurt her granddaughter.

'I knew I had to get her out. You were the only person I could trust.' She leaned her head against Vanessa's. 'I'm sorry I didn't keep in touch but I was angry with you at first and then, the longer it went on, the harder it seemed to say sorry.'

Vanessa nodded. 'I can see that. But why didn't you come to England with her?'

Brigid ran her hand through her greasy hair. How Vanessa itched to wash it for her!

'It would have attracted too much attention and then they might have got both of us.'

'What about the police?'

Brigid laughed. 'It works differently out there, Mum. A friend of mine was going back to England so he agreed to take Sunshine. There wasn't time to let you know. Things were getting really nasty.'

She stopped.

'How nasty?' asked Vanessa with a horrible feeling in her stomach.

'They burned our house down.'

'NO!'

Sunshine stirred again. Brigid put a finger to her lips. 'One of my other friends, Simon, and his wife owned a house further inland; they suggested I hid there until the fuss died down. It was really remote. No mobile phone signal or anything like that. I managed to send you a postcard, though.'

'We got it.'

Brigid looked relieved. 'I was scared you'd think I'd abandoned my own daughter but on the other hand, I couldn't tell you what had really happened.' She gave a little shudder. 'I began to attract quite a lot of curiosity in this other place and I was worried about being tracked down. Then I met Malik.'

Her voice grew softer. 'He grew up in the village I was hiding in and had gone off to university. He'd come back briefly to see his parents who lived in the shack next to mine and we got quite friendly. When I explained the situation, he said he could get me out of it.'

As Brigid spoke, she looked down at her hand. Heavens! How had she missed that simple narrow silver band? 'It was the only way.' Brigid shrugged. 'He needed to get to Britain and I needed his protection.'

'A marriage of convenience?' Vanessa couldn't keep the disapproval out of her voice.

Brigid made an amused face. 'You could say that. But the funny thing is, Mum, that I actually rather like him. And I think he likes me.'

But what about Sunshine, Vanessa wanted to say. What about me! You can't just take her away!

'I'd like you to meet him. He went off for a walk just before you arrived; he knew I'd need time with you. I'm to ring him when you feel ready.' Brigid's eyes were on hers, hopefully. 'Is it OK if he stays with us for a bit?'

MOTHER'S DAY – THE MOST SPECIAL DAY OF THE YEAR!

Don't forget to buy a card!

Special offer:
Two for the price of one

As seen in the window of Corrywood Newsagents.

Chapter 43

ANDY

'You want to report a crime that happened twenty-five years ago?'

The policewoman on the other side of the desk, who hadn't looked much older than Mel, had taken in Andy's weekend jacket, the well-cut brown cords and his expensive loafers. Don't waste our time, he had almost heard her thinking. He'd leaned across the desk to talk more quietly as someone came in behind him. 'I didn't exactly *do* this thing . . . I witnessed it. But I *should* have done something. That's the whole problem.'

Ah, her expression had said. Another rich Corrywood resident who had suddenly developed a conscience now they had a Porsche in the drive. 'Fill in this form, would you?' she had said politely. 'We'll be in touch.'

Was that it? Andy had expected someone to haul him away and throw him in a cell for questioning. He had his lawyer's number at the ready on his BlackBerry. He'd even imagined calling Pamela from the station to break the news that he'd been arrested. But instead, the police officer had gone on to deal with the agitated elderly man behind him. 'Bloody commuters,' he had heard the man grumble in an accent that suggested a far superior education than Andy had had. 'They park here to avoid paying at the station. Then I have to look out of my window and see a red Fiesta blocking my view.'

If only his own problems were as simple! Then again, it was all a matter of perspective, wasn't it?

That had been a week ago. Since then, so much had happened! Pamela was due to return to the clinic for three days next week and, frankly, he was almost looking forward to it. It wasn't easy to cope with this new unpredictable wife. And, unfair as it sounded, she was invading his space! He'd got used to emptying the dishwasher or putting on the washing machine. But so was she. 'Sorry,' he found himself saying politely when they ran into each other.

'I have to say, Andy, you've become very domesticated!' she said with an amused smile. But it wasn't her old sardonic smile; it was a genuinely nice one. At night, she actually cuddled up to him, instead of lying flat on her back to avoid 'pillow marks' on her face.

It was impossible to sleep with her so close! So he started to wait until she fell asleep and then quietly turned over to have some breathing space. Yet this morning, he had woken up to find himself cuddling her! Was that a subconscious sign that he *did* want his wife after all?

'Of course I care for her,' he said when he rang Bobbie after trying – and failing – to resist the temptation. 'But it's weird being under the same roof all day, every day. We've never done that before. Besides, I can't just go on as though nothing has happened.'

'Of course you can't!' Her lovely voice, something he'd always admired about her, made him feel better instantly. 'But you have to give her a chance. And maybe you'll learn to *like* the new Pamela.' She suddenly sounded girlish. Skittish, even. 'Rob is different too. He's started to make a real effort. The other night, he was actually home by nine o'clock to kiss the children goodnight.'

Secretly, Andy had half believed (almost half hoped, to be honest) that Rob *had* had someone on the side after all.

'And I've just had another scan!'

He could almost touch her excitement. Feel her joy. Taste her new lease of life. One that didn't include him any more.

'You can see them sucking their thumbs! It's amazing. By the way, there's something else I've got to tell you.' There was a more sombre note now. 'Don't tell anyone but I gave Rob a bit of an ultimatum. I sort of hinted that I wasn't sure if I wanted to stay with him. Of course I didn't mean it but it shocked him into applying for another job. It's with a smaller agency; one that's more family orientated. It would be a much easier journey to work so Rob wouldn't be so stressed.'

'Sounds great,' he said, trying to mean it.

'I'm sorry', she continued, 'about Pamela.'

'We'll be all right,' he said, deliberately not mentioning their financial problems. He'd already asked Pamela not to tell her brother or mother until he'd sorted out some kind of plan. Considering his wife's family hadn't accepted him when he'd been wealthy, they'd probably advise Pamela to cut loose. In fact, it was amazing she hadn't already done so.

'What have you been up to?' she asked chattily.

'Apart from getting used to having Pamela back? Just the usual stuff.'

For a moment, Andy considered telling Bobbie about the 'Know of any jobs?' phone calls he'd been making. Describing the gushing estate agent, who had virtually rubbed his hands with glee when they'd told him they needed 'an urgent sale'. Confiding in her about Mel who was out more than she was in, with that awful boyfriend of hers, sporting rings in his nose and probably other bits too disgusting to mention. Sharing his hopes and fears about Nattie, who was floating around in a state of dreamy excitement because she was, according to her new agent, going to be Very Big. Telling her about his visit to the police station.

'By the way, I meant to say. I've asked Pamela if . . .'

'DAD! DAD!'

Mel's voice was yelling angrily down the stairs. Andy walked quickly with the phone into the conservatory for some privacy. 'Afraid I missed that. What did you say to Pamela?'

'DAD! NATTIE'S STOLEN MY NEW JEANS AND I'M GOING OUT RIGHT NOW! MUM SAYS YOU'VE GOT TO SORT IT OUT!'

'Sorry. Have to go. We'll speak another time, shall we?'

Mel was standing there, arms folded. 'Who was that?'

He wouldn't lie any more. He'd told himself that in the police station.

'Aunty Bobbie.'

His lovely daughter's face frowned. 'So you've heard, have you?'

Andy felt his heart do a karate kick of fear and apprehension. 'Heard what?'

Mel scowled. How was it that teenagers could be so nice one minute and so scary the next? 'We've got to go to lunch with them on Mother's Day. And some psycho's going to be there.'

'What?'

'He's actually a psychoanalyst!' cooed Pamela, swanning in. He had to say, she looked amazing. Much nicer; more attractive with that extra stone or so. Then he took in the glass in her hand with the slice of lemon at the bottom. Water? Gin? Vodka?

'Bobbie's mother is dating Dr Know,' trilled his wife. 'The man who does that television series where he moves into people's homes and tells them how to bring up their children properly.' She gave him a knowing look. 'But you probably know all that from Bobbie herself. Personally, I think it's going to be rather fun.'

'Fun!' Mel scowled again. 'You can count me out.'

Andy's breath caught in his throat. So he'd be able to see Bobbie again – quite soon! But he wouldn't be able to talk to her properly. Not in front of the others. Not next to some smart alec telling them how to bring up their kids.

'Don't be silly, Mel,' Pamela was babbling. 'Of course you'll come. Why don't you bring your boyfriend? The more the merrier.'

Was she serious?

'I can't wait!' Pamela was getting really hyper now. 'Can't imagine Bobbie's timid little mother with someone so famous.' She tapped her glass. 'By the way, just in case you're wondering, Andy, this is water. Sparkling water! Try some if you don't believe me!'

Two hours to go and they'd be here. Why wouldn't this wretched chicken cook?

'IT'S MINE!'

'NOT IT'S NOT, IT'S MINE.'

'I HAD IT FIRST!'

Crash!

Bobbie paused, mid-baste, and waited. Since the parenting course had ended, she had tried, really tried, to let the kids sort it out for themselves instead of rushing straight in. Sometimes it worked. Sometimes it didn't. One of these days, she was sure, her new non-intervention policy would result in another emergency trip to A & E. In London, she'd virtually earned loyalty vouchers thanks to Jack's various scrapes.

'NOW LOOK WHAT YOU'VE DONE – YOU'VE BROKEN IT.'

Objects could be replaced but not people. Wasn't that what Matthew had said once in class? Thank goodness little Lottie was out of the woods, although, as Sarah had said on the phone the other day, they'd only just caught her appendix before it got serious. Almost as serious as Sarah and Matthew seemed to be getting.

'I really like him,' her friend had confided girlishly. 'And I think he likes me.'

'That's wonderful!' Bobbie had paused, wondering how to phrase the next bit. 'By the way, I loved that jacket you were wearing. Where did you get it?'

'Bermondsey market. Quite a bargain, actually.'

So the person she had sold it to must have sold it on!

'MUM! IT'S IN BITS!'

Daisy's voice brought her back to the present crisis. Uh oh. Shoving the still-pink-in-the-middle chicken back in the oven, Bobbie put her head round the corner of the lounge. Blast. A large blue and yellow china bowl lay in fragments on the carpet, mixed in with bits of phone. Jack's new all-singing-all-dancing phone which Rob had brought back from the office as a freebie, along with one for his sister too. One of the advantages of working in advertising was that you got to try out the products. Perhaps the manufacturers could test-run the kids. See where she had gone wrong. 'Your aunt gave us that bowl. She'll be expecting to see it out on display.'

'So?' Daisy gave her a withering look. 'You've always said you hated it.'

'MY PHONE'S BROKEN!'

Well, at least it wasn't his head.

'It's all right, Jack, I'll fix it. Or maybe we'll ask Claudette.'

There was the clunk of footsteps down the stairs followed by a square-shaped jaw and a pair of heavy blue denims. If it hadn't been for Jilly from parenting class who had been desperate to rehome Claudette (the last family 'hadn't worked out'), Bobbie wouldn't have considered having an au pair. How could she live with a stranger when it was hard enough surviving with her own flesh and blood?

'It's only for the Easter holidays until her new family can take her on,' Jilly had pleaded. So she'd given in. So far, it was an unexpected success. The kids were scared stiff of Claudette so they did exactly what she said. Fantastic!

'It is imperative that you do not argue!' Claudette shook a thick finger at both children. 'You attend to your mother, yes? Especially on this special day! You have given her your mothering cards, yes? The ones we make together out of dried spaghetti?'

'They were lovely,' said Bobbie quickly. 'Thanks so much! Are you sure you can't stay for lunch? I could really do with you to make sure the kids behave.'

'I cannot.' Claudette shook her head fiercely. 'I do not desire to meet this man who eats children.' What had Jack and Daisy been saying? 'In addition, it is mandatory that I attend my kick-boxing class.'

On a Sunday? But Claudette was off, marching down the path with her bag slung across her chest and music blasting out of her headphones.

'How about laying the table without stabbing each other?'

488

suggested Bobbie to the kids. On second thoughts, forget that.
It would be easier to do it herself.

Ding dong. Either Claudette had changed her mind or . . .
oh shit. They were here early! There was Mum, looking like
a star-struck teenager, holding hands with a short squat man
who just about came up to her shoulder. He looked much
smaller than on television. Fatter too. And she could see what
the critics meant about that goatee. It was almost devil-like.
Still, if he made her mother happy, that was all that mattered.

'Mum! Happy Mother's Day!' Bobbie wrapped her arms
around her, feeling a wonderful warmth seeping through. They
hadn't seen each other since Christmas, but it was only now
that Bobbie realised how much she'd missed her. Missed that
lovely kind face and rose-smelling complexion and the hug
that spelt out unconditional love. A maternal love that she,
Bobbie, still needed, despite being a mother herself.

When did you ever learn to stand on your own two feet,
she wondered. Maybe never. When her grandmother had died,
some years ago, a much younger Bobbie had been shocked
by the effect on her mother. Now she could see why. However
old you were, you needed your mum.

'Sorry we're early, darling, but the traffic was much lighter
than usual.' Mum flushed, a trait she'd passed down to Bobbie
and Daisy. 'I'd like to introduce Herbert.' She looked down
adoringly at the barrel-shaped man beside her. 'Herbert, this
is my daughter.'

Trying to hide her disdain, Bobbie put out her hand. It
didn't matter what he looked like, she told herself. It was
what he was like as a person. Besides, as Rob said, perhaps
that tough no-nonsense approach was all an act on television
to get himself noticed.

Wow! He had a tough handshake! Her bones felt crushed!
'No lock on your gate, then, Bobbie?'

What?

'Herbert, dear.' Her mother blushed furiously again. 'I did
ask you not to mention it.'

'But I must, Phyllis.' Dr Know gave her a disapproving

glare. 'Every home with small children should have a gate with a lock at the point of entry between the drive and the road. It makes common sense unless you want your kids to end up on the mortuary slab.'

How rude! He hadn't even got into their home before treating her like one of his cases on the Thursday night prime-time slot! Then again, maybe he was one of those people who began babbling out of nerves. Dr Herbert Know might be a big media name but it must be rather nerve-racking for him to meet his girlfriend's grown-up daughter.

'I'll get my husband to look into it.' Bobbie glanced at Mum questioningly. 'Please come in. Daisy, Jack, come and say hello.'

'Shit.'

Bobbie gasped. 'Jack!'

Jack grinned. 'Ohshitohshitohshitohshit.'

'Stop! Right now!' Bobbie's face was puce. 'I'm so sorry. I don't know where he got it from.'

'From you!' Daisy's voice rang out as clearly as if she was auditioning for a stage role. 'You said it just now. When the doorbell went. You said, "Shit, they're early."'

'No I didn't!'

'Yes you did.'

Mum's face was indescribable but Bobbie had to hand it to her. Ignoring Dr Know, who was muttering something about soap and mouths, she held out her arms. 'Come and give me a big hug, both of you. Goodness, you've grown.'

Then she looked up at Bobbie with an expression that her daughter could read all too clearly. Please make them behave, she was saying. This means a lot to me. 'Where's Rob?' She gave a little nervous laugh. 'Don't tell me he's in the office on Mothering Sunday.'

Daisy looked important. 'Dad's still cleaning the downstairs loo cos Jack did this big . . .'

'That's enough!' Bobbie virtually pushed her mother through the recently repaired glass doors (Jack again) into the lounge. 'Would you like a drink?' She grabbed the bottle of wine which had been breathing on the side.

'You keep wine in reach of children?' Dr Know's eyebrows were raised.

'Well, not usually.' Bobbie felt even more flustered. 'It's only because we have guests.'

'But what if they help themselves?'

Daisy did a little pirouette. 'I've tried wine before!'

There was a knotting of eyebrows and a stroking of the goatee beard. 'You have?'

'It was when Mel babysat us.'

More raising of the eyebrows followed by more furious stroking. 'Your babysitter drinks?'

'She's not our sitter any more cos she smokes,' piped up Jack.

Oh God. He was flicking bogeys at Dr Know.

Ding dong.

'There she is.' Bobbie had given up. 'You can meet her for yourself, along with the rest of her family, including my mother-in-law. Jack, can you open the door?'

'AUNTY PAM! AUNTY PAM! I'VE BROKEN THAT BOWL YOU GAVE US. BUT MUM SAYS IT DOESN'T MATTER COS SHE ALWAYS HATED IT!'

VANESSA

At times it was as though Brigid had come back as a completely different person. That old stubborn streak was still there: no, she said firmly, she didn't approve of Sunshine watching television because it might stop her reading. But at other times she was the loving daughter that Vanessa had always wanted. And she was an adoring mother.

'It nearly killed me to stay in India without her,' Brigid had said on that first night when they'd stayed up into the early hours to talk and talk and talk. 'But after they'd threatened her I had to get her out somehow. If I'd gone with her, they would have taken both of us.' She shivered. 'These men were different from the others. They were ruthless. I might have been killed if I hadn't gone into hiding after she'd left.'

So that's why the Foreign Office hadn't known anything. No one had reported Brigid's plight because it had to be kept quiet.

Vanessa had a lot of gaps to fill Brigid in on as well. 'Bastard,' muttered her daughter when she heard about Jason and the DNA test. 'He had no right.'

'Turned out he wasn't the father anyway,' said Vanessa, hoping that her daughter might come clean.

'Course he wasn't.' Brigid looked away. 'Don't push me on that one, Mum. Not now.'

Then Vanessa told her about the lump that had to come out. The lump that might or might not be cancer. Brigid cried at that, weeping like a baby in her arms, before blowing her nose and sitting up straight. 'I'll look after you,' she announced firmly. 'I'll do some healing on you.'

If only it was that simple! 'I'm sorry, love.' She shook her head. 'But I just don't believe in that stuff.'

Brigid's mouth tightened and, for a second, she could see the old rebellious Goth teenager. 'Allow your children to have their own views and don't expect them to share yours.' Wasn't that what someone had said at the parenting course?

'But it's fine if you believe,' Vanessa added quickly. 'In fact, that's great.'

'Glad you see it that way.'

Then she told her about social services. 'I'd like to see anyone trying to take my daughter away.' Brigid set her teeth. For a minute, Vanessa could see Harry in her face. Strong. Resolute. Stubborn.

'And what about this Brian?' probed Brigid. 'Do you really like him?'

She nodded shyly. 'But I'm not allowed to see him.'

'He's married, then?'

Vanessa was shocked. 'Of course not. Social services made out that he might be a threat, you see, and—'

'He didn't hurt you!'

492

'No!' She'd forgotten how her daughter would jump in and not let her finish a sentence. 'They didn't like him staying over with a child in the house.' This was so embarrassing!

'Poor Mum!' Brigid gave her another cuddle. 'It's worse than being a teenager and being told that you can't have a boy in your room.' She gave her a little look. 'I'll never forget how shocked you were when you found Mark upstairs.'

Had she? There'd been so many boys over the years in her daughter's room that she'd lost count. 'Funnily enough, I bumped into his mother at a class. A parenting class actually. She said that Mark had been quite sweet on you.'

Brigid looked away. 'It was a long time ago.'

Really? Vanessa thought of Sunshine sleeping in the next room. How long ago? Seven years? Around the time that Brigid got pregnant? Wasn't that what Audrey had implied? 'You know that you can tell me anything.' She gave her daughter a squeeze. 'Absolutely anything.'

'Thanks, Mum.' Brigid stood up and yawned. 'I'm absolutely exhausted. So is he from the look of it.' Vanessa had almost forgotten Malik, who was slumped fast asleep on the sofa. 'Let's just leave him there, shall we? I'd rather cuddle up with Sunshine, to be honest.' Her eyes moistened. 'There were times when I wondered if I'd ever see her again.'

'That's how I felt about you,' said Vanessa in a small voice.

Brigid enveloped her in another big hug. 'I'm so sorry, Mum. It wasn't until I had Sunshine that I realised what it was really like to be a mother. Can you forgive me?'

Of course she could! A week later, they were now gradually getting in a sort of routine. Brigid had spoken to social services and informed them that her mother had merely been looking after her granddaughter while she'd been away on business. Even then, it had taken a lawyer's letter to sort it out, courtesy of the solicitor mum in class who refused to charge.

Meanwhile, Brian had come round and, although Brigid had been unusually shy at first (there was something about seeing your old headmaster), they all seemed to get on really well. It helped to take Vanessa's mind off her operation which was now scheduled for two weeks' time. 'We'll still be here,' Brigid had assured her. 'I'll help to man the shop if you like.'

If only she still had Bobbie! But she hadn't seen her since Devon. Part of her wanted to pick up the phone. The other part continued to feel terribly wounded. And confused.

'There's something else.' For a moment, Brigid's eyes refused to meet hers. 'I don't want you to feel hurt, Mum, but I've decided to get in touch with Dad. All that time without Sunshine got me thinking. Family's really important, isn't it? So I've been doing a bit of research on the net.' Her eyes began to shine with excitement. 'And I think I've tracked him down.'

FIVE THINGS THAT TEENAGERS HATE THEIR PARENTS DOING

Waking them up to explain how the iPad works.
Waking them up to go to school.
Waking them up with sex sounds.
Waking them up before 2 p.m. at weekends.
Waking them up.

Chapter 44

ANDY

It had been a mistake coming here. Andy had had his doubts when he'd first heard about the lunch party, but it was even worse when Bobbie opened the door, looking slightly flustered in her pinny that said KISSES FOR THE COOK in big pink letters, and then proceeded to brush all their cheeks in greeting. Including his.

The feel of her soft skin on his – and her smell – made it impossible for him to stand there making small talk, so Andy made an excuse to slip into the downstairs loo. 'Pull yourself together,' he said, addressing the mirror sharply. 'You're married. She's married. End of.'

When he came out, Andy found a funny little dwarf of a man in the sitting room, earnestly advising Mel's ghastly boyfriend that he ought to have a Hep B test in view of his tattoos and 'numerous metallic adornments'.

Even worse, a serious-looking Rob came up to him, suggesting they 'had a quiet word'. Andy braced himself. If this was about Jack telling everyone that 'Mum had been cuddling Uncle Andy', he'd tell the truth. Well, partly anyway. He'd explain they'd just been comforting each other but leave out the bit about this stupid boyish crush. That's all it could be, he told himself fiercely. A crush.

'So,' said Rob, putting a drink in his hands and leading him towards the garden where it really was incredibly warm for this time of the year, 'what do you think of Phyllis's catch?'

Andy was so relieved that he wasn't to be interrogated at once that he knocked back half his glass. 'Bit pushy, isn't he?

He reminds me of a man in . . .' He stopped just before saying 'the home'. 'I mean, he reminds me of a man at my old school. Always critical but with a crocodile smile at the same time.'

'Exactly.' Rob's eyes were now focused on him. Andy began to feel uneasy again. 'Bobbie says you've been a big support to her in the last few months.'

He could feel the sweat running down his back. 'I'm not sure about that.' He took a deep breath. 'She's helped me too.'

'Right.' His brother-in-law's face was rigid. It had always been hard to know what Rob was thinking: a family trait which made him deeply uncomfortable. 'So long as it's not more than that.'

The words were said in such a low, steady way that Andy wondered if he'd heard them right. Forcing himself, he held Rob's gaze even though he was shaking inside. 'What do you mean?'

His brother-in-law was studying him closely. It was like a duel! Each was determined not to look away first. 'It can be easy to grow too close to someone you're working with. I see it all the time in the office and I know that you and Bobbie have been quite involved with this parenting course.'

Andy's shirt was clinging to him now with perspiration. But he had to say it. Had to be true to himself. He'd hidden too much in his life. 'Rob, your wife is a fine woman. One of the nicest, prettiest, most intelligent women I've ever met. But it hasn't been easy for her.' He shook his head, impatient with himself. 'It never is when a woman is virtually the sole carer of the kids and trying to work at the same time.'

'I'm aware of that.' Rob shoved his hands in his pockets; a gesture Andy favoured himself when making a stand. 'I've got a new job.' He spoke defiantly. 'It's in Tyneside.'

Tyneside? So far away! Andy felt a strange weight descending on his chest. A boy at the home had come from there. They'd taken the piss out of his accent until he'd stabbed one of them with a fork over tea. 'We're going to be at opposite ends of the country then.'

'Exactly.'

This time, there was no doubting the meaning behind the words. 'There's something you have to know, Rob.' He locked gazes with his brother-in-law again. 'Bobbie adores you. There's never been anyone else for her. Ever.'

Something cleared in Rob's eyes. 'I'm glad to hear that. Especially in her condition.'

Was Rob suggesting that he might be the father? That was way out of line! 'Like I said, Rob, she would do anything for you. Absolutely anything. You're a lucky man.'

Rob's face hardened again. Shit. Maybe Andy shouldn't have said that last bit. 'You seem rather familiar with my wife's views. I trust you know your own wife just as well? My sister's been telling me about rehab. Sounds as though she's really been through the mill.' He glanced through the window at Pamela, who was talking earnestly to the little man with the goatee. 'Are you two all right?'

Brilliant, Andy nearly said sarcastically. Absolutely brilliant. We had sex the other night and I only got through by thinking of Bobbie. 'Pamela's different,' he said, knocking back his drink. 'She's more relaxed, almost laid-back, and she seems to have come round to Nattie's modelling contract. She's been very good about us having to sell the house too.'

Rob's face sharpened. 'You're moving?'

So Pamela had kept her promise and not told her brother. That was something. 'You didn't know I've lost a great deal of money?'

'I didn't. I'm sorry.' Rob's eyes softened in sympathy. That was surprising too! Andy had expected a flash of satisfaction, or even fear: there were people in Corrywood who worried about losing their wealth but also took pleasure in others' misfortunes. He'd put Rob down as one of them. Maybe he was wrong. Even so, what would he say if he knew Andy had been involved in a murder case?

'It's only money,' he said, more to convince himself than Rob. 'Not health. We're still working out exactly what we're going to do and I know that's worrying Pamela, however well she tries to hide it. But I can't help thinking that there's something else that isn't quite right either.'

Rob shook his head, as though the answer was obvious. 'That's because she needs something to focus on. It's why I wanted to talk to you privately. Don't think I'm interfering, but I know my sister. And I've got a couple of suggestions to make.'

Andy came back into the lounge, feeling slightly stunned. He'd never had such a meaningful conversation with his brother-in-law before.

'Ah, there you are, both of you!' Camilla's crisp tones met him from the sofa where she was sitting with her usual erect posture, tumbler of gin in her hand, next to Bobbie's mother, who was reading a Shirley Hughes book with Jack. There was a stale whiff of BO coming from Mel's boyfriend, who was sitting in the corner with Mel on his lap. Outrageous behaviour, especially in front of the children.

'Robert, darling, do you mind if we just watch the 1.10 before lunch? I've got a little something on Upper Cut.'

'That's the name of Van Van's friend's horse!' sang out Daisy. 'He owns the front bit.'

'Don't be silly, darling. And do mind Granny's knee, won't you, or you'll ladder my stockings.'

How could two grandmothers be so different? wondered Andy. One so maternal and the other so self-centred.

'It is! It is! Sunshine's Granny's friend owns half a horse. He told us. He's going to take us to see it one day.'

'That child's imagination is too fertile for her own good, don't you think, Dr Know?'

'Please! Call me Herbert!' Ugh! He was actually kissing Camilla's hand. What a creep. 'As for imagination, in particular that of a child, it can be both a blessing and a curse.'

There was a feverish stroking of the beard. 'May I?' He sat down next to Camilla, so that Bobbie's mother had to shift along. 'There is a story I would like to tell you about the machinations of the mind.' An excited glint came into his eyes. 'A very dangerous story, which, in my view, was not handled at all well by the parents!'

Poor Phyllis! She looked like a teenager who was about to lose her boyfriend to an arch rival. 'Actually, I don't want to interrupt you, Herbert, but that sounds like Bobbie saying that lunch is ready. Shall we go in?'

BOBBIE

This was awful! Mel and that ghastly boyfriend of hers had been all over each other before lunch and even now, at the table, they simply couldn't keep their hands off each other. Everyone was doing their best not to notice, apart from Pamela. 'My time in rehab taught me how important it is to show your feelings,' she was saying loudly to no one in particular. 'It's all right, the girls know. I felt it was important to be open.'

Was this some kind of reverse psychology, intended to make her daughter stop? But her sister-in-law didn't seem to mind the smooching. Nor was she reproaching Nattie, who was texting flagrantly at the table instead of eating burnt roast chicken. Her fault for giving it an extra two hours, just to be on the safe side.

Meanwhile, Dr Know (dirty old man), was edging closer and closer to Camilla's chair so that his face was virtually in her chest. Yet instead of distancing herself, her mother-in-law seemed to be relishing the attention. 'I belong to a little arts appreciation society in Sussex,' she was gushing. 'I wonder if you might consider coming down to speak to us one day. I could put you up in the spare room. I'd make you very comfortable!'

Mum was looking increasingly miserable. Bobbie bristled. Should she say something? No. That might make it worse. Meanwhile, Daisy was pretending to be vegetarian again even though she had happily chomped through a bacon sandwich for breakfast this morning. 'I'm not eating this, Mum. I told you. I don't eat dead animals any more. Sunshine says it's cruel.'

'If you don't eat meat, you won't get protein!' Bobbie turned to Rob to seek support but he was passing the bottle of wine around: a rather sharp white which Dr Know had brought, along with a copy of his new book, entitled *How to Beat the Little Brats into Total Submission*.

'That's not exactly true, is it, Bobbie?' Dr Know's tone was so smug! Couldn't Mum see what a vain, self-important know-all he was? 'We must be honest with children, even if their personal views conflict with ours.' He turned to her daughter, flashing her a sly smile that reminded her of the snake in *The Jungle Book*. 'You can get protein, Daisy, through other food like nuts and cheese and certain energy drinks.'

'What about Red Bull?' butted in Jack. 'Can that give you pro teen too?'

All the adults gasped apart from Camilla. 'Dear me,' she tittered. 'Is this Red Bull some kind of new pâté?'

'Where have you tried it?' demanded Rob, ignoring his mother.

'Mel let us try some when she babysat us,' piped up Daisy helpfully.

Andy groaned. 'She should have asked permission first. Mel, do you hear me?'

Bobbie, along with the rest of the table, now stared in horror. Mel actually had her right hand under the table and was feeling that awful boy's . . .

'MEL!' Andy thundered, making her jump. 'WILL YOU BEHAVE YOURSELF!'

Pamela gave him a reproving look. 'It doesn't help to shout, darling. However, Mel, I do think your father has a point. If you want a room, I am sure that there are one or two upstairs.'

Her sister-in-law had to be taking the mickey! Still, it was almost worth it to see Dr Know's face. 'It is important, I believe,' he announced, brushing back that awful oily straggle of hair across the bald patch, 'for adolescents to express their sexuality. But, in my opinion, it should be done in a controlled environment.'

What on earth did Mum see in him? Was she that desperate

or was love really so blind, even at that age? Luckily, her own two chose that moment to create a diversion.

'DAISY'S KICKING ME UNDER THE TABLE,' yelled Jack.

'NO I'M NOT!' spluttered Daisy indignantly. 'It's Jason trying to touch Mel's legs.'

Could it get any worse? 'So you see,' said Pamela, leaning towards her now, beaming as though none of this was happening. 'They cured me at the centre without any drugs.' She grasped Bobbie's hand. 'We wrote our life stories instead. So therapeutic! You ought to try it.'

She snorted. 'I would if I had the time but some of us have to work.'

Rob shot her a don't-be-rude-to-my-sister look.

'Any more chicken, anyone?' she asked defiantly, deliberately changing the subject.

There was a polite chorus of 'Not for me' and 'Absolutely delicious' even though several plates still bore uneaten charred chunks.

Uh oh. There was Pongo again. Jack? Daisy? Definitely one of the two. Their esteemed guest had smelt it too, judging from the disgusted look on his face as he staggered to his feet, almost taking the tablecloth with him. Dr Know might not approve of parents drinking but he'd sunk most of that bottle single-handed. 'Actually, if everyone has finished, we have an announcement to make, don't we, Phyllis?'

Bobbie's heart turned cold as Dr Know pulled out a sheet of notes from his breast pocket, along with a mustard spotted handkerchief. 'I thought we'd decided to wait, Herbert,' whispered her mother urgently.

Oh God. Don't let this be what she thought it was . . . 'Your mother, Bobbie, has done me the honour of agreeing to be my wife!' He gave a little bow in her direction before glancing back at his notes. 'I hope you will be happy for us. Given our age, we intend to tie the knot sooner rather than later. It will be a low-key ceremony, although of course that might be difficult, given my profile.' He blew his nose loudly.

No. Please no, prayed Bobbie. Please don't let this awful little man become her step-father! She could just see it now. Years and years of family gatherings extending before them with Dr Know telling them exactly how they should and shouldn't be bringing up their children.

'Congratulations!' said Rob heavily.

Andy shot her a sympathetic look.

'Wonderful,' beamed Pamela. 'Isn't it, Mummy? Fancy having a celebrity in the family!'

'*I* could have got married again, if I'd wanted,' chirped Camilla. 'Did I tell you about the time I received two proposals in one evening at the Conservative Club ball?'

Bobbie tried to say something but failed.

'We must celebrate!' said Rob lamely. 'Open a bottle of something special! Do you want to get the champers glasses, Bobbie? I'll sort out the drink.'

Yes! At least she'd be able to get out of the room and compose herself. Maybe have a good cry in the loo. It wasn't just that it was weird to think of Mum marrying again, it was the man himself. What could you do when your parent married someone you couldn't stand? Absolutely nothing.

'Bobbie!'

Mum was close behind. 'I wanted to tell you before everyone else,' she said quietly, shutting the dining-room door behind them. 'I hope you don't mind.'

YES! YES I DO, Bobbie wanted to yell. Can't you see he's a vain, arrogant control freak? 'The only thing that matters is that you know, in your heart, you are doing the right thing,' she managed to say.

'I am.' Her mother gave a little nod. 'I'm sure I am. I've been awfully lonely on my own, you know, and, well, single men don't come along all that often. It's a big step for him too, getting married after all these years as a bachelor.'

A bachelor? 'But I thought he was a widower with grown-up children!'

Her mother looked round furtively. 'Actually, that's what his promotion people have told him to say. It wouldn't look good if he didn't have children; he could be accused of not practising what he preaches.'

How awful! 'But, Mum, aren't you upset that he's lying?'

Her mother made an uncomfortable face. 'I don't really like it.' She gave Bobbie a hug. 'But when you get to my age, you learn to make compromises.'

Everyone else seemed quite excited by the news, especially after a few glasses. 'How do you feel about having a step-grandad on the telly then?' grinned Mel's boyfriend, revealing a row of bad teeth (drugs or an aversion to the dentist?). 'Reckon he can get us some tickets for one of his chat shows? I could do something on DNA if he wants.'

Bobbie could feel her thumping headache getting increasingly worse. 'Why don't you take the kids out for a walk?' suggested Rob in a low, understanding voice. 'I'll clear up this end.'

'Won't it look rude?' she muttered back.

'Not if we say they need to let off steam.'

They certainly needed to do that! Both Jack and Daisy were jumping off and on the sofa next to their grandmother, who was sitting awkwardly with her new fiancé's arm around her while he was spouting off about the latest link between hyperactivity and summer babies.

'You could take Mel and Weasel Face with you,' added Rob. 'They'll probably be grateful for the chance to have a fag.'

He was right! The children did need to rush off judging by the way they were heading for the playground; Jack couldn't wait to get to the skate park. Mel and her boyfriend were lagging along behind her and Nattie was still texting while floating along. The park itself was absolutely teaming with couples and families and dogs.

'Bobbie!' It was Matthew, along with Lottie on a scooter. 'Good to see you.'

'We've just been to see Mummy!' sang out Lottie. 'I made her a special card which Daddy wrapped in a plastic cover so it wouldn't get wet on her grave.'

Weren't kids amazing? Bobbie wanted to give them both a hug. Every day must be difficult for these two but Mother's Day was surely particularly poignant. Still, maybe things might change now Sarah was on the scene. 'Someone seems a lot better now,' she said lightly. 'Daisy and Jack are over there if you want to join them!'

'Stay in sight!' called out Matthew as Lottie shot off. Then he fell into step beside her. 'I'm so glad we saw you. I've been wanting to ask your advice about something.' He looked awkward. 'Well, about someone actually.'

So she'd been right! It *was* very soon but when her friend decided on something or someone, she could be very determined. 'How well do you know Sarah?' he began.

Bobbie hadn't expected this! 'I don't understand.'

Matthew was shifting now from one foot to the other. 'It's just that she doesn't always tell the truth. Have you noticed that? Usually it's small things like cutting labels out of clothes and then pretending that she made whatever it is herself. But she's started to say rather unkind things about people I thought she cared for.'

Bobbie felt a nasty chill passing through her. 'Like who?'

'Well, like Vanessa. Sarah told me the other day that she was lucky social services hadn't taken her granddaughter into care. Apparently, she didn't have formal permission to look after her.'

What? Bobbie stared at him. 'I told her that in confidence!'

Matthew gave a worried shrug. 'She also told me about you and Rob's secretary and the phone call.'

She did?

'And she said she warned you against it.'

'But it was *her* idea!' None of this was making sense. Not unless Sarah wasn't the friend she'd thought she was.

'I think,' said Bobbie slowly, scanning the skate park to check Jack was still in one piece, 'I need to make a phone call.'

There once was a mum who swore –
It made your ears feel quite sore!
Her kids couldn't cope,
Washed her mouth out with soap
And now she don't curse any more.

Chapter 45

VANESSA

Harry! Ever since Brigid had uttered his name, it had rung round and round in her head. Maybe it had never really left it. Perhaps you never forgot the first person you had truly loved, even if they had lied and cheated on you.

'I'm going to write to him,' Brigid told her nervously. 'That's better than a phone call. It will give him time to think about whether he wants to see me.'

Vanessa wanted to wrap her arms around her daughter like an invisible shield. Warn her. Protect her. If only if *she* could take the pain instead! Harry would only hurt Brigid; she knew that. Just as he had hurt *her*.

'He owns this big company,' added Brigid. 'Something to do with finance in London. I don't want him to think I'm after his money.'

So Harry had come up in the world. It didn't surprise her. He'd always been bright. It was just that the booze had got in the way. Not to mention his morals. But so far there had been no contact, at least as far as she knew. Put it out of your head, Vanessa told herself. It was Mother's Day after all. Brian had come round for lunch and they were eating it on her little table in the garden. Incredible how warm it was again!

Sunshine, unusually, was playing up. Still, maybe it was to be expected, given all the changes that were going on. 'I want to see Daisy!' she whined, pushing away her bean burger that Vanessa had become rather skilled at making. 'I want to give her the card that I drew speshully *and* the present.'

'It's not Easter yet. There's plenty of time,' said Vanessa quickly.

'No.' Sunshine banged her little fist on the plate. 'I want to do it NOW. I haven't seen Daisy for ages. And anyway, I bought it out of my money. Didn't I?'

Indeed she had. Sunshine was a generous little thing. She'd been saving up her pocket money for ages. Not just for Easter eggs ('Yours is the biggest, Van Van') but also for a lovely little wooden heart that she'd given Brigid for Mothering Sunday.

'Is this your friend whose mum used to help in the shop?' enquired Brigid.

Sunshine nodded. 'She doesn't do it any more cos Van Van had a row with her.'

'I'm wondering if she's the one who rang social services,' burst out Vanessa.

'Are you sure?' Brigid's face tightened. 'Only you wouldn't want to make a mistake over something like that.'

Was she? Maybe not. Vanessa was in such a muddle that she couldn't think. Perhaps she was just being paranoid, suspecting everyone around her. But when it came to your children – or rather grandchildren – you couldn't afford to trust anyone

'We could go for a walk this afternoon,' suggested Malik, who really was a good-looking man with that lovely smooth coffee skin. She liked the way his eyes constantly followed her daughter, not lasciviously, but in a loving, caring way. He seemed good with Sunshine too, though his English could be unreliable. 'Then maybe we could drop the egg into your playmate.'

'YES! YES!' Sunshine leaped up and down. 'Let's go now. Please, Mummy. Please, Van Van. PLEASE!'

So somehow she had found herself agreeing even though her heart thumped as they went up Bobbie's path. The last person Vanessa wanted to see was the so-called friend who had betrayed her. 'We'll just leave the egg on the doorstep,' she said firmly to Sunshine.

'That's not fair, is it, Mummy?' She made a pleading face at Brigid. What a little monkey! Vanessa had noticed that Sunshine was beginning to play one off against the other.

But then the door opened. It was Bobbie's husband, looking rather friendlier than when she'd seen him in Devon. 'They're in the park,' he said warmly. 'Why don't you go and join them? Daisy's been talking about you, Sunshine. I know she'd love to see you.'

There was no getting out of it now! 'I'd like to meet Bobbie, Mum,' said Brigid grimly, linking her arm through hers. 'Tell her exactly what I think.'

Exactly. 'There she is!' Vanessa pointed to a pretty fresh-faced woman with light brown hair by the swings. 'With her niece.' Then she stopped. What on earth was Mel doing holding hands with Weasel Face?

'Jason?' whispered Brigid, turning pale. 'I don't believe it.'
Nor could she!

'Hi, Vanessa!' Bobbie stood up to greet them. Her pregnancy was definitely showing now. 'What a nice surprise. You know Mel, don't you?' Her tone altered slightly. 'This is Jason.'

'We've met,' said Vanessa grimly. Grabbing Bobbie, she steered her away. 'We need to talk.'

'I know.' Bobbie's eyes were bright. 'I've just been chatting to Matthew. And I think I know who's been trying to cause trouble. I'm going to ring her now. For you and for me.'

BOBBIE

'I've just spoken to Sarah on the phone,' said Bobbie sadly as they walked past the skateboard park. 'She insisted she bought the wretched jacket from a London market. However, she did admit that she rang social services after the school fête. It was almost as though she was proud of it. Came out with all this stuff about being a "responsible citizen". Frankly, I think she's one of those people who just like to cause trouble because they're not happy themselves.'

She looked downcast. 'Looking back, I can see the signs.'

'Some people do indeed like to cause trouble,' said Vanessa

quietly. 'Like your niece's boyfriend, Jason. He's the boy who claimed Sunshine was his child. The one who insisted on a DNA test.'

Bobbie looked shocked. 'You're joking?'

'Afraid not. You'd better tell your sister-in-law.'

'In the mood that she's in, she might think it's "liberating for the soul".' Then Bobbie made a sympathetic face. 'How are you? It's quite soon, isn't it?'

No need to say the word 'operation'. There were some things that friends didn't have to say, thought Vanessa gratefully. For that's what Bobbie was again. A friend.

'I'm sorry I didn't believe you before.'

She shrugged. 'It's OK.'

'No. It isn't. I've got it all wrong, haven't I?' To her distress, Vanessa felt her eyes welling up. 'First Brigid' – she gestured towards her daughter who was having a furious argument with Weasel Face – 'and then you.'

'Looks like your daughter is giving Mel's boyfriend a going-over.'

Vanessa snorted. 'She's not short at coming forward when she wants to be. Like her father. You look a bit peaky, love, if you don't mind me saying. Are you getting enough rest?'

'It's not that,' said Bobbie, looking down at her bump. 'I'm upset because Mum's just got engaged.' She made a face. 'To Dr Know.'

Vanessa did a double-take. 'You're kidding.'

'Wish I was.' Bobbie ran her hands through her hair. Did she know it had bits of chicken in it? 'He's at home right now, telling my husband where we've gone wrong for the past eight years. And you know what? Don't tell anyone, but he doesn't even have kids himself! The worst thing is that he's really controlling, but she doesn't seem to realise it.'

That didn't sound great. 'By the way,' said Vanessa, nudging her in the ribs chummily. 'Did you hear about that mother in Andy's class? The one who looked rather bohemian? Turns out she's been supplying some of the school mums with cannabis. Got six months, she did. It was in the local paper.'

'No!'

'Honest! What's more . . .'

'Nessie!'

She spun round, her breath catching in her throat. It was Brian. And Bingo! Out for a walk, along with the rest of Corrywood. 'Guess what, love! Upper Cut has just won the 1.10!' He lifted her up and span her in the air and he actually had tears in his eyes when he set her down. Dear man.

'That's wonderful!' Vanessa couldn't help it: she reached up on tiptoes to give Brian a kiss, feeling slightly embarrassed about doing so next to her daughter.

'Wow! I wonder if that's the one my mother-in-law was backing.' Bobbie rolled her eyes. 'She makes out it's a bit of fun but Rob and I reckon she's a closet gambler.'

'It can get that way,' said Brian cheerfully. 'Any road, reckon I can afford to buy ice creams all round. How about it?' He glanced at Jason, who was walking off now towards the other side of the park. 'By the way, looks like the police aren't going to take that young man's accusations any further.'

'That's wonderful!' She felt a huge wave of relief.

'Is it?' Brian shook his head. 'I shouldn't have pushed him. Still, we all do stuff we're not proud of. Don't we?'

ANDY

They weren't going to do anything about it! Andy stared at the letter disbelievingly. *Following enquiries, it appears there is no case to be answered.* What did that mean?

'Don't ask,' warned his lawyer. 'You've done your bit. Appeased your conscience. Now leave it at that.'

But he hadn't been able to. He'd gone down to the police station again and told the young girl once more that he had contributed to someone's death. 'It might be twenty-five years ago but aren't you going to do anything about it?'

Then she'd given him a strange look, the type that one might give someone who wasn't quite right in the head, and

511

repeated the jargon in the letter. There was nothing else for it. He had to follow Plan B. It was the only way he was ever going to get any peace of mind.

'If you think I'm coming with you, mate, you've got a second think coming,' scoffed Kieran when he rang.

Incredibly, however, Pamela thought he was doing the right thing. 'I want to see this place for myself,' she said unexpectedly. 'After all, it's part of your life.' She tucked her arm in his. 'I always felt there was more to you than met the eye.'

So they drove across country to Essex, with Andy saying all the way that it was probably a waste of time and that the supermarket would have been knocked down or sold on years ago, only to find that it was still there. A bit smaller than he remembered but it was the same place all right. Bang on the corner next to a betting shop. His heart pounding, Andy went in. The counter had been moved to a different place. It was smarter now. More upmarket. At the till hovered a man who was probably around his age.

'Can I help you, sir?' he asked politely.

Andy froze; he might even have chickened out but Pamela took over. 'We're trying to find out about a shopkeeper who used to be here twenty-five years ago.'

The man nodded as though this was a perfectly reasonable request. 'That would have been my father.'

Andy groaned. This had been a mistake! Too late, he could see that. What on earth should he say now? *Hi. My name used to be Barry. I watched your dad die.*

'You would like to speak to him? Yes?'

Andy stared at him and then Pamela. 'But he's dead!'

The man laughed. 'My father, he is very much alive! I fetch him!' Then he stopped. 'Why you want to speak to him?'

His mouth was dry. Alive! The man was still alive. It wasn't possible. There had to be some mistake. 'I, er, I need to explain something.'

It seemed an age until there was the sound of shuffling from the back of the shop. Andy took Pamela's hand (for

512

reassurance, he was ashamed to admit) as an old man with a stick appeared.

It was him. Those features had been etched in his mind for years – the slightly large nose, the high forehead – and they took him straight back to the night. The night when he had done something that he would be ashamed of for the rest of his life.

'Yes?' The old man squinted at Andy as though he couldn't see him properly. 'You want to talk to me?'

'Go on,' whispered Pamela reassuringly.

'I . . . I thought you were dead!'

The old man put his head to one side as though studying him in great detail. 'And why would you think that?'

'Because I saw you lying in a pool of blood!'

Suddenly something cleared in the old man's face. 'You were one of those boys who gave me trouble? You? You were one of them? The gang that raided my shop and made me hit my head?'

His son made to pick up the phone. 'No.' The older man raised his hand. 'No, do not do that. I want to know: why are you here?'

'I want to say sorry.' How inadequate those words sounded. 'Ever since it happened, I thought we'd killed you.' A huge weight suddenly lifted from his chest. 'I cannot tell you how relieved I am. For years, I have lived with the guilt of watching someone die without doing something. Then I realised that the only way forward was to come clean. That's why I'm here with my wife.'

'You hurt my father!' The younger man looked stern. 'He had concussion and had to go to hospital, you know. He could have died. There is no excuse for that. '

'Yes, son, there is.' The older man shook his head. 'These boys, they were from the home. The one that was closed down. It was not a good place. But I do not understand. Who said I was dead?'

'The older ones! The ringleaders! They said that if Kieran – the other boy – and I said anything, they would kill us!'

The desperation, combined with the embarrassment and the horror, made him need the loo. Urgently.

'Did you read of my death in the paper?' The old man sounded amused.

'Well, no.' Andy desperately tried to remember the sequence of events. 'We didn't get the papers and we weren't allowed to watch television. But the older boys said you'd copped it. Those were their words. They also told us that if we talked about it, we'd get thrown straight into the nick.'

The old man shook his head. 'I think those boys were using you.' He tutted, but not in a condemning way. 'I was hurt, but not badly. Now I think you have been punished enough. Go home, my son.' He patted Andy's shoulder. 'You have said your piece and I forgive you.'

'But, Dad . . . !'

'That is enough. I admire you for coming.' The old man nodded in Pamela's direction. 'I am glad you have a good wife.'

Andy stumbled out of the shop, not knowing which direction to go in. 'They lied to us,' he kept repeating. 'The other boys. They lied to us!'

'Children can be very cruel,' said Pamela gently. 'They obviously told a porky to make you do whatever they wanted.' She shuddered. 'But it's fantastic news, isn't it, darling? I mean I know it's been a horrible sword of Damocles hanging over you but your man is alive! And he's forgiven you! Rather sweet, really. So why are you crying?'

Because of everything, he wanted to say. Because he'd lost his parents, or as good as. Because he'd had a shitty childhood. Because he'd carried that guilt over the old man for years; unnecessarily as it turned out. Because his family – his immediate family – weren't what he thought they were.

'Come here.' Pamela was holding him as he let it all come out, hugging him like a child right there on the street while people walked past, staring. Telling him it was all right now. And that what he needed to do was leave it all behind and start afresh.

'I want that too,' she said briskly, walking him back to the car. 'You're not the only one with regrets. There are some things in my past that I'm deeply ashamed of.' She jutted out her chin, defiantly. 'Things that I don't want to tell anyone about, not even you. But I'm going to move forward now.'

He knew it! She was going to leave him! Not long ago, Andy might have left her himself. But now he'd got his head straight about Bobbie (well, almost) and was getting a bit more used to this new Pamela, he couldn't imagine life without her. It wasn't weakness, he told himself fiercely. It was because he loved her, despite everything. And because he wanted to keep his family together. 'Please don't go.'

'Go? Whoever said anything about going?' Pamela gave him a playful pinch. 'I've decided to go back to work. I'm going to set up an agency for mature models. What do you think? Andy? Are you listening?'

But he was staring at a newspaper placard. Unable to talk. Then her eye caught it too. 'My God,' she breathed. She clutched his arm. 'I don't believe it.' He could feel her shake as she leaned into him. Felt the new Pamela draining away into the old.

SOCIETY PHOTOGRAPHER ACCUSED OF TEENAGE RAPE – AFTER HIS DEATH.

Andy picked up the top paper on the pile. There it was. A picture of a beautiful former model, Pamela's age, who had decided to break her silence. *Now he's dead, I know he can't hurt me any more*, ran the caption.

Below were similar quotes from other models. All young girls at the time, who had been too terrified to make a fuss because the photographer had been so powerful. So revered in the fashion world. 'I worked with them all,' whispered Pamela. 'I didn't realise it was happening to them too.'

Andy pointed to the paragraph at the bottom. 'There's going to be an inquiry,' he said gently. 'They're asking for anyone else who was molested to come forward.' He held her close. 'This could be your chance, Pamela. Your way of facing the truth. Of banishing the past for good.'

She was shivering so much now that she could barely talk. 'But what about Mel?'

Andy thought of all the secrets, all the lies that had been told. Not just in their family but in others too, if the class had been anything to go by. 'Maybe it's time for us to tell her the truth. After all, we've got to do it sometime. Haven't we?'

FIVE THINGS THAT GRANDPARENTS SHOULD NEVER DO

Have sex.
Forget birthdays.
Stop talking to their children.
Pinch their children's iPads.
Buy Easter eggs for next-door's children and not give
    their grandkids anything.
Get divorced.

Chapter 46

ANDY

'You mean those buggers made us think the old geezer was dead so they could boss us about?' bellowed Kieran down the phone.

'Possibly. You know what they were like.'

'Bastards!'

Andy could almost see Kieran spitting.

'But I wasn't much better either. Look, mate. I'm sorry. I did wrong by you, threatening you with blackmail and all that. It's just that I saw what you had and I wanted a piece of it meself. But we've made up, haven't we?'

His old enemy sounded genuinely remorseful. 'Yes. Forget it. Anyway, I've lost it all now.' Andy gave a dry laugh. 'I'm broke, Kieran. We're selling up. Pamela's organising a car boot sale as we speak.'

'Bloody hell.' There was a short shocked silence. 'Listen, mate, can we have a pact, like? Neither of us will mention the shop stuff to anyone else. Right?'

'Sorry. Can't do that.'

'What do you mean?'

'I've told my wife. Just like you told yours.'

'Fucking hell, mate! Well, make sure she doesn't tell anyone. I've been thinking about a lot of stuff recently and I don't want that shit coming up and hitting me in the face. I've got an example to set my kid. And my missus has got her job to think about. Get what I mean?'

Andy knew exactly what he meant. But setting an example meant telling the truth, however painful and however overdue. 'When do you think we should tell Mel?' Pamela had asked later that evening when there was just the three of them at home. Nattie was still away on her first job (thank goodness the agency was limiting work to holidays and had encouraged her to stay on at school; they seemed more responsible than he had thought) and Mel was out with Weasel Face. Camilla showed no signs of wanting to go home just yet.

'I'm not sure.' Andy felt a nerve in his cheek twitching, the way it used to in the office when he was under pressure. He'd seen Mel as his own child for so long that it didn't seem possible she was really someone else's. Besides, it was he who had brought her up, wasn't it? He might not have been there as much as he should have been but he would always be her daddy.

'Why not leave it for a bit?' Camilla's clear, confident voice cut in. 'What you don't know doesn't hurt. After all, Pamela, your father never knew the truth about your real parentage and it didn't kill him.' Her eyes grew misty. 'Wonderful man, Johnnie. But we were both married and in those days it was for life. Sorry, darling. I thought you'd guessed by now.'

VANESSA

'Mum. Can you hear me?'

It was Brigid. At least it sounded like her but Vanessa was in that rather pleasant dreamy stage you find yourself in when coming round from an operation. She could remember the nurse telling her that she was in the recovery room but then she must have fallen asleep again because here she was, in a different place with jaunty floral curtains and her daughter sitting by her bed.

'You're going to be all right, Mum.'

Going to be all right? It's what she used to say to Brigid as a child when she fell over and grazed her knee or got a shiner on her forehead. But the truth was that no one knew if she was going to be all right now. Not till they'd analysed that lump.

'Can you feel something warm over your chest?' whispered her daughter.

She could, actually. Rather like a two-bar electric fire: the type that she and Harry used to put money in the meter for.

'It's my hands,' murmured Brigid.

But she wasn't touching her! That was amazing. Still, nothing would surprise Vanessa at the moment. Her mind wandered back to those days before the operation. Brigid had announced that she and Malik were going to rent their own place – with Sunshine obviously – but near enough for them all to see each other every day if they wanted. The pair of them were going to train as teachers, she told her. But they were going to take on part-time jobs too, to pay the rent. Would Vanessa mind looking after Sunshine after school? Perhaps she could go into the shop with her?

Vanessa, who had been steeling herself for the horrible possibility that Brigid and Sunshine might move far away, had felt so relieved that she'd burst into tears. 'Why are you crying, Van Van?'

'Because I'm happy!'

'Grown-ups are *weird*! My friend Daisy says so and she's right.'

Maybe she was. Maybe, too, it had been a mistake to ask Brigid outright if Mark (Audrey's son) was Sunshine's father. 'It's none of your business, Mum, although I will say you're wrong.' Brigid could be so sharp at times! 'I don't want to talk about it. OK?'

Perhaps there were some things that a daughter had to keep from her mother, just as she, Vanessa, had done with hers.

Then Brian had announced over a pint that he'd like her to move in with him. It was very sweet of him, as she explained, but he didn't have to worry about her. She'd managed when she'd been ill before and she'd manage again now.

'It's not because you're poorly, lass. It's because I want to be with you.'

But she'd got too used to her independence over the years. 'I'm not sure I'm ready to give it up,' she told him gently.

Brian had been crestfallen. 'If you won't move in, will you consider being a partner in a different way?' he'd asked.

And that's when he'd told her exactly how much his horse had won. She hadn't realised the prize money was that big when you were an owner. Even a part-owner. 'I know you've been worried about the lease running out on the shop,' he added. 'Why don't you let me help you rent a bigger place?'

She'd been thinking about that already. But rents were so expensive! On the other hand, did she really want to accept Brian's financial offer and give up the independence she'd worked so hard to get?

And then Brigid had dropped her bombshell.

BOBBIE

'Please tell me you're joking, mum!' Bobbie felt one of the babies leap in protest. 'Dr Know has invited us to appear on *The Worst Family in Britain* show?'

Her mother sounded mortified at the other end of the line. 'Of course I said no. And to the programme too.'

'Good . . . hang on. What did you say?'

'I told Herbert I couldn't marry him.' Her mother's voice bore only the slightest twinge of regret. 'I think I knew it from the beginning but when we came to lunch with you, I realised it would never work. You come first in my life, Bobbie. You and the children, no matter how appallingly they behave. You always will. I couldn't sit by and hear Herbert criticise you like that – either in or out of your hearing.'

'But, Mum . . . !' Bobbie was in tears now. Tears of relief, it had to be said. The thought of that man in the family was unbearable. 'I don't want you to sacrifice your life for us.'

'I'll find someone else.' Her mother sounded a bit brighter now. 'In fact, your friend Vanessa – I'm so glad you introduced us at Easter – has emailed me details of the site where she found her Brian.'

Whoever said the older generation moved slowly?

'What about you, dear? I don't want to pry but I've been

521

worried about you. Have you and Rob sorted out your differences?'

Bobbie thought of the long talks that she and Rob had had, deep into the night. Talks that they should have had earlier. Frank, honest talks about work and sex and children and boundaries. Discussions that would, they'd promised each other, lead to changes and compromises. On both sides.

'Actually,' said Bobbie nervously, 'I've got some news for you! Remember I said Rob had an interview in the north? Well he's got it and—'

'MUM! WHEN WE GO AND LIVE NEAR GRANNY, CAN WE HAVE A PONY?'

Shhh, Bobbie tried to say to Jack as he swung into the room. Not yet. Not until she'd broken the news.

Too late! Mum had heard. 'You're going to come up here?'

Was she shocked or excited? It was hard to tell. 'Is that all right, Mum? We won't get in your way but it might be nice if we were nearby. JACK, GET OFF YOUR SKATEBOARD!'

'I can't believe it.'

Stunned maybe. But in a good or not-so-good way?

'Jack and Daisy every day.' Her mother let out a nervous laugh. 'Running in and out of my house. I can't . . . I mean, I can't wait!'

VANESSA

Vanessa hadn't wanted to come but Brigid had persuaded her. Told her that she *had* to. That she'd regret it if she didn't. Pointed out that, rather like her, Harry hadn't been so lucky with his health.

Now Vanessa could hardly believe her eyes. Was this really him? She stared at the horribly thin man with the round shoulders and bald patch talking earnestly to her daughter in the restaurant. She would never have recognised her 'husband'. Might have walked past him in the street, even! What a terrible thing, not to recognise the father of your child.

For one awful moment, Vanessa thought he was going to

kiss her on the cheek. She didn't want that. It would have seemed unfaithful to Brian. Stunned, she watched him pull out her chair before the waiter could do so. The old Harry – the dancing-eyed, dark-haired, self-centred Irish charmer – wouldn't have done that. He'd have been tossing back the bed covers instead. Now he needed a stick to return to his own seat.

'Did you really used to be married?' asked Sunshine, looking from one to the other with a puzzled expression.

Vanessa nodded.

'We certainly did,' said Harry. His voice was gruff. Husky from the cigarettes. She'd warned him when they were younger. Told him they'd kill him one day.

'So why don't you have the same surname then?'

Harry laughed. That was better! The laugh hadn't changed. Deeper maybe but with the same joy. That Irish joy that had flipped her mind at twenty, kicking out any common sense. 'Your grandmother went back to her old name. Thomas. And she changed your mum's name too.' He gave her a disappointed look. 'But she's really a Screws. Like me. And you.'

Brigid began to look uncomfortable. 'I've just found out the most amazing coincidence, Mum. Dad's company used to belong to a relative of your friend Bobbie. Someone called Andy. Andy Gooding. Isn't that funny?'

Yes. And no. Nothing would surprise Vanessa now. Not after this. There was something really weird about sitting next to someone whom you hadn't seen for years. Someone whom you used to curl up to at night; who had stood next to you in the labour ward, mopping your brow; who had told you that he would love you until the very day he died. That he was sorry he'd misled you.

'Do you need the loo, Sunshine?' said Brigid sharply.

'No!'

'I think you do!'

'But . . .'

'No buts.'

Partly amused and partly apprehensive, Vanessa watched

her daughter shepherding Sunshine towards the Ladies. Brigid wanted to give them space. Space that she wasn't sure she wanted.

'Are you happy, Harry?' she asked quietly, picking up her napkin and then putting it down again.

His eyes pinned hers. They were still the same blue, but there were so many lines around them that they seemed smaller. Older. In her memories, Harry remained the same age as when she had left him. 'Not as happy as I would have been if you'd allowed me to stay with you and our girl.' He made a small gesture with his hands. 'Still, water under the bridge now. What about you?'

She thought of Brigid. And Sunshine. And her shop. And Brian. And even Bobbie. 'I'm good, actually. Very good.'

'Listen, Vanessa.' He looked as though he was reaching for her hand but then thought better of it. 'I'd like to make things up to you. I'm a wealthy man.'

'Stop. Please.' She felt cross now. 'Don't think you can buy forgiveness. I don't want your money. But if you want to help your daughter and our granddaughter, that's up to you. They could certainly do with it.'

They both looked across at Sunshine who was coming back to the table, clutching one of those keep-the-kids-quiet colouring sheets along with some wax crayons. '*See*. I said I didn't need to go.' Plonking herself next to Vanessa, she whispered loudly. 'Have you had enough time to talk now? Mum said we had to leave you alone.' Then she began to draw, sticking her tongue out in concentration. 'I'm going to make you all a very speshull picture.'

'At least we did something right,' said Harry quietly.

Vanessa took in her daughter, who was bending over Sunshine with a wonderfully tender look on her face. 'We did, didn't we?'

And then, on the spur of the moment, she reached out for his hand after all and gave it a little squeeze, before making her excuses and nipping out to the Ladies to ring Brian.

GLAMOROUS GRANNY SAYS 'NO' TO DR KNOW!

Scoop in Charisma *magazine.*

525

Epilogue

BOBBIE

'I WANT THOSE SWEETS! I WANT THOSE SWEETS!'

She should never have come in here, Bobbie told herself ruefully. Not when the removal van was ready and waiting. But she'd been desperate for certain essentials to get them through the long journey up north. Like marshmallows and poppadoms and sardines.

'WHY CAN'T I HAVE THEM? WHY?'

The woman behind began tutting and muttering the usual rubbish about things being different in her day. Bobbie waited until she couldn't stand it any longer and then whipped round. 'Actually, it's not easy when they put sweets by the checkout.'

The young mum whose toddler was having the paddy threw Bobbie a grateful look. 'I don't know what to do with my daughter,' she said desperately. 'We've only just moved here and I don't have any friends to help.'

Bobbie delved into her bag for the leaflet that Vanessa had given her: *Parenting Classes For All Ages. Contact Brigid Thomas for more details.*

'Spread the word, can you?' she'd said, with an enthusiasm that hadn't left her since Vanessa had got the all-clear for that lump. Such a relief! 'My friend's daughter – one of the helpers – she's got a great way with kids.'

The girl was studying the leaflet doubtfully. 'Where's it being held?'

'Corrywood. It's one of the local schools.' Brigid glanced across at the little girl who had dived into the Reduced Bread shelf. Her left arm and leg were coming out at the same time, just as Jack's had done, nearly nine months ago. Where did they learn it from? Naughty School? 'It's got a really good playgroup too,' she added. 'Anyway, give the class a go! It will help you find new friends, if nothing else. Good luck!'

Then she paid for her shopping and waddled out to the car outside where Rob was waiting. Jack and Daisy were plugged into their new iPads, a leaving present from Sunshine's new granddad. They didn't seem to have moved since she'd left them.

'No arguments?' she asked Rob.

'Not yet.'

Maybe it was a slow burner, this parenting-course business. Perhaps it took time for changes to be made, on both sides. But there was no doubt about it: Daisy and Jack were getting a bit easier to handle.

'MOVE OVER.'

'NO. YOU MOVE OVER.'

'MUM, SHE KICKED ME!'

'HE DID IT FIRST! ANYWAY, I HAVEN'T GOT ANY ROOM WITH HIS SKATEBOARD ON MY LEGS!'

Maybe not.

'Ready?' said Rob, patting her knee.

'Ready,' said Bobbie. She felt excited, but also apprehensive. Still, that was normal, wasn't it? They were moving to a new area, where she'd need to make new friends. Friends that were hopefully more trustworthy than Sarah had been. Friends that were, with any luck, as warm and loving as Vanessa.

'We'll miss you,' the older woman had said as she'd hugged her goodbye.

'We'll miss you too.' Bobbie hugged her tightly back. 'But you will come and visit, won't you? All of you!'

She'd miss Andy as well. Of course it was Rob she loved. Yet at the same time, Bobbie was aware that she had been able to talk – really talk – to Andy. Maybe that's why it was right to move. Best, as Vanessa had said with the wisdom that came from being a grandmother, to put temptation out of reach. A bit like sweets.

Besides, Pamela and Andy were making a fresh start now.

Not just with their venture in Devon but with the degree course in September. Psychology! She could just see Andy doing well at that.

'Are we nearly there yet?' demanded Jack, breaking into her slightly wistful thoughts.

'Course not, silly. Google says we've got two hundred and forty miles to go.'

'Everyone got their gluten-free snacks?' Bobbie turned round to check. It was amazing what a difference it had made to their digestive systems. All of them, actually. Without mentioning names, it turned out that Jack wasn't the only culprit. Pongo seemed to have completely disappeared from their lives.

Ouch!

'What's wrong?' Rob looked across at her, alarmed.

'Just another kick.' Bobbie placed a protective hand on her stomach. 'These two seem to have a mind of their own.'

Rob gave her a kiss. 'I wouldn't have it any other way.'

'I hope you mean that.' She shot him a conspiratorial smile. 'Because it's going to be pretty manic when they arrive. Even with the new au pair.'

Rob started the engine. 'Four kids *is* quite a handful.' Then he said firmly, as though to reassure himself: 'But we'll cope.'

Would they? wondered Bobbie as they drove through Corrywood for the last time, passing a very slim Not Really Pregnant Mum who was waving back furiously. Yes of course they would! They had to.

Besides, who wanted to be a perfect parent anyway? After all, Happy Families come in all kinds of shapes and sizes, don't they?

PS

BOOK YOUR PLACE NOW FOR THE PERFECT PARENTS'
ANNUAL RETREAT REUNION! NO KIDS OR PARTNERS
ALLOWED! Email Paula@Jilly'saupairagency.com
*

DR KNOW TO HOST NEW CELEBRITY PARENTING
SHOW IN NEW YORK
*

Bobbie and Rob Wright are delighted to announce the safe
arrival of Bruce (otherwise known as Bruiser) and Lucy
(meaning 'Light of the World'). Instead of flowers, the Wrights
would appreciate donations to the Sibling Rivalry Fund.
*

CORRYWOOD ADVERTISER
The wedding took place quietly on Saturday 9 April between
Vanessa Thomas and Brian Hughes. Sunshine Thomas and
Daisy Wright were bridesmaids. The happy couple will
honeymoon in the Maldives where the bride (a keen swimmer)
has already booked a snorkelling course.
*

TOP TEN B & Bs IN DEVON
For a perfect break, why not visit Gooding Towers, which
offers luxurious accommodation including a hot tub and
childcare? Also available for business conferences.
Recommended by *I Can't Cope With My Kids* magazine and
Recovering Alcoholics.

Gooding Towers is also proud to be part of 'Give a
Child a Break': a new government initiative to enable
children in care to have a week's holiday every year in the
country.
*

To Miss Mel Gooding:

An appointment has been arranged at the antenatal clinic of the R, D & E Hospital. You are welcome to bring a supporter with you. (Maximum of two.)

*

PA EXECUTIVE MONTHLY
Congratulations to Araminta Avon, who has been promoted to junior account executive. (See feature on 'How to Sleep Your Way to the Top' on page 15.)

*

WORK FROM HOME AND EARN MONEY WHILE YOU'RE LOOKING AFTER THE KIDS!
Research Trivia helps you combine the best of both worlds. Apply now online! References essential.

*

SHOCK NEWS – DR KNOW'S NEW SHOW CANCELLED, AMIDST ALLEGATIONS ABOUT WILD PRIVATE LIFE

*

EMAIL FROM BOBBY WRIGHT TO ANDY GOODING
Hi! How are you doing? Pamela says you're really enjoying running the B & B. Rob and I would be delighted if you'd consider being godfather to the twins. Both of them. We know you'd do a great job.
Best, Bobbie
PS We love it up here although I miss our chats.
PPS Please delete this email.

*

CHARISMA MAGAZINE
EXCLUSIVE INTERVIEW WITH FORMER FAMOUS LINGERIE MODEL, PAMELA GOODING
'It has been incredibly painful to tell my story. But I have to do so for my daughters. I want them to learn how important it is to say no, however stupid you feel. One of the most important lessons that a parent can pass to a child is that of self-respect.'

530

A fee for this interview has been donated to Rape Victim Support

*

CORRYWOOD ADVERTISER

A woman has been charged after confessing to nineteen counts of theft and fraud committed at a variety of shops in outer London. Miriam Marbella admitted to pretending that she 'lost' items of clothing while taking them off to try on new ones. Her co-conspirator would then buy the garment, after negotiating a knockdown price, and re-sell it to unsuspecting buyers. Meanwhile, Ms Marbella would sue the original shopkeeper for loss. A large number of related stolen jackets has been discovered at a stall in Bermondsey Market.

*

SKATEBOARD MONTHLY MAGAZINE

Congratulations to Jack Wright, winner of the Under Nines Skateboarding Championship! The prize is a family holiday at Skateboard City in Florida!

*

YOU ARE CORDIALLY INVITED TO A FASHION SHOW AT 'VANESSA'S' TO CELEBRATE ITS NEW PREMISES, AS WELL AS ITS NEW 'JUST PREGNANT' RANGE AND THE 'FABULOUS AT FIFTY' COLLECTION

Proceeds to Cancer Research

*

CHARISMA EXCLUSIVE

MOTHER AND DAUGHTER MODELS, PAMELA AND NATASHA GOODING, TAKE THE LONDON FASHION FAIR BY STORM!

*

How To Be a Hands-off Grandmother by Camilla Ponsonby-Pilling-Poop. Foreword by Dr Know.

*

NOTICE AT CORRYWOOD MEDICAL CENTRE

We would like to wish every success to Dr Macdonald, who is taking early retirement and moving to Wales, where she and her husband Kieran intend to foster children from troubled backgrounds.

*

FACEBOOK MESSAGE FROM DAISY WRIGHT TO SUNSHINE THOMAS

We've got a puppy! He's called Pongo and he's *real* this time. Can't wait for you to visit so you can see him!

*

EMAIL FROM JILLY'S AU PAIR AGENCY TO BOBBIE WRIGHT

Hi! How are you doing? My partner Paula and I have been thinking of setting up a branch in the north. Would you be interested in running it? You'd be able to work from home, which is great!

*

COULD YOURS BE THE WORST FAMILY IN BRITAIN? IF SO, THE BBC WOULD LIKE TO HEAR FROM YOU

*

BOOK NOW FOR THE NEXT COURSE OF IMPERFECT PARENTING AT CORRYWOOD SCHOOL

To be run by Brigid Thomas and Gemma Balls. Places limited! Meanwhile, we have had several enquiries about refunds for the previous course. We are afraid that Corrywood School is unable to offer compensation (see the small print in the original ad for details). We would also like to point out that the new course is very different. After all, there's nothing like a fresh start!

The Playgroup

Janey Fraser

'A must-read for anyone who has children' Katie Fforde

It's the start of a new term at Puddleducks Playgroup

For Gemma Merryfield it'll be her first year in charge. Watching the new arrivals, she can already tell who the troublemakers will be, and not all of them are children!

What Gemma doesn't realise, though, is that former banker Joe Balls, now head of Reception at the neighbouring school, will be watching her every move. As far as he's concerned, Puddleducks puts too much emphasis on fun and games, and not enough on numbers (preferably squared).

But when one of the children falls dangerously ill and another disappears, Gemma and Joe have to set aside their differences and work together.

'A terrific story and enormous fun' Judy Astley

arrow books

ALSO AVAILABLE IN ARROW

The Au Pair

Janey Fraser

'A must-read for anyone who has children' Katie Fforde

Apparently anyone can set up an au pair agency around their kitchen table. So when money gets tight, Jilly does exactly that. But she hadn't reckoned on Marie-France, a sparky French girl, signing up in the hope of finding her father, twenty years after her own mother had been an au pair in the same town.

Then there's Matthew, a confused widower whose daughter has driven away a string of au pairs. Can Jilly ever find him the perfect match?

And let's not forget the rest of the au pair mafia, including Heidi, Fatima and Antoinette who 'likes children but not very much'.

The Au Pair is a hilarious but truthful romp through the world of au pairs and their unsuspecting families.

'A terrific story and enormous fun' Judy Astley

arrow books